A former actress, Valerie Georgeson is an experienced radio and television scriptwriter, whose credits include the BBC series *Angels*, *Juliet Bravo* and *Ellen Wilkinson M.P.* This is her first novel.

Born and brought up in the Shields area, where *The Turning Tides* is set, she now lives in South West London.

Valerie Georgeson

THE TURNING TIDES

Futura

A Futura Book

The author and publisher acknowledge permission from
Campbell Thomson & McLaughlin for use of an extract from
EYE DEEP IN HELL: Life in the Trenches 1914–18
by John Ellis, © John Ellis 1977

First published in Great Britain in 1985
by Futura Publications, a Division of
Macdonald & Co (Publishers) Ltd
London & Sydney

ISBN 0 7088 2698 9

Printed and bound in Great Britain by
Collins, Glasgow

Futura Publications
A Division of
Macdonald & Co (Publishers) Ltd
Maxwell House
74 Worship Street
London EC2A 2EN

A BPCC plc Company

'There is a tide in the affairs of men,
Which, taken at the flood, leads on to fortune;
Omitted, all the voyage of their life
Is bound in shallows and in miseries.'

Julius Caesar, IV, iii, 217.

PART ONE

CHAPTER ONE

'Eeh, Henry, you shouldn't!' Lily Straker's greedy eyes scanned the folds of cloth spread out over the table. She nodded approval at her husband. 'Mind, you've got beautiful taste, I'll say that for you.'

Henry's face expressed profound relief. He had scoured the souks and markets of the Far East in search of something that would satisfy his wife. And she was hard to please, was Lily Straker, very hard. Always picking holes, as his sister, Hettie, would say.

'Real silk, eh? That'll knock them for six at "The Rooms".'

She thought. Already the vibrant silk was made up, in her mind's eye, draped elegantly round her bosom, swishing deliciously at her feet, as she and Henry swept through the great doors into the hall for the Mayor's Reception.

'By, it's lovely, Lily.' Hettie too, could see the splash her sister-in-law would make, and a wistful look came into her eyes. Lily was so lovely, so slim and erect, so proud of herself. She made Hettie feel drab and small in comparison. And so she was, coming from the humble docklands of Shields, while Lily had inherited a house in the rich man's retreat of Westoe Village and a place among the gentry.

'Aren't you going to open yours, Hettie?' Henry asked.

'Oh yes, Hettie. Open it. Open it!' All eyes turned on the bright face of the child at their feet. Little Catherine Straker, all of five years old, entranced by the mystery of unopened parcels brought home by her sailor Daddy.

'Watch she doesn't get too excited,' Lily frowned. 'You know what's she's like. Too much imagination. She'll not sleep tonight!'

'You'll not send her out, Lily!' Tears came to Hettie's eyes on the child's behalf, as the bright face clouded.

'Open yours, Hettie.' Henry, wise in the handling of his wife, diverted her attention back to the parcels on the table. Hettie stretched out her hands and picked up a bundle of green tissue. The child's eyes rounded in anticipation. Henry grinned, pleased with himself. And Lily watched, fearful lest the mysterious wrapping should contain the equal of her own expensive gift. The tissues were pulled off, pieces of coloured paper drifting down, like confetti, round the child's head. Oh how exciting it was! Cathy's hands reached out to catch the floating fragments, her mother's frowns forgotten in the magic of the moment.

'Oh, Henry!' Hettie gasped, as she drew the silk out of its folds. Lily's face dropped, then rose again as she saw that it was, after all, only a shawl, a silk shawl, with fringing round it, in garish colours, picked up, no doubt, at the last minute on the quayside at Hong Kong. The fringing touched Cathy's cheek as her auntie swept the shawl round her shoulders. Auntie Hettie was pleased as punch.

'Thank you,' she beamed at her brother. 'It's beautiful. Really beautiful.'

'She looks like a gypsy, doesn't she Henry?' Lily laughed. Cathy couldn't understand why her aunt should look so hurt at this remark. 'You'll be able to wear it for consultations.' The shawl dropped from Hettie's shoulders, and she stroked the shining cloth with her hand. 'All she needs now is one of them handkerchiefs, with coins dangling off it, to wear round her head.'

Henry gave his wife a sharp look, and Lily shut her mouth at last. He turned, his expression clouded, to the face of his sister.

'Don't you like it, Hettie?' he asked.

'It's lovely, Henry.' Hettie smiled up at him quietly, reassuringly. And the wife, excluded from the tender moment, bent down to gather up the discarded paper in angry movements. She should never have lowered herself. And she couldn't say she hadn't been warned. 'You're marrying beneath you,' they'd said.

Left orphaned at sixteen and fed on romantic notions by Great-Aunt Jessie, Lily had seen the world, and men in particular, through rose-tinted spectacles. And with no one to guide her but her spinster aunt, she had allowed the attentions of a young adventurer to go to her head. He had had such a passion for her, handsome Henry Straker, and she had let him sweep her off her feet. What if he *was* poor? He had ideas! Oh yes, Henry Straker was full of them. Shipping tycoon by the time he was thirty, he'd be . . . with her money behind him. Investment it was called, and after all her money wouldn't do her any good just sitting in the bank. But the visions of glory were brutally shattered through the years to come. The wedding night alone! Where was the chivalry, the romance? Like the brute beasts he was with her! Great-Aunt Jessie had not led her to expect that. And then there was Hettie, Henry's sister, a working-class woman if ever there was one, actually running a boarding house on the quayside, reading the sailor's palms! And she just would not keep away. Especially after Catherine arrived. If Lily hoped to drag Henry up to her own level, Hettie was completely out of the question. And what about Lily's dreams of wealth?

Henry did well at first, well enough to want to expand. He took on a partner, and together they bought a second ship. 'Things are tickin' over nicely, pet,' he'd reassure her, when she asked; she'd just have to be careful till the profit margin increased. Ah well, Henry should know, and Lily couldn't look after everything. She had enough on her hands with this wilful child of hers. Lily glanced up from collecting scrap paper to see her daughter absent-mindedly screwing up her mother's new silk cloth in her grubby hand.

Lily slapped out at the child's leg.

'You leave that be, Miss,' she shouted. And Cathy, her leg smarting, started to cry.

'Ah, come to Daddy, then.' Henry lifted her up onto his hip, allowing her to bury her tears in the lapels of his suit.

'You're too soft with her by half!' Lily snapped. 'Look at this.' She yanked the silk off the table and displayed the ruched corner where Catherine had spoilt it.

'She's only a bairn, Lily.'

'And what has it got to do with you, Hettie Straker, I should like to know?'

'Nothing, I'm sure.' Hettie, miffed, went off towards the door.

'Look at her now!' Lily stood, hands on hips, for all the world like one of the fishwives down on the quay. 'The Grand Duchess, if you please, goin' off in a sulk!'

Hettie, on her dignity now, turned to face her sister-in-law.

'I was goin' to ask the maid to light the gas,' she said. 'It's gettin' dark.' Then she left them, but not without a warm smile at the staring eyes of her niece.

'I wish you wouldn't get at her, Lily,' Henry sighed, setting his daughter down on an easy chair. 'You make her feel inferior.'

'Do you know, Henry,' Lily's eyes challenged his, 'I think you love her more than you do me!'

He looked away. The same old jibe. And it wasn't true. He worshipped the ground Lily walked on, and she knew it.

'I sometimes wonder if you've got any feeling for *me*, never mind Hettie,' he whispered back.

This was unexpected. Lily had wanted to hear his vows of everlasting love, have him at her feet, so to speak. But he had turned on her instead.

'What do you mean, Henry?' she asked. 'You know I do.'

'Do you?'

'Yes! I married you, didn't I?'

'Ha!' Henry turned away angrily. In the half dark Lily watched his back, silhouetted against the bay window. The trees outside moved whisperingly in the wind. Her heart sank. She had gone too far. He might refuse to go with her to 'The Rooms', and she did so much want to wear her lovely new silk. She would have to make it up with him. Resigned to humbling herself, Lily rustled over to stand at her husband's side.

Nestling between the wings of the great chair, Cathy watched. Her hand comforted her still smarting calf. She knew she had been forgotten. She should get up now and leave the room, but she couldn't bring herself to break the spell. No, better keep still and just pretend she wasn't there. Her eyes glanced towards an unopened parcel still lying on the table. How she longed to go over and take it. If only she could, without disturbing her parents. It was her parcel. It must be. It was the only one left, and Daddy never came home from the sea without a present for Cathy.

'I'm sorry, Henry.'

Her mother's voice drew the child's attention back to the window. Her father's head inclined sadly, and he turned to look at her mother, questioning.

'Do you love me, Lily?'

'I love you, Daddy. I love you,' Cathy wanted to cry. But, child as she was, her instinct told her that her kind of love was not enough for him.

'Of course I do.' Lily's voice was light, evasive. And Henry moaned, burying his face in her breasts, his hands searching her clothes, drawing her closer to him. 'Not now, Henry.'

'You said you loved me!'

'Yes, but why does it always have to come to that! Men've got a funny way of showing their love, that's all I can say.'

Again, Henry turned from her. But she touched his arm, knowing the price of her forgiveness.

'All right, Henry. Just this once.'

'Thank you, Lily. Thank you.' And he was kissing her all over, crying in his relief, as he scurried his wife out of the room. Cathy listened to their steps, then she rose from the chair and approached the table.

The tissue paper crackled under her fingers. The thing inside was hard, with sharp edges; such a strange shape. She pulled away the layers of paper carefully, revealing the object beneath. It was a shell, a huge shell, it was as big as her own head! She had never seen anything like it. She took it to the window and saw the peachy-coloured roughness of the outside, shading down into the rosy insides. It was beautiful! She lowered her head to it, and sniffed, hoping to smell the salt of the Southern Seas. But there was nothing. Perhaps if she licked it. The little tongue flickered out and felt the roughness of the texture, and yes, there unmistakably was the tang she knew from her walks with Hettie on the seashore at Marsden. Gently, she shook it next, wondering if it rattled. And then she bent her ear towards it. There was a funny sound, a swishing, murmuring noise. She pressed the shell closer to her ear and her face lit up. Oh it was wonderful! How clever of her Daddy! What she wanted most was to know the seas he travelled, to see and hear the exotic things in the other half of the world. And here it was in her very own shell, the South Seas. All for her.

Cathy rushed out of the parlour, clutching the big shell in her arms.

'Daddy, I can hear the sea! I can hear the sea!' But he was not there. The hall was dark, and the big oak staircase loomed up to the gloomy upper floor. Suddenly, the child was afraid. She was all alone! Then she put the shell to her ear again, and whispered, 'I know you're there. I can hear you. Fish and dolphins, playing in the waves, diving to the bottom of the seabed. I can hear you.' And the shell whispered back.

The little nightdress was white and prim, the sheets clean and crisp, and Cathy crawled in between them.

'I suppose you'll be wanting another story!' Hettie said as she tucked her in. Cathy's eyes sparkled. 'All right, tell me what you want then.'

'Oh, Auntie . . . something about the sea . . .'

Hettie picked up the storybook and flipped through the pages.

'Here's one,' she said, '"The Little Mermaid".'

'What's one o' them?' Cathy asked, frowning.

'Well, pet, it's a kind of woman, except she isn't, because she's got a fish's tail.' The child's eyes opened wide. 'Look, there's a picture.' Hettie held the illustration in front of her, and Cathy gazed down at the fairytale princess, her long blonde hair flowing down over her naked body to a long, green tail.

'Where do they live, Auntie?'

'Oh, in the South Seas, I think, at the bottom of the ocean. They swim like . . . well, fish, I suppose.' Cathy giggled. 'They sing like the sea when the waves move along the surface in the moonlight, and sometimes they sit on rocks, like her, and comb their hair with starfish.'

'Oh Auntie! That's lovely! I wish I was a mermaid!'

'You'd catch your death, pet, in that cold water.'

'I wouldn't be one here. Not in the North Sea, Auntie.' The child frowned at her aunt's stupidity. 'Has Daddy seen one?'

'I don't know, pet. You'd better ask him.'

Cathy knew her father was wonderful, but oh, she never knew how wonderful! To have seen a real live mermaid! Yes, she would ask him tomorrow.

'Shall I read now?' Hettie asked.

Cathy nodded, and lay back against her pillows as Hettie settled on the edge of her bed to read to her.

'Far out in the sea, where the water is blue as the loveliest cornflower and clear as the purest crystal, where it is so deep that very many church towers must be heaped one upon the other to reach from the lowest depths to the surface above, dwell the Merpeople . . .' Hettie's hair, as she read, fell in wisps from her bun, and her new silk shawl had slipped to rest over her arms. Her face was gentle and her voice warm as buttered scones; comfortable, familiar Hettie. Even the gaslight lost its greenish, livid hue and glowed round her head; or so it seemed to Cathy. Then the child's eyes closed, and she was in the South Seas, where mermaids played, oyster shells on their tails, in beautiful palaces, with flowers growing out of the walls, fish swimming in through the windows, and eerie music blowing from shells just like her own. Oh it was wonderful. How she would love to be a real mermaid!

'Are you asleep, pet?' Hettie listened to the steady breathing of the little girl, then gently eased the huge shell from her grasp. She tiptoed to the chest of drawers and set it there, where Cathy would see it in the morning. Then, turning the gas down low, she noiselessly left the room and made her own, lonely way back to Thrift Street and the quayside, where her chores waited.

CHAPTER TWO

'A shell? What? You mean coral? He brought you a nice coral necklet, eh?'

Cathy shook her head. Her mother wouldn't understand, she knew. She would spoil it, but there was nothing for it. She had to be told.

'No, just a shell. Auntie Hettie says it's a conch shell.'

'Oh, so she's in on the secret, is she?'

'Fetch it down, pet. Show your Mam,' Henry said.

Reluctantly, Cathy left the room and dragged her feet up the stairs. The shell lay where Hettie had left it, displayed on the chest of drawers in pride of place. Cathy took it up, heavy as it was, and carted it back downstairs to show her mother. The voices were loud as she approached the parlour.

'You shouldn't encourage her, Henry. She's too much imagination as it is. Why could you not have brought her something more fitting?'

'She's only a bairn!'

'You don't understand, Henry. These are her formative years. You've got to start as you mean to go on. You don't know what she's like. You're always away. She's wild, Henry.' Henry snorted his disbelief. 'She is! She takes after you, that's her trouble! Why could you not have brought her something dainty, some handkerchiefs, or . . . well, a little necklet. Something ladylike!'

Lily's jaw dropped as Cathy tottered in, the shell hanging from her straining hands.

'Where did you get that? Whitley Bay?'

Cathy looked agonisingly at her father. He hadn't, had he?

'I got it from a sailor I met in Hong Kong. He'd just come back from the South Seas.'

Cathy sighed with relief.

'Listen, Mam. You can hear the sea!' She tried to push the shell up to her mother's ear, but Lily shook her off.

'Take it away!' she cried and held it from her with disdain. 'You don't know where it's been!'

'It's an exotic specimen, Lily.'

'Aye, well. Put it in a glass case where it belongs.'

'It's mine!' Tears smarted at Cathy's eyes. 'You're not havin' it put in a glass case!'

'You mind your manners, Miss! I'll dispose of this!' And Lily put the shell out of reach, behind the glass door of the display cabinet, turning the key in the lock before depositing it in her skirt pocket. 'Hear the sea, indeed. I told you. That child has far too much imagination.'

'What's mag. . .nation, Mam?'

'What you've got too much of!'

None the wiser, the child sighed and stared at the magical shell encased behind the glass of the cabinet door.

'Never mind, pet. Your Daddy'll make it up to you,' Henry said, as father and daughter crept out of the house and out of Lily's road, into the mist. Sea fret billowed in from the sea and the sharp cries of seagulls, seeking refuge from stormy weather, squalled overhead.

'By, I'm glad I'm not out in this!' he said, taking Cathy's hand. 'Now, what'll we do? I know, we'll go and see your Auntie Hettie!'

'But me Mam says you're not to take me there.'

'Well, don't let on then. It's a secret between you and me.' Cathy grinned broadly. 'And you know what going to see your Auntie Hettie means, don't you?'

Cathy was wild with delight.

'A ride on the tram!' Her mother never deigned to ride on public transport, but Cathy loved it. Her bottom wriggled on the seat beside her Dad, and she craned her neck to look out of the window behind her. Mist swirled all round them, so that she could hardly see the shapes of the trees as the horses drew them on from country village into the township of Shields. They might as well be high up in the clouds for all she could see of the scenery around them. Disappointed,

Cathy turned back and settled at last, remembering the question she had wanted to ask her father.

'Tell me about the mermaids, Dad,' she demanded gravely.

Henry was visibly taken aback. He looked out of the window, as though he might see them there, then shook his head, puzzled.

'What mermaids?'

'The mermaids that live in the South Seas!'

'Oh!' Henry nodded, as though he'd really known all along. '*Those* mermaids!'

Cathy gazed at him, waiting for him to go on.

'You know, she's right.'

Now it was Cathy's turn to look puzzled.

'Who?'

'Your Mam. You *have* got too much imagination.'

'Dad, what *is* magnation?'

'Well . . .' It wasn't easy to explain. 'It can get you into trouble.'

Cathy stared at him, worried. *She* had too much magnation, her mother said so, and that meant *she'd* get into trouble.

'It's when you pretend things're not what they are really.' The child's steady gaze made him falter. 'You make things up to suit yourself, like.'

'You mean, like tellin' lies?' Cathy asked, hurt that her father should think she told 'untruths'.

'Well, yes and no.' This was getting them nowhere. Cathy sighed in annoyance. 'It's when you don't see what's in front of your nose, what's real, and you see what you want to instead.'

'You mean like when Mam pretends we're not there and won't speak to us?'

Henry laughed delightedly.

'Aye, pet. Somethin' like that.'

'But there *are* mermaids, aren't there?' She willed him to say there were, and Henry hesitated. Lily was right again, he thought. Cathy *is* wilful. But he could not deny her, since she wanted it so passionately. After all, wasn't he just like her? Lily had seen it, in her wisdom. Cathy took after him, with his visions of grandeur, sailing the seven seas, seeing only success ahead of him when all the signs told him otherwise. He should nip this trait of 'magnation' in his little daughter now. He knew it. Her very future might depend on it. But, looking back into her desperate eyes, he could not. The moment was gone. He looked away.

'Aye. There are mermaids.'

Cathy sighed with relief. Her spirits bubbled up excitedly.

'Have you seen them, Daddy?'

Ah well, Henry thought, in for a sheep . . .

'Aye. I have.' Cathy was all round-eyed attention. How it pleased her to be told what she wanted to hear. 'Mind, you don't see them straight off, you only hear them! They sing these strange songs you see, and they do say that if a sailor hears a mermaid singing, he's doomed; you see, at first you think it's only the call of the sea . . .'

'Like in my shell, Daddy.'

'Aye. Like in your shell. But it isn't, and slowly you realise it's a voice, half human like, drifting across the waves to you, luring you on to your death.'

Cathy gasped in horror.

'But you're not goin' to die, are you?'

'No. Not me, pet. In fact I don't believe any of that. I think the boot's on the other foot. What I think is, it's a sort of swan song, see? You know that a swan sings just before its death?' Cathy didn't but she nodded just the same. 'Well, I think a mermaid does that an' all. You see, it's fatal for them to fall in love with a human.'

'That's what Auntie Hettie said in the story last night.' So that's where she got this mermaid business from, Henry thought. He might've known! 'The story said it was all right to love a man, but only if he loved her back, because otherwise she'd turn into the foam on the sea.' Henry nodded.

'That's just about the top and bottom of it,' he said.

'Will *I* turn into foam?' Cathy asked. Henry looked at her seriously and bent down to inspect her legs. 'What're you lookin' at?'

'Where's your tail, then?' he asked. Cathy burst out laughing. Oh how she loved her Daddy!

The tram filled up as it trundled on into town. Women with shawls round their heads, women in bonnets carrying shopping, men in work clothes on their way to the docks and West Holborn, with its busy streets, jam-packed with people and shops, trams and barrows. You could buy anything there from a tin bath to a hatpin, from a dress to a brush head. There were posh folk and workmen, fishwives and the hoi polloi, jostling together from Market Square all the way down King Street to the poor end of town and onto the quayside, where Hettie lived. The smells were strange and exciting; wet clothes, tar, horse dung, oil and sawdust all mixed together with the tang of the sea. You couldn't see it, but it was there. It dominated the little town like a master dominates his ship.

Before going down to see Hettie they called at the office in Union Lane, 'For an alibi', as Henry said. It was in a little cramped building, with a painted sign, 'Straker and Wapping', over the door. And Cathy was given a toffee to keep her quiet while Henry did some work.

'Mind you don't clag your teeth up,' he warned her.

'What's that mean, Dad?'

'Clag means . . . well clart . . . stick something up, like. It's Geordie. Eeh!' he laughed, 'your Mam doesn't half neglect your education!'

Savouring new knowledge, Cathy stayed quiet till they were, at last, in sight of Thrift Street and Hettie's boarding house.

Thrift Street was a wide street, built on the slope going down towards the river. It was cobbled, as all streets were in the 1890s, and lined with shops and seamen's lodgings. The smell of tar and the sea were stronger there than elsewhere, and the people frequenting it were of a different class. There were seamen, foreigners, 'scrubs' as they called the Icelanders, tall men from across the sea in Norway. There were Arabs, come to settle in Shields, starting up in a small way with corner shops and cafés. Local men hung around in the hopes of a ship, whiling away their time in the pubs. And there were women, encased in sombre shawls or with their man's cap on their heads, pushing bogies down the street because there wasn't enough money for a horse; and, of course, there was Auntie Hettie, who had inherited her 'doss house', as Lily called it, from her and Henry's parents, and who ran it now as her only source of income.

Number 15 Thrift Street was a tall house, with a lot of stairs and a narrow hall. It had a yard at the back with a lavatory and a washhouse. There was always a shining white line clean across the doorstep. Hettie was very proud of that.

'Watch me step!' she warned as she opened her door to Henry and Cathy that afternoon. 'I've just soap-stoned it.' So they carefully stepped over it and walked down the dismal hall into the kitchen, where they sat and warmed themselves before the range. Henry settled there, more comfortable than he ever felt in his wife's grand house, but Cathy wandered off. There was much for her to inspect.

Like a forbidden fruit, the house was all the more exciting for her mother's prohibition. Cathy wandered around it, half hoping, half fearing that some great bearded seaman would emerge from one of the rooms and frighten her. But they were all drowning the sea fret in the bar down the road. All except one. Cathy spied his sea boots in the hall. Great big things they were, with the tops turned down. They came almost up to her waist. She peered down into one of them and drew back sharply at the smell. She coughed, swallowing a whole piece of toffee and almost choked. She stood still, hoping Hettie wouldn't hear and come out to see what she was up to. But Hettie and her Daddy were deep in conversation. She could hear them arguing, their voices muffled by the chenille curtain that hung over the door.

'What's this I've been hearing down at the docks, Hettie?' Henry demanded.

'I'm sure I don't know what you mean!'

'You know very well, our Hettie. It's that Johnny Beale again. Aye! I saw his boots in the hall there. Hidin' from me, is he?'

'Now why would he do that, Henry?'

'Because he knows I'll wallop him if I set eyes on him, that's why! Muckin' around with my sister!'

'Sh! He'll hear you!'

'I want him to hear me! Hettie, man, you're crackers. What if his wife finds out?'

'What the mind doesn't know, the heart doesn't grieve over,' Hettie retorted.

'There's plenty as'll tell her. Honestly, I don't know what you see in him.'

'You want glasses, then!'

'Oh I see. Prince Charmin', is he? Handsome is as handsome does, Hettie.'

'He's nice to me, Harry. He is! He makes me . . . oh, come alive again.'

Henry was silent. How could he chide her for that? He knew what she meant. He only wished Lily could be more like her.

'I can't help me feelin's. I can't. I get carried away. That's the way I am.'

'Aye, but it's your future I'm thinkin' of. Now what about Tommy Minto, eh?'

'Huh! What *about* Tommy Minto!'

'He's a canny lad, is Tommy. And he's gone on you. You know he is.'

'He's a twerp. Not all there.'

'He's a ship's engineer, Hettie. You've got to be all there to be an engineer.'

'Well, he looks daft, then,' Hettie sulked. 'He's got a hump back an' all.'

'You're being silly, pet.'

'It's my life! It's incurable, his back you know. His Mam told me. They tried everythin' when he was a bairn, strapped seaweed to his back and everything, but it got no better.'

'Well, you wouldn't expect it to!'

'No, well, I'm only sayin'.'

'And I'm only sayin' that Tommy Minto is not to be sniffed at!'

'I love him, Harry. I love Johnny Beale.'

'Love! Look where it got me!'

'It got you a lass with money, Henry Straker, and that's not to be sniffed at neither. And look how you've let *her* down. Eeh, sometimes I feel sorry for that lass, in spite of her snotty ways.'

Cathy frowned as the voices rose again. Auntie Hettie feel sorry for her Mam? What did it all mean? Hettie was the poor relation. Her Mam was rich and beautiful. It didn't make sense.

'Don't change the subject,' Henry snapped. 'Hole-in-the-corner stuff with a married man. You're a disgrace, Hettie.'

Then Hettie started crying. Cathy frowned, again disturbed, her heart reaching out to her auntie with the voice like melting butter, who read her stories and held her close.

'You live in a dream, make-believe, telling lies to cover up.'

'You need talk! It'll be dark days ahead when Lily finds out what *you've* done. It will that! I wouldn't like to be in your shoes!'

Then Hettie jumped up and threw back the kitchen door as though panting for air, and saw Cathy up to her armpits in Johnny Beale's wellies.

'That bairn!' she cried. 'Look at her!' Henry came out, and the worried lines of his face gave way to a smile.

'Eeh, Cathy Straker! What *are* we goin' to do with you!'

Henry yanked his daughter up into the air, clear of Johnny's boots, and set her down on the lino floor, laughing.

'We'll have to set her on possin' the mucky clothes in the washhouse!'

Cathy looked up at her father, in horror. Her possing dirty clothes! Her Mam'd go mad if she heard such a thing so much as mentioned. She was going to be a lady and ladies never soiled their hands possin'! Why, even Auntie Hettie had a 'girl', Jessie Lidell, to do the washing and scrub the wooden steps that went down into the cellar.

'Eeh, don't look so worried, Cathy,' Hettie smiled. 'Never fear, I wouldn't dare risk it. I'm too scared of your Mam!' But Hettie, good humoured, didn't look scared at the moment, that hunted look only came over her face in Lily's presence. 'But mind . . . curiosity killed the cat! Today it's a strange man's boots, tomorrow who knows, if you're not careful! You've got to learn to mind your ps and qs, hinny. I mean, would you see your Mam tryin' on a pair of fishermen's smelly boots?' Cathy shook her head. 'And you do want to turn out like your mother, don't you?' Henry groaned, but Hettie gave him a look and he held his tongue. 'Because I do.'

Cathy looked up at her auntie disbelieving. How could she wish such a thing! Hettie! When her mother treated her like the dirt from under her feet? She was a saint, was her auntie, a real saint!

'Aye, Cathy. I do. And so does your Dad. He wouldn't want you to turn out like me.'

Henry hung his head. It was true. He didn't. He wanted better things for his daughter than a life of drudgery, running a boarding house, no man behind her, and a reputation soiled by 'goings on'.

'Do you, Daddy?' Cathy asked, alarmed.

'Yes, Cathy,' he said quietly. 'You have to keep yourself like a lady, fit for a prince, when the time comes.'

'Like the little mermaid?' Cathy asked, suddenly enthusiastic.

'Aye.' Hettie smiled, remembering the story from the night before. 'That's right, pet. And that means not doin' things like tryin' on other people's boots.'

'What *am* I supposed to do then?'

'Sit still and be quiet, lookin' as pretty as you are.'

'But that's borin', Auntie!' Hettie glanced at her brother.

'Aye, well,' she said. 'There's a big price to pay for adventure.'

The look on her face told Cathy she mustn't ask any more questions. It was always the same. Just when you were getting to the nitty gritty, grown-ups would clam up and not tell you any more. She sighed, and resigned herself to not knowing. It was hard work, being a lady, minding your ps and qs all the time, especially when you didn't know why you should.

'Haway, pet,' Hettie said gently, 'it's not such a crime. It's just your Mam wouldn't like it. So don't tell her, eh?' And she winked.

Cathy was relieved. So that was it! It was all right to have adventures so long as you weren't found out! Then you could be a lady and get your prince and that, and enjoy yourself on the quiet as well! Now that wasn't so bad!

It was dark as Henry Straker led his daughter by the hand to the tram. She was tired now. Her head snuggled down against her father, breathing in his warmth. She sighed. She'd never be able to work it all out. What price would she have to pay if she failed to be the lady her father wanted her to be? And what were 'dark days', when they were at home? It sounded nasty, did that. 'Dark days'. Cathy yawned and nestled closer in. The tram lurched as the horses plodded onwards up the hill from King Street. She was fast asleep when they halted at the arch. Her father held her still in his arms as the passengers waited for the horses to be changed. Through the steamed up window he watched the man emerge from the shadows, drawing the two fresh horses, and help as the old ones were unbuckled and replaced before they could all set off again, dragging on up the hill towards Westoe Village.

Aye, Henry had gone up in the world in more ways than one. But he was never cut out for a safe life, living in idle luxury. He *had* to gamble. And by, but he had! And Lily'd gone along with him, longing to equal Lady Readhead herself, their neighbour in the village. Her husband ran 'Readhead's Shipyards'. Such dreams of grandeur! Poor Lily. Hettie was right to feel sorry for her. If only she knew! But she didn't. Not yet. And, maybe, with a fair wind, she wouldn't have to, either. He could still pull things off. And his daughter would grow up to hobnob with the best of them, aye and marry a Readhead too if she liked! Then Lily'd be pleased! By heck she would! The horses strained up the steep slope. There were times when it felt like they'd stop altogether, and then, maybe, they'd all start slipping back down to the bottom of the hill. But they didn't. They went on till they were safely at the top, and stopped to let the passengers alight. Henry picked up his sleeping daughter and stepped down onto the road. He could hear the horses wheezing, harsh, panting breaths from the strain of the climb. By, but it was a wonder they didn't drop down dead with the effort, Henry thought. Cathy stirred in his arms. He looked at her sleeping face in the light from the lantern. She was a bonny lass, his Cathy. Aye, she would grow up to marry a prince, and live happily ever after, or she would if he had his way. Gently, he carried her down the tree-lined street, past the Readhead residence, and on to the smaller but still impressive house that was his wife's. He stood outside, staring up at it, frowning. Then, as though a decision had been reached, he strode purposefully in.

CHAPTER THREE

Cathy did her level best to behave like a lady. She let their maid, Ellen, twist her wild copper hair into rags every night, and slept uncomfortably on them so that the shining ringlets would please her mother the following day. Hettie was under orders from Lily to read to her from *Little Women*, and Cathy tried to see herself as Amy, the artistic sister who married the rich neighbour, because she knew that that, too, was what her mother wanted. And if her mother wanted it, then her Daddy also wanted it, for hadn't he said so? For Christmas she made samplers, one for her mother, one for her father, and one for Hettie, though her stitching was far from neat, and her fingertips were raw from the needle. And when the posh Stoddards down the street invited them to the same party as Lady Readhead, Cathy's mother thought they had arrived at last.

Henry, for all his efforts, had not been able to secure a cargo for some time. His rivals offered cheaper rates than he could afford with the interest on his debts. He put a cheerful air over his troubles when he was with Lily, but became increasingly silent and morose when he was alone with Cathy. He spent long hours in the office, 'doing his sums' as Cathy was told, and his face looked grey and drawn. But always they would call in on Hettie and that would cheer him up, sitting in her scullery, drinking tea, listening to the dull thud of the iron as Hettie smoothed the many shirts that came her way. Always, there was that pair of boots in the hall. Henry would purse his lips when he saw them as he passed along the dark corridor to the kitchen, and Hettie would throw her chin in the air and refuse to speak of the matter. Cathy longed to see the owner of those boots. Only once, when Henry had come early and Hettie, all flustered, had tried to stuff the hair back into her bun, did Cathy glimpse a pair of big feet stumbling up the scrubbed back stair, out of the way, as she and her father entered the room. Henry had made the visit short that day. He had been sharp with his sister, gone on about Tommy Minto, now first engineer, and chewed his lip. Hettie, flushed and wilful, as ever, looked happy, for all her brother's jibes, and Cathy marvelled to see the plain face come alive, and glowing. They talked as though she wasn't there, and without being asked Cathy knew she had to keep this secret alliance of Hettie's under her hat. Her mother knew Henry sometimes dropped in at his sister's. No one told her so, but she guessed, and when they got back she would question Cathy.

'Did you see . . . "anything"?' she'd say pointedly. And when Cathy asked what 'anything' meant, Lily would draw in a breath and say, 'Well . . . a man.' And she would hiss the word as though it described some green-eyed monster from the lower depths. And Cathy would just shake her head. Then Lily would look hard at her. 'Are you tellin' me the truth?' she'd say. And Cathy would nod, then say, 'I haven't seen no man, Mam.'

For it was true. She hadn't. Even when they'd got there early and surprised Hettie and Johnny Beale, all she'd seen was his feet, and you couldn't call that having seen 'a man' could you?

'You know what happens to little girls who tell lies?'

'They get into trouble, Mam.' And Cathy added to herself, 'If they get found out.'

But Hettie wouldn't get found out. At least not through Cathy. She would be loyal to her auntie, even if it meant telling an 'untruth'. But Henry, worried now after the 'feet' business, started cutting down on his visits to his sister, making them short and sweet when he did.

'It's not right, Hettie,' he said, when he thought Cathy was out of earshot. 'Our Cath's not daft. She knows there's somethin' going on, and it's not fair on her, askin' her to keep it quiet. I feel fair ashamed in front of her. I do!'

But then Johnny Beale went away. His boots no longer stood in the hall, and Hettie looked sad. But Henry was happier, and took his daughter to visit her again. There was an atmosphere of relief everywhere. Even Lily failed to get at her husband about his trips to Thrift Street. Johnny Beale was away, and the tongues would stop. She had to be thankful for small mercies. And Cathy was turning out nice. She was proud of her, especially since the Readheads had asked her round. Lily would see to it that she was decked out in her finest for the occasion, and got Ellen and Hettie to join her in choosing an outfit for her.

So there were some advantages in being a lady after all, Cathy thought, as she sat patiently in front of her bedroom mirror while Lily herself combed through the bright ringlets. Ellen had set out her finery on the bed, she could see it reflected in the mirror: her emerald velvet dress, trimmed with fur; her little black kid shoes; her fur cape; and her emerald hat, trimmed to match the dress, with a muff made out of the same material. Cathy itched to get it on. But her mother bade her be still, and yanked her head back so that she was looking straight in front at her own face.

'Eeh, there'll be no flies on you tonight, Cathy Straker. You're bonny. No doubt of it. You'll be driving men to drink by the time you're seventeen. You will!'

Lily dropped the comb for a moment and stared at Cathy's face. She was peaches and cream, only a few tiny freckles to mar her complexion; the velvet eyes loomed out of that paleness like dark pools, and the hair, oh the hair was bright as a copper kettle, shining round her head like a halo, startling in the intensity of its colour; but its wildness was tamed now. Tortured by rags and subdued by comb, it hung graceful and ladylike down the child's back in well-arranged curls, not one out of place.

'Mind, they do say redheads are hot tempered,' Lily mused, almost jealous of the copper strands, knowing her own dark, fine hair was as nothing in comparison. The colour of Cathy's was inherited from the Straker side, from Henry's mother.

'But I'm not sure that's right,' Lily went on. 'It's something else, more dangerous by far.'

Cathy wondered if it had anything to do with 'dark days' and looked fearfully at her copper hair. The little mermaid had had to cut hers off and give it to the seawitch along with her voice, so she could have legs and win her human prince. And then she'd gone and lost him, and faded into foam on the sea. But *she* wouldn't do anything so silly. Oh no. She liked her hair far too much to part with it.

'You're a big girl now,' her mother was saying, 'so you must remember your ps and qs.'

Always those 'ps and qs'.

'Yes, Mam.'

'More hangs on this do tonight than you know. And call me 'Ma' not 'Mam' while we're there, will you?'

'Yes Mam, I mean Ma.'

Just then Ellen, scuffing her heels as she walked, came into the room, her arms laden with freshly ironed underwear for Cathy. Lily frowned at those heels, wearing out her good carpets.

'Miss Straker called,' Ellen announced, 'and asked me to give you this, Miss.' And she handed a small parcel over to the child. As Cathy undid the wrapping, Ellen talked on. 'She said she wouldn't bother you by coming in, but she wanted Miss Catherine to have this tonight. I believe it's something for the party, like.' Ellen was laying the underclothes over the fender to warm.

'It's a handbag!' Cathy screamed with delight. 'A real handbag, with 'broidery on it and everythin', to go with me outfit!'

Lily pursed her lips. Always Hettie had to put her oar in, vying with her for her own daughter's affection. Even now, Cathy had no eyes for her new clothes on the bed, but was up in the air over having a real grown-up bag of her own.

'Very nice. You'll have to keep your hanky in there. Like ladies do,' Lily said, going to the fender to check the underthings. She raised them to her cheek to test their dryness. 'These underpants aren't properly aired, Ellen!' She frowned.

'I'm sorry, Ma'am, I'm sure,' Ellen said, put out.

'Never mind. We'll just have to leave them till last.'

And so saying, the two women set to dressing Cathy in

her finery, and then left her sitting on a hard chair by the window till her parents were also ready.

Henry looked his handsome best, and Lily, her fine dark hair adorned with flowers, was discreetly elegant in a blue silk dress. They surveyed each other in their bedroom mirror. Both smiled, their faces softened with the memory of their first meetings and their early love. She turned towards him and fiddled with his cravat.

'You will take the chance to get in with Stoddard, won't you?' she pleaded with him. 'I've heard tell he has more cargoes than he can handle, and you never know, he might throw something your way.'

Henry frowned. Taking charity from Lily's high-flown friends! Still, needs must. He sighed. Yes, he would humble himself. He had to. Lily didn't realise just how much he had to. Then they went down to the hall and waited while Ellen went to fetch Cathy.

Ellen was all of a fluster, what with her master and her mistress both wanting her at once, and then the range going out down below just when she'd needed hot irons! She fairly pushed Cathy out of her room and down the stairs. Lily surveyed her daughter proudly. She looked very nice. Henry, too, nodded his approval.

'Now, are we sure we've got everything?' Lily demanded.

Ellen frowned. She was sure there was something, if only she could remember what. Flustered, she looked at the girl, who was also racking her brains.

'Me bag! Me bag!' Cathy yelled suddenly.

Oh yes, of course. That was it. Ellen had laid it on the chest. Quickly, she went back upstairs and brought it down. Then she helped Lily on with her cloak and stood back to admire them all.

'Eeh!' she thought, 'but it's nice to work for the gentry!'

Then out they all swanned, taking a cab to go the half mile down the road to the mansion at the other end of the village.

It was a grand affair. Cathy was shy at first. She knew some of the children by sight and had joined them playing with their hoops in the street from time to time. But she had never seen them so dressed up before, nor they her. Her father watched her fondly as she mixed with the boys from the Stoddard and Readhead families. Henry turned to his wife and whispered in her ear, 'Look . . . that lad's sweet on her!'

'He's never!' Lily laughed. But she looked pleased all the same. 'That lad' was Gilbert Stoddard, eldest son of the shipping magnate and a real catch. He'd do! Never mind the Readheads!

'How old are you?' Gilbert, round-eyed at the shining curls, demanded.

'I was six in November,' Cathy replied. 'How old are you?'

'Nine.'

'Oh.'

'Would you like some toffee?' He held the sweet out to her.

'No thanks. It clags your teeth up.'

Gilbert frowned.

'D'ye not know what "clag" means?' Cathy asked as though the lad must be a dimwit.

Gilbert shook his head.

'It means the same as "clarts".'

Still the boy looked puzzled. Cathy sighed at his stupidity.

'It's Geordie, man. It means sticky and that.'

'Oh.' Light had dawned. 'We don't use words like that in our family.'

'Oh neither do we,' Cathy put in quickly, sensing she'd put her foot in it. 'Only me auntie does sometimes.'

'Oh.' Gilbert paused, nonplussed, and looked round at Mr and Mrs Straker, and then at his own parents who were talking with them. Ah well, he could always ask them later.

'Will you marry me?' he said.

'I'm not old enough,' Cathy answered him.

'Yes, but when you are,' he put in.

'I'll think about it.' Cathy smiled benignly on him, and let him serve her with ice-cream and trifle from the table.

Lily had engineered Henry into conversation with Mr Stoddard, and she herself was engaged in polite repartee with his wife when a loud scream distracted their attention. It had come from the other half of the room, where the children played. A child was heard sobbing loudly and a girl cried, 'Give it back! It's mine!'

Cathy, tears racing down her cheeks and red in the face, grabbed out at the bag in the girl's hand. It was the pretty bag that Hettie had given her, the one she had embroidered with her own hands.

'Findies keepies,' the girl said, holding it further from Cathy's reach.

'It's only a bag, Catherine, for heaven's sake.' Lily hurried in, alarmed. 'I'll get you another one. A better one.'

'I want *that* one!' Cathy stormed. It rent her small heart to see it being bandied about from pillar to post, always out of her reach, smeared with ice-cream and spoiled.

'I want it back!' she screamed.

The adults all stopped talking, and watched as Lily caught hold of her daughter's skirt, trying to restrain her, hissing at her through her teeth to be quiet. But Cathy was beyond everything now. She would have murdered to get her bag back and no power on earth could stop her, let alone Lily.

The bag was thrown high in the air and landed over the great fender, close to the fire. A woman screamed as Cathy leapt after it, and Mr Stoddard himself tore after her, grasping her legs and lifting her clear of the fire, the bag clutched victoriously in her hand. As he did so, the velvet skirt fell round Cathy's head amid layer upon layer of petticoat, to reveal a bare, pink bottom underneath.

Mr Stoddard was surprised, as well he might be. There was a gasp from the ladies, and then Henry, close behind in the bid to rescue his daughter, burst out laughing. The rest of the men followed suit, apart from Gilbert, who looked most embarrassed. Lily wished that the floor would open up under her. Together, she and Henry turned their daughter the right way up, revealing the dishevelled mass of red hair, mercifully hiding the tear-stained, flushed face beneath.

'We'll have to go,' Lily hissed at her husband.

'I don't see why,' Henry answered her. 'Mr Stoddard and I are doing very nicely. I'd prefer to stay.'

But Lily, feeling she could no longer hold up her head at the party, dragged Cathy away, bag still tightly grasped in her hand, put her cape round her and took her home.

'If only you'd behaved like a lady!' Lily wept. 'Nobody would have known.'

Cathy sighed. She had committed the crime of crimes. It was not so much being without her underpants that mattered. It was being found out.

Ellen was summarily dismissed, but Henry was none the worse for the incident. He and Stoddard struck up a friendly acquaintance, and his old rival put a little business his way from time to time. But although Henry had a cargo to take out, he rarely seemed to pick up another to bring back. It was wasteful of manpower and steam. If only he could drop his price! If only he had not got himself into debt!

Hettie was in the doghouse with Lily because of the bag business, but Henry still visited her on the quiet. It was a long time since Cathy had seen those boots in the hall, and she had almost forgotten about them, when, one day, she and Henry were surprised to find Hettie's front door open. She was usually very careful about locking it. 'You never know what might breeze in,' she'd say. Concerned, Henry went into the house without knocking, Cathy close on his heels. There were voices behind the scullery door. He opened it wide. There, bang in the middle of the kitchen, stood Hettie and Johnny Beale, locked in one another's arms and kissing for all they were worth. They jumped a mile apart as Henry flew in, and stood, dishevelled and guilty looking, waiting for him to speak. Cathy, forgotten, peered out at them from behind her father.

'He's just got in, Harry,' Hettie explained tremulously.

'I wash my hands of you, Hettie, I really do.' And Henry turned, banging into his daughter, before hurrying her out and away from the street.

It was a while before Cathy saw her Auntie Hettie again. She spent a lot of time at the Stoddard house, in spite of her rude display at Christmas, and she loved the great swing in their garden. She would make Gilbert push her on it for hours on end, and he never tired of doing so. Lily always checked Cathy's underthings most carefully whenever she went out, and no similar incident threatened to nip this hoped-for relationship in the bud. But Cathy missed the stories her auntie used to read to her. Sometimes, sitting quietly in the parlour at home, she would glance over to the big shell, still behind the glass of the display cabinet, and remember the strange music it made. She missed the tar smells and the adventure of Thrift Street, and plagued her father to take her there again.

It was summer now. Henry picked his way hesitantly amongst the Thrift Street bustle, Cathy's hand in his. He wasn't sure of his reception, nor was he sure if he was doing the right thing by calling there. He had his daughter to think of. He had told Hettie so, quite plainly. 'What an example you're setting her!' he had said. 'If you don't care about yourself, you might at least think of her!' And Hettie had cried then. She hated to think she wouldn't see her Cathy again, but she couldn't help herself where Johnny Beale was concerned. She just couldn't help herself. Henry knocked on the door and waited a long time for Hettie to open it. When she did, he gasped at the sight of her. She was grey looking, red-eyed and tired out.

'What's the matter, Hettie?' he asked anxiously.

'Nothing,' she said, then silently led them through the passage and into the scullery. There were no boots in the hall. Father and daughter sat in uneasy silence. Finally, Hettie spoke.

'You needn't worry, Cathy'll not get contaminated here. We'll not be seein' Johnny . . .' the word was hard for her to say '. . . again.' She sobbed, then gulped it down, refusing Henry's words of sympathy with a gesture.

'I don't want to speak of him,' she said.

'When?' Henry asked.

'Couple of weeks back.'

Then Hettie put the kettle on the hob to make some tea. Her movements were slow. She was obviously very tired.

'Are you eating and sleeping, Hettie?'

'Aha,' Hettie nodded, and sat back in her chair, waiting

for the water to boil. 'I just feel so sick all the time,' she whispered.

'Cathy, leave the room,' Henry said sharply.

Surprised, Cathy got up and went out into the hall. She heard her father close the door firmly and pull the curtain across, blotting out all sound from within. And she wandered aimlessly, playing with walking sticks and umbrellas left by the front door, then settling finally upstairs at a landing window, where she could put her head under one of the nets and stare out into the street. Her father was a long time coming for her, and when he did, his look was heavy and pained.

'I've to get a doctor to your auntie, Cathy. So I'm sending you home in a cab.'

Hettie was never the same after that. Cathy heard her Mam and Dad rowing over her often, late at night, when she was in bed. Her mother's voice was bitter and hard, but Henry fought her passionately. And, for once, Lily found herself having to give way. But it was autumn before Cathy saw Hettie again, when Lily finally allowed her to come to the house in Westoe. She wouldn't speak to her sister-in-law. Hettie, looking very thin and washed out, far older than her years, flinched in Lily's presence. Henry was kind, and brought his daughter to her, while Lily looked on in stony silence.

Cathy looked up into Hettie's face.

'Have you been sick, Auntie?' the child asked her.

'Yes, pet.'

'What did you have?'

'A fever, pet.'

'You look very pale, Auntie.'

'I lost a lot of blood, that's all that is.'

'That's enough of that!' And Hettie clammed up, sitting miserably, the fight gone out of her with her life's blood.

Cathy looked from Hettie to her mother, to her father, then back to Hettie again. Something dreadful had happened. She knew that. But what? Suddenly Hettie took hold of Cathy's hands and held them to her face, kissing them and crying loudly.

'She's not right!' Lily shouted. 'It's turned her brain.'

Henry gently parted the auntie from the niece, as Hettie sobbed out, 'My little girl. My little girl.'

Tears sprang in Cathy's eyes in sympathy, and she was taken away to her room by the new maid, Maisie, crying her heart out, without the faintest idea why.

CHAPTER FOUR

Henry went away, far away on business put his way by Stoddard, and Hettie spent a lot of time at Westoe. Lily complained of her extravagance. Once she had come home to find every lamp in the place on. They were on in the kitchen, in the parlour, and on the stairs. There was even one on in the lavatory. And Lily had been furious, 'Burnin' money is what you are, Hettie Straker! It's as well to be seen it isn't yours!' And Hettie had gone from the sublime to the ridiculous. Now she wouldn't put the lamps on at all if she could help it. She brought her own candles from Thrift Street and strained her eyes over the magazines and papers she hoarded in the kitchen. It annoyed Lily even more, and so the downtrodden woman got her own back. And she and Cathy conspired. *Little Women* was the prescribed reading for Lily's daughter, but Cathy insisted they continue to read the fairy stories. 'The Little Mermaid' was still the favourite and the small girl knew it almost by heart. And then someone returned the big rosy shell to Cathy's room when she wasn't looking. There it was, on her chest of drawers, where Hettie had first put it, large as life. Cathy stared at it in disbelief, and Hettie caught her looking at it, but said nothing, only smiled quietly to herself. Late at night, when Hettie had gone home to tend to her boarders and she was supposed to be asleep, Cathy rose from her bed and went across to the shell. It weighed heavier than she remembered, and she almost dropped it. But it still had the same music. She wished she could sing like that, like the mermaidens, far out at sea. Her heart yearned for her father, and her soul, the soul that the seawitch would never take from her, tore at its moorings in Cathy's small frame, passionately reaching out to her father across the wide sea. As she put the shell once again in its place and padded back to her bed, Cathy reflected that soon, very soon, she too would be grown up, and like the little mermaid, she would go out into the world, and maybe even find her prince.

Cathy's seventh birthday had come and gone, and the excitements of Christmas were drawing near. She went to the Stoddard house often, to play with Gilbert, who treated her as though she had a label pinned to her back saying, 'Fragile. With care.' 'He treats you like a lady,' her mother said. But it was boring; Cathy wanted to climb trees, and fight and kick, and release the emotional energy that seethed inside her. Her mother decided she was 'highly strung' and the doctor added his weight to the verdict. 'Send her for music lessons, dancing lessons, something like that. Steady her.' So Cathy was sent for singing lessons given by a lady who used to be on the stage. Her name was Fanny Liddell, and she lived on the hill between Westoe and the town. Lily had visions of musical evenings at home. But Cathy's eyes gleamed with thoughts of the bright lights and the music hall which she had never seen but which Miss Liddell told her all about, and Cathy practised hard at her singing, as much in the hopes of pleasing her father on his return as to prepare for her future career. Ah yes, this was the world for her, she decided. Fanny Liddell's voice rose and fell like music even when she wasn't singing. It had waves of emotion in it, and she felt passionately about many things. They were two of a kind, the singing mistress and the little girl; kindred spirits. But Fanny Liddell wasn't a lady. Oh no. She was an actress, and that was very different. Lily treated her like a servant when she took her daughter there, and Cathy was relieved when she left them, as she usually did, to go shopping in the town. 'Ladies don't show their feelin's, Cathy,' she'd say as she walked her daughter home after a particularly exciting tale told by the mistress. 'It's not nice.' And Cathy began to realise that at heart she wasn't a lady. But she had to behave like one all the same. And so she did. Even when, allowed downstairs after an illness, she had spied the conch shell, her conch shell, back in the display cabinet in the parlour, she had bitten back the outburst that came to her lips and swallowed her feelings. 'You must learn to suffer in silence, Cathy. It's more ladylike.' Her mother's voice echoed in her mind and she stifled her feelings accordingly. And, later, she was glad she had, for when she got back upstairs, her shell was back in its place on her chest of drawers. What a mystery! How had it flown from the parlour cabinet to her chest in the time it had taken her to walk up to her room? The next day, the truth dawned. There were now two shells. But which was hers? She dared not ask for fear that, reminded of the offensive presence in her room, Lily would have it removed, and for a long time afterwards Cathy pondered silently over those two shells and how they came to be.

Her father was expected home for Christmas, and in the New Year she was to be sent to school. Miss Liddell laboured hard to teach Cathy a new song to sing to the returning sailor at the Christmas celebration. It was a popular song and it was called, 'The Waters of Tyne'. The first verse went like this:

I cannot get to my love, though I would dee,
The water of Tyne runs between him and me,
And here I must stand with a tear in my ee,
Both sighin' an weepin', my true love to see.

Lily's back stiffened as she listened in Miss Liddell's parlour to these most unsuitable sentiments for a little girl to be singing. And Cathy's thin voice strained at the leashes of the notes pitifully, but her soul expressed itself through the lyrics all too clearly, and Lily privately decided that when her daughter went to school in the New Year she would discontinue the lessons with Miss Liddell. Most unsuitable! Cathy looked in vain for encouragement after her rendering, and received none from Lily. The hearts of both mistress and pupil sank to their boots.

The tree was in place in the downstairs hall, and the box of toys with which to decorate it stood close by. Cathy's underpants were checked carefully, for Gilbert Stoddard was invited to tea and to help with the Christmas ritual, passing up coloured baubles to his adored Cathy, who's artistic eye never failed to find just the right spot in which to place it. Hettie, in the kitchen with Maisie, cackled over the budding 'love story'. At teatime Lily let the pair take their plates into a corner to whisper secretively between themselves, as they usually did; Cathy telling Gilbert all about her plans, confiding in him as she would confide in no one else, about her dream of going on the stage. And he listened, round-eyed. He had no doubt of Cathy's ability to be an actress. He had no doubt of her ability to do anything she liked. And he begged her to sing for him, for, he was sure, her voice was wonderful. At first, Cathy was demure.

'Oh go on, Cathy. Sing for's,' he pleaded. And finally, after he had begged hard and long enough, she gave in gracefully. The music was far beyond her childish reach, and without the accompaniment of Miss Liddell's piano it wavered uncertainly from time to time, but Gilbert didn't notice such minor flaws. Her voice was clear and pure, and her eyes! Oh her eyes! They flashed like the sun, only to mist over as she pleaded and pleaded with the boatman to take her across the water to her lover on the other side. 'Showing off', her mother would call it later. But Gilbert didn't think of it that way. Cathy was his idol. He worshipped her, and his soul responded to the outpourings from her heart. He never cared about whether it was ladylike or not; nor that her hair was out of place. He loved it like that, wild and free like a copper halo round her head, tiny curls on the forehead teased out of her ribbon, tousled and wild and passionate, and beautiful. He would love her for ever. He knew he would. And Cathy knew it. She played him like a bow on a fiddle, aware of her surprising power over him.

Watching her, Lily felt a conflict of feelings inside herself. Her little girl would be able to have anybody she liked, with her looks and her compelling attraction, apparent in its childish way even now. But it was not Lily's way. And it was this that nagged her. It was not ladylike. No, Cathy's power was the power of the mistress, not the wife. And it could get her into trouble. And then Lily knew in her heart that her daughter outshone her by far. Lily had been beautiful, still was. But her beauty was of a cold and distant kind, while Cathy's was warm, startling the onlooker with its intensity. The difference was the difference between a meteor and a distant star. If a meteor flashed across the sky, the star didn't get a look in. And so there was jealousy in Lily's soul; jealousy, and hope and fear. That little girl, trilling out 'The Waters of Tyne' for her admirer, could break his heart even at her youthful age, but what would happen when she was older? Her wildness bore the seeds of her own undoing. Cathy sailed close to the wind, and Lily would have to watch her like a hawk while she grew up. The Straker in her daughter must be subdued.

Cathy sang on, unaware of the machinations of her mother's mind, knowing only that Gilbert Stoddard adored her and she gloried in it, forgetting even the absence of her father for a while, as the fragile glass baubles winked amongst the candles on the tree, and the golden coins shone on the branches.

It was Boxing Day when the glass shattered and the candles went out. They had had a quiet Christmas, the three of them on their own, with no news of Henry. His presents sat, still wrapped, under the tree, and Cathy felt a gnawing fear growing deep inside her. But she dared not speak of it. Hettie also longed to put her anxieties for her brother into words. But Lily was silent, and they took their cue from her. So Christmas Eve passed, and Christmas Day, and Boxing Day, the day of the Stoddard's party, came and still no one had spoken. And then Lily calmly summoned Hettie and Cathy and made them sit in the best chairs in the parlour while she sat down facing them, a piece of brown paper in her hand.

'Cathy, your father's dead,' she said.

Cathy stared at her, her face white against the vibrant colour of her hair. Hettie moaned and raised her hand to her head, as though to check it was still there.

'It's true,' Lily went on in a flat voice. 'I had a telegram from Lisbon two days ago. I thought to spare you the news till after Christmas.'

'How could you, Lily! How could you!' Hettie wailed.

And Lily blanched at the accusing tone in her sister-in-law's voice.

'What do you mean, how could I? You should be grateful!'

'How could you!' Hettie howled again, and reaching forward she snatched the paper from Lily's hand, though her eyes were too blurred by tears to read its contents.

'I see! I'm in the wrong, am I? Never a thought for me, have you! Never a thought about how I had to bottle up my feelings so's you two could enjoy yourselves.'

But Hettie was beyond rational discussion. Tears streaming down her cheeks, she thrust the paper back at Lily.

'What happened?' she sobbed. 'Was there a storm, or what?'

'A storm? No, Hettie. Henry got peritonitis. Died at sea. They stopped off at Lisbon, gave him a Christian burial, then put out again.'

Hettie wailed louder at this news. How could they, after burying her brother, just leave him there and put out to sea!

'Well, they did have a perishable cargo,' Lily reasoned.

'Oh dear,' Hettie sobbed. 'To think, Lily, Henry's dear bones rest on a foreign shore.'

'Well,' Lily snapped, annoyed at this display of grief, when she herself had been so restrained in her sorrow, 'I don't suppose he minds. And anyway,' the voice rose, 'it'll save us the expense of a funeral.'

That was one in the eye for Hettie. No matter that Lily broke down straight after she had said it and had to blow her nose hard several times to set herself to rights, in Hettie's view that had been a horrible, callous thing to say, and in front of the child too! But the child just sat, staring in front of her, looking for all the world as if somebody had just hit her over the head with a sledgehammer.

'Never mind, pet. You might be an orphan now, but you'll always have your Auntie Hettie.' Hettie took her limp and cold hand and brought it to her lips, kissing it and wetting it with her tears.

'She is not an orphan, Hettie. I, I might remind you, I am still very much alive!'

'I wonder this bairn isn't weepin',' Hettie said at last.

Lily looked at her daughter and frowned. She had expected a tantrum. She knew how much Cathy had worshipped her Daddy, even at her own expense. It was always him she wanted, never her. And yet now, having just been told that he was dead, she sat like a stone, without any feeling at all.

'It'll be the shock,' Hettie said. 'It'll come out later.'

Cathy let her auntie take her in her arms, and hold her close, and rock her knowing that Hettie needed her, just as she herself had sometimes needed a teddy bear when she'd been a baby. And the woman worked out her grief on the little girl who had no way of working out her own grief.

Lily watched her daughter over the following days, but still there was no display of emotion. It all seemed so unreal to Cathy. It was as if her father had suddenly gone off in a puff of smoke. There was not even a funeral to bring it home to her. He had simply been put out of her reach just like her conch shell, encased inside the glass cabinet. Gilbert, when he heard, was all attention. He would have laid down his life to make Cathy happy, but all he could do was to stand in the garden, blowing warmth into his fingers between the pushes he gave to the garden swing, as Cathy swayed, back and forth, her face still, in a world of her own. The only outward sign of unease in the little girl was that she had started to suck her thumb again, just as she had when she had been tiny. She would shut herself in her room, her thumb in her mouth, and read and read till her eyes dropped out. And always she turned back to the tale of the mermaid. She felt it to be hers alone, and through it she found the only outlet for her grief. The familiar words echoed through her mind: 'The mariners fancied their song was only the whistling wind, for if their ship was wrecked, all on board were drowned. For none but dead men enter the Mer King's palace.' 'None but dead men.' Her father was dead. Her mother had said so. He had died of a burst appendix and been buried at Lisbon. Not for him the encircling arms of a mermaid, then. 'None but dead men.' 'Dead.' But still Cathy couldn't cry. Her face might pale and swell with unshed tears, but even the story could not help her to unburden all the pent-up grief. Like the little mermaid, 'She would have wept, but mermaids cannot weep and therefore, when they are troubled, suffer infinitely more than human beings do.'

And then her mother came into her room. Lily had been crying. Cathy could see that from her red eyes, and the way her bottom lip trembled as though at any moment she'd be off again. She sat tremulously on the edge of Cathy's bed and took her daughter in her arms, rocking her as Hettie had done when told of her father's death.

'I want to talk to you, Cathy.' She spoke in a trembling voice and Cathy's heart lurched, wondering what more dreadful news was coming. 'I know you're only little, pet, but though I'd spare you this if I could, I'm afraid you've got to be told.'

Already Cathy's soul urged her to close her ears against what was coming. Something inside her warned her that she would not want to hear it. But her mother held her close, and insisted on telling her tale.

'I've been to the solicitor's this morning. You know what they are, don't you?'

Cathy shook her head.

'They deal in, well . . . the law, and that sort of thing. They look after your affairs for you. I had to go, you see, to find out how we stood, now that Hen . . . your Daddy's not with us any more, and . . . and . . . I'm afraid I got some rather bad news.' She paused to control the rising tears and anger in her breast, and Cathy's chest tightened with fear. 'It seems that Hen . . . your Dad borrowed money against this house, it's called a mortgage, without telling me. I mean,' and now Lily was telling herself, the walls of the room, imagined throngs from Westoe Village as much as her own daughter, 'I knew things'd been, well, a bit difficult last year, but I thought they'd bucked up. I mean, Mr Stoddard got him going again, so I thought . . . Anyway, apparently I was wrong. Things were worse than I'd thought. And this last trip he was on was a desperate bid to rescue the firm. And then he went and died and that's properly put the cat among the pigeons, hasn't it! Because now all the creditors are callin' in their debts, and we can't pay. So you see . . .' her voice rose in anguish, 'we're goin' to have to sell the house.' Sobs reached through her words, making the phrases jagged and almost incomprehensible. 'And, and . . . everything. We'll have nothing left, Cathy! Nothing but the clothes we stand up in!' Then she stopped and howled, wrenching up her grief from the depths of her being, her hands twisting in her daughter's hair, hurting her and pulling her head painfully towards her.

Gradually, the crying subsided. But still, the little girl sat, with no display of feeling. Her mother drew back from her, holding her at arm's length.

'Mind, Cathy,' she said, shaking her head in wonder, 'you're a tower of strength. I'll say that. I'd never've thought it. Cool as a cucumber, and I know how you loved your Daddy.' Again she shook her head and stared in amazement at her daughter. 'I'm proud of you, pet. I really am. I thought . . . Well, never mind what I thought. You're takin' it like a real little lady. You are that!' She sniffed the tears back up her nose, then searched for her handkerchief, already sodden with previous crying, and blew her nose on it. 'But there's worse to come, pet.' She took Cathy's hand and held it in hers. 'Have you thought where we'll have to live?'

Cathy looked at her, waiting to be told.

'Eeh, the shame! Me Dad'd turn in his grave!'

Still Cathy waited.

'There's nothin' for it, pet. We'll have to go and live . . . live . . .' Lily gasped for the words, 'with your Auntie Hettie in Thrift Street.'

The words 'Thrift Street' came out in a shriek of dismay. Lily stared at the impassive face of the child.

'Do you not mind?' she asked in disbelief.

Cathy shook her head, and Lily's mouth hardened. What was this? she thought. It wasn't natural. The child just wasn't natural!

'I like Auntie Hettie's house,' Cathy said belligerently.

This was too much. Lily's mouth dropped open. This was worse than she'd ever dreamed. The child wanted to descend to the squalor of the quayside. Yes! That was it! Her heart was there. After all, she was a Straker. Yes a Straker, and she'd never be a lady now!

Cathy's face was sullen and downcast. Lily moved herself away from her so that she could look at her face more easily.

'I know you thought the world of your Daddy, Cathy.' Again the warning voice told the child to shut her ears. 'But he was only a man, after all. And they're not made of sugar and spice, you know. Oh yes, when I was younger I thought they were as well. They're all right when they're boys. I mean, look at Gilbert. Butter wouldn't melt in his mouth now. But wait till he gets a bit bigger! Oh, it's a different story then, I can tell you.' She paused, gathering steam. 'And I want you to know what your Dad did to me, Cathy, so's it'll be a warning to you, for the future. I didn't have the benefit of a mother like you, you know. Oh no, my Mam died when I was fourteen and me Dad passed on soon after, in the cholera epidemic, but anyway that's all water under the bridge now. But, well . . . what I'm tryin' to say is, all I had was a spinster aunt, me great-aunt she was, Aunt Jessie, to tell me about . . . things. And she was a romantic fool if ever there was one, and she had me full of the same nonsense. Well, then your Dad came along!'

Cathy groaned. Her hands shot up to her ears, but her mother pulled them away again.

'No. You must listen. You must. It's for your own good! Well, I was full of romantic nonsense and he . . . well he was like all men. You see, pet, they confuse love and passion. Now, your Dad had a . . . passion for me. And being young I didn't know what that meant. I thought it was romantic love, you know sugar and spice. And I was flattered, I must say I was. So I let it go to me head and when he asked me to marry him, I said yes.'

Lily paused and looked at the tightly closed eyes of her daughter.

'Well,' she went on, 'once we were married he soon taught me different. He was a cruel man in some ways, Cathy. He was!' she insisted, as Cathy shook her head. 'He hurt me . . . physically, I mean. Well, all that's rather rude really, but that's not all. He mortgaged my house, without telling me, and risked everything for his own selfish dreams with no thought for either of us. Oh no Cathy, not even for you!'

A small tear squeezed out from under the clenched eyelids of the little girl. Her mother had found her mark at last.

'I'm tellin' you this for your own good, you know, pet.' And in her way she was. She paused to let the fact sink in. 'You see, pet, I've got to be sure that *you* won't be as daft as I was and let your romantic little heart get carried away with you, for I know you. I do. You've got to realise, pet, and the sooner the better, so you get used to the idea, that in the matter of men, you've got to be ruled by your head. When your time comes, and I'm relying on you for this, Cathy, I'll expect you to choose someone sensible . . . no matter what he looks like or how charmin' he is or isn't as the case might be. Just so long as he's respectable, and keeps you as I want you to be kept. Like a lady.' She paused and sobbed before going on, 'And then, maybe, we might even get back here, where we belong. Have a house in Westoe . . .' Then she cried again, before taking Cathy's arm and gripping it tightly. 'Promise me, Cathy. Promise me, on your immortal soul, that you'll do as I tell you and choose somebody sensible!'

It was a cry from the heart. But Cathy sat, bolt upright, without saying a word, tears smarting at her eyelids. Lily sat for a while, staring at her, then got up and left the room without another word. Days later, when she was clearing out, ready for the coming auction, Lily found the expensive china doll she had bought Cathy for her birthday stuffed, head down, into the rubbish. Its legs stuck up out of its petticoats and it had no bloomers on. Lily bit her lip, pulled it out, then stuffed it back the right way up.

It all happened very quickly. Hettie came up and helped, and even Maisie, knowing she'd get no wages for her work, sorted and sifted their possessions. Lily was worse than useless. She kept disappearing to the water closet to be sick. But Cathy knuckled down, sorting out the toys and clothes she would take with her to Thrift Street. She wouldn't be allowed her fur cape. That would be sold along with her mother's furs. But she was allowed to take the green velvet dress, hat and muff with her. Her heart was torn over the shells. She packed the one in her room, but kept going back to the cabinet in the parlour to look at the other one, unsure which of them was the genuine article. In the end, Hettie managed to get the keys to the cabinet from Lily and got it out for her. Then it was packed, alongside the other, to be taken to their new home. The day before the auction, they left Westoe Village. Lily was 'dosed up to the eyeballs', as Hettie put it, for they'd never've got her away otherwise. And Maisie was there to help load the trunks and parcels onto the bogie. A bogie in Westoe Village! It was as well Lily *was* dosed! Even Hettie and Cathy felt the shame as they hitched up to sit themselves on the back, while Lily joined the driver at the front, and the horses set off down the tree-lined street.

Curtains twitched at the windows, and Lily hung her head as they passed the houses of their old neighbours. As they turned the corner out of the village and faced the long hill down into Shields, Lily clenched her teeth and swore that somehow, some day, they would ride back up that hill, not on the back of a bogie as now, but in style, and enter Westoe Village once again, as rightful residents of that exclusive domain. She turned her head, and beyond her daughter's shining, copper hair she saw the small figure of Gilbert Stoddard racing out of the village after them. As they gathered speed and descended the hill, he stopped, took out a handkerchief and waved, staring mournfully at the ever increasing distance between himself and his idol.

PART TWO

CHAPTER FIVE

The seaman tucked his paper under his arm and bent down in the hall to put on his boots. It was a nice day and he had time to spare. He thought he might just take himself down to Beacon Lawe for a look out to sea and a sit. It was a better place for picking up bits o' news than any newspaper. Aye, they all gathered there, rivermen and seamen, old men and kids, all drawn by the spell of the sea. As if they hadn't had enough of it, sick to their eyeballs of being prey to its whims and fancies, still they couldn't forget it. It drew them like a woman. They cursed it and loved it in the same breath. Even when they were in the drink, there was no getting away from it. For their eyes would mist and they would sing the sentimental songs of their calling, their voices cracking with emotion, great soft men that they were.

There was a flurry in the kitchen. The heavy curtain was drawn aside and the kitchen door flung open. Before he knew it, the seaman found himself cracking his head against the wall, pushed out of the way by the figure of a young girl in a tearing hurry.

'Hoi!' he yelled.

But she had gone, and the front door had clanged shut behind her. Quickly he hustled on his remaining boot and snatched open the door to look out after her, rubbing his throbbing head.

'What's the marra?' he called after the flying petticoats. 'Devil after you, is he?'

The hand, holding on the straw boater, dropped, and the girl turned, still walking backwards up the street.

'Sorry Mr Miller,' she shouted back. A sudden gust of wind caught under the rim of her hat and she whipped round to catch it as it sailed off her head, revealing the bright red curls underneath.

The seaman shook his head. You couldn't be angry for long, not with Cathy Straker.

'Late again.'

The woman sitting knitting outside the front door made a space for him on her stool, and he sat, looking after the disappearing girl.

'Goin' at a rate of knots, eh?'

'She is that. Aye, frightened she'll miss the tram, I shouldn't wonder. It's her mornin' for helpin' in the wash-house. Half day from work, like.'

'Pity she couldn't get work nearer home.'

'Her mother wouldn't hear of it, Mr Miller. Not good enough for her.' And the woman sniffed her disapproval as she counted the stitches on her needle.

The tram was rattling away from the stop, when Cathy reached it. Winded already, she leaped after it, pelting down the tram lines, sparks flying from the electric cable overhead, and, before it gathered speed, she managed to jump onto the platform with the timely assistance of a young gentleman who had watched the race from his seat on the lower deck. Wheezing like a ferryboat, Cathy sank thankfully into the place he had vacated for her and smiled her thanks. He smiled back, his eye caught by the little dimples that showed at each side of her mouth as the pink lips curled. The conductor was upstairs, on the open top deck. She had time to gather herself before he came for her fare. She took one last deep breath to steady herself, and her bosom rose and fell again under the neat blouse. The young man couldn't keep his eyes off her, and the whole tram knew it! He was standing next to her, holding onto the leather strap above her head, and he swayed against her with the movement of the carriage. His knees brushed hers, once, twice, and then she pulled her legs back clear of him, and made a show of arranging her skirt demurely over them. Then she raised her head and gave him a warning look. To her surprise, he winked at her. Actually winked! In full view of all them people! Cathy gasped. What did he think she was? Could he not see she was a lady? To her horror, his feet shuffled closer, and her legs, pressed back against the seat already, could retreat no further. Then the tram swayed, and once again his knees grazed hers. Wriggling uncomfortably in her seat, Cathy's eyes pleaded with his to let her off, to leave her be.

'Please,' she hissed. 'You're squashing me!'

And then his foot moved and brushed the toe of her shoe. Angry now, she bent down to dust the leather with her gloved hand. They were good shoes. She didn't want scuff marks on them!

'You're no gentleman,' she cried indignantly.

'And you're no . . .'

'Is this man troubling you, Miss Straker?'

Cathy's head swung round to see the bared head of Joe Robson at her side. Her heart sang with grateful relief.

'Yes, he is,' she announced.

'Then I'd be warned if I was you.' Joe's chest pushed against the man's fancy waistcoat. 'This young lady is a relative of mine and I'll thank you to leave her alone.'

Everybody was watching them. The young gent in his felt hat and suit, and the workman in his shapeless jacket, cap in hand, who dared oppose him. Their eyes locked for what seemed to Cathy an age, and then the 'gent' shrugged and sidled off further down the tram.

'Thanks, Mr Robson,' she said, and he swelled visibly with the pride he felt in defending her.

The tram swayed round a corner. Joe, gripping the leather strap, pitted his strength against gravity and avoided touching so much as the edge of Cathy's skirt. Cathy saw the straining muscles of his thighs through the slack trousers and knew that he worshipped her, this man she hardly knew, this young cousin of Auntie Hettie's from North Shields, on the other side of the river. Why, he would lay down his life for her if need be. They had hardly passed more than half a dozen words together when they'd met the summer before on the *Ha'penny Dodger*. She had been sixteen then, and her form just beginning to round into womanhood. It had been one of those rare occasions when Hettie had asserted herself. She wanted to go over the water and visit her relatives on the other side.

'I don't know why you bother, Hettie,' Lily had said. 'They don't bother about you, do they?'

And it was true. Hettie never saw her relations from one year to the next. But she'd made up her mind. She had family other than her sister-in-law, and she wanted to show her that. So Lily sighed and hummed and hawed, and muttered things like, 'North Shields!' as though it was the midden of the world, and 'Now, if it had been Whitley Bay!' as though that salubrious resort was the acme of modern civilisation. But in the end she gave way. She even let her take her young niece along with her for the ride. For Cathy was always pestering on about boat trips and such like, asking the seamen that lodged with them to take her out, and mooning round the quay and the seashore. She'd long ago tired of the little paddle boats on the lake at Marine Park, and now it was a proper ship she hankered after. So, Lily thought, maybe a ride on the ferry would keep her quiet for a while. And Cathy and Hettie had dressed in their Sunday best, swanked their way down to Comical Corner, and descended the steps to the riverside where the ferry, the *Ha'penny Dodger* as they all called it, boarded. Oh but it had been exciting! As they waited on the planks and watched, the ferry churned in, chucking up bucketfuls of dirty river water in its wake, steam puffing from its chimney. A man stood ready to take the great thick rope thrown out to him and haul with all his might, as the boat glided in to bounce gently off the wooden sides of the platform, and then secure it to the capstan in strong sweeping movements. When the North Shields folk had got off, the South Shields folk got on, and made for their favourite places from which they could watch the drama of the embarkation.

Seagulls screeched overhead, following the ferry as it chugged across the river, diving down for crumbs when some old bloke shared his bait with him. He didn't get much of them sandwiches eaten, Cathy remembered. Not with so many gulls waiting to be fed. Cathy made her way to the stern, with Hettie close on her heels, and leaned over the side to stare, as though mesmerised, at the churning, oily water in their wake. Schools of dolphins swam in the river in those days, and Cathy watched as they threw themselves up out of the water and dived down under it, their tails flicking up out of the grey river. Like mermaids' tails they were, Cathy thought idly as she watched them. All too soon, the engine's noise deepened, and the ferry manoeuvred towards the landing stage at the other side. There was the return trip to look forward to, of course, but now Cathy was filled with the anti-climax of happy landings, as they waited to be let off onto the quay.

Suddenly Hettie shouted out, 'Look! There's our Joe!' and she called over the heads of the crowding people, 'Joe! Joe!' And a young man in dirty overalls looked up, dazzled by the sunlight, to see where the voice had come from. He was wiping his hands on an oily rag, and his face was streaked with black.

'Joe! Joe!' Hettie was waving now, dragging Cathy from the front of the queue to the back of it, away from the disembarking passengers.

'Whey if it's not wer Hettie!' He grinned as he saw her.

'What are you doin' here, Joe? You're not workin' on the *Ha'penny Dodger* are you?'

'Aye,' Joe nodded, lookin' down at his filthy clothes. 'Stoker. I've just come up for a gulp of air between trips like.'

Hettie frowned.

'But I thought you'd got set on a trawler,' she said, 'fishin'.'

'Aye. I did. But there's more sense in this, Hettie. You see, I'm savin'.'

Hettie's eyes questioned him.

'Aha. Savin',' he went on. 'Goin' to go shares in a boat of me own.'

Hettie gasped.

'Eeh, you're never! Well, all power to your elbow, Joe.'

And they'd smiled at each other. Ten years younger than her, she'd always looked on Joe more like a nephew than a cousin, and though they hardly saw each other, living on different sides of the river as they did, Hettie had always had a soft spot for Joe Robson. But now he looked uneasily at the girl restlessly silent behind her.

'Who's this then?' he'd asked.

'Eeh, I'm sorry. I forgot in all me excitement. You've never met, have you? This is Cathy. Catherine Straker. You know, Henry's little lass.'

Joe shyly put out his hand to her, dazzled by the copper hair and huge brown eyes.

'Pleased to meet you,' he said. But Cathy had drawn back.

'You'll dirty me frock,' she had said, and his hand had withdrawn as though stung by a nettle.

'It's all right, pet. Nowt to be afraid of. It's honest muck, any road.' And he had smiled sheepishly as the girl retreated from him. Poor Joe. He was smitten on the spot. And judging by her nice clothes and the proud tilt of her head, she was as out of his reach as a Russian Grand Duchess.

'Bonny lass that!' His eyes followed Cathy, though he spoke to Hettie.

'Aye. She'll make somebody a fine wife some day, Joe,' she said. And both of them knew, though neither said it, that Joe hadn't the ghost of a chance of being the lucky man.

'Aye well,' he sighed. 'I'd better get back down. Stoke up for the next trip. Tarrah Hettie.'

Then, with one more glance in the direction of Catherine Straker, Joe Robson turned and went back down into the bowels of the ship.

Hettie hurried to catch up the queue of disembarking passengers.

'Eeh, our Cathy. D'ye know?' she whispered in Cathy's ear, 'I think he took a shine to you?' And she giggled delightedly. 'You're growin' up, pet! Eeh, who'd've thought it!'

Cathy was angry. How dare he! A stoker on the *Ha'penny Dodger*! Not even a proper sailor on a proper ship on the real sea! How dare he! And her thought was reflected in the tilt of her chin. Hettie saw it, and was hurt for the lad.

'You needn't turn your nose up like that, our Cathy! Who d'ye think you are, eh? By, lass! You'll have me thinkin' you take after your Mam after all!'

And that had been enough to make the young lady hang her head in shame.

Such had been her first meeting with Joe Robson.

'I'm surprised you knew me, Miss,' Joe bashfully broke the ice between them, as the tram swayed on. 'Out of me muck, like.'

And Cathy deigned to smile at him. She'd been grateful enough of his presence today anyway, she thought.

'Good job you were there, Mr Robson,' she said politely. 'I didn't see you when I got on.'

'I was upstairs,' Joe explained.

Cathy flushed. Then he too had seen her running, her skirts flying and her hair streaming from the ribbon that caught it back.

'I knew you at once,' he said.

Cathy gave him a cold look and he realised his mistake.

'Ocean Road,' the conductor called. And Cathy, getting up from her seat, said a civil goodbye before easing out of the tram and stepping onto the cobblestones outside. She looked every inch a lady now. Holding her head high and ignoring the desperate eyes trying to catch hers for a last wave from the tram windows Cathy walked sedately across the road to Miss Hutchinson's hat shop.

'Nice day,' she said as she took off her gloves in the shop.

'Very,' said Miss Hutchinson. 'Like spring.' And she set a bunch of silk snowdrops into the brim of a powder-blue hat.

But it wasn't spring. Not yet. The day had dawned clear and bright, with blue skies, and the people of Shields felt the warmth of the sun on their backs after the coldness of winter. It brought them out onto the streets to promenade in spring clothes, or to sit on their doorsteps pondering the mysterious revival of the year. But a false spring was not unknown. A dangerous thing it was. And it was not just the risk that the likes of Catherine Straker ran, in putting on a light dress too early in the season. The worst they were likely to catch was a cold. No. It was the seamen who had the most to lose, seduced by a lying day into setting out during the treacherous month of March. 'Dead March' they called it. 'Dead.' More boats were lost in that month than at any other time of the year, when sudden winds whipped up the waves far out in the North Sea, and fogs sped down the river to catch you unawares. But it was the time when Hettie, at least, did good business. They all came, captains and cabin boys alike, knocking on her door.

'Lodgin's or consultation?' she'd ask.

And they'd look up and down the street before lowering their voices to whisper in confidence, 'Consultation.'

Then Hettie would nod, and lead them inside, through the hall and up the dark stairs to disappear into her darkened room, the lampshade mysteriously green, to mutter over the Tarot cards and the upturned palms. Was it safe to go out? Would they miss a catch if they didn't? Would the young lad find a boat, or a lover? Was the world at their feet, the devil at their back, or would the magician conjure away their wives and sweethearts leaving them with the hanged man and the death card.

Cathy had pestered her auntie for years to do her a reading. But Hettie had shaken her head and said, 'The cards are not to be taken lightly, Cathy.' And anyway, she knew what Lily would have to say if she did. But Cathy persisted, creeping up the stairs to hang around in the passage outside Hettie's room till her mother came and chased her away.

'Come away from there, Catherine. It's not nice listenin' at people's doors.'

Then there was the chink of coins changing hands. Cross my palm with silver. And the door opened to the departing client, his face plainly showing what the cards revealed. Cathy got to be as good at reading faces as Hettie was at cards, but her aunt never told her how close she was to the truth.

'It's sacrosanct, Cathy,' she would say. 'Like the confessional.'

On this false spring day of March 1913, a seaman dragged his hopes over the cobbles to knock on the door of Number 15 Thrift Street. He was tall and blond, and came from over the sea. A captain he said he was, and he was young. Hettie took him up, as usual, and read his palm, while Lily seethed in the kitchen, acting the skivvy, and getting their teas ready for Cathy coming in.

It was a quarter to nine. Where was the girl? The mist had

come in from the sea, and the air was cold and damp. She was sure her daughter had left without a jacket on her when she had rushed out at dinner time. Headstrong and wilful as ever. 'She'll catch her death,' Lily thought as she turned the cabbage in the frying pan.

But she needn't have worried. Cathy was even now alighting from the tram, warmly wrapped in a shawl lent her by her solicitous employer, Miss Hutchinson. She was clutching a piece of paper in her hand and her step was light as she hurried away from the main street towards the gaslit reaches of the quay. It had come at last. To Shields itself! The bioscope was opening at the Queen's. And she wanted to go. Her mother had never let Hettie take her to the music hall, but in spite of her Cathy knew the names of all the artistes that appeared at the Tivoli and the Empire. She bought postcards of them all and kept them in a tin box in her drawer. Surely she would be allowed to go to this! The bioscope, opening in Shields, who'd've thought it?

Panting and happy, she skirted round the back of the street, up the yard, past the washhouse and up the scrubbed wooden steps into the scullery. Her face fell. Her mother was in a mood. She could tell. No use asking her just now. Quickly, she hid the paper behind her back, then, turning to take off her shawl, she folded it and slipped it in her bag.

'Tut!' Lily eyed the unfamiliar shawl. 'The folly of it. Goin' out without your jacket.'

Cathy said nothing.

'That one of hers, is it?' Lily indicated the shawl lying on the chair by the window.

'Aha. I'll take it back tomorrow.'

'Mind you do.'

'What's for me tea?'

'Bubble and squeak,' said her mother, scraping the onion and cabbage across the hot frying pan, and turning it to brown the other side. Cathy sighed. She might've known. It was washday. They always got bubble and squeak on washday. Cathy shivered. She would have liked to get near the range, but it was fenced off by mounds of airing clothes, laid across rails, chairs, clothes horses, anything that would serve. The combination of steam and frying cabbage, her mother's hands, red up to the exposed elbows from the washing soda, and the martyred face above, brought down Cathy's heart.

'Mr Miller's got a lump on his head the size of an egg,' Lily announced.

Cathy frowned. She felt accusation in her mother's tone and wondered why.

'It's a wonder we've got any lodgers at all, the way you carry on. Tut! You'll have to say you're sorry.'

And Cathy remembered. She hadn't realised she'd hurt him. She liked Mr Miller. He was a canny old soul. Retired from the sea, he had taken the Captain's room, him with the nasty habits and the chamber pot, and had stayed with them all through the Captain's long absence at sea, so that on his return there had been 'no room at the inn' as Lily had said victoriously. He'd never stayed with them again and 'good riddance to bad rubbish' they all said. They liked Mr Miller. He played the piano and had nice manners, keeping them entertained in the long winter evenings.

'I'll tell him I'm sorry,' Cathy said. Lily sniffed. 'Would you like me to see to the fire in the parlour?'

'If you like,' came the terse reply. And it meant, as Cathy well knew, 'Yes and be quick about it.' So Cathy wrapped a pinny round her skirt, made her way through the hall and opened the sacred door to the parlour. 'The Sanctuary', Hettie and Cathy called it, though never in Lily's hearing. The room had been used for the boarders in Hettie's day, a place where they could sit and while away the evenings. But when Lily came all that was changed. 'I'm not goin' to spend the rest of my days cooped up in a scullery,' she insisted, and immediately set about banishing the men from the room, flinging windows open to get rid of the terrible smell of pipe tobacco that clung to the drapes, and setting Jessie the scullery maid to scrub and polish and generally restore the room to its former glory. That is, until Hettie had gently pointed out that now the boarding house had to support the three of them they couldn't afford a scullery maid, but would have to do all the work themselves. Mortified, but not beaten, Lily fairly strangled the sheets soaking in the washhouse and left them limp and lifeless in the tin bath at her feet. Watching her, Hettie would wonder just who Lily had in mind when she wrung the laundry so viciously with her bare hands. The elegant white hands roughened and grew red. At night she larded them and put on a pair of linen gloves in the hopes that in the morning they would have returned to their old lilywhite appearance.

'We must struggle, Catherine, to remember who we are,' Cathy recalled her saying, over and over again. 'We must keep our dignity.' And Lily would lie awake through the long nights, listening to the sound of fog horns mournfully calling out to the ships at sea, and bitter tears silently stained her cheeks.

In the beginning, Lily had been drawn back to Westoe. She would put on her best and take the tram up the hill, to walk among the trees, the young saplings that grew on either side of the street. She stared forlornly at the old house and the carriage horses that grazed on the green in the centre of the village. But it was a bitter pleasure. Her heart burst with the pain of it, and always there was the fear of bumping into old neighbours. Once, Mrs Stoddard had seen her, tears welling up in her eyes, looking up at her old house, and had gently pulled her away and taken her in to give her a cup of tea, before sending her on her way back into Shields. Lily felt the woman's kindness more keenly than her loss. It was a humiliation to her to be treated with such charity, and she never went near the old shady haunts again. Unwittingly, Mrs Stoddard had cured her.

But she made the best of Thrift Street. She had rescued one or two pieces of her own from the Westoe house. Things that she could prove were hers, for her private use; nothing to do with Henry at all. And they let her take them. The chaise longue she had used as a day bed became the centrepiece in the parlour of 15 Thrift Street. And her piano, which she had never played but which had been her father's, stood stately in the corner, the brass candlesticks ornamenting the polished wood on its front. And how she nursed those pieces. She polished them weekly, put a dustcover

over the chaise longue and kept the curtains permanently drawn to prevent the wood from fading, and the outside world from coming in. 'The Sanctuary.' It was well named. For it was here that Lily came when her work was done, to sit in state and preside over the teapot. The lodgers called her 'Lady Muck' on the quiet, but they deemed it an honour to be invited into the parlour, to be 'received' by Lily. They put on their best bibs and tuckers then. Hettie was encouraged to play the piano. She had a musical ear, though no training, and Lily's dreams began to extend to musical evenings. Always, she kept her head up and her sights set on her daughter's future prospects. There lay her hope. With her copper hair, which had not dulled with the years, her sweet oval face and natural grace, Cathy would haul her mother back up the hill to Westoe. If only she met the right people. That was the difficulty. The job in the milliner's was a start. It was a high-class establishment, Miss Hutchinson's, attracting the better class of people. There were the public 'dos' too, where Lily could parade her daughter, and bow to old acquaintances, hoping that somehow they would think to send an invitation to an 'at home', or a dance, where her daughter might finally meet the 'right' man. But Cathy had to be trained for such society. Hence the idea of musical evenings. With Hettie on the piano, Cathy would be able to polish her singing and shine in the drawing rooms of the upper classes. So Lily dreamt and worked for Cathy's future, and her own.

Raking the cinders, such dreams of grandeur were far from Cathy's mind. All she wanted was permission to go with the girls from the shop to the Queen's. The moving pictures had come to the town, and she was going to see this phenomenon or die! The paper flared. The sticks caught and the coal spat. Wiping her hands on her pinny, Cathy cleared the debris away into the pail and rose to leave the room.

A door opened upstairs and steps were heard coming down into the hall. Cathy opened the parlour door and bumped into a young seaman on his way out. Her attention was on the pail, which nearly flew out of her hand, and she simply muttered, 'Sorry', before going on back into the scullery. But he had noticed her all right. He peered after her down the dimly lit hall. He could swear that hair had been red, the colour of copper. He would have liked to see it in daylight! A neat little figure she had, and a slim ankle, above which a well-formed calf rose enticingly, only to disappear under her skirt. Hettie, pocketing a silver threepence, came down after him to show him out.

'Thank you so much, Miss Straker,' he said in the lilting accent of his country.

'Don't mention it,' Hettie replied, and shut the door against him, bracing herself for the storm which she knew awaited her in the scullery.

The seaman looked back at the closed door, then up at the sign which hung above it. 'Straker's Lodgings' it said. Then he turned and made his way back down the cobblestones to the quayside, a smile twisting at the corner of his mouth.

CHAPTER SIX

'I don't know why you don't hire a caravan, put coins on your scarf and be done with it, Hettie!' Hettie sniffed in a corner, where she had retired with one of her magazines, and Cathy sat silently, eating her bubble and squeak. 'Who d'ye think washes up, peels the vegetables, washes the mucky sheets from all them filthy sailors, eh? While you sit upstairs, like . . . like . . . Lady Muck, playin' cards!'

Cathy starting at the use of Lily's own nickname, choked on a bit of cabbage and coughed hoarsely.

'And you! Runnin' round with no clothes on.'

'Don't exaggerate, Ma,' Cathy gasped.

'And don't you answer me back. It's no wonder you catch colds!'

'I haven't caught cold. I got a bit of me tea stuck!'

There was a moment's pause while Lily racked her brains to remember where she'd got to. Like a fool, Cathy thought, Hettie went and reminded her.

'I don't play cards, Lily. I read fortunes.'

'It's not even Christian!'

'They believe in it, Lily. They always come in 'Dead March'. They need to know. You can't deny them that.'

'Tut! What rubbish! It's moonshine. That's all it is. Moonshine.'

'It's a different story when you need the money, though, isn't it!'

Lily refused to answer this just remark.

'We need the extra cash, Lily. Our Cathy's growin' up.'

Cathy sighed. As usual when the women quarrelled, the truce was called only at the mention of her name. It was always the same. If it was for Cathy, then it was all right. They'd each put up with whatever it was they didn't like. Cathy felt the weight of this responsibility like a load on her back. How she wished she could get away and just leave them to it. They could fight like cat and dog then, and she wouldn't care. She'd be far away instead of being pig in the middle like she was now. Suddenly, feeling an urgent need to get out of the close, steaming kitchen and the two rowing women, Cathy rose.

'I'm going up,' she announced, making for the scullery door. Her mother looked up, surprised.

'Are you not goin' to sit in the parlour, pet? You've lit the fire, haven't you?'

'I'm tired.'

Cathy got the door open and went out without more ado, dashing quickly up the stairs to the privacy of her own room.

She stood leaning against the door in the darkness for a while, listening to the foghorns. The mist had thickened into a fog which had swirled up the river and swelled now at her window, mizzling the panes. She walked towards it and peered out. But there was nothing to see. Feeling for the matches on the mantelpiece, she lit the candle by her bed and looked round the little room. The wallpaper was old and faded, but at least there was wallpaper. A damp patch darkened the corner of the chimney breast where it joined the ceiling. The little iron grate was empty. There was bare lino on the floor and a clippie rug by her iron bed, on which she sat now. But at least she had the luxury of a real feather bed to lie on. She leaned back on it and rested her legs, weary from a day in the shop. She closed her eyes for a while and listened to the sounds in the house. Pigeons nested in the loft above her and perched on the dormer window. She could hear them scuffling. The steep slope of the walls reflected the slope of the roof and she heard the birds sliding from time to time from top to bottom, down the damp tiles. A floorboard creaked on the stair as Old Man Jock climbed up to his 'Look Out', as he called his room, to splutter and spit noisily behind his closed door.

'I don't want your sausages,' she heard him mutter grimly, then his bed twanged as he threw himself down and began to snore almost immediately. The front door banged and someone came in, singing. Mr Hills that was, with a skinful already. And then her mother's sharp tones rebuking him rising up the three floors. And then the foghorns. Always the foghorns. She loved them really. Late at night, when the house was asleep, and she lay awake thinking, she would listen to them, waiting for the next blow of the warning horn, familiar, like an old companion, making her feel safe and less alone. They were like an old friend, like Rag Doll Mary, sitting at the bottom of her bed, and the two shells on her chest of drawers.

Cathy pushed her chin down towards her neck and strained to see them through the bars of the bedstead. There they stood, glowing by the light of the single candle, rosy as ever. One was bigger than the other, something she hadn't noticed when she'd been a child and they'd been kept separate, one in the cabinet downstairs and one on her chest of drawers. They looked funny together, as though one had somehow spawned the other. If that was so, she thought idly, then the big one must have been the original. But she never knew, not really, which was which or where the second one had come from. She got up now from her feather bed and went across to them; taking one in each hand, she raised them to her ears and listened, as she had a thousand times before, to the music trapped inside them. 'Moonshine.' And she remembered the words of the story Hettie used to read to her when she was little:

'When you are fifteen, you will be permitted to rise to the surface of the sea; you will then sit by moonlight in the cleft of the rocks, see the ships sail by and learn to distinguish towns and men. "Oh if only I were fifteen," sighed the little mermaid. "I know that I should love the upper world and its inhabitants so much."' She, Cathy, was seventeen now. When would the day of her release arrive? And what would she find when it did? Putting down the shells, Cathy, fingers sore from sewing flowers on hats, undid her blouse, unbuttoned her skirt, unhooked her corset and loosened her hair, letting it hang like a curtain over her face, and shaking it free of its bondage. How she would like to escape from the pent-up streets, the pent-up lips of the people who lived in them, the smug little parlour, and the steaming kitchen. Her mother sought to marry her off to some old fogie. She was sure of that. It didn't matter what he was like just so long as he was rich. She shivered at the thought, and dived under the bedclothes. Not what she had in mind at all. If only she had let her keep on with her lessons at Miss Liddell's. She had offered to take Cathy free when she'd got to know of their plight, but Lily had turned her down. The offer had been like a slap in the face to her. She wouldn't even consider it. How dare someone like that offer them charity? Bad enough that Mrs Stoddard . . . Cathy often wondered how that unfinished sentence of her mother's should have ended. Mrs Stoddard . . . Mrs Stoddard . . . she remembered her vaguely, from the dim and distant past. She remembered the affair of the bloomers, certainly; she had never been allowed to forget it! And there had been a little boy. What was his name? Graham? George? What was it now? Cathy yawned. Well, what did it matter? It was all past and gone, like the story of someone else's life. Nothing to do with her.

Cathy frowned and felt for her bag, by the side of her bed. It clanged against the chamber as she caught it up and laid it on the coverlet. If only she had continued with those lessons. She might have been somebody then. Like Miss Liddell had been. Like Vesta Tilley, like Violet Vanbrugh, like Cissie Loftus and Mabel Love. Instead of being here now with an old fogie in prospect. Untrained as it was, her voice was good. It held its own even against Hettie's accompaniment! Deaf to the noises in the house, Cathy quietly sang, as she opened her bag: 'I cannot get to my love, though I would dee, The water of Tyne runs between him and me . . .'

She had forgotten to mention to Hettie that she'd seen her cousin, Joe. Ah well. No matter. Cathy fished the bill out of her bag and smoothed it with her hand. It was an advertisement for the new programme at the Queen's: 'The Greatest Exclusive Picture Ever Produced – East Lynne' it read. She sighed. Perhaps her mother would be in a better mood tomorrow. She'd maybe get the chance to ask her then.

Then she reached for the old, battered storybook and leafed through the familiar pages. It comforted her like the sound of foghorns on the river, and she read of the little mermaid:

'If a mermaid can win the affections of a human being as to become dearer to him than father or mother, if he loved thee with all his heart and promised, whilst the priest joined his hands with thine, to be always faithful to thee; then his soul would flow into thine and thou wouldst become partaker of human bliss.' The book dropped from Cathy's hands, and her head fell back onto her pillow. 'His soul would flow into thine.' Now if she could have that . . . Cathy sighed.

In the parlour, Lily sat in solitary state, doing the mending. Hettie, crouched by the still warm stove in the scullery, devoured the lurid romances of her favourite magazines, and three flights up, in her attic room, Cathy smiled sweetly in her sleep, her copper hair spread across the expanse of her pillow, like seaweed at low tide, swathed across the rocks at Marsden.

The next day dawned with a lugubrious light, for the fog had still not lifted. The weary foghorns sent their intermittent warnings out to sea, and the ships, feeling their way into port, answered dismally. Cathy yawned and stretched luxuriously on her soft feather bed. Her legs explored the wide expanse at either side of her. It was warm and soft and spacious, like a world of its own, till she opened her eyes. She had always slept in this room; ever since they had come to Thrift Street. In the beginning her mother and she had had to share this bed in the attic, there not being enough rooms to spare in the house at the time. Her mother could have shared the bed in Hettie's room, of course. But there were 'reasons', as Lily had put it, why not. Cathy had supposed it was because Hettie snored, that her mother preferred her daughter's company in the cramped little room at the top of the house to her sister-in-law's more spacious apartment on the first floor. But it was not. To tell the truth, Lily just could not bring herself to sleep in 'that bed'. The one night she had tried she had lain stiff and fully dressed on her side of the dividing bolster, imagining the scandalous goings on that had caused the horsehair mattress to dip so perilously in its middle. Next morning she had packed up her belongings and carried them up the narrow stairs, to dump them on the floor of Cathy's room. It had been a desperate act. For she didn't want to live in this garret and be kept awake night after night by the pigeons in the loft. She hoped that Hettie would take the hint and suggest that she herself change rooms, leaving the large room on the first floor to Lily and her daughter, while Hettie took the attic. Of course, Lily dreamt of having the large bedroom to herself but could not really hope for such a thing. As it turned out, however, Hettie refused to take the hint at all, and having departed the first bedroom in high dudgeon, Lily was forced to stay in the garret with her daughter permanently. Where Cathy did benefit from the arrangement, though, was in the matter of the feather bed. For Lily absolutely refused to sleep on itchy horsehair. She had salvaged some of her jewellery from the wreck of her fortunes, unknown to the receiver, and had sacrificed a ring in order to buy the feather bed Cathy slept on now. For some years Lily and her daughter had slept, the bolster between them, in that one small room. Hints, ever more obvious as time went on, were dropped from time to time about people selfishly taking up a lot of space while others were cramped up together. But Hettie never let on that she had understood, if indeed she had. And Cathy couldn't blame her. It was her house after all, left her by her parents, and it was good of her to have taken in her destitute family as it was. But then, when Cathy started working and bringing in a wage, it was agreed that when one of the lodger's rooms fell vacant Lily should have it. They could now afford to do without the extra rent. And so it was that on this foggy morning Cathy found herself alone in her own double bed up in the attic.

She smelt the dank smoky odour that fog has even before she opened her eyes, as the yellow pall seeped in under the sash. Then she registered the foghorns and she knew, without looking, that it was a dismal day. If only she could stay in bed. But she had to be up and dressed, ready to help with the breakfasts and the cleaning, before the long trudge up the hill to the tram stop and her day's labour at the shop. But Cathy didn't mind the drudgery itself. It was just the boredom, the lack of colour in her life that rankled her. Her wild, restless nature longed to be up and doing. Her expressive features longed for something to express and someone to express it to! She ached for adventure, romance and glamour. She was only seventeen, she was beautiful, and everyone liked her. But when she looked at Hettie and her mother, her heart sank, and she was afraid. She didn't want to end up like them.

Yawning, she threw her legs over the side of the bed onto the cold linoleum. She had slept in her camisole and underpants, dozing off without even blowing out her candle. It was gutted now. She bit her lip. Her Mam would go mad at the waste. Quickly, she dressed; not in the light frock of yesterday but in the worsted skirt she had worn most of the winter, drab and boring as it was. She yanked the brush through her hair. It stood out wild from her head, like a mane. She laughed when she saw it in her little mirror and reached for the Macassar oil which she used to tame it. It made the copper light shine so. She loved it. The girls at work admired it, and yet it didn't always please Cathy. Her hair restricted her. She could never wear the vibrant scarlets and pinks that they wore, and there were only so many variations of blue and green after all. 'You should wear brown,' Miss Hutchinson had told her, 'dark brown. The colour of your eyes. You are a brown velvet lady.' It sounded lovely that. But fat chance she had of getting a velvet suit, and brown flannel or worsted just wasn't the same. Ah well. She picked out a navy ribbon to match her skirt and drew back the long ringlets neatly. Then, pulling on her boots and tying up the laces, she was ready to fly down the flight of stairs, candle secreted under the jacket on her arm, and into the kitchen where she could get rid of the evidence of her wastefulness without her Mam being any the wiser.

Hettie was there before her, raking out the stove. She glanced at the gutted candlestick but never said a word. And

Cathy scraped the dead wax out into the bowl kept for the purpose, so that later they would be able to melt it down and make rough candles with bits of string for a wick. Then she put on her pinny, fetched coal from the cellar, sticks and paper, and set to lighting the range, while Hettie laid the big table in the lodgers' dining room.

It was the usual routine. Lily came down later, after the fires were lit, and, yawning, fried the bacon for the breakfasts. Hettie served up and made tea. Cathy acted as waitress. Poor Mr Miller came down, looking rather dazed, and pointedly rubbed his head when Cathy came in with his bacon and dipped bread.

'Eeh, I'm sorry, Mr Miller. I didn't realise,' Cathy said at once. Mr Miller sighed and looked disconsolate. Cathy put the plate before him. 'Shall I rub it better?' she said, smiling. He made a sort of 'If you like' expression and Cathy rubbed it gently. 'By, but you've got a cracker there,' she said. 'Never mind. Kiss it better.' Then she leaned forwards and he bent his head towards her as her mouth touched the bump. 'There now. All better,' she said, as if to a child. And Mr Miller was consoled. He nodded his satisfaction and dug into his breakfast, while Cathy went out, smiling, for his tea.

She sang as she helped with the washing up.

'What have you got to be so cheerful about?' her mother demanded.

'Nothing,' Cathy said, 'just fighting the miserable weather, that's all.' And she smiled at her mother. Lily looked at her in wonder. How could she keep so cheerful under such circumstances? You just couldn't keep the lass down.

Bait box and tram money waited on the table. Cathy slowly put on her jacket and watched till her mother's back was turned, then slipped the bill about the Queen's out of her bag and laid it on top of the dresser where her mother would see it. Maybe, if she had the idea of going herself, it would be different, she thought. Whereas if Cathy suggested it Lily would 'pooh pooh' the idea straight away. Then she picked up her box and her money, snatched a bit of bread and dripping and hurried out into the dank morning air for her tram.

As the tram scuttled away into the town, Lily put away the pots. Bending down to open the dresser doors, her eye was caught by the piece of printed paper on the top. She picked it up and strained to read it. Eeh, but her eyes were going to the dogs. They were. She reached for her glasses and read: 'The Greatest Exclusive Picture Ever produced – East Lynne'. The first moving picture to be shown in Shields. That was an event all right. The bioscope, eh? The world and his aunt would be there on the first night. Aye, maybe even the Stoddards! How had the bill got there? Hettie obviously didn't know anything about it. She'd been too curious when Lily had picked it up and started reading it.

'What's that, Lily?' she'd asked.

And Lily'd answered, 'Nowt,' and put the bill in her pocket.

Mabel Chapman and Ethel Williams were all agog about the new bioscope. Miss Hutchinson had already seen a moving picture, in Newcastle, and told them all about it. It was hard for them to imagine what it could be like, this new phenomenon.

'It's like . . .' Miss Hutchinson sought for a suitable image to explain it to them, 'It's like a magic box. Now you've seen one of them, haven't you?'

Mabel and Ethel shook their heads, but Cathy bent over her work and said nothing.

'Well, it's a sort of barrel-shaped thing, with a handle on the side. Inside are a series of cards with a picture on each of them. When you turn the handle the pictures go round and it looks like it's one picture that actually moves and changes.'

Still the two girls looked puzzled. Miss Hutchinson sighed.

'Do you know what I mean, Catherine?'

Cathy shook her head. She knew exactly what Miss Hutchinson meant, but she wouldn't let on. She'd had a toy like that as a child, when they lived in the village. She remembered it well. It had been a picture of a boy with a ball, and he had seemed to throw it up and down as the cards revolved quickly. But it was a rich child's toy, and neither Mabel nor Ethel had ever been rich, so Cathy didn't let them know that she had. It would have seemed like lording it over them, and she didn't like doing that. Already they admired her for her good looks, how much worse it would be if they realised that she had once lived in the lap of luxury! Cathy wanted to be one of them. She wasn't 'snotty', as they'd have called it, not with anyone. She had a facility for mixing with anyone, whether they were above her or beneath her in station. It just didn't matter to her and that was the truth of it. When she had turned her nose up at Joe, it had been because he lacked romance. As a brother she would have accepted him gladly, but as a young man with his eye on her, well, that was different. She wanted more for herself than to settle for the stale routine of being a stoker's girl! The man she married would take her out of all that, or she wouldn't marry at all. She'd shock them all instead by going on the stage!

'Isn't it a kind of toy?' Cathy volunteered at last. Miss Hutchinson frowned.

'Do you know, now I come to think . . .' and off she went upstairs into her private quarters and they heard her scratting around above their heads.

At dinner time, Cathy opened her bait box to find the same old paste sandwiches inside. She sighed, and offered them to the other girls. Ethel, who was a maid of all work and rarely touched an actual hat, took one eagerly. She always seemed to be hungry, that girl, and she was always thin. But Mabel disdained the thin slices smeared with paste.

'I have to think of my figure,' she said. For Mabel fancied herself, and well she might. For she was the one Miss Hutchinson trusted with shaping the felt, while Cathy was confined to decorating them afterwards.

'Mabel has the skill, Cathy. But you have the eye,' Miss Hutchinson would say as she surveyed a new creation, which owed its life to the combined efforts of the two girls. She was a kindly mistress, and the atmosphere in the shop was always 'congenial', as she put it, but she worked them hard all the same. She was a good businesswoman and got every ounce of labour out of them that she paid for.

Now, as Cathy fingered a paste sandwich without interest, she was glad of the diversion when Miss Hutchinson came bustling in with a huge cardboard box in her hands, set it down before her staff and carefully lifted out a strange round object. Ethel's jaw dropped.

'Them's never the spring fashions!' she said.

Miss Hutchinson almost dropped the battered old object and Mabel and Cathy fell from their chairs, near to wetting themselves with laughter, as Miss Hutchinson set the thing down on the work table before them.

'See if you can work it out for yourselves,' she said smiling, then left them to it.

Cathy set down her sandwich and brought it towards them.

'I suppose,' she said, as though she was just guessing, 'you're meant to turn this.' And she took the handle and turned it round. Ethel gasped. In the viewer at the front she could see the picture of a little girl. She had a skipping rope, and when Cathy turned the handle the little girl seemed to be actually skipping, the rope moving round and round, and the legs moving up and down. It was amazing!

'That's what the moving pictures are like,' Miss Hutchinson popped her head round to say, 'only much much better.'

All through dinner the girls played with the toy, taking turns at the handle. And then their dinner time was ended, and work began again on the hats for the Easter Parade. But all the talk was of the toy and the new bioscope.

It was almost three, when the shop bell clanged and two people came into the shop. Miss Hutchinson was there to serve them, and the girls behind the baize curtains held their tongues as the business went on in the front. It was a young man and his mother. The young man spoke little, and when he did it was in a quiet voice. He obviously didn't like being in such a female environment. But his mother talked enough for the pair of them. She was a new customer, obviously rich, and from the upper crust. But it was a sweet, gentle voice, strangely familiar to Cathy. Miss Hutchinson was bowing and scraping before the gracious lady.

'You'd think she was the Queen!' Mabel whispered, sneeringly. But Cathy did not reply. The voice brought back memories; memories of sun through leafy shades, dappling its light on grass. Laughter echoed in her memory too, the laughter of children. There was a swing. Yes. In a garden.

Miss Hutchinson had nothing made up which pleased the lady.

'I'll just get one of my assistants to help you, Mrs Stoddard.'

Cathy jumped.

'What's the marra?' Mabel asked.

'I pricked my finger,' Cathy lied.

Then the baize curtain was drawn aside.

'I'm sure we'll be able to create something special for you.'

Miss Hutchinson put her head round and in her genteel voice, the one reserved for serving customers, she said, 'Will one of you two young ladies step this way, please?'

Ethel, of course, was not even considered for such an honour. Her duties extended only to sweeping the floor, washing, tidying up and helping upstairs in the 'rooms'. So it was always left to Mabel and Cathy to compete for helping Miss Hutchinson in the shop. Usually they rushed at the opportunity, fairly pushing each other out of the way in their eagerness. But not so today. Cathy stayed where she was, as though she hadn't heard. Miss Hutchinson and Mabel looked at her amazed, and it was Mabel who walked with ladylike demeanour, into the shop.

As the curtain fell Cathy looked round briefly and caught a glimpse of a young man standing self-consciously in a corner of the shop. He was tall and slim, but had good wide shoulders. His hair was brown, and his face bore a patient, amused expression. It was a handsome face; not strikingly so, perhaps, but a strong bone structure, and an open, frank look in his wide grey eyes. Cathy smiled to herself. Mabel would be making eyes at him all right.

Cathy wished the young man would speak, so she could

hear his voice. What was his name? It began with G. She was sure of it. George? Geoffrey? Ge . . . Oh what was it?

Miss Hutchinson was getting irritated with her assistant. She wished fervently that Cathy had come in instead. What was the matter with her anyway? Sitting there like a lump of suet as if she hadn't heard. Mabel was showing a switch of cloth to the young man, asking him whether he thought it would suit the lady.

'I'm sure Mrs Stoddard is quite capable of asking the gentleman's opinion for herself, Miss Chapman!' her employer reprimanded her sharply.

'No no, my son has excellent taste. I often ask his opinion. Gilbert, do tell us what you think!'

Gilbert! Yes, that was it. Gilbert Stoddard. In a flash of memory Cathy saw him, a white handkerchief in his hand, waving as she descended the hill on the day they left Westoe. She hadn't seen him since. Cathy smiled. Gilbert. Yes.

'Gilbert has a penchant for colour, I find,' Mrs Stoddard was saying. 'He hates anything dull and drab. "I want life," he says.' Mrs Stoddard laughed.

'Good old Gilbert,' Cathy thought wryly, as she stitched a grey ostrich feather along the brim of a silver-grey hat.

'It is heartening, certainly, to find such taste developed in one so young,' Miss Hutchinson said obsequiously.

'All things bright and beautiful, eh, Gilbert?' Mrs Stoddard laughed. 'My, it doesn't seem five minutes since he was singing that, such a sweet little boy, and here he is, twenty-one next month!'

Miss Hutchinson made a suitable noise, her mouth full of pins. There was a moment's silence.

'And is the young man marking the occasion with some sort of gathering?' Miss Hutchinson ventured to ask, as soon as her mouth was free of pins.

'Oh yes! We're holding a reception and dance at the Queen's Hall,' she said jubilantly. She was obviously looking forward to it very much. 'Everyone will be there.'

'Not quite,' Cathy thought, and laughed to herself. But then, she wouldn't have wanted to be. Mrs Stoddard was friendly and chatty enough with everyone, it was true, just so long as they knew their place. Oh yes, kind though she was, the third verse of that children's hymn, which she remembered so nostalgically, certainly applied to Mrs Stoddard if it applied to anyone. It expressed her attitudes exactly:

The rich man in his castle,
The poor man at his gate,
God made them, high or lowly,
And order'd their estate.

She had made Cathy welcome enough, but then a child was of no consequence, socially speaking. It would be different now that Cathy was almost grown up. Her instinct told her to keep out of the woman's way and to avoid making herself known to her. She had no desire to be the poor man at her gate, or at Gilbert's come to that. Riches were all well and good, but not if you had to beg for them. She wished him joy of his birthday reception, and was glad when they both left the shop.

Cathy was unusually quiet for the rest of that afternoon. Miss Hutchinson noticed it and wondered why. But Mabel, too full of the young Mr Stoddard, didn't question her companion's reticence. Ethel, bored by the talk, for she had been upstairs cleaning during the greater part of the visit, preferred to talk about the bioscope.

'We must get up a party an' go, Cathy,' she said.

'I wonder if Mr Stoddard'll go?' Mabel reflected aloud. 'He winked at me, you know, Cathy. Honest! He did!'

Cathy's heart was heavy as she walked for the tram that night, though she didn't quite know why. The magic box had reminded her of her childhood and her father, and then when the Stoddards came into the shop, somehow it had made her feel uneasy. The daily grind seemed more irksome than before, the world more dull and colourless. Gilbert wanted 'life' apparently. 'He hates anything dull and drab.' Well, he wasn't the only one, but his chance of getting what he wanted seemed far greater than hers. Even the bioscope was denied her.

But that night when she got in it was a different story. Wearily, Cathy drew off her jacket, folded her pinny round her and sat down, ready for her meal. There, on the table facing her place, was the bill she'd left on the dresser that morning.

'What's this, Mam?' she questioned innocently.

Lily gave her a long, hard look. Apparently she didn't know anything about it, either.

'I found it this mornin', when I was puttin' the pots away,' Lily said. 'What do you think?'

'What do you mean, "What do I think?"'

'I mean, would you like to go?' Lily said, irritated.

Cathy's eyes opened wide in astonishment, and she had a job to keep the enthusiasm she felt out of her voice.

'Eeh, I don't know,' she said, as if she couldn't care less. 'I mean, who would I go with?' And she paused as her plate of Pan Haggerty was put in front of her. 'I suppose, mind, the girls from work might want to go.'

'You never think of me, do you,' her mother snapped.

Cathy now did not hide her astonishment.

'You, Mam? Honest? Do you want to go to the Queen's?'

Lily nodded. She supposed the pink flush in the girl's face was caused by the hot steam that rose from her dinner. 'But I thought you said that place was a flea pit!'

'That was the Empire. Eat your dinner.'

Cathy picked up knife and fork and held them aloft.

'Well,' she thought to herself, 'it didn't half show you, you shouldn't give owt up, no matter how impossible it seemed.'

It was her favourite meal, sausage, onion rings and potato slices, laid in layers and cooked in the oven. The top layer, potato, was crisp and brown. Slowly, smiling with the thought of pleasures to come, she began to eat.

'We'll go on the opening night,' Lily said. 'Only don't tell Hettie.'

CHAPTER SEVEN

For some unknown reason, Cathy's mother insisted on decking her daughter out for the occasion. Not that Cathy was complaining. And Hettie wondered what was going on, what with the whisperings, the secret meetings in Lily's room, and the scufflings and rustlings behind the door. It was something to do with a new dress, she could tell that by the pins Lily forgot to take out of her bodice, but she couldn't understand why she wasn't in on the act, and when she asked Cathy, all casual like, about it, Cathy just blushed and said, 'Me Mam's altering something. That's all.'

And it was true, in a manner of speaking, but it wasn't just anything that Lily was refurbishing. It was an old suit of her own, from 'the good days', as Lily thought of them. She had kept many of her best things, untouched, in her trunks all these years, taking them out twice a year for a shake and an inspection, then putting them back, with fresh mothballs and a sigh, to languish in the darkness for another six months. It was like an Aladdin's cave to Cathy when her mother had finally sprung the locks and opened up the trunks for her.

'Choose something,' she had said. 'Choose something we can make up for you for a special occasion. A day dress.'

And Cathy had sifted through her mother's treasures, oohing and ahing over the evening dresses, the lace, the velvet suits, the hats, the silk gowns and shawls. Shyly she looked up at her mother. Lily's face was tightly drawn as it always was, but there was the ghost of a smile on her lips today as she remembered the figure she had cut in those dresses.

'I'd forgotten, Ma,' Cathy whispered. 'I'd forgotten how lovely you were.'

'Aye. "Were" is the right word.' Lily laughed dryly, and

looked at her chapped, roughened hands. 'Come on. Get on with it. I haven't got all day.'

It wasn't an easy task, choosing from so much wealth. But as soon as it had caught her eye, Cathy had been drawn to it. 'It' was a dark brown velvet suit. It had jet beading at the neck and on the cuffs, and dainty tucks in the bodice.

'I like that,' Cathy said.

Lily frowned.

'Isn't it a bit . . . well . . . old for you, pet?' she asked. 'I mean, it's so dark!'

'Miss Hutchinson said I was a brown velvet lady.' Cathy blushed at repeating such an exotic statement about herself.

'Brown velvet lady, if you please,' her mother mocked. But she was pleased with the idea all the same. She held the velvet up to her daughter's face. It showed off her hair nicely, and the pale cream of her skin seemed luminous beside it. Perhaps if she was to take off that black beading . . . yes, and maybe . . . Lily fished round in one of the trunks. Ah yes, there it was. Maybe if they added a little of that nice cream lace, to trim the neck and hang down a bit at the throat. Oh, that was fetching, and no mistake. No man could resist that. She would have to alter it, of course.

'Eeh, you'll have to watch your weight, our Catherine,' her mother said as Cathy tried on the suit.

Cathy frowned. The waist needed pinching in a good three inches. Then she followed her mother's eye, further up the jacket.

'I can't help that, Mam,' she protested. 'That isn't weight.'

Lily only sniffed, to indicate she didn't altogether approve of such exuberance in her daughter's flesh, and Cathy wondered, not for the first time, or the last, if her mother wasn't just a little bit jealous. The tucks would have to be let out over the bust and taken in at the waist, and the skirt would have to be revamped altogether to bring it up to date. But when it was finished, it would be the bees knees. There could be no possible doubt about it.

The 'brown velvet lady' was made to wash her hair in coconut-oil shampoo the night before the 'treat'. Lily had searched high and low for the stuff, but she knew it made your hair shine like nothing else. She had even saved rainwater for her daughter's use; rainwater being so much softer than the stuff that came out of the tap in the yard.

'I'm not goin' to lower meself to ask,' Hettie sniffed as she watched this procedure from her corner in the scullery. 'So if that's what you're waitin' for, you'll have to wait!' The threat was met with a haughty silence from Lily.

'Oh go on, Mam. Tell her,' Cathy pleaded. She hated being part of a conspiracy that made a point of excluding her Auntie Hettie.

'If you *must* know,' Lily said, exasperated, 'we're goin' to the first night of the bioscope.'

'Eeh, never!' Hettie dropped her magazine with the shock of the statement, and banged her head on the range as she bent to pick it up. 'I'm coming with you, then!' she announced. The bang had brought tears to her eyes, but it wasn't going to put her off insisting on her due.

'You can't, Hettie,' Lily said. 'Somebody's got to look after the place.'

'It'll be all right for once!' Hettie cried.

'Anyway,' Lily's face was as tight as a drum, 'we'll be sittin' in the best seats.'

Silence greeted this remark. Cathy couldn't bring herself to look at Hettie's face. She pulled her hair across her face as she dried it at the fire. And then she heard a sob, a strangled, miserable sob. Cathy's face creased. She couldn't bear it.

'Mam, why can't she go?' she cried. But Lily only gave her a look that sent her back, with her head down, out of it. But from the corner of her eye she could see Hettie's hands working at the corner of her paper. Cathy wanted to cry out, to comfort her aunt, throw her arms round her and tell her she loved her, but the constraining influence of her mother was there, and she could not. Instead she suffered silently, as Hettie's glasses steamed and the tears edged their way out from under the rims and down her cheeks. Then a quivering voice gasped out, 'I know what you're gettin' at, Lily Straker!' Hettie paused, gathering her strength, to screech, 'You think I'm not bloody good enough for you, don't you? Not good enough to be seen with you in the best seats. Frightened you'll bump into some of your old friends, eh?'

The outburst surprised them both. They stared at Hettie. Her face was white and she was shaking. They couldn't see her eyes for the steam, but the fingers worked on, tearing at the edges of the paper on her knee. Lily was shaken. But she couldn't back down now. She had said. And that was that. Cathy, kneeling at Hettie's feet by the fire, felt a sense of deep shame at her involvement in the affair. She looked at her mother, and there was disgust in her eyes. Lily flinched before them both, and took a step back.

'I'm goin' into the parlour,' she announced, then turned and went out of the kitchen. Cathy watched the door for some seconds after her mother had gone, then turned her hair back to the fire. In the silence, Hettie gulped down another sob. Cathy's hand reached out and touched hers. She was surprised by the strong grip it received in return. Neither of them said anything.

The joy had gone from the occasion for Cathy. Hettie had recovered herself, and got in some beer as a companion during their absence. She would sit as usual, on her own in the scullery, reading her magazines by a solitary candle and drinking her stout. Cathy wanted to speak to her but felt too ashamed to, all dressed up in her brown velvet finery.

'You look very nice, pet,' Hettie said to her when her mother was out of the room. And Cathy only hung her head.

'We'll not be late,' Lily stated, as she pulled on her gloves.

Hettie steadfastly read her paper.

'Tut, sulkin' like a two-year-old!' Lily sneered at her sister-in-law, then turned on her heel and left her to it.

Cathy stayed for a minute, hoping her auntie would give her a last look. But she didn't, and the girl sadly followed her mother out into the night.

The picture pleased Lily. She thought its sentiments very respectable. Tears stung Cathy's eyes as the flickering pictures unfolded a tale of deserted maiden, abandoned with her lover's child, banished from home, to live her hard and solitary life as best she may, returning through the snow to her old home for a glimpse of her child, exhausted and fainting with hunger, to die, with the terrible cry, 'Dead! And never called me "mother"!'

Most satisfactory, Lily thought. The just deserts of wantonness. But Cathy's tender heart went out to the poor woman, in the snow, and her cheeks were stained with her tears when the lights went up.

'Eeh, look at you!' Lily said, getting out her handkerchief to give her daughter a 'cat lick', dampening her hanky with her spittle and scrubbing the cheeks clean. Cathy was mortified at this behaviour. And her mother had kept jumping up and down in her seat all through the film, apparently more concerned with who was in the audience than with what was going on on the screen, and the couple behind had had to hiss at her to keep still. And then, of course, Lily had retorted, 'You need talk. I wish you'd keep your mouths shut, so we can hear the music.' For all through, the old man had read aloud the captions to the woman at his side, and she had made answering noises back. They were in the best seats, and Lily didn't think much to people who complained at you moving about yet made a noise themselves!

'Never mind, Mam.'

And then, at the end, Lily had made indecent haste to be out of the main hall, only to hang about in the foyer till almost everybody had gone.

'Smile, Catherine,' she'd said through clenched teeth. 'What're you lookin' so miserable about?'

'People're lookin' at us,' Cathy complained. 'Let's go home, Mam.'

'Of course they're lookin', pet,' Lily said smugly. 'You shouldn't look so attractive if you don't want folk to look.' And then Cathy had felt more conspicuous than ever.

Suddenly, Lily completely changed her tune.

'Come on, lass,' she said almost angrily. 'What're you doin', hangin' about here. Let's get home.'

Cathy opened her mouth to retort, but thought better of it. Her mother had had some purpose in this 'treat', she was sure of it. But what? She seemed cross with herself all the way back in the tram, and when Cathy spoke about the amazing new wonder they had just seen, her mother seemed preoccupied, scarcely answering her.

'It's a long time since I saw a play,' she announced at last.

Now what was she thinking of? Cathy gave her a look, but thought better of asking. She'd know, all in good time.

Hettie was still up on their return home. She pretended not to have heard them coming in, and sat, intent on her paper as before, as they entered the scullery. She didn't look up. Cathy went to warm her hands at the range, and Lily, deep in thought about something, sat in a chair by the table.

'I've got you some cocoa, pet,' Hettie said in a taut voice.

'Thank you, Auntie Hettie,' Cathy said, and watched as her aunt poured the milk from the pan, then took a fork to froth it up. Cathy felt guilty that Hettie should take the trouble for her when she had been part of a plan to deprive her of enjoyment. She took the mug gratefully.

'Thank you very much,' she said and meant it.

Hettie sat, and Cathy drank from the mug, but no one had spoken about the evening and it hung like a sword between them. Cathy decided to break the ice.

'Don't you want to hear about the film, Auntie?'

Hettie said nothing.

'Shall I tell you the story?'

Lily jumped up and started taking off her jacket.

'It's too late for tellin' tales now,' she snapped.

'Go on, pet,' Hettie said, more to spite Lily than anything else.

'Well, there's this young girl and she falls in love.' Hettie's eyes were misting over already. 'But he's not a gentleman, and she gets . . . you know . . . and her parents banish her from home, because she's going to have her lover's child. Oh, and I should've said, he went and left her, abandoned her . . .'

Hettie put her hand on Cathy's, and Cathy stopped in mid-sentence. Her aunt looked up at Lily, who was standing in the shadows, a sympathetic expression on her face.

'Would you like a cup, Hettie?' Lily asked.

'No thank you, Lily.' Hettie answered nicely, 'don't bother.'

Cathy was mystified. She felt as she had done when she was a little girl, when they had left her guessing at dark mysteries, and she knew she wasn't allowed to ask. She sighed, and drank down her cocoa. Hettie removed her glasses and wiped her eyes with her pinny.

'Are you all right, Auntie?'

'Why aye, pet. Gan to bed now.'

Cathy put her empty mug on the table and went upstairs. It had been a funny day, one way or another. She twisted herself to see her reflection in her little mirror. 'Brown velvet lady!' she snorted.

It was a busy time in the shop. The whole of Shields took part in the Easter processions, and all the women who could afford them wanted new hats. So Miss Hutchinson had the girls working late and even Ethel was let loose with a needle and thread, to sew various themes of fruit, flowers, ribbons and feathers onto the brims. The bigger the better seemed to be the motto this year, and half-finished creations festooned the workroom, like cartwheels gone mad. Miss Hutchinson was increasingly tetchy. The strain of the seasonal work load, her employees thought. But it made life in the little shop less pleasant than it had been of late. She kept getting headaches, and was always at the girls to 'hold their tongues and get on', instead of joining in the usual chatter. Ethel and Mabel had gone to see *East Lynne* together, and went on and on about it, so that Cathy had some sympathy for Miss Hutchinson's point of view and was rather glad, herself, when silence fell and she could be left to her own thoughts.

And there was plenty to think about. Though at work the atmosphere might be less 'congenial' than it had been, at home all was sweetness and light. Cathy couldn't understand it. She quite missed the old fractious atmosphere between her mother and her aunt. They were falling over themselves to do things for each other, and actually smiled, saying 'please' and 'thank you' from time to time at the dinner table, or as they passed one another going about their chores. Cathy felt uneasy, left out of things now, for the two women suddenly had no need of the young girl to act as umpire. The pig in the middle suddenly found herself pig on the outside. Of course it wouldn't last. She knew that. And the pair of them must be finding all this niceness quite a strain, when all was said and done, since it was so foreign to them!

Lily, downcast at first after the trip to the new bioscope, had soon brightened up. She had a gleam in her eye, which Cathy didn't trust, especially if the thoughts that caused that gleam concerned herself. Lily scanned the papers, every night for a week, and then announced to her daughter, 'I think it's about time you saw some Shakespeare, pet.'

Cathy, lost for words at this sudden interest in her education, looked up from the ironing and stared at her mother.

'I see here they're doin' *Romeo and Juliet* at the Tivoli. Quite a good company, I'm told.'

Cathy looked at Hettie, but her aunt turned her head away. Was she in on this secret, whatever it was? The pair of them had been whispering in corners ever since the night of the 'truce'.

'I thought we might go on Saturday.' Decisively, Lily put away her spectacles. 'You'd better get some wear out of that suit now you've got it,' she added, as though that ought to explain everything.

So she was now to go to the theatre! Heaven knows why what had been frowned on as wanton extravagance and sheer vulgarity should suddenly have become respectable; but who was Cathy to question why? It was something to look forward to, at any rate.

The same ritual preceded the trip to the Tivoli as had preceded the trip to the Queen's, but there was no secrecy this time. Hettie accepted that she was to remain behind, and made no bones about it. After all, she probably wouldn't understand half of what was said, so it wasn't as if she'd be missing much. No, she was looking forward to the processions on Good Friday, with the bands and the kiddies, and the women decked out in their new costumes and hats. She didn't want to go with them to the theatre. And the Tivoli, in Laygate Lane, was too grand for her. It had been opened some ten years before, with great acclaim, when it had been described as the 'Prettiest Bijou Palace in the North of England'. It catered for the 'West End' of Shields, and put on a better class of entertainment altogether. Since Cathy already had her clothes for the occasion, Lily was able to concentrate on herself this time, updating her old finery and letting it out at the waist. They'd make a splendid pair, though Cathy did think her mother might have chosen something with a bit more colour in it. After all, they weren't going to a funeral and black looked a bit sombre for a theatre outing. Still, her mother seemed more than satisfied as they stood side by side before her bedroom mirror. She gave a decisive little nod of the head to signify her approval and off they went in their 'glad rags', as Hettie put it.

And it was a pretty little theatre. Cathy delighted in the warm colours and the gilt, the shades on the lamps and the nice carpets on the floor. 'Plush' was the word for it. Her mother seemed to grow three feet as she walked into the foyer and went up to the box office.

'Have you a box, my man?' she asked.

'Certainly, Madam. We have just one left,' the man replied in posh Geordie. 'That'll be two shillings, Madam.'

Cathy gasped. Her Mam was never going to squander two bob on a box, was she? But, calmly as if it was something she did every day of her life, Lily felt in her beaded black bag, pulled out the little silver chain purse, and counted out two shillings for the ticket. As the bag was raised to the level of the counter, the ticket man flinched. A whiff of mothballs had gusted under the glass partition to assail his nostrils. He coughed and drew back on the pretence of marking the ticket, and Cathy bit her lip, trying not to smile. It gave the whole show away, that stink. Unmistakable, it was. They were not two ladies of means and fashion at all, but a pair of Geordie women, out on the town in their best, kept for high days and holidays and preserved, like the mummies of centuries, in mothballs. Lily didn't seem to notice the smell, and ignored the wrinkling nose of the attendant who showed them to their seats. 'Lady Muck.' Cathy smiled. The nickname could not have seemed more appropriate tonight.

As they settled in their seats, Cathy surreptitiously sniffed at the sleeve of her own jacket. The fumes had almost overwhelmed her during all the trying-on sessions she had suffered at her mother's hands for the trip to the bioscope, and she had taken the precaution of airing her suit beforehand. But even so, it had smelled strongly of mothballs, and she'd doused herself in lavender water to combat the horrible odour. Her clothes were now almost free of it, but her mother, unaware of the pungency of her costume, had taken no such precautions, so that the reek followed her wherever she went. It was just as well, Cathy thought, that they *were* in a box!

'Can you see all right, Mam?'

'Oh aye,' Lily replied. 'Don't worry about me.' She was getting her old opera glasses out of her bag now.

'Are you sure? I'll swap seats with you if you like.'

'I'm all right!' her mother snapped.

Cathy shrugged, and laid her gloved hands on the velvet-covered ledge before her. Her eyes were bright, dancing here and there as they found new sights to interest her. She was glowing with anticipation; her cheeks were flushed and the pale skin gleamed against the copper hair and the velvet suit.

In the gallery a young man and his mother were just arriving. They had missed the last box and had had to make do with the best the theatre had left for this sole performance of the Shakespeare play. The mother was displeased at this inconvenience, and wondered who had had the affrontery to take her usual place. So that no one would be left in any doubt of her displeasure, she made as much fuss as possible in finding her seat and settling into it. Lily's attention was immediately caught by the sideshow in the gallery and her glasses swung to take it in. They stayed there some time, inspecting the young man first, who's frank eyes looked about him, searching out his acquaintances and waving to them. In the restricted view of the opera glasses, Lily suddenly saw a gloved hand come across the young man's chest and point in their direction. She swung the glasses to the right then, and took in Mrs Stoddard's angry face. Lily dropped the glasses as though they were a hot cinder.

'Sit further forward, pet,' she hissed at her daughter, pushing and shoving the girl till the gaslight caught the shine of her hair. 'That's better,' she said. Then the mother leaned back, her black clothes a foil to Cathy's brighter looks. Lily smiled grimly to herself. She had done it, after all. She had done it at last. Then the lights dimmed and the curtain went up as the play began.

Cathy had never seen the piece before, and she sat entranced as the tragic love story unfolded before her. The passionate yearnings of Juliet echoed in her like old familiar friends, they sucked her into their intense emotions so that she lived inside the play, and when the lights came up it was with great reluctance that she tore her eyes away from the stage.

'Hurry up, pet. Or we'll miss it.' Lily hastily gathered up her bag and dug her daughter between the shoulder blades. Cathy jumped.

'Why? What's the matter? Where're we goin'?'

'Nowhere!' Lily hissed. 'Just for a bit of a walk round, that's all!'

'Ah, Mam, do we have to? It'll break the spell.'

'Come on!'

'We'll miss wer refreshments, mind.'

'I see. Ashamed of bein' seen with your Mam now are you?'

Cathy pulled a face. The same old bit of blackmail. Reluctantly she rose from her chair and stood beside her mother while she opened the door to their box. She became aware of the smell again and her heart sank.

'Ah Mam . . .' she pleaded. She dared not tell her to her face that she stank to high heaven. Her mother would have been so ashamed at the knowledge that she would have stopped enjoying the evening altogether. And yet Cathy would have liked to have spared her mother the indignity of finding out the hard way. But Lily insisted.

'Get a move on!'

So Cathy allowed herself to be hustled out of the box and down the corridor to the milling crowds behind the gallery.

Cathy saw them almost at once, and her heart jumped in horror. Gilbert Stoddard, balancing a cup of coffee in each hand, was threading his way back to his mother who stood, fanning herself, on the edge of the crowd. Cathy had stopped in her tracks.

'See anybody you know?' her mother asked with assumed innocence.

Cathy shook her head and turned, as if to walk the other way.

'And where are you waltzin' off to?' Lily asked. 'You're goin' to leave me on me own, are you?'

'You deserve to be left,' Cathy thought angrily, as she walked slowly back to her mother's side.

'Smile, can't you! What've you got to be so miserable about?' And they walked further towards the crowd, as though the refreshments were their only object.

'Only gentlemen go up to the bar,' Cathy hissed between clenched teeth. Her mother hesitated for an instant, then stopped, looking longingly towards a cup of coffee in a lady's hand.

From the corner of her eye Cathy saw Gilbert Stoddard watching her. He was looking at her hair. Her red hair! How she wished she'd dyed it black! He made a step towards her, but a hand on his arm restrained him. Then Lily turned and looked straight at him.

'Well, Catherine,' she said in great surprise. 'If that's not the Stoddard boy!' And she danced forwards to greet them, the crowd receding and making way as the cloud of mothball wafted from her moving body. 'It is, isn't it?' Lily put out her hand to the lady, who smiled graciously, only the slightest rise and fall of her well-mannered nostril betrayed the fact that she had caught the faint trace of something unpleasant. 'Mrs Stoddard, how *are* you?'

'Extremely well, Mrs er . . .'

'Straker.'

'Ah yes. That's it. Well, hasn't it been a long time!'

Lily eyed the young man at her side.

'You remember Gilbert, of course.'

The young man bowed his head and smiled in some amusement, coughing slightly as Lily moved closer to him and offered her hand.

'And this is Catherine.' Lily smiled broadly and put her arm out to encourage her daughter further into the little group. Gilbert's eyes widened. He came forward eagerly.

'I thought it was!' he said warmly. 'The hair!'

Cathy managed to smile, though she felt she could die of shame.

'And where are you living now?' Mrs Stoddard's eye appraised the costumes of the two ladies. 'Still in the same place?'

Lily glossed over the question.

'My I *am* thirsty,' she said pointedly.

'Of course. Let me,' the young man volunteered.

'Such a nice boy,' Lily said, after a brief silence.

'Yes.'

Another silence. Lily was becoming unpleasantly aware that her own accent had slipped dreadfully during the years at Thrift Street. Try as she might, she couldn't erase the Geordie traces from her voice. It was a humiliation for her, but bravely she battled on.

'How old is he now?' she enquired.

'Almost twenty-one.' And Mrs Stoddard smiled. She was always pleased to talk about her beloved son.

'And are you having some sort of celebration?'

'A dance.'

'Oh?'

Another long pause. Then Lily turned to her daughter and said pointedly, in an attempt to get Cathy to talk, 'Isn't that nice, Catherine?'

'Yes, Mam,' she muttered in reply, hanging her head.

Mrs Stoddard looked at Cathy and her face softened. She had always liked the girl, in spite of the 'bloomer' incident. Such a pity that her stock wasn't up to scratch. She obviously had excellent taste too. She looked very fetching in her plain velvet suit, and her hair, rather too vibrant in Mrs Stoddard's view, was piled neatly on top of her head.

'You look very nice, my dear,' she said kindly.

Cathy smiled gratefully at her. The compliment had made her feel more at ease, more welcome. But the conversation had ground, once again, to a complete halt. Eventually, after a painful silence, Gilbert returned with the coffee and handed the cups to Cathy and her mother.

'I hope you ladies've been getting on all right without me,' he joked.

'Oh yes. Been chatting nineteen to the dozen,' Lily smiled.

Cathy avoided Mrs Stoddard's eye.

'I hear you're to have a dance for your birthday!'

Gilbert nodded.

'Yes. Oh yes. At the Queen Victoria Rooms, opposite Fowler Street, you know.'

'How lovely,' Lily enthused. And she turned to her daughter. 'Our Catherine loves a dance, don't you, dear.'

Cathy wished the floor would open up and swallow her. Her mother could not have been more obvious if she'd tried. She felt for the Stoddards in their dilemma.

'Oh, really?' Gilbert said. 'Then she must come!'

He turned to his mother, who said not a word.

'Mustn't she, mother?' he insisted.

'It's entirely up to you, Gilbert.' Mrs Stoddard could not have expressed her disapproval more plainly. 'It's your party.'

'Then that's settled! You will come, won't you?' He looked down at Cathy's lowered face. 'For old time's sake,' he added gently.

Cathy's face was red. She was only too aware of the stony face of Gilbert's mother at his side.

'I'm not sure, Gilbert,' she replied.

'Of course she'll come. Very nice of you, I'm sure,' Lily answered for her. Mrs Stoddard pursed her lips.

'Have we an address to send the invitations, Ma?'

'Yes,' Mrs Stoddard said with some distaste, 'we have an address.'

Cathy could not have believed that her embarrassment could have deepened. The phrase 'saved by the bell' might have been invented for just that moment. For the interval bell sounded to announce the beginning of the next act, and polite goodbyes were all that were needed as the Strakers and the Stoddards parted company. Gilbert stared after his childhood sweetheart with frank admiration. But Mrs Stoddard merely sniffed.

Cathy cringed as she heard the parting shot: 'Let's hope the dear lady's evening wear is slightly less well preserved.'

Gilbert laughed, and mother and son followed the stream back into the gallery.

So that was what it had all been about! Cathy prayed for the lights to dim so that she could hide her shame. To be paraded like some prize cow before a bull! And poor Mrs Stoddard! She could hardly be blamed for being peeved at her mother's behaviour. How ridiculous she had looked, putting on airs and graces, poshing up the Geordie, stinking to high heaven of mothballs, and to top it all, acting like, like . . . If Cathy had known such a word as 'pimp' she would have used it. As it was, she had to be content with finishing off the phrase with 'like a trollop'. Tears stung her eyes, and the rest of the play passed over her head as she recalled the scene in the interval, again and again.

'*Now* what have I done!' Lily demanded to know as they trundled home on the tram.

Cathy gave her a look, and subsided into silence for the rest of the journey.

'Were *you* in on this?' she asked Hettie angrily after her mother had gone up.

'She means it for the best, you know, pet,' Hettie said soothingly. 'She's got your interests at heart. And from what I remember, you used to like that little lad.'

'Little lad!' Cathy fumed.

'Don't turn your nose up at him, just because he's got money now!' Hettie warned her. 'You know your trouble, pet, always cuttin' off your nose to spite your face!'

Cathy said nothing, though she recognised the truth of what Hettie was saying.

'Don't be too proud. That's all.'

Cathy smiled. It was true. It had been her pride that had been hurt.

'And don't think your Mam hasn't got her pride either. Think how much it cost her to face them two the night! Eh? Just you think of that!'

Cathy took her cocoa up to bed with her and undressed slowly by the light of her candle. She hadn't expected Hettie to come to her mother's defence, and her words bore all the more weight because of it. Poor Mam! She remembered how proud her mother had been when Cathy was little, and how it had hurt her to be brought low. She'd nearly died of shame when Cathy'd forgotten her underpants at that Christmas party! Cathy's eyes filled with tears. Her poor Mam, with the red chapped hands, the pitiful lahdy-dah accent, and the mothballs! How she'd been brought down low. Cathy threw on a wrap and rushed towards the door of Lily's room. She would tell her, tell her now, before she settled down to sleep.

Lily looked up, surprised, as her door flew open. She opened her mouth to snap, but shut it again in surprise as her daughter flung herself onto her bed.

'I do love you, Mam. Honest,' Cathy said, tears flowing down her cheeks.

Lily looked at her in astonishment. Her hand itched to stroke her daughter's bonny head, but somehow she couldn't.

'What's got into you then?' she asked, more sharply than she wanted.

'Nothin'. I just love you, that's all.'

Cathy longed for her mother to make some response, to demonstrate her affection, so that she, in turn, could kiss her, and hold her in her arms. But they just sat there in an awkward silence. Finally Lily found words to speak.

'I thought I was in the doghouse,' she said timidly.

Cathy looked up at her mother's face. It was suddenly vulnerable, trembling, the skin thin with cares.

'No, Mam. Of course not.' Then, with a great effort, and solely to please her mother, Cathy managed to say, 'I'm lookin' forward to that party, eh? Aren't you?'

Lily smiled.

'If they remember to send the invitation,' she said wryly.

'Aye, "if".' Cathy smiled back. Then she leaned forwards and kissed her mother lightly on the cheek. 'Night night, Mam.'

'Aye. Don't let the bed bugs bite, pet,' her mother laughed.

Then Cathy gently closed her mother's bedroom door behind her and went back up the stairs to her room, feeling as she was to feel time and again later in her life, that strange and poignant mixture of happiness and sadness, a feeling that just as her heart's desire was finally within her reach it would float away again, leaving her hand grasping at the air, pining for what she never really had.

'We'd better get somethin' sorted, just in case,' Lily said as she rummaged through the trunks again. 'White'd be nice for you.'

Cathy sat quietly, fiddling with a silk rose that had fallen from the bodice of a dress. Days had passed since the play. Surely, if it was coming at all, the invitation would have arrived by now? At first, Cathy had hoped it wouldn't come, that they would simply forget and she could put the whole thing out of her mind. But after a couple of days she had begun to feel disappointed. She'd got used to the idea of going and was looking forward to it. Gilbert had been nice to her at the Tivoli, and he had always had a bit of a thing about her. When she'd been little, she had taken Gilbert's crush for granted. His adulation had come so easily, and she had accepted it as a matter of course. Gilbert adored her and that was all there was to it. But it was different now. She was in no position to take the attentions of a handsome and highly suitable man for granted any more. She tried to remember how he had looked at her when he had handed her the coffee. His voice had been kind, but his eyes . . . ? Surely they had liked what they'd seen? They'd seemed to, anyway. And she had looked nice, no one could've denied that, not even Mrs Stoddard. Perhaps that was the trouble. Yes. Cathy felt cheered at the thought, and wondered why. Mrs Stoddard was afraid that her son might be attracted to her, and that meant that he *was* attracted to her. Her heart rose at the thought. He was so nice, was Gilbert! And he had grown up into such a strong-looking young man. He had an air of confidence, as though he was at ease with the world, which he never was as a child, she was sure. She had been the leader then. But now . . . ? She was smiling, without knowing it. Lily looked up, and her frown melted as she saw the look on her daughter's face.

'Haway, lass! It's *your* frock we're lookin' for!'

Cathy started out of her thoughts, and throwing the rose to one side she started to inspect the dresses her mother had laid aside for her.

Even Lily's hopes had begun to flag when, finally, the invitation came. The dance was to be on that same Friday, and there was a bustle to get things ready in time.

'They've not given us a lot of notice,' Lily complained. Secretly Cathy suspected that Mrs Stoddard had not intended to invite them at all. She looked at the writing on the card. It was a free-flowing hand, with strong, determined vertical lines and generous loops; more like the hand of a man. But she said nothing to her mother, and wrote their acceptance quickly, flying out to the post to get it off as soon as possible. Hettie teased her endlessly.

'It says Mrs and Miss Straker,' she pointed out, as she looked at the card propped up on the mantelpiece. 'Well, *I'm* Miss Straker, now, aren't I?' And they all laughed. Though Cathy did wish that somehow her aunt could come to the dance. It was impossible. She knew that. And Hettie would have felt more awkward and out of place than either Cathy or her mother, and not really enjoyed it because of that. So it was no good wishing. Only it seemed so hard for her that she always had to be the Cinderella left behind while Lily and her daughter went off to the ball. She mentioned this to Hettie once, when she was raking out the ashes.

'Eeh, no pet. You're the one that's doin' the rakin' out, and it's you who's goin' to find your Prince Charmin'. I'm past all that now.'

The night of the dance Hettie surveyed the departing ladies with unfeigned admiration as they paraded before her.

Lily was fussing about not having the proper furs to wear over their dresses.

'It spoils the effect,' she complained, 'puttin' ordinary cloaks over your evenin' dress.' But all the furs had gone with the crash of their fortunes and nothing could be done about it now.

'You look smashin', Lily,' Hettie soothed her, 'just how you used to look.' She could not have said anything kinder, and Lily was visibly moved by the remark. She 'pooh poohed' it of course, but it comforted her and gave her confidence all the same. For, deny it or not, Lily dreaded this dance. She was as nervous as a kitten. But she looked nice enough in the burgundy silk she had chosen for herself. The long kid gloves hid the roughness of her hands, and instead of jewels she, like Cathy, had tied a velvet band round her throat. She had pinned a piece of jet to it, with the bitter statement, 'Well! They won't be able to complain at that, will they!' For Lily had one or two small pieces of her old jewellery left and would have loved to wear it, but she was afraid that some of the old creditors would be there at the dance and would look askance at the gemstones, sticking a price ticket on her necklace as she walked about!

Cathy was gorgeous in cream silk, a dress so simple as to be stunning in its effect. Lily and Hettie were proud, and rightly so, of their combined efforts there. It had been Lily's wedding dress, long ago, and they had revamped it, cutting away the sleeves and the neck, Lily clicking her tongue at the décolletage but revealing as much of her daughter as seemed modest all the same. They swathed lace round the edge, so that it seemed like creamy froth, half hiding the bosom, which rose and fell underneath tantalisingly as Cathy breathed. Her only ornament was a moss-green velvet ribbon at her throat, on which her mother had pinned a silk gardenia, and Hettie, who had had the happy idea of dying an evening bag to match the ribbon, adorned that in the same way. The copper curls were piled high on top of Cathy's head and held in place by combs. No one would be able to touch her for her beauty or her style.

They took the tram and Cathy wrapped her cloak round

herself, hiding her slippered feet from the dirty great shoes of workmen, and hiding her décolletage from their dirty great eyes! They alighted at the stop before 'The Rooms' and walked the rest of the way, in case any of Lily's old acquaintances should see them.

A man took their cloaks as they entered and inspected their invitation. Then the doors opened and they walked into the hall. Several heads turned at once. And by the time Mrs Stoddard deigned to come over to greet them they were beginning to feel like prize cattle at a public show.

'Hold your head up, pet,' Lily whispered, as she herself bravely ignored the stares and the sizing up.

'I feel like a tin of milk stood here, Mam,' Cathy whispered back.

'They wouldn't stare if there was nowt to stare at,' her mother said, instilling courage into her. 'None of them could hold a candle to you.' And then, finally, their hostess appeared.

'So glad you could come,' she said to Lily, but her eyes were on Miss Straker not her mother, and Cathy felt her disapproval as it expressed itself perfectly in the raising of her right eyebrow. Still, snob though she may be, Mrs Stoddard knew her manners, and since they were here she drew them into the room, introducing them into little groups of people, breaking the ice for them. Lily, only too aware of how her accent had roughened, kept her words to a minimum, giving her a cold, stand-offish appearance. But Cathy, at ease in any setting as long as she wasn't being patronised, more than made up for her mother. She was warm and friendly, smiling graciously, the soft, gentle tones of her voice smoothing the edges of her accent so that it mattered less. The men accepted her at once, but the women were more distant and cold. They were at a loss what to say to Lily, and her to them, especially if they had known her in the old days. There was a gap between them like the Grand Canyon. Still, Lily braved the women, just so long as Cathy was all right. She watched with pleasure as her daughter was whisked off to do a 'Dashing White Sergeant' by one admiring young man. Once one had asked, others would follow. And her foot tapped perkily under the burgundy silk as Cathy moved gracefully at her partner's side.

Lily hadn't realised it before, but Cathy moved beautifully. She made the other girls look like wooden dolls next to her. They danced well enough, certainly, but Cathy had something extra. It was the way her head tilted, and her back swayed, her arms moving like fronds of seaweed borne on the ebb and flow of the tide. And Cathy loved to dance. Even at a Sunday School party she had felt herself come alive as the music started up and her limbs responded to its rhythm. It was like the pulse of life in her, taking her out of the ordinary routine of her life and her drab surroundings into colour, excitement, whirling motion, where she could express her inner self at last. And that was it. Cathy danced expressively, at one with the rhythm of the music and the rise and fall of the movements of the dance. The 'Dashing White Sergeant' might have been a minuet, for all the grace Cathy put into it.

Panting and flushed, Cathy had hardly regained her seat when Gilbert Stoddard was at her elbow asking her for the next dance. Cathy smiled at him as she rose to take his arm and walk back to the centre of the floor. For a merciful moment the dancers waited for the band to rearrange their sheets of music and Cathy got her breath back.

'I haven't brought you a birthday present,' she apologised.

Gilbert laughed.

'Do you remember my tenth birthday?' he asked.

Cathy frowned, then put her hand to her lips, giggling.

'Yes,' she laughed, 'I brought you a huge box of chocolate soldiers, didn't I?'

'Yes. And then proceeded to bite off all their heads one by one.' Cathy hung her head in pretended shame. 'Your mother was furious.'

'Eeh, but they tasted nice,' Cathy responded in broad Geordie, her eyes sparkling, and Gilbert roared with laughter.

As the band struck, they fell easily into one another's arms as though the years between the birthday party of the chocolate soldiers and this one had never happened, and they swung into the broad movements of a Grand Valse. On the sidelines, Mrs Stoddard's eyes narrowed as she watched the spinning couples on the floor. She turned to the woman on her left.

'I thought Gilbert was promised to your May for this dance,' she said.

'Oh no, Edith,' the woman smiled knowingly. 'It's for the quadrille he's promised.'

Mrs Stoddard nodded her head, satisfied. The quadrille was a very long dance.

Cathy was happy. She fairly beamed her pleasure, so that the other guests couldn't help but smile at her. She had never enjoyed herself so much. She was promised to a young man called George for the quadrille, a dance she didn't know very well, and she took her place beside him with some nervousness. She could see Gilbert in the next set, at the side of a tall blonde young woman in a turquoise gown. She caught his eye and they smiled at each other through the crowd of dancers. She wondered who the girl was, but her attention was soon caught up in the dance as she followed the figures round, concentrating on the other ladies in her own set and copying what they did. It was all far more complex than she had realised. She knew the Lancers pretty well, but the quadrille! At the third set, Cathy was forced to admit defeat, and she and her partner gave way to another couple who had not been able to find a place in a set and gratefully substituted for the departing pair. Released, Cathy and George made their way towards the refreshment room. Mrs Stoddard watched Miss Straker's exit with some contentment.

'May's doing very well,' she commented to May's mother. 'I don't know how she stands the pace. Miss Straker has had to leave the floor exhausted!'

'May has great stamina,' the mother replied.

Cathy couldn't believe it when the evening ended. The time had flown so rapidly. As they waited for the attendant to fetch their cloaks, Gilbert tumbled down the steps after them.

'It's been just marvellous,' he said. Cathy's eyes shone up at him and he shrugged, as though words couldn't express his joy at having seen her again. 'Like old times,' he added, 'only better.'

'Yes,' Cathy agreed. 'Thank you for asking us.'

'Perhaps we could meet again?' Gilbert ventured.

Lily felt her chest tighten. Oh God, where, how would they meet again? She surely couldn't ask a Stoddard to Thrift Street? She had not been able to see beyond this evening, hoping against hope for its success, but not a thought for thereafter. Gilbert sensed her dismay.

'A drive, maybe?' he looked at Cathy, and she smiled.

'That'd be lovely,' she said.

'Sunday?' Cathy nodded.

'Pick her up after Church, why not?' Lily put in. Gilbert smiled at the quick thinking of Cathy's mother with some approval. 'We attend Saint Hilda's in Market Square as a rule. We're usually out by half past ten. Early service, you know.'

Gilbert nodded.

'I'll be waiting for you, Miss Straker,' he said formally and bowed. Cathy nodded her head in acknowledgement and Gilbert hurried on before them to order a cab.

'How are we goin' to pay for it, Mam?' Cathy muttered as they walked out after him. But their attention was diverted by a voice from behind. It was Mrs Stoddard. She was holding a brown paper bag in her arms. She held it out towards them.

'I thought you might like to take some home with you,' she said.

Lily took the bag and looked into it. It contained leftovers from the supper table. She looked Edith Stoddard straight in the eye.

'Thank you most humbly, Ma'am,' she said wryly. 'The dogs'll enjoy it.'

Mrs Stoddard pursed her lips angrily and marched back into the hall as the Strakers climbed into the cab. As soon as 'The Rooms' were out of sight Lily leaned forward and shouted, 'Cabby! Stop round the corner. We'll get out there.'

In some surprise, the cabby shouted back, 'But the gentleman gave me the fare to Thrift Street!'

Cathy didn't know whether to feel ashamed or grateful.

Hettie dug into the scraps provided by their hostess.

'Eeh, mind,' she said with a full mouth, 'this was kind of her!'

'I don't think!' Lily sneered. 'Huh! Tryin' to put us in wer place, that's what she was doin'! But mind, you should've seen her face when I said "The dogs'll like it". I thought she'd wet herself!'

Cathy laughed and nodded.

'What dogs, Lily?' Hettie asked, puzzled.

'Tut! It was just somethin' to say, to get at her!'

'Oh I see.' Hettie dug further down into the bag and fetched out a piece of chocolate cake, oozing with liquid. 'I'll have to eat this with a spoon,' she said, rising to look in the dresser drawer. 'By, they did you proud, mind. You must be burstin' with all this food.'

Cathy shook her head.

'We didn't eat much, did we, Mam?'

Hettie turned to look at them in amazement. 'Why ever not?'

'Scared we'd not look ladylike,' Cathy laughed.

Shaking her head, Hettie fetched three spoons and gave them one each.

'Dig in and the last one finished's a Jessie,' she said. Laughing and giggling, the three of them demolished the cake together.

'By, it was wet mind,' Hettie said. 'What was the stuff?'

'Rum,' Lily smiled broadly. 'It was laced with rum, Hettie.'

'Eeh! No wonder I'm half tiddly!' She giggled and picked up a chicken leg, all set to ravish that. 'And how was the young Mr Stoddard?' she teased Cathy.

'All right,' Cathy replied shyly.

'Alreet!' her mother nearly shouted. 'Eeh, it was love at first sight, Hettie,' she announced. 'Not that I hold with that sort of thing,' she added.

'Eeh, Mam. Don't exaggerate!' Cathy protested. 'He's a canny lad, Hettie. That's all.'

Lily snorted.

'Don't believe her, Hettie. He's as gone on her as he ever was.'

Up in her room, as she brushed her hair lazily in front of her mirror, Cathy pondered idly on her mother's words. 'Gone on her' was he? Her brush stopped in mid-air, and she let the copper strands fall from it in a veil. 'Gone on her as ever.' It sounded nice. It gave her a warm glow all over. It was lovely to be wanted, and admired. He had brought her out of herself, made her come alive, dancing and laughing and enjoying herself as she hadn't done since she could remember. It was funny really, but when she thought about it she knew she felt sort of at home with Gilbert. As though she belonged with him somehow. And she knew he felt the same way. They didn't have to pretend when they were with each other. All they had to do was be themselves. Ah well, she shrugged, what will be will be. All that mattered now was that she felt happy.

In fact, an unusual situation had arisen in the Straker household. They were all happy, and in agreement for once. They even joked about it between them.

'It'll not last!' Lily laughed, as the three of them talked and smiled and helped one another along with the chores. No aggravation! What an unusual state of affairs. And Cathy no longer felt out of the arrangement as she had done after the bioscope. She herself was the pinnacle of all their hopes, and the centre of their world. It made for a happy atmosphere in the house, which even found its way into the lives of the seamen who lodged there.

On Sunday morning Hettie dolled herself up to accompany Lily and Cathy to the church in the town. It was not their usual church. Hettie preferred the drama of the Sally Army meetings on the pier, or the Jehovahs at Jerusalem Hall. But she wanted to get an eyeful of Cathy's young man, as she said. 'See if he's good enough!' and she winked at her niece, glad for her, and thrilled that things were going so well. She sat impatiently through the service. 'Too High

Church for my taste,' she muttered, 'all that bobbin' up and down,' and she kept one eye on the doors 'in case he thought to come in.' But he didn't. When they finally emerged from the long service they found Gilbert waiting, hat in hand, by a brand new motor car.

'Birthday present,' he explained, abashed at the admiring faces.

'Here, Cathy, wrap this scarf round your hat.' Lily, ever practical, removed her own scarf and gave it to her daughter. 'Your hair'll be all over.' And the pair got in, started up and jolted off out of the town as Hettie waved excitedly after them.

'Where would you like to go?' Gilbert asked.

Cathy tilted her head to one side, and thought.

'The sea,' she said decisively.

'The sea?' Gilbert questioned, surprised. 'I thought you'd get enough of that, living near the quay!'

'Huh! That's just the river!' Cathy said. 'I've not seen the sea, the proper sea, for ages.' She sighed. 'I miss it, you know. In the winter, when she won't let's go out.'

'Where do you go?'

'Oh, just walkin'. You know, along the cliff tops, or round Trow Rocks way, down by Gypsies' Green. There's a heavy tow there, an undercurrent.'

'Is there?' Gilbert was surprised at her knowledge. 'I don't know much about the sea.'

'Don't you?' Cathy looked up at him and smiled, sensing that he was playing a game with her. For Gilbert *did* know about the sea. It was his father's business and therefore his own. He was a master of ships! For a moment, she saw a facet of his life that sparkled for her. Gilbert knew more than she would ever know about the eddies and currents of seas far beyond Trow Rocks. But he also knew eddies and currents of a more subtle nature . . . how to play the exciting game of drawing her to him. Well, she would respond and play it with him, enjoying every minute! She put her hand through his arm.

'Never mind, pet,' she said teasingly. 'I'll teach you!' And he smiled down at her, almost driving the car up onto the kerb as he did so. Gilbert had turned on the lights in her life, and she danced for him.

Cathy returned windblown and bright-eyed from her trip. Gilbert had brought her to the door and sent in his excuses, knowing Lily would be embarrassed if he called in. Cathy was grateful for his consideration. He wasn't a bit snotty either, unlike his mother. It was a pity about her, Cathy reflected. The only fly in her ointment; they could all have such nice times together if Mrs Stoddard would only unbend a little. And she could be nice if she chose, Cathy knew that. Ah well, maybe she would come round. And so she dismissed the problem and braced herself for the coming week.

Good Friday was coming up at last. Miss Hutchinson's shop was a hive of activity. Customers breezed in at all hours, demanding to know how their hats were coming on, changing their minds about the trimming, or the shape, or even putting in last-minute orders that put the workroom in an uproar. Miss Hutchinson's headaches got worse and she was positively snappy by the end of the week. On Maundy Thursday the shop was officially closed, but the bell kept ringing as people turned up for their orders, and the girls remained busy in the workroom at the back. Miss Hutchinson's head got worse with the clanging of the bell, and she retired upstairs for a lie-down in the mid-afternoon. Mabel, Ethel and Cathy were working silently, their fingers sore and their tempers tried by the overwork and Miss Hutchinson's shortness. There was still a lot of work to get through. Then the bell clanged. Mabel looked at Cathy. Her legs were swollen, and she was fed up with getting up and down to answer the door. Cathy sighed and rose to do it. She drew the baize curtain aside, and walked wearily and slowly to the door. As she opened it, an angry voice snapped, 'You took your time, didn't you?'

It was Mrs Stoddard.

CHAPTER EIGHT

The two women stared at each other across the open doorway. There was an embarrassed silence. It was the older woman who recovered first.

'I beg your pardon, Miss Straker.' She spoke in an exaggerated, formal tone. 'I didn't realise there were other customers in the shop.'

Cathy opened the door wider and let her in.

'There aren't, Mrs Stoddard,' she said quietly. Edith Stoddard looked at her sharply, and Cathy took the look unflinching. 'I work here, Mrs Stoddard,' she said. The woman gave a snort and set down her handbag. She muttered something which Cathy couldn't catch. Then, bowing her head slightly, the girl excused herself and went behind the curtain to fetch the customer her hat.

When she returned, Mrs Stoddard had had time to gather her wits. She stood tall and erect, her back to the workshop, as Cathy re-entered.

'Here we are, Mrs Stoddard,' she said. 'I hope it's to your satisfaction.'

The lady took the hat and glared at it for a moment.

'Where is the proprietress?' she demanded to know.

'Miss Hutchinson has had to retire with a bad head.'

In silence, Edith Stoddard turned to the glass and placed the hat on her head, looking this way and that.

'Are you quite sure that it's as we planned it?' she asked.

'Well, I wasn't here when you came for the fitting, if you remember, Mrs Stoddard. But I can soon fetch Miss Chapman . . .'

'It doesn't matter.' She removed the hat from her head and studied it for a moment before looking back at the girl. 'And have you been working here long, my dear?' she asked, her voice softening to a patronising kindness.

'Since I was sixteen.'

'And do you enjoy the work?'

'I'm not ashamed of earning my living, Mrs Stoddard, if that's what you're gettin' at.' The defiant tone in the girl's voice surprised her.

'Is your hat all right?'

'It'll do,' Mrs Stoddard admitted grudgingly.

'Then I'll just put it in its box.'

Mrs Stoddard shuffled awkwardly as Cathy performed this operation in total silence. Really, Gilbert had put her in a spot. She hardly knew what to say to the girl. A shopgirl, if you please! All the same, it might make things easier for her. After all, a shopgirl could hardly be thought of as a serious contender for her son, and he was allowed his fling, she supposed. May was a patient girl. She would bide her time, no doubt. And she, too, would be patient. She smiled as Cathy handed her the box.

'Thank you, my dear,' she said graciously.

Cathy noticed the gleam in her eye.

'Now what's she thinkin'?' she wondered.

'I do admire your spirit, Catherine,' said Mrs Stoddard. 'So attractive.' She smiled encouragingly.

Cathy frowned as she showed her out of the shop. What on earth did she mean by that?

Hettie put as many streamers as she could on her bonnet on Good Friday. She resembled a maypole. Lily looked at her askance.

'It's a religious occasion, Hettie,' she remonstrated, but let it drop, knowing how Hettie loved the show and razzmatazz of the parades. But when Cathy wanted to follow suit, she put her foot down.

'Auntie Hettie's put streamers on hers!' Cathy pointed out.

'Aye well,' Lily said firmly, 'it doesn't matter about her.'

'Thanks very much,' Hettie pouted, but she wasn't greatly bothered by what Lily said. Hettie was going to enjoy herself no matter what, and Cathy had caught her mood.

'You've got to look like a lady,' Lily reminded her daughter.

Hettie sided with Lily.

'She's right, pet. Your Gilbert wouldn't like it.'

Cathy pulled a face and removed the offending streamers. Her boater looked so dull without them.

'Come on, pet,' her mother consoled her. 'Let's stick a few flowers on it. That'll cheer it up.'

It was a lovely day for once, but then Easter fell late that year and the usual freezing cold winds that dogged the processions were absent. The processions were sober, being a Holy Day and all, and the bands played soberly to match, but the faces of the people were smiling as they waved to friends and relatives in the crowd, and the flower gardens burgeoning on the women's hats gave the whole thing a truly festive air.

'You want to watch it, Hettie,' Lily laughed at her, 'or the Boy's Brigade'll start dancin' round you!'

Hettie gave her a look, and tossed her streamers haughtily in the air. Who cared if she looked silly? She didn't, for one. Why should she? She was enjoying herself.

Cathy and Gilbert had agreed to ferry their respective parties in the same direction, in the hopes they might eventually meet up somewhere on the corner of Fowler Street. As the Strakers went up the hill from the town, the Stoddard's walked down the hill from Westoe. Cathy laughed delightedly as she saw Gilbert waving.

'Eeh!' she said, in mock surprise. 'There's Gilbert Stoddard!'

'Well now,' said her mother. 'Fancy that!'

The young pair pushed their way through the crowd lining the road towards each other, 'grinning like a couple of school kids' as Hettie fondly remarked. Their families followed them more reluctantly, but eventually the two sides met.

'By. That's a corker!' Gilbert said, eyeing Hettie's hat.

Lily and Mrs Stoddard chose to ignore the remark, but everyone else, including Mr Stoddard, laughed. Even Hettie felt more at her ease, especially as Mrs Stoddard was being so civil.

'I believe we met on one of your visits to Westoe, Miss Straker, in the old days,' she said kindly.

'That's right, Missus,' Hettie replied as politely as she could. 'Our Cathy was always round at your place, playin' in the garden. I came to fetch her a few times.' Mrs Stoddard nodded and smiled. 'Childhood sweethearts they were.' Lily dug Hettie in the ribs, and she winced painfully.

'Childhood sweethearts?' Mrs Stoddard reflected, smiling. 'Yes. Yes, I suppose they were really! Good playmates, anyway!'

They turned to see the 'childhood sweethearts' laughing together as Cathy mischievously tried to tickle her admirer, her hand darting out to catch him at his sides, where she knew he was ticklish of old.

'Catherine!' her mother shouted. But Mrs Stoddard surveyed the pair pleasantly.

'We mustn't be spoilsports, Mrs Straker,' she said easily. 'Let them enjoy themselves. It's all innocent, clean fun.'

But Lily wasn't so sure. Innocent it might be, but her Cathy, acting the goat like that in full view of everybody? There she was now actually dancing down the street behind a group of disapproving women from the Church Union. And Hettie, unaware of any indiscretion, running out into the road to join them, her streamers flying behind her in the breeze. Gilbert welcomed her in his usual open-hearted fashion.

'I was thinking,' Mrs Stoddard was saying in Lily's ear, 'Why don't you bring Catherine to tea on Easter Monday.'

Lily stared at her, astonished.

'Oh,' she said, 'that would be very nice. Thank you.'

'I believe you and Ma met up yesterday,' Gilbert whispered in Cathy's ear as they bowled along behind the Church Union. Cathy gave him a look. 'Oh. Like that was it?' he laughed. 'You didn't tell me you worked in a hat shop.'

'It's nothing to be ashamed of!' Cathy said sharply.

'Keep your lovely hair on,' Gilbert soothed her. 'I never said it was. Only it was a bit of a shock to her, that's all.'

'Not good enough for her. That's it, isn't it?'

'Don't be daft, Cathy. You're worth a dozen of her or

anybody else,' Gilbert said warmly. 'And I don't care. I admire you, really I do. In fact,' he said reflectively, 'Ma rather surprised me. Know what she said?'

Cathy shook her head.

'She said you had a fire in you that'd never go out.' Cathy looked at him, pleased. 'I take it you gave as good as you got,' he laughed.

Cathy flushed.

'Well!' she said, tossing her hair.

'And she's right,' Gilbert gave her an admiring look. Cathy smiled.

'Oh I do feel happy,' she announced. Then she flicked Hettie's streamers in the air. 'Don't you, Auntie?'

'Gerroff!' Hettie shrieked, and Gilbert and Cathy laughed.

Easter Monday was warm, with only the slightest breeze which swayed the still bare branches of the trees. The green buds swelled, and the snowdrops had given way to a few daffodils and narcissi in the gardens. Lily had mixed feelings as she walked down the tree-lined street in Westoe Village. She was ten years older than she had been when she left the place, and the trees had grown from young saplings into sturdy trees, casting dappled shadows across their path as they walked. She had got over her grief, of course, but the place still had the power to draw a nostalgic lump to her throat, and she had to remove her glasses to wipe a tear from her eye more than once. Cathy took her arm encouragingly. And Lily patted her daughter's hand.

'I'm happy, really, pet,' she said. And her look pleaded with the girl to make her dreams come true for her and banish the last ten years of drudgery in a blaze of glory that would send them back where they came from, where they belonged.

Gilbert was at the gate, and greeted them enthusiastically.

'Ma's decided to risk the rheumatism and have tea in the garden,' he said.

'I'm glad I kept me vest on,' Lily whispered in Cathy's ear as they were escorted through to the garden.

Mrs Stoddard was very kind to them. She pushed cakes and sandwiches at them till they were full to bursting. Mr

Stoddard cracked jokes and had them all laughing. It was homely and nice. All that strain and disapproval that had emanated from the mistress of the house previously seemed to have disappeared, as though it had never been. Even Lily began to relax and be herself more, while Cathy literally let her hair down as she and Gilbert hunted in the bushes and the orchard for the hidden chocolate eggs. Gilbert sighed, kicking at the long grass with his shoe.

'You'll have to forgive Ma,' he said. 'She can't get used to the idea that we aren't in nappies any more.'

Cathy, dishevelled, her hair wild about her face, laughed.

'What's the matter, Gilbert? Frightened I'll bite the heads off your soldiers again, are you?'

Gilbert smiled, then looked at her seriously.

'Don't you see what she's at?'

'Who?' Cathy asked, puzzled.

'Ma.' Cathy shook her head. 'She's trying to get us to behave like children. Instead of developing a more . . . well . . .' He searched for words that would embarrass neither of them. 'A more adult relationship.'

Cathy shrugged and smiled at him. Their eyes held together for a brief moment, then Cathy looked away.

'Perhaps, if we play her along, she won't mind us being friends,' she volunteered ingenuously.

'Yes. Maybe you're right.' He took her hand for a moment, and fought with a desire to raise it to his lips. Cathy watched him, transfixed. Then he actually did it and his lips brushed the back of her hand. His eyes sought her approval of the gesture. Cathy let her hand drop once more to her side, and tilted her head. Then she smiled.

'Come on,' she said. 'Let's find them ruddy eggs.' The word, picked up from seamen living in the house, was used purposely. They both laughed, and the difficulty of the moment passed.

Lily could hardly believe their luck. Edith Stoddard seemed to be actually encouraging this relationship with her son. She couldn't fathom why, but, as she said to herself, 'Ours is not to reason why', and she couldn't but be glad that things seemed to be going so well. Cathy was always up there these days. Having a high old time of it, she was, going for rides, visits to the theatre (though never the music hall, Lily always put her foot down about that. It had to be 'proper plays'). The only nagging doubt in Lily's mind was the knowledge that soon, very soon, she'd have to ask Gilbert's family round to Thrift Street, and she paled at the prospect. What sort of entertainment could she offer them? It was then that her long cherished dreams of musical evenings began to take shape.

Hettie was made to practice at the piano 'till me fingers bled', she complained in a pained and exaggerated voice. Cathy was allowed to call on her old music teacher, Miss Liddell, who was delighted to give her talented pupil some lessons 'on the cheap'. On enquiry, it was found that Miss Hutchinson had won a prize for the recorder as a child. Why, the place was packed with untapped talent! Mr Miller could play, Lily could recite verse. All they wanted was somebody to lend a bit of 'real class' to the proceedings. Cathy balked at the very idea. 'Musical evenin's in Thrift Street?' she snorted. What was her mother thinking of?

Neither Lily nor Gilbert could understand Cathy's overt irritation. Something had to be done to bring the two sides together if ever they were going to make a thing of it. Nothing had been said, of course. But Cathy had sensed a change in the air, and she wasn't sure she wanted it. It had been a lovely spring, being with Gilbert so much. Work had been a weary occupation lately. Miss Hutchinson was ill; she was in pain and the girls knew that as their employer's hand reached down to touch her side they had to be silent. For Miss Hutchinson's mood would change drastically. She flew off the handle at the slightest thing, screaming with rage. She even slapped poor Ethel once, and made her cry. Afterwards Miss Hutchinson was devastated at what she'd done. She took the girl in her arms and soothed her.

'You'll have to make allowances from now on,' she said in a shaky voice. 'You see, I'm not very well, and I suffer such pain. You don't know. It's terrible.' She shook her head and a tear rolled down her cheek. 'And then . . . then I'm driven that mad, that I just don't know what I'm doin'!'

Ethel found herself comforting the woman. Her own distress was temporary and passing. Miss Hutchinson's was ever present and far more dreadful. Then Ethel was gently pushed away and Miss Hutchinson wiped her eyes and sniffed.

'Well now you know,' she said. And so they did. But their days had lost the natural joy that they once had had, and they found themselves nursing their employer through the long hours, taking her tea, applying poultices, and soothing the puckered forehead. They didn't know what it was that was wrong with her. It would have been bad manners to ask, but it wasn't bad manners to empty the pails of vomit from her bedside and hold a bowl in front of her when sudden nausea struck.

So the days with Gilbert seemed brighter by comparison with the usual grind in the shop. Gilbert often waited for her outside till she had finished for the day, and took her home, usually staying for a cup of tea these days. There was a lot of whispering among the girls. Mabel was positively jealous.

'I'll be glad when you've gone and got yourself wed,' she snapped. 'Then maybe I'll get a look in!'

And Cathy, annoyed, had replied, 'Don't be daft, Mabel. Gilbert and me're good friends, that's all.'

Then they all, including Miss Hutchinson burst out laughing.

'Pull the other one!' Ethel cried. 'It's got bells on.'

'Well it's true!' Cathy insisted. 'It's true.'

As Gilbert met her outside, Cathy was decidely out of sorts. He opened the door of his car to let her in and pecked her on the cheek as he usually did.

'What's the matter?' he asked. 'You've got a face like the back of a bus.'

'Thanks for nothing!' Cathy said sulkily.

'Only jokin',' Gilbert reassured her as he jumped into the driving seat. She expected him to start the engine, but he just sat there.

'Are we goin' or aren't we?' she asked, trying to smile.

'Haway,' Gilbert said, dropping into the Geordie to set her at her ease. 'Tell's all about it.'

'Oh it's nothin'. Just that daft lot in there.'

'Why? What did they say?'

'Oh, they were goin' on about you and me.'

Gilbert looked away.

'Ah,' he said.

'I mean, I told them,' Cathy said, 'I told them, we're good pals. I mean we are, aren't we?' She looked at him for reassurance.

'Are we?' He asked quietly. Cathy frowned.

'What do you mean?'

'Is that all we are?'

Gilbert's voice slithered beneath her defences and she flinched at the sudden excitement of it. The lights he had switched on were too bright. She felt caught out by them, naked, and was afraid. She had been so happy. But now he was forcing her to own up to the meaning of the game they had been playing with their emotions. It had all turned serious. Her breath caught in her throat, and Gilbert watched her apprehensively. What was the matter? Was she embarrassed? He had thought they had been playing in the same sea, that the eddies and currents of her emotions were the same as his. Was he then, merely floundering in a duck pond after all, kidding himself about her feelings for him? Disappointed, Gilbert got out of the car and started up the engine, ready to drive Cathy home.

Lily noticed Cathy's long face at once, and noted Gilbert's polite refusal to come into the house when they got back to Thrift Street, but she was wise enough to say nothing. And when Sunday came, she was relieved to be told that 'he was coming at two to take her out'. She contented herself with asking, 'Where're you goin', pet?'

'I don't know. By the sea, walking, I suppose.'

'Why don't you walk down to Gypsies' Green? I used to love it there as a girl.' And she crossed her fingers as the pair went off.

They walked in silence for a while. Then, as if to reassume their usual close companionship, Cathy threaded her arm through Gilbert's and smiled up at him cheerily.

'I do like being with you,' she said.

'Do you, Cathy?' he asked.

'You know I do. I hadn't realised,' she said thoughtfully, 'how lonely I was before.'

They stopped, and he smiled down at her. There was a chill wind coming off the sea. Cathy shivered.

'How would it feel if I went away, Cathy?'

Cathy's mouth opened in horror.

'No! Oh no!' she cried.

'It's what Ma wants,' he said.

'Do you? Where would you go? You wouldn't, would you?'

Cathy was seized with panic at the thought. She would feel bereft without him. Her feeling flung itself at him like a rope to a drowning man. He grasped at it, no master of ships now, but a man who had chanced the sea and was at its mercy.

'Do you love me, Cathy?' he asked her.

'Yes, oh yes, you know I do!' she cried, her arms flying to his neck. She had hauled him in and Gilbert was safely back on board. His body relaxed against hers and he almost wept with the relief of it.

'I'll not go, if you don't want me to,' he said. 'I'll tell her no.'

'Yes. Tell the old faggot where to get off!' And they both shook with laughter, rocking in each others' arms.

'I'll have to break it to her gently,' Gilbert said, straightening up to look at Cathy's face.

'What? Break what, Gilbert?'

'You and me,' he explained, surprised. 'Well, we can't go on like this, you know.'

'No,' Cathy sighed.

'I love you.' Gilbert took her face in his hands, and bent his head towards her. A chill gust came between them for a second, making her shiver, then he put his lips against hers and kissed her long and gently. When he moved away, he saw her sweet face smiling at him.

'Leave it to me,' he said. 'I'll talk the old faggot round.' Then they laughed again, and walked arm in arm along the shore.

Now that it had been decided, Cathy felt quite happy about the arrangement. She loved Gilbert. She was sure of it. She'd be heartbroken if he ever left her. The very thought turned a day grey and desolate. And then there was her mother and Hettie. She laughed at the thought. They'd never forgive her if she didn't nail young Gilbert! It had all come so easily, much easier than she'd expected, perhaps almost too easily. She couldn't believe her luck. She loved Gilbert. Gilbert loved her. He even wanted to marry her in spite of his mother, in spite of her circumstances, in spite of what people would say. Life with him would be full of joy and pleasures. She would never want. Neither would Hettie or her mother, she was sure of that. And she would never be lonely again, that above all. Just to be with Gilbert felt like coming home. She wondered why she had hesitated so long. But she wouldn't tell her mother. Not yet. There was Mrs Stoddard to be brought round, and that would take time, heaven knew! Leave her to me, Gilbert had said. And so she would.

Walking in the garden at Westoe, Gilbert drew Cathy along the lawn in front of the house. From the corner of his eye he saw a curtain twitch and he knew his mother was watching. He put his arm round Cathy and drew her closer to him. They stopped walking, and Mrs Stoddard watched tight-lipped as he kissed her, slowly, deliberately, right in front of her. Her eyes were cold.

Later that night Gilbert faced a scene that would have made many a man blanch. His father and mother had summoned him to the study, and they stood there, ranged against him.

'Friendship's one thing, son, but kissing her right in front of the French windows! Well!'

'I want to marry her, father.'

There was a deathly hush.

'Have you asked her?' his mother's voice was tinged with hysteria.

'Yes. And she agreed.'

'She would!'

'Be quiet, Edith.' James Stoddard assumed mastery of the situation. 'She's an attractive lass. I'll give you that. You've got taste, me lad! But can't you just . . .' His tone suggested what a gentleman couldn't say.

'Just what, Dad?'

Mr Stoddard raised an eyebrow and tried another tack.

'She seems willing enough, I must say, kissing right in front of the windows!'

'She didn't know anyone was watching.'

'Maybe not but . . . a bit importunate.'

'I kissed her, Dad, not the other way around.'

'A shopgirl, son! You're in love. I know. Oh I know. But you don't have to *marry* the girl!'

'I will, Dad.'

'Give it time, son. Don't rush.'

'We've known each other for years!'

'As children, yes, but . . .'

'Catherine Straker is going to be my wife. The sooner you both get used to the idea, the better!'

Gilbert slammed the door behind him. He had told Cathy he would break it to them gently. But he knew it would have done no good if he had. They'd play for time, pushing other girls at him in the hopes of distracting him, playing games with his happiness. And Gilbert was not in the mood for playing games. He knew what he wanted, and he was going to get it. A head-on collision was the only way. If he wanted Cathy, he would have to fight for her and fight hard. He had said that about breaking it to them to reassure Cathy, for that was the kind of man Gilbert was. Cathy would never know of the fight he was putting up now. He would protect her pride, he would make everything as easy for her as he possibly could. That's how much Gilbert Stoddard loved Catherine Straker.

'We could always cut off his allowance,' Mr Stoddard said.

'No. Only encourage him. Takes after you. Pig-headed,' Mrs Stoddard answered him.

'What then? Ban her from the house?'

'Don't be silly, dear.'

'What then?'

'Play for time. That's all. Give her a long rein. She'll do the rest.'

PART THREE

CHAPTER NINE

The water reared. Joe Robson spread his weight and clung with raw hands onto the rope. And then came the slide, as *The Shieldsman* turned into the wave and began to swing towards the sky. Nose, lips, eyes were filled with spray from the approaching crest. He looked up into it, as though daring it to crash down upon him, and then, poised on the brink, the boat held its breath. Time stilled, man and vessel suspended high above the world. Joe's mouth spread and a laugh burst from his throat. This was living, living on the edge of life. It was what he wanted, where he felt at one with himself and the sea and everything that was ever born or died. On land, he was a man and only a man. The sea was his element where his soul soared. The timbers creaked, stomachs heaved, the tension of the water strained and broke. And they were dropped from the high peak, plunging down into the gorge that lay on the other side.

'By, but that was a big'n!' Alec MacGowan gulped his stomach back into place. 'Are you enjoyin' your holiday?'

Joe grinned.

'Haway, man. Help's with the lashin'. It's comin' adrift!'

Alec hauled himself along the rope towards Joe.

'You know, if I didn't think you had more sense, I'd suspect you were enjoyin' this!' Then the two caught at the free rope and lashed it back into place.

Below deck, they pulled off their oilskins and crouched over mugs of hot tea.

'That's better!' Alec smacked his lips, and sighed. 'Och, but it comes to somethin' when even your tea tastes salty!'

'What's the matter with you?' Joe laughed. 'You tartan Johnnies put salt in your porridge, never mind your tea!'

'Aye well. That's different.' From a dark corner, Eddie

Pope groaned dismally. 'You're makin' good music, Eddie!'

'He can't help it, man. Let him alone.'

Alec gritted his teeth. 'It gets on my nerves.'

'Do your deep breathing, then! Calm you down.'

Alec nodded. One hand held onto his mug, the other he raised to his face. Then, closing one nostril with one finger, he breathed in deeply, held his breath, then closing the other nostril with another finger he exhaled slowly.

'Has it got a name, what you're doing?'

'Yoga.' Alec breathed again and Joe watched till a sudden movement of the boat lurched Alec's mug from his hand and it fell down his trouser front. 'Hell!' Joe laughed as the Scotsman held his trousers away from his skin. 'You'll laugh on the other side of your face when I've done with you, Geordie!'

'Sorry. I'll get you some more tea.' Joe reached for the mug which was clattering about the floor and, waiting for the moment of suspension at the height of the wave, he poured quickly and held on till they were back down in the gulley. Alec took the mug and drank it quickly.

'What's yoga?' Joe asked him.

'What the Indians do, sittin' cross-legged and all that. Very good for you. You'd never know I was in pain, would you?' Joe shook his head. 'That's the sort of control a yogi gets over his own body. You do that by learning how to breathe. Breath is life. You control your breath, you can control your life, and you can control your pain if you have any.'

'Is that a fact?' Joe asked him, amazed. 'Will you teach me?'

'Aye. If you like.'

There was a pause as the boat rose again. Joe's brow puckered.

'Why're you in pain, Alec lad?'

'Bloody tea! Hit my vital parts, didn't it?'

It was to be only a short trip. Joe doubted if they would reach the herring grounds. But it made a change from stoking the boiler on the *Ha'penny Dodger*. He was soaked to the skin, pink from the raw air, bedraggled. What would

Miss Straker think of him if she were to see him like this? He wasn't fit for her parlour before. He remembered how she had flinched when he held his hand out to her, afraid he'd dirty her dress. He'd be a lot dirtier on his return home with the stink of fish on him. He laughed at himself. She'd never so much as look at him, a lass like that! And yet, when he saw the sunset touching the horizon he was reminded of the red lights in her hair, wave upon wave of red gold fire. And the fire was inside her too. It sparked him. That was the pity of it. Madge, who served teas at the mission, had a shine for Joe. And he liked her all right. She was a good lass, was Madge. She baked a good cake. She kept her mother's house nice. She had a warm smile, and a welcoming body. He could always have a good laugh and a bit of carry on with her. But she had no spark. No, it was young Cathy Straker who drew him to her pinnacle like the wave drew the boat to its crest. He had only to rise higher, and he would have his day. The boat, his boat, that he slaved for day in day out on the *Ha'penny Dodger* would carry him to her. A stoker on the ferry was one thing, but the owner of a boat, even if it was part shared, was another! Whether he smelt of fish or not! She might think herself far above him, but by, wouldn't she be surprised when he landed on her level, up there on the crest of the wave. Then she'd look at him. He'd make her!

Who'll buy caller herrin'?
They're bonnie fish an' halesome farin';
Buy my caller herrin',
New drawn frae the Forth.

When ye were sleepin' on your pillows,
Dreamt ye aught of our puir fellows,
Darkling as they face the billows,
A' to fill your woven willows?

Buy my caller herrin',
They're bonnie fish and halesome farin'
Buy my caller herrin',
New drawn frae the Forth.

Alec's voice rose above the creaking timbers, borne on the breeze to where Joe stood watching on deck. Alec MacGowan. A crazy Scotsman if ever there was. Money flowed through his hands. He couldn't hold onto it. Either the breweries took it off him, or his 'mates' with their hard-luck stories. Which was why Joe relieved him of the greater part of it at the end of every trip, and stashed it away with his own for that boat. Alec MacGowan, Jim Webster and Joe, three men, of one mind but differing temperaments. Jim ran a wet fish shop in Wallsend, and had a few bob put by already. But he got sick lookin' at the park lake. He'd stop onshore and look after the business side while Alec and Joe put out to sea in the shared trawler. Joe had a lot to learn before that fishing boat of theirs became a reality. Alec was the real seaman amongst them. The one with all the experience. He was always in demand for work, while Joe had to wait till the skippers were short-handed and be content to fill in, where he could, navvying the rest of the time in the ferry boiler room. Alec would therefore be the skipper. Joe would be first mate. Meanwhile, Joe learned from Alec, and not just seamanship. The wild, gentle Scotsman guided him into the unknown waters of the mind; lent him Nietzsche, Plato, Homer, political tracts, books on economics and history. Joe raised his right hand to his face and covered one nostril with his forefinger. Then he breathed slowly and deliberately, changed fingers, closed the other nostril and exhaled. Yoga! Whatever next!

Caller herrin', caller herrin'.
An' when the creel o' herrin' passes,
Ladies clad in silks and laces,
Gather in their braw pelisses,
Toss their head and screw their faces.

Aye. It would take more than yoga to dull the pain in Joe's heart. Cathy was a lady all right, with her face screwed in disgust at him. But she was a woman too. And Joe was a man. And he wanted her. He would learn, he would grow, and one day his chance might come. And when it did, he'd grasp it, with all his might, see if he wouldn't.

Across the now still sea, Joe's eyes picked out a place ahead where the waters seemed choppy. He focused his attention on it. It was alive, thrashing; it was what they had been looking for.

'Herring! Herring!' he yelled across the boat. Alec flew to his side.

'Where, man?' Joe pointed.

Alec's face lit up, and he whooped with delight.

'We'll be takin' a packet home after all, lad!' And the crew set to to land the catch that made their trip worthwhile.

The dawn was like a dusk. Cathy rose to it wearily. Saturday was a busy day at the shop. Lily and Hettie were already up, and the smell of boiling sheets filtered up the stairway. She looked out of her window at the grey sky, the colour of the North Sea. If they lived on the seafront, she would be able to see it from her room and she wouldn't feel so trapped. She would be able to watch the ships and the little boats coming in and out between the harbour walls. If, if . . . If pigs had wings, if women had mermaid's tails. If she had been born a man, then she might have gone to sea and even now be tasting the salt on her skin, adrift on the free ocean.

'Wake up! You're late!' Lily's voice rasped against the door. 'If you and Hettie want to go gallivantin' tonight, you'd better get crackin'! There's a lot to do today!'

Cathy yawned, and pulled her nightdress over her head. 'Gallivanting' if you please! A trip to the market with Hettie, the high spot of Cathy's week! If that was 'gallivanting' then Cathy was not impressed. She pulled the brush through the tangled mass of her hair and braced herself for the day.

The Shieldsman, laden with herring, looked insignificant as it came in between the harbours of North and South Shields and made its way towards the quay. Jim was waiting as they flung the rope around the capstan and jumped off ship.

'Better you than me, me bonnie lads,' he said smiling. 'I thought I'd join you for a cuppa down at the mission before I open up shop, like.'

Joe slapped him on the back.

'Haway, then! Alec! You comin'?' And Alec bounded after them, his legs giving on the unfamiliar stability of dry land.

Madge was waiting. News of their landing had come ahead of them. Her face beamed over the tea urn, and her hands lashed the greasy bacon onto the bread.

'Get that inside ye!' she ordered, pushing the plate at Joe. Joe winked and took it to a table close by where he could look at her as he ate. She was a bonny lass!

'You're in there!' Alec nudged him.

'Shurrup, man!' Joe silenced him.

'Joe's savin' hisself!' Jim laughed.

'Don't be daft!' Joe gave a sidelong glance at Madge, who winked back at him.

'Did ye see that, Jim?' Alec said, amazed. 'He's a mighty dark horse, is our Joe.'

'She'd have anythin' in trousers, man,' Jim teased.

'Show a bit of respect!' Joe upbraided the pair of them.

'Women like a bit of rudery! Take my word for it!'

'You show him, Alec.'

Alec rose with his empty plate and approached the counter.

'Gimme a bit more hen, and I'll make it worth your while!' His hand reached round the counter towards Madge's backside. Joe blanched. Madge turned, arms flailing, and fetched him one round his whiskers. Alec went flying, while Jim and Joe laughed and clapped, and Madge glared.

'That'll teach you!' she snapped. But she smiled afterwards and gave in about the bacon. Joe watched in surprise. She had objected to Alec taking liberties, but once put in his place, she had immediately relented and gone soft on him. And now, here he was, coming back to the table with a second helping of greasy bacon and another mug of sweet tea.

'You don't know how to handle women,' Alec told him.

'You want to ask Madge whether I can handle her or not!' Joe snorted. 'An' you don't have to take liberties to do it!'

'Aye. He's a devil on the quiet!' Jim backed him up.

'Madge is a canny lass,' Joe said. 'I feel comfortable with her. But we all know Madge is no lady!'

'So what?' Alec said. 'Ladies are nae different! You handle them the same way! I mean, they're not made of sugar an' spice!'

'Maybe, Alec. But that doesn't mean they're made of puppy dog's tails either.'

Cathy might have disagreed with Joe as she strove to please a particularly difficult customer at Miss Hutchinson's.

'Perhaps a little veiling?' she suggested, arranging a swathe of net across the woman's face. 'Ah, that's better.'

'Nobody can see me now!' the woman objected. Cathy tried not to smile, and removed the veil. 'I shall speak to Miss Hutchinson when she returns from her walk, Miss! I find you hopelessly inadequate to your task!' So saying, 'Madam' dropped the hat to the floor and swept her skirt over it as she stalked out of the shop. Cathy suppressed a scream of rage and bent to rescue her creation.

'She looks like the back end of a tram anyway!' she snorted.

Jim had gone to open up his shop, but Alec's money was burning a hole in his pocket and Joe knew that if he didn't watch over him it would all be gone by nightfall. He was forced to be his brother's keeper and followed him along the quayside to the pubs. The Abbey Arms was followed by the Alexandra. The Alexandra was followed by the Norseman, and the Norseman was followed by the Capstan. Coming out of the Capstan in a drunken stupor, Alec saw a woman, dressed all in black, sitting on a box. She was waiting for someone; a quiet body with a sad face, and her clothes, though far from new, were well mended and decent. Before Joe could stop him, Alec made a bee line for her.

'Cheer up, hen,' he was saying. The woman averted her face from his breath. 'Look at me when I'm talkin' to you.' She edged further along the box.

'Come away, Alec. She doesn't want us.'

'Oh aye she does! Don't you?' His hand reached out to touch her chin. Suddenly she rose, trembling. But he did not want to let her go.

'Leave her, Alec!' Joe's voice was sharp.

Alec turned on him angrily, his fists flailing, and the woman fled. But Joe was ready for him and undercut his defence with a sharp right to Alec's jaw. The big Scotsman tottered backwards and fell, a surprised look on his face.

'I didn't know you had it in ye, lad!' And Joe stood, ready, his fists up, waiting for him. 'I'm bigger than you! You know that?'

'Aye. I know. But I'm tougher. You don't stoke boilers without gettin' a few muscles, Alec. D'ye want a fight or not?'

Alec shook his head.

'I don't want to fight with you! But Joe,' his voice was pained, 'what d'ye mean, givin' me orders, Joe! Givin' *me orders!*'

'You can't force yourself on a poor defenceless woman like that. It's not right!'

'I was only tryin' to cheer her up!'

'*She* didn't think so! You behaved like a roughie!'

'Are you a man or what?'

'Of course I'm a man!' Joe shouted.

'You don't show it!' Alec sat on the pavement's edge, looking up at him.

'Don't I though?' Joe's voice was menacing. 'I just don't happen to think it's manly to boss women about, that's all!'

'Don't come that, son! You canna tell me you've never forced or hit out at a woman!'

'I have not!'

'You dinna ken what manly is!'

'You don't mean what you're saying, Alec. You're drunk. You wouldn't force a lassie any more than I would.'

'All right! I wouldn't. I'd persuade her! Come on son, let me give you a bit of advice. You with women, son, you're like a fish out of water. You don't know how to handle yourself. You're your own worst enemy, you know that?'

Joe sat on the pavement beside him.

'Well, I'm no ladies' man, I'll agree with ye . . .'

Alec snorted.

'Ladies man! Hah!' He smiled gently. 'That's half your

trouble. You think you've got to be a gentleman to please them, all airs and graces! But really, Joe, you only have to be a man, whether it's Madge you're talkin' about or some fine lady!'

'Aye, but what's a man?' Joe asked quietly.

Alec was silent. He had reached the other side of drunkenness and was sobering up. He resisted the impulse to say 'If you dinna ken I'm not tellin' ye!' and considered a while before he spoke.

'I reckon it's a matter of just being yourself, and not ashamed of it,' he said. 'You and me, we're as good as the next man. Better maybe.'

Joe nodded. He had never felt ill at ease with another man. It was 'ladies' who made him feel awkward, made it impossible for him to be himself. They always seemed to 'expect' something of him. Only Madge liked him for what he was, Joe Robson, a navvy with dreams.

'Who is she?' Alec probed into his thoughts.

'What d'ye mean?'

'The lady. Who is she?'

'It doesn't matter. She's way out of my class!'

At sea anything had seemed possible. But on land, literally back to earth, Joe floundered once again in a sense of social inferiority and lack of worth.

'Ye know what they say about "faint hearts",' Alec reminded him.

Joe smiled.

'Oh I'll not give up. I've got me plans!' Then he held out his arm. 'Haway, Alec. One for the road before I pocket that money for ye! We're goin' to get a boat if it's the last thing I do!'

'Meanwhile, you'll make do with Madge!' Alec winked at him and allowed Joe to drag him to his feet.

On the south side of the river, at last, Alec and Joe sat over their pints in the White Horse. Had they been counting, pint by pint, Joe was well behind the Scotsman. All the same, he felt the floor move under him like the ocean and the sea of faces blurred around the bar. Still, one voice sounded clear above the rest. A familiar voice.

'Another'n?' Alec nudged his arm.

'Sh.' Joe shook his head, listening. That voice bothered him. He strove to shake off the affects of the beer and remember. He waited for the man to speak again.

'Have you heard anythin' of Hettie Straker?'

Yes. Of course! Joe had him now. He would know *that* voice anywhere!

'What're you puttin' on your glad rags for?' Lily asked as Hettie arranged her best hat on her head.

'I'm meetin' me boyfriend, Lily,' Hettie teased her.

'Huh! I don't think!'

Hettie smiled and tilted the brim. Lily was only jealous. She, Hettie, was having an outing with Cathy, and Lily felt left out of it, that was all. Hettie wasn't going to let her spoil her pleasure.

'Skivin' off to the market! They sell nowt but rubbish there, any road!'

Hettie gritted her teeth. No she would *not* let Lily spoil her fun. Without a word, she reached for her purse and left the house and its miseries behind her.

Cathy was late. Miss Hutchinson had held onto her till the last minute, and Hettie was annoyed at having to wait. Then, when finally the girl did turn up, she wanted to go in search of a cup of tea!

'We've not done any shoppin' yet!' Hettie objected.

'I'm parched, Auntie. I've come straight from work ye know! Ah come on!'

But Hettie would not be persuaded. She'd come to shop and shop she would.

'You go and have one if you like!' she said huffily. 'I'll be at the haberdashery stalls.'

'All right! All right!' Cathy too was annoyed, annoyed at being kept late, and a cup of tea would calm her. 'I'll see you in a bit, then.' So the two parted company, Cathy to the tea stall and Hettie in search of a special bit of something for her winter dress.

The stalls were like small theatres, lit up, the occupants clearly visible from the darkness round about. A man emerged from the shadows and idly made his way towards the centre of the market. His eye appraised the little stalls, seeming to size up the extent of their trade and the manner of displaying their wares. Those with perishable goods were beginning to cut their prices. For it was late on a Saturday evening, and the crowds were thinning. A flower seller pushed a box of red carnations to the front, hoping to attract the dandies on their way to the theatre. The man eyed them, then went up to the stall and bought one which he immediately put in his buttonhole. He looked at the girl. She nodded her approval, and he smiled at her, holding her eyes long enough to make her blush and turn away. Then he turned from the glare of the acetylene lamps back into the shadows and watched the cluster of women still gathered round the haberdasher's stall.

Beads, crystal and paste, glittered in the lamplight. It drew the women like a gaudy flower draws the bees. Hettie's fingers searched through the box of oddments, looking for a clasp. She wanted something bright, something to enliven her old flannel dress. It was October, and there'd been a frost that morning. She had taken her winter things out of storage and stared at them mournfully. They looked dead as autumn leaves, walked on, rained on and faded. The colour of the cold earth. Perhaps russet or copper, something that recalled the vibrant shades of the leaves before they fell, if there was such a thing in this miserable little box. Her eye strayed upwards to the card hanging across the front of the stall. On it was a gilt clasp, shaped like a butterfly; that was the one she'd really set her heart on. But it was too expensive. No. There must be something in the box. People were going home, packing up. And where was Cathy? If only she would come and help her make up her mind. Her hands dropped the oddments into the box, and she looked around her. The lamp above her head flared dangerously, lighting up the dark corners round the fringes of the stall. She couldn't see among this crowd of women gathered in the light. Perhaps out there in the dark spaces between the stalls Cathy was waiting for her. If only she could see. A sudden flare illuminated a corner by the awning. The man was there. Hettie gasped. His face was clear as day; he was looking straight at her in some surprise, and he seemed to smile. But then he looked away again, and when the lamp flared up a second time he had turned his back and was walking off into the dark.

'Auntie Hettie, have you not found one yet?' Cathy, at her elbow, made her jump.

'There you are!' she snapped. 'I thought you'd got lost!' Cathy raised an eyebrow but said nothing. Hettie seemed upset. 'There's nowt here anyway. Nowt worth havin'.' And dismissing the stall, she took Cathy's arm to lead her away and get the tram home.

All night that face flashed across Hettie's mind, a snapshot, coming up in her restless thoughts like a ghost, determined to haunt her. She knew that smile, those eyes, half-amused they always looked. There could be no mistake. And yet there had seemed something different about him. He was dapper, sported a red carnation in his buttonhole, and he had lost some weight. He looked younger, and she, she knew, looked older. Had he recognised her? Hettie didn't know whether she wanted him to or not. Tossing in her bed, emotions long since buried and forgotten surged up inside her, ebbing and flowing like the restless sea.

The next morning Lily was on about her musical evenings again. Hettie turned a weary eye to look out of the scullery window into the yard. She noticed it had begun to drizzle again, leaving the slate top of the midden and the washhouse with a greasy dampness on them.

'If you'd only show a *bit* of interest!' Lily complained. 'Our Cathy's a proper wet blanket. Heaven knows what's goin' on between them two!'

Hettie sighed, and picked up her cup of tea in both hands, watching the steam rise before she drank some down.

'They're all right, Lily. She's only a bairn. Give them time.'

'Huh! Who's side are you on, might I ask? That's what *she* wants!'

'Who?'

'Edith Stoddard. She's not daft, you know. She thinks he'll cool off, I bet; puttin' spanners in the works, so they'll not name the day. If I was him I'd elope!'

'Aye, and we'd all end up where we started, Lily. Except our Cathy'd have a husband, I suppose. You could be right.'

'What do you mean, end up where we started?'

'Why, man, they'd cut him off!'

Lily said nothing. The thought had been niggling her for some time. She drank the hot tea and smacked her lips decisively.

'He's their only son,' she said knowingly. 'They need somebody to run the firm after he's gone! And he's not too well! Walkin' with a stick now, so Cathy says.'

'Aye,' Hettie sighed, 'I expect you're right.' Lily looked at her suspiciously. She looked pale and drawn, weary.

'Are you sickenin' for somethin'?' she demanded.

'Oh, Lily, I wish you'd mind your own business.' Hettie got up from the table and flew out of the room, leaving Lily to stare after her.

'I only asked!' she said, amazed.

Cathy and Gilbert had settled into a routine of courtship. It was accepted in Thrift Street among the lodgers and the family, and tolerated in Westoe Village, though nothing was said about any engagement. And Gilbert had been content to let things slide for the summer, let his parents get used to the idea, showing by his steadfast behaviour that he wouldn't waver in his choice of a partner. Mr Stoddard was coming round, he was sure of that. His father had grown to depend on him more and more in the business, as his legs began to fail him, and it saddened Gilbert to see him like that, hobbling along with a stick, frustrated and helpless. It made him go more gently than he might have done, out of consideration. And then, Gilbert was busy at work. The freight business was booming, and he had his hands full learning the ropes, doing deals and handling the men. Cathy'd pestered him to death to take her with him when he went on board his father's ships. 'Just to show me around, Gilbert. I'll not stow away, honest!' But he had not allowed himself to be wheedled by her charms into saying yes. 'It's no place for a lady, Cathy,' he'd say. 'Maybe when we're married. It'll be different then.' And Cathy had sighed loudly and complained. 'You mean never!' she said. And then Gilbert had looked at her very seriously.

'I think it's about time we let your Mam in on the secret,' he said.

'Tell her we're engaged, Gilbert?' Cathy smiled, pleased at last.

Gilbert nodded.

'This musical evening she's on about . . .'

Cathy sighed with some irritation. 'You're not takin' that seriously, are you?'

'What else is there? My lot've got to visit your lot before we can make any sort of official announcement.'

'Musical evenin's in Thrift Street. Folk'll kill theirsel's laughing!'

'There's got to be something your mother can invite mine to.'

'She'd never come.'

Gilbert considered the possibility.

'No matter. At least it'll make our intentions clear. And then, when we announce the engagement . . .'

'We'll be just the same as we were.'

'Oh no we won't. I'm not going to ask permission, Cathy. They've known long enough. I shall simply tell them.'

Cathy looked at Gilbert and smiled. He was so strong and sure of himself. In the past, when they'd been children, she'd led him, but now she was more than happy for him to lead her. He seemed to know just what he wanted and how to go about it. She could always depend on him.

'Oh Gilbert! I do love you!' she cried and threw her arms round his neck. His mouth searched for hers and they kissed, their lips touching, then receding again, only to touch even more lightly, sending a frisson down Cathy's spine. Surprised, she looked up at him as she nestled in his familiar arms.

'That was particularly nice,' she said giggling.

His hand silently touched her hair, and eased under the

loose copper mane to stroke her neck. Immediately, her feelings stirred, and she moved against him sinuously, moaning with delight. Gilbert, his eyes closed, basked in the warmth of their closeness. He would go gently, carefully with her. They were both so innocent, it would be a shame to rush in and spoil it. No, they would find each other through scattered moments like this one, growing ever closer and more desirous of one another. He sighed with contentment. He'd been patient so far; this long sweetness that they both felt in the embrace was proof, if ever proof was wanted, that his own restraint had paid off. She was coming to him, slowly, in her own good time.

Cathy came round lazily, her head light and spinning from his touch. Her eyes were hazy and a smile played about her lips, savouring the memory of Gilbert's touch. He kissed her lightly on the top of her head.

'When shall we announce it?' he asked.

'I don't know,' she sighed dreamily.

'It's nearly your birthday.'

'I'll be eighteen.'

'I know.'

Cathy drew apart from him, a pleased look on her face.

'Oh Gilbert, what a smashing idea! Let's do it then!'

And Gilbert pondered the ring he would buy her. He would keep it to himself, not tell her, just seek out some special stone that was hers and, on her birthday, present it to her. What a day that would be, his ring on her finger, symbol of their trust, which they would keep no matter who or what tried to come in their way.

Lily was all agog at the prospect when they told her.

'That's the way to do it!' she cried. 'Get the bit between their teeth and they'll *have* to bite on it!' Gilbert laughed. 'Not that I mean any disrespect, pet, to your Mam and Dad I mean.'

'No, Mrs Straker. I know you don't.'

'I mean, I like your mother. She's a canny soul.'

Cathy whooped with mocking laughter.

'She's not nasty, you know,' Gilbert said, trying to make

amends for his mother. 'It's just she's got these funny ideas. She can be quite nice sometimes.'

Lily remembered her kindness all those years ago when she had stood outside her old Westoe home and cried.

'I know she can,' she said softly, and the young couple were surprised at her tone. Then suddenly she brightened up. 'By, but I'm glad you've got the spunk for it. You're a good lad.' She looked approvingly at him. 'She'll take some keepin' in check mind! Where are you plannin' on livin'?'

The question was asked innocently, but both Gilbert and Cathy knew of Lily's pretensions to find her way back to the village. Poor Lily. She couldn't see beyond that, not to actually living there, alongside Gilbert's mother, seeing her every day and feeling her disapproval.

'We've not actually thought about it yet, Mrs Straker,' Gilbert said kindly. 'First things first.'

'Aye. I daresay you're right,' Lily reluctantly admitted. 'Mind he gets you a nice ring!' she said to her daughter, smiling.

'Mam!'

Hettie cried when Lily told her.

'Nothin' pleases some folks,' Lily complained. 'I thought you'd be happy.'

'Oh I am! I am!' Hettie sobbed. 'It's the most wonderful news I ever heard.'

'Mind you keep it under your hat, though. It's not official yet. And we don't want to upset the apple cart.'

'Oh no, Lily,' Hettie shook her head. 'I'll not tell a soul.'

It was such a relief, the news that Gilbert and Cathy had finally settled what to do. Hettie'd never gone much for elopements. She wanted a wedding to look forward to, memories to cherish of the blushing bride. And she'd make a lovely bride, their Cathy. Hettie'd gladly work her fingers to the bone on a dress for her. Her eyes misted with visions of lace and apple blossom, all the trimmings. No expense spared, she hoped. Then she blew her nose and set about cleaning 'The Sanctuary' for Friday evening. They were having a trial run at a musical evening, and the place had to look like you could eat off the floor.

The morning of the do Hettie got up very early, long before it was light, and went down to Comical Corner. She heard the *Dodger* steaming its way across the river, and the funnel blowing. It was cold again. She could just make out the sparkling crust on the pavement by the light of the stars. Her breath steamed on the air, and she watched it rise and disappear into nothing. She remembered the day at the market the Saturday before. It seemed like a lifetime ago now, what with the news of Cathy and Gilbert and then with 'The Sanctuary' to scrub and polish for tonight. She'd never've believed it, but she'd almost forgotten! And now the picture of his face flashed across her memory once again. He had come and gone again like a puff of smoke, like her breath upon the air. Ah well, best forget all about it, she thought. Think of it as a bad dream. The ferry was docking. Hettie clattered down the steps to the landing stage and waited. Joe came rushing out, a parcel in his hands.

'Here y'are, Hettie. Smoked mackerel. And I've had them put in a few kippers for you an' all.'

Opening the parcel, Hettie examined the contents.

'Eeh, mind they're lovely, Joe. Be sure an' say thanks to your friends now.'

'It's nothin', Hettie,' and he refused the money she held out to him. 'Look, pet, I've not got long, so I'll come straight to the point, like.'

Hettie, surprised, peered at him in the half dark.

'It's like this, Hettie. Well, ye know I call in at the pub sometimes for . . .' he cleared his throat, 'for me dinner like.'

Hettie nodded.

'Well, I heard this bloke, talkin' like. And I pricked me ears up when I heard your name . . .'

Hettie drew in a sharp breath.

'Who was it?' she whispered.

'Whey, he looked different like. Kind o' dapper and that, but I'd know him anywhere. It was Johnny Beale, Hettie. I'm sure of it.'

Hettie's throat ached. She wanted to cry out. Her eyes seemed to search for some means of escape. Joe, distressed for her, spoke as kindly as he could.

'He was askin' after you, Hettie. Were you wed, your circumstances, whether you had any kids and that. Mind I thought that last one was a bit funny like, just after he'd found out you weren't wed or owt!' Joe tried to laugh. But Hettie said nothing. After an awkward moment, he said, 'Look, hinny, I've got to go now,' and he turned as if to go back to the ferry. But Hettie caught his arm.

'Thanks Joe. If there's ever anythin' I can do for you . . .'

Joe hesitated, weighing up in his mind whether to mention it or not.

'Well, as a matter of fact, Hettie,' he said slowly, watching her, 'there is. I've been thinkin' about it for a long time. It'd be easier for me if I lived this side of the river like, and I thought if you had a room free, for rent like . . . I mean I'd pay the goin' rate.'

Hettie's eyes lit up.

'Eeh, Joe, we've got a room free now. It'd be smashin', that. Mind, I'll have to ask Lily!' Her eyes shone at him out of the darkness. And he smiled, relieved.

'Thanks, Hettie,' he said. Making for the ferry, he turned back an instant to shout, 'Watch yourself hinny! There's some funny folk about!' Then he was gone, and the ferry churned on over the dark waters.

Hettie walked slowly up the hill in the pale light of the stars. As she looked up at them, wondering, she felt her heart breaking. She had no fight left. It had drained from her all those years ago. How would she keep him from her now?

Miss Hutchinson let Cathy off early that day and closed the shop long before the usual time. To Mabel and Ethel it was like a holiday, and they whooped joyously as they left the shop.

'Like a pair of school kids!' Miss Hutchinson reproved them, shaking her head.

'Are you all right now, Miss Hutchinson?' Cathy asked solicitously. 'Do you want me to do anythin' before I go?'

But Miss Hutchinson had shaken her head and shooed her out. Her hand had slipped to her side. Cathy noticed it and sighed. She hoped her employer would be all right for tonight, for she was invited, along with her old recorder, and her Mam would be very disappointed if she didn't turn up. Miss Hutchinson locked and bolted the door, turning the sign 'Shop Closed' to face the glass. A pain gripped her and held her rooted to the spot for an instant, then she turned and walked briskly through the curtain into the workroom and upstairs to her own rooms. There she poured some water in a glass and to it added a measure of kaolin and morphine. She looked at her pale face in the glass of her dressing table, then drank the liquid down. She would feel better shortly.

When Cathy reached home, her mother was in a flap.

'Eeh, am I glad to see you, pet. Your Auntie Hettie's been in a dream all day. We're miles behind. Kept sayin' she wanted to talk to's, if you please! Today of all days.'

'Is the Sanct . . . parlour done?'

'Oh aye. That's all finished. Just help me cut the crusts off the bread. We're still doin' the sandwiches!'

Removing her hat as she went, Cathy followed her mother into the scullery and set about slicing crusts off the already sliced bread. Hettie was beating up some mackerel with butter and vinegar to make a paste, and Lily was cutting up cucumber as fine as she could.

'I wish we could run to a bit of salmon,' she muttered. 'We'll have to try, for *them* comin'.'

'They're not comin' the night, are they?' Hettie asked.

'Oh, still in the land of the livin' are ye? I did wonder. No, of course they're not. This is wer trial run.'

'Mind,' Cathy warned them, 'I wouldn't bank on them comin' at all. It's just we've got to ask.'

Lily bit her lip. She knew that. She knew very well she'd have to work herself half to death just in case their highnesses deigned to show their faces in her humble dwelling.

'Never mind, Mam. It'll be different when we're wed,' Cathy comforted her.

'Aye,' Lily replied, slicing viciously through her cucumber. 'I'm bankin' on that.' Cathy smiled. 'And now, Madam,' Lily turned to Hettie, 'what did you want to talk to's about?'

'Nothin'.'

'Nothin'? What a carry on about nothin', eh?'

There was a pause and Cathy, working at the crusts, looked sidelong at her auntie. She had stopped beating and, Cathy could swear, a tear fell down into the bowl.

'Only . . .' Hettie spoke up at last, 'you know that room we've got spare?'

'Aha.'

'Well, Joe . . . you know he got us the fish from North Shields. Nice fish an' all an' he never charged us a penny . . .'

'Get on with it, Hettie.'

'Well, he's lookin' for a room, and . . .'

Lily looked up sharply.

'I see. Gives us free fish so he can get free lodgin's, eh?'

'No, Lily. He'd pay.'

'Too true he would,' Lily sighed exasperated.

'Hettie thinks he's gone on me,' Cathy laughed. Hettie gave her a dirty look. 'Now what have I said?' Cathy protested.

'That settles it.' Lily finished the chopping and inspected the shorn-off bread. 'I'm not havin' him here, tryin' to get his feet under the table.'

'It's my house, Lily.'

There was a silence. Lily had almost forgotten that. And it hurt her pride to be reminded they were there on sufferance.

'I see. So it's back to that, is it?'

'You two!' Cathy tried to ease the atmosphere. 'We're supposed to be havin' a party!'

The row subsided. Hettie sniffed but said nothing, and Lily's lips tightened over her tongue. Cathy sighed. She might've known it wouldn't last. The old, old story, sniping at each other, and her in the middle, watching.

Cathy oiled her palms and was passing her hands lightly over her hair when she heard the car arrive. Quickly, she finished her styling and washed her hands in the bowl, before running down the stairs to meet Gilbert.

'More haste less speed,' Mr Miller called as she hurtled past him.

'Sorry, Mr Miller,' she called over her shoulder, and

continued on, to arrive out of breath in the hall, where her mother was taking Gilbert's coat.

'Step into the parlour, Gilbert,' Lily said pompously.

Gilbert gave Cathy a sidelong smile and they went in to wait in solitary state for the other guests to arrive.

Cathy hadn't expected to enjoy the evening at all, but in fact she and Gilbert were in such high spirits they would have enjoyed anything. They had begun with the joke of 'The Sanctuary', Gilbert bowing and scraping about on the floor when they were on their own at the beginning. Then Mr Miller had walked in and found him grovelling there, at her feet as it seemed, and he coughed and went quite red, which made them laugh more.

'And who's going to give you away, Cathy?' he teased.

'Why, what do you mean, Mr Miller?' Cathy said in mock amazement.

'I'll willingly volunteer myself,' he said, 'when the time comes.' The old man threw his shoulders back, ready for anything. Cathy smiled warmly at him.

'Why, I can't think of anybody I'd like for the job more than you, Mr Miller,' she said gently. Mr Miller positively glowed.

Then Lily ushered Hettie in. Hettie wasn't keen to join the proceedings at all. That was obvious. The two had had a tiff in the scullery, but Lily put a smile on her face as she entered bearing plates of sandwiches, which Mr Miller eyed hungrily.

'They'll not last long,' Gilbert laughed in Cathy's ear.

Then Miss Hutchinson arrived, looking quite chalky. Cathy was seriously worried about her and sat her near the door in case she had to make a sudden exit. Miss Liddell, though invited, had made her excuses. She was attending the theatre tonight.

'Music hall,' Lily sneered. 'She would have found it more select in here!'

Mr Miller played a very long piece. Hettie, of course, managed to applaud in the wrong place and looked quite abashed when he gave her a filthy look before continuing with reassumed dignity. She looked so miserable throughout. And Cathy deeply regretted saying that about Joe Robson. She hadn't realised his coming had mattered so much to her. She wondered why. Surely it couldn't just be that that was making her so unhappy tonight? Miss Hutchinson was so dopey, she almost dropped off. But she revived enough to give a shaky rendering of some bird calls she used to do on her recorder as a child. They were very good, and the party clapped loudly. It made her day. You could tell. It brought a pink flush to her white cheeks, and though her hands shook from the nerves and the effort, she had enjoyed herself, all the same. She left soon after. It was the mackerel sandwiches that did it, Cathy thought. The pinkness left her cheeks at once as they were passed under her nose. Cathy rose and saw her out to the door, Gilbert following.

'I'll give her a lift,' he whispered.

'You can't. There'll be no one left,' Cathy hissed.

'I won't be long,' he reassured her. Between them, they got the lady into Gilbert's car and he drove off with her, having arranged the rug to keep her warm.

Lily was peeved he'd gone, though her annoyance mollified when she was told he would be returning.

'He'll miss his tea,' she said. But she wasn't sorry about that, because the rate Mr Miller was eating them sandwiches, there wouldn't have been enough to go round anyway. When Gilbert returned, Hettie was persuaded to accompany Cathy, who hadn't performed yet. Suddenly Cathy felt very nervous. She coughed just as Hettie plonked out the opening chord. The performers glanced at each other, and started again. It was to be 'The Waters of Tyne'. Gilbert suddenly realised he hadn't heard Cathy sing since that time under the Christmas tree, when she'd sung this very song, her childish voice shrilling without the help of a piano. The lyric must have seemed odd coming from the mouth of someone so very young, he realised, though he hadn't noticed it at the time. But there was no such oddity now. Shy at first, Cathy was soon drawn into the emotions of the song, her mellow soprano flowing with the rise and fall of the piano, expressing a depth of emotion which left his knees weak as water.

I cannot get to my love, though I would dee,
The water of Tyne runs between him and me,
And here I must stand with a tear in my ee,
Both sighin' and weepin', my true love to see.

Oh, where is the boatman, my bonny hinny,
Oh where is the boatman, bring him to me,
To ferry me over the Tyne to my hinny,
And I will remember the boatman and thee.

Oh bring me a boatman; I'll give a' my money,
And you for your trouble rewarded shall be,
To ferry me over the Tyne to my hinny,
Or scull him across that rough river to me.

It was too much for Hettie. She rushed from the room weeping, and was heard running up to her room, sobs heaving out of her convulsively. They heard her door bang and looked at one another, dismayed.

'I wasn't *that* bad,' Cathy said at last.

Everyone laughed and the atmosphere was relieved, but the musical evening was definitely over.

'How did you think it went?' her mother asked as Cathy cleared away the plates from 'The Sanctuary'. Cathy gave her a look and smiled. 'Ah it wasn't *that* bad, pet. If your Miss Hutchinson'd been a bit steadier on her pegs . . . was she tiddly or what?'

'No Mam. She gets this pain. I think she was, you know, doped.'

'Oh.' Lily considered her. 'Has she said anythin'?'

'What about?'

'You know, the shop. I mean, if she gets any worse . . .'

Cathy frowned.

'I don't know, Mam. I suppose the three of us'd just have to struggle on. It's her livelihood. I can't see her givin' up easily.'

'No,' Lily sighed. And then there was Hettie. 'I don't know what's got into her.'

'Ah Mam, can ye not give in about that Robson bloke, eh? It's no skin off our noses.'

Lily pursed her lips.

'I don't know, Cathy. It's not just, you know . . . what you said. He's family, and once in we'll never get rid.'

Cathy refrained from pointing out that the same could've been said about them.

'Anyway, I don't think that's all it is, do you?'

Cathy shook her head.

'No Mam. I don't. Is it the change do you think?'

Lily was struck by the thought.

'She's thirty-five. It's a bit young, but still, after what she went through . . .' Then she closed her mouth and could not be persuaded to clarify her remark. 'Aye. That's it pet. Fancy you thinkin' of that! That's what it'll be. We'll just have to be a bit tolerant like.' Then Lily sighed. She felt the approach of her own change of life. She hoped she wouldn't be taken that way. Eeh well! 'What we need,' she went on, 'is somebody with a bit of life about him. A real man, a gentleman, mind, with a voice and a bit of swank about him. That'd get the evening goin'.'

'What about my Gilbert?'

Lily smiled at her.

'Other than *your* Gilbert,' she said.

CHAPTER TEN

It was a day of secrecy all round. The lad had been told to 'go the back way', and he had found Hettie in the yard, on her own, hanging out the washing.

'What do you want?' she asked as he poked his head round the yard door.

'Are you Miss Straker?' he said, staying where he was.

'Depends which one you want.' Hettie continued to hang out her washing.

'Oh. I don't know.' And the lad looked nonplussed.

Hettie stared at him. He had a note in his hand, with the name written on it, but of course he couldn't read.

'Give's it here,' she demanded, putting out her hand.

Reluctantly, the lad handed over the paper. Hettie looked at the name, but there was no initial, so she ripped it open to read what was inside.

'Here! I'll get told off if he finds out!' he cried.

Hettie gave the lad a sharp look.

'Keep your hair on,' she said. 'It's for me all right.' Her breathing came hard and fast. 'What are you hanging about for?'

The lad looked angry and Hettie went into the scullery to fetch him a slab of bread and butter pudding.

'Thanks, Miss Straker,' he said gratefully and started eating it at once.

When he went Hettie looked up at the house windows to see she wasn't watched, and then she took herself into the midden and sat with the door half open so she could read by the daylight. 'Dearest Hettie,' it began, 'I know how you must feel, but if you knew my circumstances, you wouldn't blame me. I have never forgotten you. There will never be any other woman for me, you know that. And I hope you still have some regard for me, at least enough to be friends. I thought of you every day, believe me, and thought of nothing but seeing you again, which, I hope and pray, may be soon, if you will. That's all I ask, Hettie, dearest love, just to see you once more and know you forgive me for the past, which I am sure you will, when you know. I will be at the bridge on the pier head (south pier) at 11.30 this morning, unless the weather's bad, when I will be at the bandstand in Marine Park. Please come, dearest. My heart yearns for our meeting. Hoping this finds you as it leaves me, well and longing for our meeting. Your own, Johnny (Beale).'

Hettie had known he'd get in touch somehow, after what Joe had told her. And yet she felt shocked now it had happened. What could he want with her after all these years? She remembered how he'd looked at the market, well suited, with a flower in his buttonhole, man of the world with a bob or two to his credit, by the looks of him. And he knew about her; he'd asked around. He'd seen her, looking plain and old, her looks neglected since . . . since that terrible time. Could she believe him? After what he'd done to her? What circumstances could he mean? What reason would excuse his past behaviour? She could not imagine. And yet . . . 'Dearest Hettie'. The words shot through her. No one had called her that for years and years. She had thought nobody ever would again. And, God help her, she liked it. She wanted to be called 'dearest love' and all the rest of it, and why not? Wasn't it just what everybody else wanted too? What was so special about her that she had to turn her back on a little bit of lovin'?

Hettie rocked to and fro on the midden, keening till her heart was ready to burst. He was a philanderer. She knew it. It could bring her nothing but harm. But what if . . . what if there *had* been some good reason for his disappearance? Might she not be turning her back on her one chance of living if she didn't even go and find out? He hadn't left her any time to think. God knows what the time was now. What should she do? What in heaven's name should she do? 'Dearest Hettie . . . dearest love.' Her heart lurched. Paralysed by indecision she sat on in the midden, her mind blank, smelling the dank earth, cold and frightened.

'Hettie? Hettie? Where are you?' Lily came into the yard in

search of her, found the clothes left in the basket and looked round the corner. She saw Hettie's feet through the open door of the midden.

'You've been in there a long time, Hettie.'

Hettie pulled the door shut against her but Lily wouldn't go till she'd said her piece.

'I thought you were sickenin'. You want to get some syrup of figs down you. That'll sort you!'

And then, thank the Lord, Lily went. Was that all she was? Just a soulless body in need of dosing? Was that all they thought could ever be wrong with her? They never even considered her feelings, did they? No! Hettie never had any, or if she did they never mattered. Hettie's life's over, finished, dead. Well it wasn't. Hot tears stung her cheeks as she rose stiffly from the midden seat. She gasped out a cry, settled her skirt, and emerged into the daylight. She'd better hurry if she was to make the south pier by half past eleven. She looked up at the sky. It was grey, overcast, but it wasn't raining. Not yet anyway. Then she dashed upstairs to ready herself, well as she might, for the meeting with Johnny.

She almost fell over a seaman at the door as she opened it to run out into the street.

'What do you want?' she asked him automatically. 'Lodgin's or a consultation.'

'Lodgings,' he said.

Then Hettie shouted back towards the scullery.

'Lily! Come and see to this man, will you? I've got to go out.'

Before Lily could get there, Hettie was off, rushing for the tram that would take her to the south pier.

At half past eleven Gilbert was just approaching Scotswood Bridge. He found himself singing as he drove slowly along, 'I cannot get to my love, though I would dee, The water of Tyne runs between him and me.' Gilbert's voice hardly matched the emotions of the words; it was positively chirpy, and as he looked out over the sides of the bridge he greeted the river with a tweak of his cap and a smile. He had not a care in the world. Today he was buying his love a ring, a ring to plight their troth on her coming birthday. And what if the 'old faggot' did kick up a fuss! He laughed as he remembered Cathy's phrase for her; 'old faggot' indeed! She couldn't seriously stand in their way. Not now Gilbert had made himself so useful to the firm. He'd worked and worked through the last months, aiming to make himself indispensable. And though he would never have wished his father's crippling illness on him, it did mean that the old man leaned more heavily on him than before. And his father, at least, liked Cathy. He had noticed the way his eyes lit up when she came to the house. He found himself talking to her, as they sat in the garden, telling her all the tales of his youth. Even his mother hadn't heard some of the things James Stoddard told Cathy. The young woman was warm, and open. She didn't judge anybody, and so he had been drawn to unburden himself of some of the thoughts and memories from the past which he had kept hidden from his wife for years. Yes, there was a growing fondness between the girl and the older man. He would not have dared to cross his wife in the matter, but once the engagement was a *fait accompli* he would be a good ally in helping her to accept it. Nothing could go wrong now. He and Cathy were made for one another, and nothing could stand in their way.

Hettie was late as she got off the tram and hurried along to the pier. The wind was strong on the unsheltered promontory, and the air damp with the promise of rain. There was someone standing up by the bridge, further along. It must be Johnny. Her heart lurched, and she slowed a second to get her breath, before hurrying along again. The strain had given her a pain across the chest. She held her hand under her breast to steady herself as she approached. The man turned towards her. Her breath caught in her throat, then he walked on past her. It wasn't Johnny. Hettie turned and frowned as she looked about her. There was nobody else in sight. A drop of rain touched her nose. A panic gripped her and she fished out the note, reading it for the umpteenth time. 'Unless the weather's bad, when I will be at the bandstand in Marine Park.' That was miles away! Her feet longed to take her there, running hard so as not to miss her old lover, but she had no breath in her body and, anyway, he might just as likely turn up here. Just like him to be vague about their meeting place and put her in a quandary. Her breathing eased and she felt the perspiration on her body turn cold and clammy. Her feet suddenly seemed like blocks of ice, and the cold wind made her eyes water. A bonny sight she must look, she thought bitterly. She must walk to keep warm.

Hettie rubbed her arms and crossed to the other side of the pier, looking out over the grey sea to the town. At least the air must be doing her good. They did say that ozone was excellent for the health, so she breathed deeply of the pungent smell of rotting seaweed which lined the rocks on either side of the pier. If only there was some shelter to keep the wind off her. The wind was coming from the southwest. She could maybe scramble down the side of the pier and sit on a rock, and then the pier would shelter her. Fairly blue with cold, Hettie awkwardly picked up her skirt and climbed down the side, backwards, till she was in the lee of the stone wall, and there she huddled, her feet among the seaweed. Was it the wind that brought the tears to her eyes? Her hand reached out towards the weed and drew a long ribbon towards her. Automatically her fingers worked their way along its length, popping the bubbles, something children did, unable to resist the way the tiny swellings burst under pressure from their fingers.

Suddenly, there was a blast from a ship's funnel. Hettie frowned, then realised that of course the ship would be none other than the ferry, coming in from Newcastle. The seaweed still clutched in her hand, she hurried back up the stone wall, and stood watching as it steamed across to the landing stage at the end of the bridge. It reached out sideways from the pier to the landing stage, which stood in the deep water, where the ferry could stop. She stood leaning on the rail on the north side and watched while passengers picked up from every landing stage on the river, from Shields to Newcastle, disembarked and clattered across the little bridge towards her. A tall figure ambled close behind, dapper and handsome, with a parcel in his hand. It was, at last, Johnny Beale.

Gilbert was humming to himself as he left the bank and made his way towards the jewellers' shops of Grainger Street and Northumberland Street. He wouldn't stint on this important gift. Only the best would do. He hummed and hawed over tray after tray which the patient assistants spread before him. They all looked so ordinary, so dull to his critical eye. The assistants retired to make way for the managers who tried their luck with this young man, his money burning a hole in his pocket. At first he thought only a diamond would do, a single solitary stone, its brilliant flash reflecting the fire of Cathy's eyes. They showed him pear-shaped diamonds, emerald-cut, marquise, and round solitaires. They danced and sparkled before him, each vying with the other for his attention, dazzling him with their glory. But their brilliance was a dead brilliance. There was no real life in them. The light that blinded him was merely reflected in their many facets, not intrinsic to the stones. They were cold, mere ostentation, he decided, and he waved them away, and after them the diamond clusters, shaped like flowers and bows, half-hoops, designs of all sorts. Perhaps, the jewellers suggested, a sapphire encased in a diamond surround, or a ruby. Gilbert thought them better. 'The sapphire set in diamonds is very popular,' the manager encouraged. Ah but, Gilbert thought, if it's popular then it's not for my Cathy. She must have something out of the common mould, something special. No, they would not do; and so they too were waved away. Doggedly he searched on. There had to be something better than this. His offering to his love was not to be picked up like some bauble at the fair, ten a penny. It would be a statement of the depth of his love for her, and by it she would know him always.

On the south pier, as the other passengers walked away, shivering against the cold wind, Johnny held out his peace offering to Hettie. She looked at it with some surprise, then took it in her hands, the brown paper crinkling as she held it to her.

'Open it,' he said. 'I know you wanted it.'

Puzzled, Hettie awkwardly removed the wrapping and the wind took it away, whipping it up into the air, light as tinsel, playing with it a while only to discard it among the rotting seaweed on the rocks. Inside she found the clasp she'd been looking at at the market. The gilt had come away on one of the corners to reveal a grey-black metal underneath. It was still on its card, and pencilled in the corner was the price, '1s 11d'.

'Oh Johnny, you shouldn't,' Hettie shook her head. 'I thought it was expensive at the time.'

'I wouldn't stint you, Hettie,' he smiled, knowing Hettie was pleased.

'I thought it was you,' she said. 'Why didn't you stop and speak.'

'I couldn't be sure you were on your own.' Hettie's look was suspicious. 'I didn't want to compromise you now, did I? For all I knew you were married with fourteen kids.'

'I've got no children,' Hettie told him sharply.

There was an awkward pause. The pair could not look at one another but fixed their gaze out to sea, where a single ray of the sun had pushed its way through the thick cloud and lit up a patch of the sea, like a spotlight on a stage.

'What happened to it,' he said at last.

'I lost it.'

His head turned to look at her.

'That was a stroke of luck.'

Hettie snorted, and refused to meet his eyes. It was tougher than he'd thought.

'Don't you like the clasp?' he asked.

Hettie looked down at it and a scalding tear fell onto the gilt. Then she sobbed, one gasping sob.

'It's very nice,' she said. 'It'll brighten up me maroon dress.'

'Good.' Then he took her arm and guided her gently to one of the seats that were placed periodically along the length of the pier.

'You're cold,' he said as her hand brushed against his to fall in her lap. And he reached out, taking both her hands, and held them between his own, rubbing and chafing them into life. Hettie's teeth began to chatter. She could kick herself. At such a moment! But Johnny laughed, and she too smiled. She couldn't help it. He held her hands in front of his mouth, and blew into them, warming them with his breath. 'Better?'

Hettie nodded. 'Thanks.'

Then he gave her back her hands, and put an arm round her to keep her warm. They sat like that in silence for some minutes, both staring out to sea, where a small tug was chugging out between the piers. They heard its engine, and it filled the space between them for a while. When it passed, Hettie asked, in a quiet, apologetic voice, 'Why did you leave me, Johnny?'

His arm tightened round her, and he began his story.

Gilbert was beginning to despair of ever finding what he wanted. His mind was dazed with looking, and the images of all the rings he had seen jostled for attention in his memory, till he decided that the only thing to do was to drop in at the Eldon for a spot of lunch. Then he could return to the search with a clearer mind. He was just turning the corner from Northumberland Street, in the direction of the Eldon Grill, when his eye was caught by Samuel's window. He frowned, and walked closer. There was a tray of emeralds, set amongst the usual diamond clusters it was true, but the gems themselves called him to them. His eyes narrowed as he considered them, and then he turned briskly and walked into the shop.

'A single emerald, all on its own is rather unusual,' said the manager anxiously.

'Exactly,' his customer insisted.

'I might have one or two unset stones,' he volunteered. 'But of course you'd have to, er, pay for a special setting . . . ?'

'Excellent idea!'

The manager nodded, more enthusiastic now, and hurried into the back room, unlocked his safe, and brought a tray of the green gems. Together the two men pored over each individual emerald, discussing its merits and its defects. They were all sorts of shapes and sizes, but the square cut suited them best, and Gilbert, with his keen eye, picked out one in particular. It was a large stone, cut square with facets only on the sides so that it did not sparkle as the diamonds did. Instead it drew you down into it. It invited you, a pool of green water, to dive deep into its depths and lose yourself among the delicate fronds of blue that lurked beneath the surface. It held a mysterious life all of its own, far superior to the flashy diamonds that vied for Gilbert's attention. He smiled quietly to himself. This was Cathy. This was the Cathy that he loved. Not the flashing beauty that had first turned his head at the dance, but the warm Cathy with the unplumbed depths who was slowly emerging into womanhood before his eyes. This was the woman she would become, a woman of compassion and wisdom, vision and understanding, above the common mould. The copper hair would fade, and the flashing eyes would dull, but the inner beauty, which Gilbert saw echoed in this stone, would remain for ever, nurtured by his love.

'This is quite nice,' he said casually. The jeweller's sharp eyes watched Gilbert's poker face. But Gilbert gave nothing away. He was a man of business, used to clinching deals with men harder by far than this one. He hummed and hawed, and put it down to inspect far lesser stones, diverting the jeweller's attention away from the real object of his search. But nothing suited him. And in the end Gilbert agreed he would have to make do with this square-shaped stone which was perhaps a little too large for his taste and contained too many threads of blue running through it. And then there was the price to negotiate. Of course he could always take his custom elsewhere, but no, the jeweller would come to some arrangement with him, and finally, when Gilbert's stomach was rumbling and complaining at the lateness of the hour, a figure was agreed on. Now there was only the design of the setting to be decided, and Gilbert chose the plainest that was offered, one that would not compete with the beauty of the jewel that it served. It would stand alone, like Cathy, transcending the dullness of its surroundings.

Satisfied at last, Gilbert left the shop, the happiest man in England, to celebrate his purchase with poached salmon and a glass of wine at the Eldon Grill.

On the south pier the man behind the fish counter handed Hettie her plate of jellied eel, and demanded to know if she wanted vinegar.

'Yes, please,' she said. And he shook the bottle over the fish for her, before she took it to stand close by Johnny, huddled under the awning and eating whelks. Hettie's nose was red, but her eyes were brighter and her mouth had softened from the hard, set look which it had worn before. She looked young and vulnerable, for all the rings under her eyes and the pallor of her skin, like a schoolgirl out for a treat. Johnny smiled at her encouragingly to eat her food, and Hettie dug in with relish. She'd always liked a good jellied eel.

'You haven't changed,' he said gallantly, trying to catch her eye. It was a lie, and Hettie knew it, but it was a nice lie and it brought a blush to her cheeks all the same. Then he took her plate and fork, returned it to the counter, and walked her back in the direction of the tram.

'Is it not out of your way, Johnny?' she asked, concerned. He shook his head and smiled at her. 'I mean, have you got somewhere to stay like?'

'I've got a room,' he said. 'It isn't much. But then, bein' on me own, I don't need much.'

'In Shields.'

'North Shields,' he said. 'I came off the ferry, if you remember.'

'Oh aye.' She hesitated, then added, 'I've got relations over that side.'

She thought he looked a little alarmed at that, but he explained his distress.

'Things aren't just as they look, Hettie,' he said sadly. 'I know I put on a brave show, but, you see, you have to, if you want business credibility.'

Hettie nodded as though she understood.

'It's all right, Johnny,' she said. 'I won't press you, pet. It's no skin off my nose where you live. Though I hope, for your sake, you'll soon be out of it, if it's as bad as all that.'

Johnny smiled bravely.

'I've got great hopes, Hettie,' he said. 'I've got ideas.

There's a man in Cullercoats lookin' for a partner, fish merchant, like. Well, I've got contacts, ye kna, from workin' on the quay. I could be useful to him.'

'Eeh, that's smashin', Johnny. I am glad for you.'

'Aye. Only trouble is, like, he wants me to put up a bit of, well . . . capital.' Then he sighed, as though this was quite impossible. Hettie said nothing, but kept her eyes fixed on the ground as they walked along.

'Still,' Johnny said, smiling again, 'it's good to know *you're* all right, Hettie.' And he nodded as though the news pleased him greatly. 'I'm glad you got on, runnin' the lodgings. I only wish I could've been there to make things easier for you.' Then he sighed. 'But at least now you know what happened to me.'

There was silence between them as they walked towards the tram. Hettie ran over in her mind the long tale that Johnny had told her on the south pier. She had never met Johnny's wife. She only knew she was a harridan and held the purse strings tight, refusing him the comfort of her bed, and even the warmth of her less intimate affections. But Hettie had never known how unstable she was, or how ruthless. And to think that Hettie bore the blame for what had happened! Yes, she herself was responsible for the woman's mental state, and the knife had turned in her when she'd heard. She accused herself now of her selfishness, her lack of thought for the other woman's feelings. For she did have them in spite of her cold outward behaviour, must have done to have been brought to such an act. There were women like that, physically cold, but kind and loving at heart. Polly Beale must have been like that. And when she had found out about Hettie she had been so anguished as to mutilate her own wrists with a broken bottle, so that she needed seven stitches in each arm to sew her up again, and she lay for days, balanced between life and death while Johnny watched over her. And he had blamed himself, and himself only, sparing Hettie any responsibility for what they'd done, suffering such remorse that Hettie had cried openly before him on the pier, she couldn't help herself. And Polly had made him promise that the affair with Hettie was over at last. Johnny, believing her to be dying, had promised, and when she had finally recovered and been found guilty in the courts for her criminal attempt to take her own life, Johnny had felt bound by his promise. The terrible wounds she had inflicted on herself had made her weak. She never recovered, and the constant care she had needed had used up all Johnny's resources, till now he was reduced to keeping up appearances and living in a dingy room in a North Shields slum.

'You never said what happened to her,' Hettie said at last as they stood waiting at the stop. 'Did she die?'

Johnny sighed, reluctant to tell her, but knowing he must.

'She's in a home . . . Polly had to be put away. She couldn't be trusted, you see, not to try again. It had become an obsession with her. I had no choice, you see, for her own good.'

Hettie nodded, bleakly.

'No,' Johnny sighed, 'she'll outlive me. I'd put me last farthing on that!'

Hettie said nothing. She felt so responsible. Hard though it had been for her, it'd been worse for them. And he bore no grudge against her for what had happened. He'd even bought her her dinner. Suddenly realising, Hettie felt in her bag for her money, dropping her parcel and the strand of seaweed which she still carried with her.

'Here,' she said, holding the money out to him.

Johnny shook his head and pushed her hand away gently.

'No. No, I couldn't,' he said firmly. And then he stooped to pick up her things for her.

'It's been very nice,' Hettie said as the tram approached.

'I must see you again, Hettie,' he urged. 'I must.'

Hettie wavered, but the tram was nearly there. She nodded.

'But you must let me pay for the . . .'

'No, no. All I want is to see your sweet face, Hettie.' And then he kissed her lightly on the cheek and she flushed as the whole tram looked on. She scrambled onto the platform without daring to look back.

The new lodger was ensconced in their spare room when

she got home, and Lily was huffed with Hettie for leaving all the work to her. Hettie was tired and confused. Absent-mindedly she set her things down on the scullery table and went to fill the kettle for some tea.

'What's this?' Lily asked, holding up the strap of seaweed as though she had a fish by its tail.

'What does it look like!' Hettie snapped. She had forgotten she had it with her, and only now became aware that it betrayed where she'd been.

'What's it in aid of?' Lily wanted to know.

Hettie snatched it up and took it out into the yard to hang it over the midden door.

'It'll tell us what the weather's doin',' she announced as she came back in. Everybody knew that it changed when rain was on its way. It plumped out and became slimy to the touch, whereas when it was dry it was wrinkled and brittle. Lily sniffed.

'Buildin' sandcastles, while I'm workin' me fingers to the bone!'

'I wasn't buildin' sandcastles. I went to see . . . wer Joe.'

'Oh? And what did he want?'

'He had something he wanted to discuss with me.'

'Oh well. Don't tell me!' Lily said. '*I* don't want to know!'

And with that the whole thing was allowed to rest, and Hettie drank her tea in peace.

Cathy was out of sorts when she came in from work that night. Gilbert had met her at the shop as usual but he hadn't been able to fetch her home in his car. 'The engine's boiled, again,' he'd said. 'I'll have to look at it.' Not only that, he had told her he was going to be away. 'In Liverpool,' he said, something to do with the business. She had complained, but he had whispered in her ear, 'It'll mean me taking on more of the business, Cathy. And that's good for us, isn't it?' She hadn't been able to deny him that. But he'd seemed far too happy in the arrangement for her liking. In fact he seemed far too happy in general, as though he had something up his sleeve.

'There's somethin' you're not tellin' me,' she had said suspiciously.

And he had only winked and said, 'It's a secret,' leaving her to the work of her own imagination.

'Oh well don't tell me,' she'd answered. '*I* don't want to know.' And then he'd only annoyed her all the more by laughing at her.

She flung herself down now at the table and drank her tea.

'The parlour fire's lit,' her mother said. 'Why don't you and Gilbert go and sit in there?'

'Gilbert's not here,' Cathy answered her. 'He's tinkering with his car.'

'Oh well, then, I think I'll go in.' Lily wearily raised herself from her kitchen chair and went out into the hall.

Cathy, sitting with her back to the open door, felt the cold draught on her, and she turned to shout to her mother, 'Don't close the door, will you?' when she saw a man standing in the hall talking to Lily. He was tall and blond, and somehow, she could see, he'd got her mother eating out of his hand. He was asking if he might 'avail himself', as he put it, of their piano in the parlour, 'when it isn't an inconvenience, of course.'

'You play?' Lily asked, as though it was a miracle as big as seeing Hettie flying past the scullery window on a broomstick! The Captain, for Captain he was, bowed his head humbly and declared that he could play, yes, but singing was his first love, and did Lily know the works of Schubert, or, light of his life, the celebrated Wagner?

Lily turned, and shouted, 'Just fancy! The Captain's a singer!'

'Fancy!' Cathy shouted back.

'Be a good girl, Catherine, and fetch us some tea through to the parlour. You will join us, Captain, I hope.'

The Captain smiled and humbly offered his thanks before opening the door for her and following her into 'The Sanctuary'.

Cathy rose and prepared a tray, doing up the blouse she had carelessly unbuttoned when she'd come in from work. When she took the tray into the room she found her mother and the new lodger deep in cultural conversation. He turned his grey-blue eyes on her.

'I hear that you yourself are quite a songstress, Miss Straker,' he said in a strong Scandinavian accent.

Cathy felt herself blushing, and almost dropped the tray.

'Not bad,' she said quietly, and turned away from him to set the tray on the table. She felt his eyes still on her, even through her back, and she leaned against the table to steady the shake in her legs. Why was she so nervous? Why be afraid? She didn't even know him! Resolutely, she turned, and asked, 'Milk and sugar?' in her best parlour manner.

Something, though she couldn't imagine what, seemed to amuse him, for his eyes twinkled, willing her to share some mysterious joke with him. Bemused, she poured him his tea and handed it to him.

'I was just saying, the Captain must feel free to play the piano whenever he likes,' Lily told her.

Cathy gaped at her mother. Who was this man who had such power that her mother had offered him free use of 'The Sanctuary'?

'Of course,' Lily went on, as Cathy turned back to pour her a cup, 'I don't allow just anyone in here. The other, er, lodgers are rarely invited. But I can see at a glance that you're a gentleman.'

'I am most honoured.' The Captain bowed his head.

'In fact, I was wondering if you'd care to attend one of our little soirées. We have them from time to time. A sort of a musical evening, you understand.'

Lily took the cup Cathy offered. Again Cathy felt his eyes on her, and again she blushed. His manner was perfect, but his eye made her feel naked before him, as though she wanted to pull down her shining hair and cover herself with it. She shivered, and quietly sat herself by the teapot to wait for their second cups. But the Captain, having finished his tea, did not want any more. He rose to go, talking all the time to the mother and ignoring the daughter, who suddenly felt slighted by the negligence. She felt disappointed, somehow, as he went to the door without so much as a glance at her, and then, when he was almost out and she had risen to collect the teacups, he surprised her by calling, 'Good evening, Miss Straker.' Cathy's startled look was met with a smile which told her that she was the only person in the room.

Or so it seemed to Cathy. She couldn't get that smile out of her mind. As she sat in front of her mirror that night, brushing through her hair, she did not see herself reflected there in the glass, but the face of the Captain. She quailed, the brush held still in mid-air, and remembered how his eyes had seemed to undress her. She rose and picked up her wrapper from the end of her bed. The dead note of a foghorn sounded out at sea. The clouds of the morning had gathered and come down, blanketing the river and the sea. The foghorn sounded again, calling out, till at last the answer came, a different note, eerie on the still air. Cathy pulled the wrapper round her, got into bed, and sat huddled, staring into the candle-lit shadows of her room. The two shells sitting on her chest glowed between the rails of her iron bed. She stared at them bleakly and wondered how long it had been since she had listened to their music.

CHAPTER ELEVEN

'You're never goin' out again!' Lily caught her sister-in-law scuttling down into the hall just as she emerged from laying the fire in the parlour.

'Why? There's no law against it, is there?' Hettie said tartly.

'Who's it this time? Joe Robson again, is it?' Hettie pulled on her gloves, obviously not wanting to talk about it, but Lily wouldn't let it go. 'Him again, is it?'

'Yes.' Lily opened her mouth to say something more, but Hettie cut her short. 'Now *if* you don't mind, Lily, I'm late!' And with that she wrenched open the front door and escaped out into the street.

'It's the change. Must be,' Lily said as she carried the ashes through to the scullery. Cathy was standing at the window, staring at the drizzle falling on the midden roof. 'Well, don't say anything, will you?' her mother snapped. 'Standin' there in a dream. You'll be late again!'

Cathy came to and got her things together.

'I thought we'd discuss the do the night,' Lily went on. 'For the Stoddards comin', seein' as Gilbert's away. Where did you say he was?'

'Liverpool.'

'Oh aye. I thought we might as well, seein' as you'll not be out courtin'.'

Cathy sighed.

'If you want.'

'It's for your benefit, Miss,' her mother said, balked at the disinterested tone of her daughter, who took not a scrap of notice. 'Mebbes the Captain'll sit in with us and offer a few suggestions?'

'Why d'ye have to bring *him* into it!' Cathy snapped suddenly.

'By, you've suddenly woken up.' Lily, taken aback by the onslaught, stared at her.

'Sorry,' Cathy sighed, and, like Hettie before her, escaped out of her mother's presence by muttering something about the tram. But Lily caught up with her at the door.

'You've forgotten your bait,' she said, holding it out to her. 'You'd forget your head if it wasn't screwed on.'

Cathy looked at the box without enthusiasm.

'What've I got in me sandwiches?'

'Paste.' Cathy screwed up her face in disgust. 'What did you expect? Caviare? You're not married to Gilbert Stoddard yet, you know!'

Snatching the bait box, Cathy opened the door and flew out into the street. Lily shook her head, muttering, 'Honestly! There's a pair of them! They're both crackers!' Then she smiled as Captain Christiansen came down the stairs, late, for his breakfast.

The tram swayed and trundled on into the town. The windows were steamed and people stood, pressing against her. Cathy, encumbered by the bait box, had difficulty holding onto the strap, and an old man rose to give her his seat. She smiled her thanks and sank down gratefully into the oblivion of her thoughts. 'Paste' again. Was life always to be like this? With paste in the middle of it? Fish paste, meat paste, and nothing to choose between them, each as bland and uninteresting as the other. She wished Gilbert would come home again. It had been a dull Sunday at home on her own, the very first without him for months on end. She needed him now. Sitting cramped on the tram seat, Cathy realised that her hands were cold and clammy, that she had nervous butterflies in her stomach, that she needed her Gilbert there beside her to put the colour back in her life and to reassure her. For Cathy was afraid. What of? There was nothing to be afraid of, was there? Only something was happening. Her every instinct was alert and sending messages to warn her. Run, run, they said, before it's too late. But where could she run? Or to whom? To Gilbert if he was here. Yes, her Gilbert. She imagined herself in his arms, and felt all the warmth and safety of a homecoming after a long absence in foreign lands. Her pulse slowed, and she felt at peace again. If only he would come back soon.

Hettie sat bolt upright, tense against the movement of the tram as she approached Marine Park. This time he was there before her. She could see him from the window as he turned the corner towards the park, and she fought against the desire to rush as she got off and walked in the same direction. The wind played havoc with her umbrella and the leaves were chasing off the trees. But the park looked bonny in spite of the dirty mess of trodden leaves under her feet. He heard her coming after him and turned, all smiles. Then, throwing restraint to the winds, Hettie ran to meet him, and he took her in his arms and kissed her.

'Your nose is cold,' he said.

Hettie laughed.

'Let's go somewhere for a cup of tea,' she suggested. 'My treat!' And then she took his arm to guide him back into the busy streets.

Cathy had gone past her stop. She fretted and fumed as she ran through the drizzle, retracing her steps to the shop. She was late and Miss Hutchinson was annoyed with her. She had to go out, she said. She had an appointment and Cathy had held her up. Cathy apologised, and stifled a yawn.

'What's the matter with you, child?' her employer asked her. 'Too much canoodling with your young man, eh?' But her voice was kind. Gilbert had given her a lift home, and she thoroughly approved of him.

'No,' Cathy snapped. 'He's away in Liverpool. I just didn't sleep last night, that's all.'

Why was it that everybody wanted to know about Gilbert all the time? As though she was tied to him by a bit of string and hadn't any life of her own. Always it was Gilbert Gilbert Gilbert. Well, she wasn't married yet!

While Cathy struggled with ostrich feathers, Hettie laughed and joked with Johnny Beale. While Cathy sulked over paste sandwiches, Hettie dug into a cream slice and a cup of tea. And all the time, on her own at the Thrift Street boarding house, Lily Straker battled on, doing enough work for all three of them and praying to God that when her change of life came it wouldn't make her as flighty as their Hettie. By, but it was hard to make allowances when your back was breakin' from bendin' and possin' and brushing and scrubbing! But she would try. By God she would try not to shout when Hettie eventually deigned to show her face in the house again. Just so long as Cathy had cheered up a bit, because if she carried on, moonin' about the place like she'd done all day Sunday, just because her Gilbert was away, well, Lily wouldn't be able to answer for what she might do! She had enough to cope with with the Stoddard do on her mind.

Hettie was in far better spirits when she arrived back at Thrift Street. She had returned, all sweetness and light, soon after dinner, and insisted Lily take a lie down while she turned out the lodgers' rooms. Lily had looked at her suspiciously.

'By, you've changed your tune since this mornin',' she observed. And Hettie had laughed and said something about a 'woman's prerogative'. Cathy, too, had undergone a mood swing as the day wore on. And as the hour of release from the shop approached, she grew positively chirpy. There was no Gilbert to meet her after work. And though, only that morning, she had been longing to see him, now, after the tedium of the day, she was suddenly glad of the change in routine. She felt free as a bird as she made for the tram and looked forward to her evening. There were plans to discuss for the do. The Captain would be there, and well, as they say, a change was as good as a rest.

The parlour fire glowed and the tea tray was put aside. Lily, revived by her afternoon rest, sparkled with enthusiasm now that Cathy's interest had revived in the forthcoming musical evening. The girl was talking nineteen to the dozen, in high old spirits, with the amiable Captain, who nodded encouragingly from time to time. He was a good-tempered man, the watchful type, always with an amused expression to his eye, and yet he inspired trust and confidence with his gentle manner. You couldn't help talking to him, and yet, after an hour or so, when he took his leave, you suddenly realised that you knew nothing about him, because you had done all the talking.

'And so, Miss Straker. You are engaged,' he said, as Cathy paused for breath. She had been talking about Hans Anderson, and the remark he had just made seemed to come from nowhere.

'Not exactly,' she corrected him.

'No. But she soon will be,' Lily butted in.

Cathy frowned. She felt the Captain's interest flag as he heard this news, and he turned to her mother.

'And this "do",' he laughed as he said the word, 'is to cement the relationship, I gather.' Lily nodded. 'Oh well, we must all do our best, eh?'

He turned, his eyes laughing, back to Cathy, who looked away in apparent confusion.

'Ah, love is a wonderful thing,' he went on. 'I know the Latin races think they are the only ones to know about love, but it is not so. Why, even the Germans, the stolid old Germans know more than they do.'

Lily raised her eyebrows unsure of whether love was a suitable subject for the parlour, but Cathy listened quietly, intently, as he continued.

'Take Wagner now. My favourite. He knew a thing or two. Ah yes.' And his eyes regained that lost look they had when he talked of the sea. 'Love and death. That is the Wagnerian theme.'

'Doesn't sound very nice to me!' Lily objected.

'Oh, but it is that way, you know, Mrs Straker. And you see it is really quite respectable, being opera!' The eyes were laughing again, and Lily was reassured. 'You see love and death are very close. After all, they both lift one out of life, do they not?' Lily laughed. 'Oh yes, because dying and loving are both a kind of an ecstasy, a union with the divine. Then we become Gods, out of the humdrum lives of ordinary people. But think of the sadness, the *angst,* after such an experience, such ecstasy, to be forced to return to these dull lives of ours. No. Far better to die in the moment of union, I think, than suffer such torture.' He leaned back in his chair, shaking his head, and Lily sniffed. 'I will sing to you, Mrs Straker, from the Meistersingers at your do and then you will believe me!' he laughed. Lily smiled, appeased, although such talk of ecstasy had made her somewhat uneasy. It hardly seemed decent, and especially in front of Cathy, who'd got that far-away look in her eye again.

'Tut!' Lily said. 'Look at our Cathy. Moonin' after Gilbert again, no doubt.'

But Cathy frowned.

'Why does everyone think that *he's* at the root of everything!' she objected. 'He doesn't own me, you know.' And then she turned to the Captain. 'Will you play for me, Captain Chistiansen? I'd like your advice on me song.' And together they went to the piano where Cathy sought out her music.

Lily, apparently listening to the rendering with rapt attention, was actually making mental lists for the catering, turning over this and that, wondering whether to give them tongue or jellied chicken, or whether sandwiches were a good idea at all. For her, ecstasy consisted of a well-laid table before the guests got at it, the silver sparkling, the china shining, the linen perfect. Everything just so. It was a bit of ground she held in common with Edith Stoddard, had she but known it. For, like her, Lily believed in a place for everything and everything in its place. The only real difference between them was that Lily believed her place was still in Westoe and Edith didn't. So, as Lily sat, her mind wandering through the linen closets and china cupboards, her soul did not soar on the wings of Cathy's song, borne up by the accompaniment of Captain Christiansen on the piano. For her, the binding of those two beings through their music did not exist, because she just didn't have the eyes to see or the ears to hear.

Cathy was in another world. The song was simple enough, 'Barbara Allen', but the Captain played the piece with great sensitivity. Even as he played the opening bars, Cathy felt the freshness of his approach, and she began to sing as though she had never sung 'Barbara Allen' in her life before. The tragic story became real to her. It drew her emotions into her voice, and the Captain, sensing the drama within her, listened to her as she listened to him, tuned in to each other to create a performance which, Cathy knew, she could never have achieved on her own. Upstairs in his room Mr Miller, playing patience, looked up from his cards transfixed by the expression of the music. In the scullery Hettie in an agony of indecision over Johnny Beale, suspended her thoughts and allowed her emotions to ebb and flow with the music which infiltrated through the kitchen door. At last the song came to an end. The rejected lover had died, and Barbara Allen now declared, 'I think I'm . . .' the musicians paused, feeling with each other the required length of the dramatic pause, then coming in again with 'dying'. The last note faded into the air, and the pianist rose to kiss the singer's hand.

Lily looked up and said, 'I prefer "Nellie Dean" meself.'

At last Cathy knew. She admitted it to herself, and having admitted it, it no longer frightened her so much. Restlessly she tossed in her bed, and then got up to look through the window. It was raining hard now. The rain fell deafeningly on the roof above her head. It sounded like a million dried peas clattering down on her. It battered against her mind, insistently, making thought impossible. Her skin was cold, but she didn't reach for her wrapper because inside she was burning. Standing impotently by the darkened window, her body was taut and geared up as if for a race. Her pulse speeded, and her eyes darted over the dark panes, though they saw nothing. Every slight gesture betrayed the wealth of energy which raged inside her, unappeased. It was late. Her candle was out, she had to be up in the morning to get the breakfasts and go to work. She was tired, weary after the sleepless night she had already endured, and still she couldn't settle or find any peace. A pain sprang up inside her as she thought of Gilbert. Dear, dear Gilbert. How she loved him. She couldn't bear even to think of life without him now, and yet, it was true, he irritated her; he was so responsible, so careful of her, so kind and gentle, so faultless that as she stood in the sleeping house, wide awake, she wanted to scream.

What did she want? What? Escape. That was it, escape

from the ordinary dull existence she knew here, and the gorgeous, luxurious, happy, predictable existence she would know with Gilbert once they were married. There would be no adventure, no excitement. And she needed that so much. She was capable of feeling that ecstasy the Captain talked of, she knew it, her whole being was reaching out for it now, and knowing it, how could she settle for any less? And yet, how could she hurt Gilbert, dear kind Gilbert? She could see his face and the hurt on it now in her imagination, and she dismissed the picture from her mind as far too painful even to think of. It would be like hurting herself, if she hurt Gilbert. It was as if he were her own familiar flesh and blood, while the Captain was alien, strange, and dangerous. He took risks on the high seas. Gilbert sat in offices and made deals. He spoke of death and love, and Gilbert asked her if she felt hungry. She was hungry, but not for roast beef, or even caviare. She was hungry for love, for danger; she wanted to know that divine union the Captain had spoken of. Suddenly, she smiled, remembering the little mermaid. What had the grandmother said? She searched out the battered storybook she used to read as a child, and it fell open, unbidden, at the page: 'It is true, that if thou couldst so win the affections of a human being as to become dearer to him than either mother or father; if he loved thee with all his heart, and promised, whilst the priest joined his hands with thine, to be always faithful to thee; then his soul would flow into thine, and thou wouldst become partaker of human bliss.'

The little mermaid had rather risked death than miss her chance for such bliss. No wonder she had loved the story as a child, no wonder she had made Hettie read it to her again and again. She would abandon herself to the wide sea of her feelings, leave hold of the safe anchorage of dear, earthy Gilbert, and find that bliss if it killed her!

Lily lay wide awake, haunted by visions of unset jellies and sad cakes, upset cups and *faux pas*. Hettie, too, lay calm and cold, her decision reached, only wondering when she would be able to put it into action. And Cathy, believing herself to be the only woman in the house, if not in the world, unable to sleep for her rioting thoughts and feelings reached at last for the shells on her chest of drawers. She could hear Hettie's voice warning her, 'You can't take them to bed with you. You might turn over on them and hurt yourself.' But she did it all the same, and holding the shells to her ears, she was lulled at last into a sleep as deep as the seabed.

It was days before Lily became aware that anything at all was going on. Cathy was pining for Gilbert, and very right and proper even if it was a little inconvenient; and Hettie was going through the change. 'It's just as well one of us has got their heads screwed on,' she said as she beat the life out of the dough. But when she caught that little lad poking his head round the yard door, she got suspicious. She'd been emptying the chamber in the midden, and she was just coming out when she saw him, and he didn't half beat a hasty retreat when he saw Lily. She'd rushed out of the yard into the lane, the chamber still in her hand, and shouted after him.

'Hoy you! What d'ye want?'

Caught by the coalman coming the other way and blocking his exit down the lane, the lad had no choice but to come back and face Lily.

'Well?' she insisted.

The lad was shamefaced; she'd obviously caught him in the act of something shady. He stared mournfully at the chamber-pot.

'Well?' she said again.

'I've come for Miss Straker, Miss.'

Lily frowned, immediately thinking he meant Cathy.

'Why? What d'ye want with her?'

'I've got a message, Missus.'

'What sort of message?'

But then Hettie rushed out. She'd seen the episode from an upstairs window, when she'd been turning a bed, and she'd known at once what would happen. And she had raced down into the yard to prevent him giving her away. As soon as Lily saw Hettie's face, she realised her mistake.

'Oh. I see. It was Hettie you were after, was it?' The lad

nodded miserably. 'Go on then. Give her your message, there's a good lad.'

The poor boy looked from one to the other. He could see Hettie was in a proper state, sending him all sorts of signals not to, but the other one looked so stern that he knew at once which was the boss, and knowing which side his bread was buttered, he blurted out, 'He says to meet you tomorrow at three o'clock at the usual place.' And then he turned on his heel and ran.

Hettie was beside herself, though it could have been worse. At least the lad hadn't given Johnny's name away. And it would have been so daft if he had, when the thing was nearly over. If only Lily would keep her nose out of things.

Lily stood square before the yard door, the chamber-pot held across her front like a barricade.

'You're not gettin' back in,' she said, 'till you tell me what this is all about, Hettie!'

'I'm not likely to give all my secrets away in the back street!' Hettie protested.

It was a reasonable enough objection, and Lily let her pass, following close on her heels till they were in the kitchen, where, at last, she put down the chamber.

'Come on Hettie Straker,' she insisted. 'I'm waitin'.'

'Well you can wait till Kingdom come, for all I care, Lily. I'm not tellin'.'

'I see.' Lily put on her all-knowing air. 'I see. It's a guessin' game, is it?' Hettie groaned with exasperation. 'It's that Joe Robson again, isn't it?'

'If you like.'

'It's not if I like!'

'Have it your own way, Lily. I don't care.'

'So it *is* him!'

No answer.

'Humph!'

Still no answer. Hettie stood unmoving as a lamppost, resisting her all the way.

'What's goin' on with him, then? Eh? Eeh, our Hettie, secret assignations, what a carry-on. I mean, not everybody's as slow to criticise as me, you know; and it does look suspicious, Hettie. Why, if I didn't know he was ten years younger than you I'd think you were carryin' on together!'

'Don't be so bloody daft!' Hettie spoke with such vehemence that Lily actually thought for a moment that her shot in the dark had reached its mark. But then another idea came into her mind; one far more likely, in her view.

'Wait a minute. Wait a minute,' she said slowly. 'Didn't you tell me he was savin' up to buy a boat?'

Hettie stared horrified at the narrowing eyes of her sister-in-law.

'Aye you did. I remember now. He was workin' on the ferries so's he could save to go half shares. That was it. The miserable little blighter! He's gone and asked you for the money, hasn't he? Eh? Isn't that it, Hettie?'

Hettie's voice was cold in reply. 'Believe what you like, Lily. You will anyway, knowing you. But you shouldn't think bad of Joe. He's a good lad.'

'Good lad, my aunt fanny. You're not goin' to give him it, are ye?'

'What I do or don't do are nowt to do with you, Lily. I'm a grown woman. And I can do what I like. So there!'

The two women glared at one another across the scullery. Cathy, bursting in on them, was surprised by a blast louder than a ship's hooter.

'And what are *you* doin' home at this hour, Madam?' her mother shouted.

'The shop's closed. Miss Hutchinson's been taken bad. They've got her at the Ingham.'

Under cover of Cathy's entrance Hettie made good her retreat and was heard running upstairs to her room, where she locked the door and refused to speak to a soul.

The next day, just after two o'clock, when Hettie was washing up after their dinners, Lily slipped up to her sister-in-law's room. The door was locked, and Hettie, pulling down her sleeves and drying her hands, listened as Lily tugged hard at her door. 'That'll teach her not to interfere in other folks' business,' she thought. Calmly, she took off her pinny and folded it before laying it over the back of her chair, and then went out into the hall to pick up her coat from the stand, and went out. Lily, still pushing and pulling at the door, heard the bang and flew downstairs to find Hettie had gone. Lily's face was pale and tight. She could get one of the boarders to break down the door if need be, but it'd only mean explanations, and this was a family affair. Cathy had gone off to the Ingham to ask after poor Miss Hutchinson. So she was out of the road, at least, but she did wish there was a man in the house she could rely on. For a brief moment she considered the Captain, but immediately dismissed the idea from her mind. She knew he was a gentleman, but it would embarrass him to be brought in on something like this.

Suddenly Lily rushed up to her own room. She always kept it locked through the day. She took the key from her pocket, opened the door, and walked straight up to her dressing table. She knew she still had it somewhere. Yes, in the little drawer at the side, there it was, the old key. Cautious as ever, Lily had had the lock on her door changed when she took over that room, believing that old boarders might have had copies made and creep in on her in the night. But she had kept the key 'just in case', though she could never imagine 'in case' what. Quickly, she put the old key in her pocket, locked her own door, and made her way back down to Hettie's room. The old key slid into the lock and fitted perfectly. The door swung open and Lily went inside.

Lily knew very well where Hettie kept her Post Office book. She'd shown her the hiding place, again 'just in case', only this time Lily knew what 'just in case' meant. If Hettie was taken suddenly, like poor Miss Hutchinson, it'd save them having to search for it when they were smitten with grief. Lily went straight to the little writing desk, opened it up, pulled out a tiny drawer at the back, then pressed on a piece of wood at the side. A small panel swung open to reveal an empty space behind. Lily was panic-stricken. It was all Hettie had! All *they* had, come to that, apart from some jewellery she still hadn't sold herself. Hettie was squandering away their only security. She was that soft, was Hettie! Simple-minded even, since that business that had left her so ill and broken. She'd fall for anything! Racing against time, Lily got herself ready. She'd have to confront him, the blighter! That was all! By God, she knew some of Hettie's relations were a shady lot but this took the biscuit! How could a man, worthy of the name, stoop so low!

Leaving the house, the rooms in a mess, the parlour fire with its ashes and the kitchen stove unmended, Lily ran out of the house. There was no time to lose. At least Hettie would have to go to the Post Office first to withdraw the money before she could hand it over. A terrible thought gripped her. Supposing, just supposing she'd got it out already and had the money in her bag when she left the house? Lily might be too late. Gasping for breath, she reached the tram stop, got on the first that came along and found her way down to Comical Corner. Standing on the steps she could see the *Ha'penny Dodger* coming in. She looked about her. No sign of Hettie. What if it was his day off and they'd arranged to meet elsewhere? In an agony of suspense, she waited, paid her fare and got on. She had never met Joe, never in all her life. How was she going to find him out? A man in some sort of uniform was on the deck, and she approached him anxiously.

'Excuse me, have you a Joe Robson on board?' she asked. 'I believe he's a stoker.'

'Aye, Missus. Who wants him?'

'I do.'

'We need him down below, Missus. We're about to sail.'

'I don't care. It's a matter of life and death. I must see him most urgently.'

The man sighed.

'And who shall I say wants him?'

'The name's Straker. Lily Straker,' she said.

Shaking his head, the man went down below, muttering 'Women! Women!' under his breath.

Joe bounded up, soon as he heard. He was cleaning his brow with a rag and looked very worried.

'Lily Straker?' he asked, as the woman turned and stared at him.

'I am. And you're Joe Robson.'

'Well, I'm glad we've got that settled, any road,' he laughed.

'And we'll have none of your lip!' Lily snapped. 'Where's Hettie?'

Joe frowned.

'What do you mean, where's Hettie? I thought you lived with her.'

'Stop bandyin' words! Where is she? Or more to the point, what have you done with it?'

'Eeh, Missus,' Joe said, shaking his head, 'you've got me proper bamboozled. And I've got to get back down, or else I'll be losin' me job.'

'She's been here already, has she?'

Joe shook his head.

'I've not seen her for . . . oh, couple of weeks or so now.'

'Liar!' Lily spat at him. Passengers were gathering, drawn by the scene, and a seaman stood by ready to step in if need be.

'Here, here!' Joe objected.

'She's gone an' given you the money, hasn't she? Couldn't wait for your precious boat could you, but you had to take advantage of a poor simple-minded soul, and take her life savin's off her!'

Joe stood open-mouthed, unable to believe his ears.

'Me?' he said at last.

'You cannot deny it, can you?'

'I've not had a penny piece from our Hettie. And I wouldn't either. I don't know what you're on about Mrs Straker, I don't really.'

Lily hesitated. Then ploughed on again.

'Well, her savin' book's gone. And that's a fact! And if it's not you's got it, then who has?'

Joe gasped. He thought for a second, then looked steadily at Lily.

'I've not seen sight nor sign of it, Mrs Straker. But I bet I know who has.' He started taking off his boiler suit, and shouted to the seaman watching, 'Take over for's Jock. I've got to go. It's family!'

Taking Lily by the elbow he guided her off the ferry and

planted her down on the landing stage. Then he turned to her and said firmly, 'Now, leave this to me!'

Lily was left gaping after him as Joe ran off down the quay. All that righteous anger had left her feeling helpless and foolish, standing there. People were looking at her, and she realised she'd come out without a hat. Her hand lifted involuntarily to her head as if to cover the oversight, then sticking her chin in the air, she walked briskly up the steps and up the hill to catch the tram home.

When Hettie got back, she found Lily sitting, arms crossed in the rocking chair by the fire, waiting for her. She had a face like a gable end, blank and forbidding. Well, it was too late. She could say what she liked. It was her money and she could do what she wanted with it. Let her think the worst or the best of her as she pleased. Hettie went to fill the kettle and make some tea, feeling that a great weight had been taken off her mind. As she plonked the kettle on the stove, Lily spoke at last.

'Well, I hope you're pleased with yourself!' she said sternly.

'Would you like a cup of tea, Lily?'

'Don't prevaricate.'

But Hettie wouldn't be drawn. Even when she went up to her room and found the door unlocked and the desk open, she just avoided Lily's eye after locking up her door again and coming down.

It was seven o'clock and Lily was just beginning to wonder where Cathy had got herself to, when Joe came banging on the door. Hettie opened to him and showed him into the scullery. She was surprised to see him. She knew he hadn't felt exactly welcome since Lily'd turned him down as a boarder. And she thought something must have happened to one of her relations on the north side.

Joe, cap in hand, looked awkward and out of place. Lily rose stiffly and asked him to seat himself. From the way he looked at her, Hettie knew that whatever it was Joe had come about, it had something to do with Lily and her.

'Well?' Lily asked sharply.

'I found out,' Joe said. He didn't want to go on. It

distressed him, and he glanced up at Hettie, a pained expression on his face.

'What's the marra, Joe?' Hettie asked.

'I warned you, didn't I?' he said quietly. Hettie went cold. She sat awkwardly in a kitchen chair, facing him and Lily. 'I said to watch yersel'.' He shook his head sadly.

Lily frowned impatiently.

'What's all this?' she butted in.

'Shut up, Mrs Straker,' Joe said firmly. Lily was taken aback, but she did as she was bid.

'Lily came to me,' he said gently to Hettie. 'On the ferry this mornin'. She thought that I . . . well anyway, she knew your book had gone. Your savin's book. She thought I . . .'

Hettie gasped and stared at her sister-in-law. Lily looked away. Whatever she had done, she had done for the best.

'I know you've been seeing him, Hettie,' Joe went on. 'I made enquiries, after Lily came down.'

Hettie looked pained at this news.

'Who's been spyin' on wer?' she said tremulously.

'Nobody, hinny. But it gets aboot. Somebody sees you and goes tappy lappy down the pub and sees somebody else and tells them, like. You know how word gets about.'

Hettie sniffed. Joe still hesitated. He felt it wasn't his business, and yet he cared for Hettie, and if some lousey blighter'd sweet-talked her out of her savings, well he didn't know what he'd do to them.

'Hettie, did you?' he asked at last. 'Did you give him your savin's?'

Hettie nodded silently. Lily looked at them both, bursting to ask who this 'him' could be, but held her peace, fearing Joe's tongue and knowing how she'd wronged him in front of all his mates on the boat. Joe shook his head.

'Why?' he asked.

Hettie sniffed, and took out her hanky. Her voice was thin and quiet.

'I felt guilty,' she said. Joe frowned.

'What about, for heaven's sake?'

'Her. What I did to her.'

'Who?'

'His wife. He told me.'

'What did he tell you?'

'Who is this man you keep on about?' Lily demanded at last.

Hettie just sat, without opening her mouth, so Joe was obliged to say, 'Johnny. Johnny Beale.'

Lily gasped. It was her turn to sit, speechless for once. She had never dreamt of this. It was far worse than her wildest imaginings.

'Come on, Hettie. Tell us what he said.' And so Hettie told them the story about Johnny's wife, her attempted suicide, her long illness. How he'd had to give up the sea to look after her, and he'd spent all his money on caring for her, only for her to be committed, leaving him destitute, desperately trying to start up again in the one opportunity that presented itself to him.

'I had to, don't you see? I had to give him the money, with *that* on me conscience! It was all my fault!'

There was silence in the kitchen. Finally Lily gathered herself together and spoke.

'I never heard such a lot of cock and bull in all my born days!'

Joe glanced at her, a warning look.

'Well I mean!' she gasped.

Hettie looked at her, shocked. 'You don't believe him, do you?'

Joe rose and put his hand on Lily's arm to keep her quiet. Hettie looked from Lily to him.

'Neither do you!' Now she was shouting, and sobs rose into her gullet.

'Take it easy, Hettie. Take it easy,' he soothed her. 'We'll get it all sorted out.'

'What do you mean "get it sorted out"? There's nothing *to* sort out!'

'What was the name of the bloke in Cullercoats? The fish merchant that was supposed to have offered him a partnership? Did he tell you, Hettie?'

She gulped.

'Why do none of you believe him? Why? Why?' She was

banging her fist on the table and crying loudly now. Joe rose and put his hands on her shoulders, soothing her as well as he could. 'Why Joe?' she screamed. Joe took a deep breath. She had to be told sooner or later, now that Lily had brought it all to a head. He had no choice.

'Because, Hettie,' he said slowly, 'I know for a fact that his wife never tried to commit suicide at all. She divorced him seven year since, and she lives in Whitley Bay.'

Hettie stopped crying. Her hands went limp on the table. She leaned back in her chair.

'It's not true. It's not true. It's not true,' she moaned, over and over again. Lily bit her lip and turned away. She couldn't watch. She found herself close to tears and trying to keep control.

'What was the name of the bloke in Cullercoats?'

'Herbie Cochrane.' Hettie spoke so quietly they could hardly hear her.

'Herbie Cochrane, eh? All right, Hettie. Don't you worry. I'll find him, sort it out.' Joe couldn't understand it. She'd cried before, why not now? She had gone so limp and cold, staring blankly at the wall ahead of her. Lily nodded to him to leave her to it, and the man, feeling helpless in the face of Hettie's misery, picked up his cap and left the house without saying a word.

Cathy came in full of herself. Miss Hutchinson had been 'opened up' but had left a message that she and Mabel were to take the keys and run the shop for her in her absence. She didn't know what it was that ailed her employer, but she'd come out of the operation all right and was sleeping.

'I'm very glad,' Lily said, almost to herself. Cathy looked at her mother. She was very pale and drawn, and her eyes were red as though she'd been crying. She was fetching a plate for Cathy's tea. Her movements were slow and deliberate, like those of a sleepwalker or a very old woman.

'Mam?' Cathy said.

'What?' The dead reply brought her daughter running to her side.

'What's the matter?'

'Nothing.' Lily's mouth closed tight. It was the signal that always told Cathy to probe no further. Cathy sighed and went to sit at the table, feeling the weight of terrible happenings in the room but unable to fathom what they might be.

'Where's Hettie?' she asked at last.

'Upstairs.'

'Is she ill?'

'Headache. That's all.'

'I'll go up, shall I?'

'No! You'll stay where you are and eat your tea!' Her mother's response was so sharp it sent Cathy immediately back to her seat. She didn't dare to question any further.

Upstairs, lying on her bed, Hettie lay still and cold. She had never felt so cold. Not even then, when he had first brought her so much grief. If it had been anybody but Joe she wouldn't have believed it. And yet Johnny hadn't *asked* her for her money. She'd had to force it on him. It was true. He hadn't wanted to take it from her. But she had insisted. Maybe Joe'd got it all wrong. Maybe it was as Johnny'd said. Johnny loved her, always had. He said so, and no other man had said as much to her! Hettie's body shook with a violent, sudden sobbing. When it had subsided, she reached her hand under her pillow and drew out a note. It was Johnny's first note to her when he had come back, as if from the dead. She opened it, and through her tear-filled eyes tried to read what it said. 'Dearest Hettie.' The words brought renewed sobbing. 'Please come, dearest. My heart yearns for our meeting.' 'There will never be another woman for me.' She *had* to believe him. Or what was there left? She might just as well be dead! If it had been anybody else but Joe! But if *Joe* said it, then it must be true. And if it was true about his wife, being alive and divorcing him, then the rest of the tale had to be a pack of lies as well. If it had been anybody else but Joe. She trusted Joe. He was honest as the day is long, she'd known him since he was a bairn. Why had Lily gone and stirred it up? Why had she gone to him with her accusations and her anger? Why had she not just left well alone! Better not to know than this! The note dropped from Hettie's hand. Her eyes closed as if to shut out the world. The candle flickered then went out, gutted in its holder. She lay unmoving in the darkness, seeing neither light nor dark, feeling neither cold nor pain. Next morning, when she stirred, it was as a dead woman that she rose from her bed to greet the world.

CHAPTER TWELVE

Gilbert had come back from Liverpool. He had had a good trip and returned with new ideas for the company's future. They should expand, he was sure of it, open up new offices in Liverpool, and perhaps even in London. He had sounded out his father at once, and they had spent the afternoon in the Shields office, going through the books. Mr Stoddard had not said yes, but he hadn't said no either. 'I'll chew it over, lad,' he'd muttered thoughtfully. 'Leave it with me.' And bolstered up with optimism, Gilbert had left the old man 'chewing' while he nipped round to the hat shop to pick up Cathy.

It had been a sunny day, after all the rain, and the atmosphere in the shop had been close. What with that and the extra responsibility, Mabel was rather tetchy. She had picked a row with Ethel, and Ethel, in tears, had been sent home early, so that now there was only Mabel and Cathy left in the shop.

'I'll see to the locking up and that, Mabel,' Cathy said. 'You get off now.'

Relieved, Mabel handed over the keys of the shop and got her things together. She watched as Cathy totted up the day's figures and worked out the work rota for the following day.

'You're good at it, aren't you?' she observed.

'Not really.' Cathy's face was serious, concentrated on the job in hand. 'I'm just play-actin', Mabel. Playin' at bein' a business woman, a proprietor.' Mabel laughed. 'No honest. That's all it is. I'm enjoyin' it really.'

'I'm glad somebody is,' Mabel sighed, and picked up her handbag. 'Tarrah then, Cathy. See you the morra!'

'Aha.' Cathy didn't look up as Mabel let herself out of the front door. The bell clanged after her. She was alone in the shop. Her pencil stopped in mid-air. Surprised by the silence, Cathy looked up. She had never been alone in the place before. It was strange, eerie. The rooms upstairs, Miss Hutchinson's rooms, were empty, dark. She put down the books and went to check the back door. It was locked but not bolted so she slid the bolts across. The felts sat piled up neatly. The drawers of feathers were arranged according to colour and size. The flowers brimmed from half-finished hats. Their presence crowded in on her, more real, more pressing somehow than they were during the day, when it was light and there were other people around.

'Miss Hutchinson must feel like this,' she thought, 'when we've all gone. Alone. Completely alone.' Cathy shivered. How dreadful to be so alone. To have nobody to fall back on, nobody to talk to, when your work was finished and you went up to your rooms at night; nobody to take away the fear of the pain in your side, or drive the bogey men from your dreams. Fear hung in the air like a presentiment. It whispered in the gaslight. It crept closer to Cathy's heart. At last, the fever that had kept her watchful, night after night, chilled. She felt herself to be on the brink of an abyss, darkness falling away at her feet, and nobody to catch her as she fell.

The bell clanged on the shop door. Cathy let out an involuntary little scream.

'Cathy?'

It was Gilbert. Thank God! It was Gilbert! He met her as she rushed through the baize curtain into the shop, straight into his arms.

'Oh Gilbert! Never let me go, will you? Please! Please promise!'

'I promise.' Gilbert quelled his surprise and whispered soothingly in her ear, 'It's all right. It's all right, love. I'll always be there, just so long as you want me to be.'

'Oh I do!' Cathy moaned, her arms tight around him. 'I do. Promise me, Gilbert, whatever I do, please promise me, you'll still love me.'

'I'll always love you, Cathy. I always have, haven't I?'

'Yes.'

'And I always will.'

'You won't let them send you away from me, will you?'

'Cathy, oh Cathy.' He stroked her hair gently, and rocked her in his arms like a child wakened from a nightmare. 'The only person who could ever send me away from you is you yourself.'

Cathy shivered. His hand moved down to warm her back, soothing her till she felt comforted at last.

'I'll never do that, Gilbert. Never.' She looked up at him, and her eyes burned with suppressed tears. 'You don't know how much I need you.'

Gilbert looked down at her pale, intense face. She looked so young, so like a child. He kissed her on the forehead tenderly, but she pulled him to her; finding his lips, she searched out his answering fire. His body moulded around hers. Her arms rose to his shoulders, and he felt the movement of her breasts lifting against him, the roundness of her belly, trapped behind whalebone and cloth, as his hands sought down the curve of her waist, and he moaned at the torture of it. Laying his hands now firmly on her waist he held her still at last. Their lips parted slowly, and she drew away feeling the pain of their separation like a chameleon shedding its own skin.

They stood staring at one another in the silence. She smiled faintly as he took a very deep breath.

'It's lucky for you I'm a gent,' he said wryly. But Cathy didn't laugh. She held him still with her gaze. Her hand rose to touch him, and quickly he took the hand in his and kissed it gently. Her eyes pleaded with him, but she knew he would not take her, not yet, no matter how he burned. Her eyes dropped away from him at last, and she turned to put out the lamps.

Outside in the lane a fire was blazing. The children had been gathering flotsam and jetsam, worm-riddled wood, ancient sofas, anything that would burn, for weeks, and now they danced round it as the guy slithered down into the flames to a roar of delight from the crowd. Gilbert laughed.

'I'd forgotten it was Guy Fawkes,' he said.

'So had I, for the minute.' They stood watching for a while, then suddenly Gilbert took her by the waist.

'If we hurry we'll be in time to catch the Corporation display in Marine Park!'

Cathy grinned at him and took his hand as they ran for the car and drove off down the road.

A fire-engine passed them, going the opposite way. A man in uniform, leaning out at the side of the vehicle, was clanging at the bell.

'Oh, they're not goin' to put it out, are they?' Cathy said in dismay.

'Well, it is a bit close to the houses, Cathy,' Gilbert said. 'Bonfires are all very well, but they've got to be kept under control.'

'Oh why do you always have to be so . . . so practical,' Cathy snapped.

'Because,' Gilbert laughed good humouredly, 'I'd hate to see poor Miss Hutchinson's livelihood goin' up in smoke, hinny!'

Cathy, smiling at his put-on accent, took hold of his arm and leaned her head against him as they winged along to the park and the bright lights of the Corporation display.

Sitting in the scullery at Number 15 Thrift Street, Lily heard a rocket going up and looked out of the window. She could just see the end of its flight, the cluster of stars, before it fell to earth again, exhausted.

'We should've gone, Hettie,' she said. But she might as well have spoken to an empty room. Hettie sat, her eyes closed, in her usual chair, hard up against the stove.

'You'll scorch yourself, Hettie, sittin' close as that,' Lily warned her.

Hettie's eyelids fluttered and opened.

'It's me circulation, Lily. I cannot seem to get warmed.'

A pink flare lit the sky. Lily turned back to watch as it faded into the blackness. She sighed.

'Ah well,' she said. 'I suppose it's like Christmas really. For the bairns.'

The do was fixed for 10 November, a week before Cathy's birthday, and Gilbert saw to it that the printed invitations reached his parents' hands personally. There could be no excuses about delays in the post to gloss over any snub given by the Stoddards to the Strakers. He set it down on the supper table like a man throwing down a gauntlet.

His mother picked it up gingerly.

'And what's this when it's at home?'

'Same as it is when it's not, Mother.'

Edith Stoddard took the card out of its envelope, and read it open-mouthed.

'What's it say, Edith?' her husband asked.

'It's from them!' she gasped.

'Who's "them"!'

'They want us to go there!'

'It's a musical evening, Dad, that's all. You're invited to a musical evening.'

'But at Thrift Street, Gilbert!'

'Maybe we should go, Edith. Broaden our outlook, eh?' James Stoddard laughed, but was subdued by a look from his wife.

'And what am I supposed to wear, Gilbert? I haven't got any old blankets to wrap round me, or will it do if I throw a shawl over my head?'

Gilbert gritted his teeth.

'If you do, you'll look out of place, Mother. They always dress for the occasion at the Strakers.'

Mrs Stoddard sniffed and laid the card back in the centre of the table, where she eyed it as though it was an unexploded bomb.

'I see,' she said at last. Gilbert raised his eyebrows and looked sidelong at his father. But James merely pushed out his lips as he did when deep in thought, and coughed to fill the silence.

'It's Cathy's birthday on the seventeenth,' Gilbert said.

'Oh?' James Stoddard was glad of a change of subject, as his wife stared bleakly at the peas. 'And what are you going to give her, lad? Somethin' special?'

'Oh yes, Dad.' Gilbert's reply was meaningful, and his mother pricked up her ears. 'Something very special indeed.'

The silence fell again, deeper this time than before. James

Stoddard had quite a fit of coughing, and the peas were thoroughly inspected by his wife. Gilbert wiped his mouth and laid his napkin beside his plate.

'Well, I think I'll nip out for a breath of air,' he said, 'it's a little stuffy in here.'

James Stoddard suppressed a smile and waited till his son was out of the room before he spoke.

'I think we'd better go, dear, hadn't we?'

Edith shot him a look. It needed no words for him to understand. 'Never!' her eyes blazed at him.

Gilbert had never seriously expected his mother would lower herself to attend the Strakers' 'soirée'. To him, the invitation had never been more than formal notice of intent. It was as though he had served his parents with an affidavit, a sworn statement of his commitment to marry Cathy. And so he was not disappointed when his mother wrote out her reply: 'We are sorry to inform you that Mr and Mrs Stoddard cannot attend the above-named function.' And then his father had added, as a postscript, 'Due to the indisposition of Mrs Stoddard.' Gilbert laughed as his father handed the envelope over to him for delivery. Mr Stoddard's eyes twinkled wickedly.

'She's a faggot sometimes,' he said, 'but she's not a bad old stick. Tell your intended not to mind her. After all, nobody else will.'

Gilbert was grateful to his father. He might not be the power in the Stoddard household, but he held sway in the family business at least, and that was far more important. Together, father and son ran through the books and the plans for the umpteenth time.

'Aye,' James Stoddard said at last, 'it's the next logical step, son. Either you expand or you contract. You cannot stop still, that's for sure. And, I daresay, with an extra family to support, the business could do with opening up a few new channels. Aye . . .' He sighed thoughtfully. In handing over the business to his son, James would be handing it over to a man of vision and sense, a rare combination indeed! And one which he could respect deeply. 'Aye . . . that's what we'll do, Gilbert. We'll expand. Like you say.' Gilbert felt his father's approbation and warmed with pride. But suddenly Mr Stoddard grinned, 'And where do you and Cathy fancy livin', after you're married, eh?' His eyes twinkled. 'London be far enough away for you, will it?' Gilbert laughed.

'There's one thing for sure, Dad. We'll not be livin' in Westoe!'

Lily sold a ring to pay for the buffet, for all Cathy's warning that they might not come, and when Gilbert finally delivered their reply, Lily was deeply upset. Cathy seemed to take it more to heart than he had expected, too. She blamed him for her mother's distress, using it as an excuse to be angry and cold towards him. He was a little hurt, but he supposed that women made more of these things than men, and he shrugged it off as well as he could. Lily complained of Cathy's behaviour. 'Blowing hot and cold' she called it, as she and Hettie prepared the food for the supper. 'One minute she's all lovey-dovey towards you and the next she's bitin' your head off! I mean I only mentioned how nice it would be if we could all move back into the old house in the village, and she went for me! "Mam, for all I know we'll be livin' in Timbuctoo," she says, "not in Westoe, mebbe not even in Shields!" Eeh, well Hettie, it knocked me for six, that did.'

Cathy felt guilty afterwards. She knew very well how her mother dreamed of returning to Westoe. She needn't have broken it to her quite so suddenly. And she was doing her best for her daughter, Cathy knew. It was all for her, this cooking, and shopping, polishing and thinking. In fact, Cathy thought, she wished they wouldn't do so much. It made her feel uneasy somehow, guilty. She felt she didn't deserve all the care and attention everyone was giving her, and certainly she didn't deserve Gilbert!

'I wish you weren't so nice,' she said one day, as he drove her up to the village for her tea. 'Maybe if you and your father weren't so nice, your mother wouldn't be so nasty.'

She sounded annoyed, and it wasn't like her to make a remark like that. For all her faults, Gilbert's mother wasn't nasty, more misguided was how he liked to think of her.

'What do you want?' he asked her. 'Do you want me to be like a docker and come home on a Friday neet, with a skinful, and me belt off ready to thrash you? That what you want?'

'No. No,' Cathy replied tearfully. 'Oh I don't know what I want.'

Gilbert sighed, exasperated, and Cathy blew her nose. They were almost at the top of the hill, ready to turn off into the village.

'Come on, pet,' he urged her gently, 'she'll see you've been cryin'. You don't want that, do you?' And Cathy shook her head, bracing herself for the hot tea and the cold reception.

She need not have worried. Mrs Stoddard had retired to bed with a headache.

'Indisposed again,' Mr Stoddard winked, and turned the tea tray for Cathy to pour the tea. He could see by her eyes that she'd been weeping, and you could cut the atmosphere between Cathy and Gilbert, with a knife.

'Had a lovers' tiff, you two, have you?' he asked good humouredly.

'No. No!' They both said at once.

Mr Stoddard frowned. Gilbert looked unhappy, at a loss. Cathy seemed strung up. Summing up the situation, he decided that whatever the problem was, it was coming from her. After they had finished their tea, he rose, patting his stomach thankfully, and said, 'Cathy, come with me for a minute. I've something to show you.' And he led her out of the drawing room and into his favourite haunt, the conservatory, the place he most liked to be, away from his wife.

Cathy had never been invited into this haven before. She was surprised at the warmth as the old man opened the door for her and followed her inside. He shut the door carefully behind him and took off his jacket, with apologies to 'ladies present', as he put it. Cathy decided to follow suit and remove her own. It was a large conservatory, with a wide variety of plants inside, all tended by Mr Stoddard himself. He took great pride in his collection, and let no one else near the place except on special invitation. Cathy felt herself honoured to have been asked, and her heart warmed towards Gilbert's father more than ever. She looked up at one huge plant which spread its soup-plate leaves up and over the glass roof. The great green hands had holes in them.

'What's that?' she asked.

'It's called Monstera Deliciosa. It grows in the rain forests of South America,' he told her. 'You can eat the fruit. Look, there's one up there.'

Cathy peered up through the searching aerial roots and saw a pale green fruit hanging there.

'I've never had one myself,' he said, 'but they say it tastes like an avocado.'

Cathy looked blank.

'No, I've not eaten many of those myself,' he added kindly.

Cathy shook her head in amazement. There was a palm tree, a fig, a peach grew along the wall of the house, an aspidistra lurked in a shady corner, ivies trailed, mosses crept, violets hid. It was a jungle of lush green, overwhelmingly beautiful. Cathy looked at Mr Stoddard and smiled.

'It's lovely,' she said quietly. 'I could sit in here for hours.'

'I often do,' he said laughing. 'But look, this is what I wanted to show you.' And he led the way past a feathery Jacaranda to where some flowers clung to the bark of an old tree stump, erected in the centre of the glasshouse. It was covered in blooms. She gasped.

'Why! They're orchids, surely!' She turned to him amazed. 'I'm sure they are. I've seen them in a shop window in Fowler Street. The woman said they were orchids!'

Mr Stoddard nodded.

'I'm rather proud of those,' he said. 'I want you to wear them at your wedding.'

It was as though he'd stabbed her with a knife. With a suddenness that surprised Cathy herself, the tears gushed out and she found herself sobbing helplessly. Alarmed and distressed at her reaction, James Stoddard's first instinct was to take the girl in his arms and comfort her, stop the crying at all costs. But he knew he must not. It was better out than in, as they say, and he must wait for the tumult to subside before doing anything at all about it. So he sat in a cane chair in the shade of some hanging ferns and waited patiently.

'I'm sorry,' Cathy gulped. 'I don't know what's come over me.'

Mr Stoddard sighed and took out his pipe, knocking it out against a stone.

'Nerves,' he said. 'Women suffer from their nerves. Or at least my wife's always tellin' me they do.' He winked, and Cathy was surprised to find herself laughing. 'It'll be the strain, the engagement and that.' He filled his pipe, then looked up at her as she fiddled restlessly with a loose pebble at her foot. 'That what it is, is it?'

'I suppose so,' she shrugged.

Mr Stoddard thought for a bit, then lit up. Sitting there, gently puffing on his pipe, he exuded a relaxed, gentle atmosphere.

'Come on and perch yourself,' he said, patting the cane stool at his feet. Cathy trailed over and sat; he was being nice to her. Everybody was so nice. And they all made her feel worse than ever.

'Come on. It's not so bad,' he said. 'She'll come round.'

Cathy looked at him, and realised that he meant Mrs Stoddard.

'She'll make the best of it.'

'Best of a bad job, you mean,' Cathy retorted bitterly.

Mr Stoddard frowned. It wasn't what he'd meant at all.

'Eeh, you're far too sensitive, lass.' He shook his head. 'You know what I think, don't you?' He waited till Cathy looked at him again before going on. Then he pointed the end of his pipe towards her and said, 'It's my belief that you don't think near enough of yourself.' Then he put his pipe back in his mouth as if that was all there was to say on the matter.

'Far too much, you mean,' Cathy answered.

'Why? What's wrong with you, like?'

There was a long silence. He knew she was struggling, and he waited, as he'd waited while she cried, till at last she was able to spit it out.

'I'm not worthy of Gilbert.'

Mr Stoddard roared with laughter! Cathy, rather annoyed at this unexpected reaction, bit her lip as though she wished she'd never let the words out at all. But when he stopped laughing, the old man adopted a stern tone.

'I never heard such a load of codswallop in all me born days!' he said angrily. 'Why? For the Lord's sake, why?'

Cathy was silent. He was pushing her too far. She couldn't tell him. She just couldn't. 'Come on!' he insisted. 'I'm waitin'. It'd better be good an' all!'

'I don't love him!' she cried.

The silence then was terrible. She felt her words hanging in the humid atmosphere like ghosts. The plants themselves had seemed to shudder as she said the words, but perhaps, she thought, it was just the loud vibrations of her voice after all.

'Is that true?' he said at last.

Cathy sighed.

'No. Not exactly. I can't explain.'

'Try.'

'I do love him, of course I do. I couldn't bear it if . . .' She trailed off miserably.

'You mean, you're not, well, attracted to him?' This was delicate ground indeed! At least it was between an unofficial father-in-law and his son's intended! Cathy could not look at him. She shook her head.

'No. That's not true either. I am . . .' she whispered, remembering the night in the shop, when for two pins . . . 'I am!' she said suddenly with such determination that the old man raised his eyebrows.

'Then I don't see what the problem is!'

'I just think,' she dragged the words up from her boot-laces, slowly and painfully, 'I just think that Gilbert loves me, well, more than I love him. That's all.'

Mr Stoddard sighed. He puffed on his pipe slowly and considered carefully before he spoke.

'In any relationship, there's always one who loves, and one who allows themselves to be loved. It's never equal. Take me and Mrs Stoddard now. It's like that between her and me. I love her, always have. Now she . . . well, she's not a passionate woman, if you understand me, but she allows me to love her. It was the same between your Mam and Dad.' Cathy looked up at him surprised. 'Oh yes. I remember. Henry loved your mother. Mad about her he was, but she, well, she . . . put up with it, if you see what I mean.'

Cathy looked away. She could not tell him that she was different from his wife or her mother. It was not that she lacked passion, it was just that her passion seemed to have a will of its own, and Gilbert was not the only object of it!

'It's usually that way on,' Mr Stoddard continued. 'The man loving, the woman being loved, I mean. Best way too. When it's the other way, well, men being what they are . . . Still, there's no need to go into that. No lassie, you should think yourself lucky that it *is* this way on. Accept Gilbert's love, and stop feeling so guilty about it for God's sake.'

Cathy looked up at the old man and smiled.

'You're smashin',' she said.

James Stoddard went quite pink, and Cathy laughed.

'You see what power you have over me?' he joked. 'Aye lass, far better you have the whip hand than the man!'

Suddenly Cathy's face fell and she looked away. The old man's eyes narrowed. 'There isn't another man, is there, lass?'

'No! Of course not!'

The answer came so quick, so sharp on the heels of his question, that Gilbert's father doubted its truth. He looked at her quietly and sadly.

'Because if that's it, then you'd better get him clean out of your system, and quick, or . . .' He sighed.

'I love Gilbert. I do. I always will. I don't want to lose him.'

'Then snap him up, lass. Snap him up.'

'It's all in me mind,' Cathy whispered. 'The whole thing. All in me mind.'

Mr Stoddard snorted. Cathy glanced at him embarrassed.

'Then it's up to you, Cathy. Gilbert's a man. Flesh and blood. Show him another man and he'll fight him. But he can't fight shadows, lass.'

'Get it out of me system.'

'Aye. Either that or give yourself a damn good kick up the trousers!'

Cathy blushed and laughed, suddenly feeling about ten years old and well and truly put in her place.

'Shadows won't keep you warm in bed!'

The old man and the young lass laughed and they were still laughing as Gilbert, uninvited, came into the conservatory, looking for Cathy.

'Gilbert! I might've known you'd come and spoil me fun!' his father teased him and winked at Cathy. Cathy smiled and rose to kiss him on the cheek.

'Thanks, Dad,' she said fondly.

'Go on, Gilbert. Find the best orchid you can and pin it on her blouse. I'd like to see that. I would!'

Gilbert took Cathy by the hand and Mr Stoddard watched as the pair wandered to the display of flowers which he had tended so carefully. Smiling and happy together, they chose a pink orchid, the trumpet shading down to cream, and the stamens yellow and bright, reaching out down the shelf of the flower. The green leaves of the palm, circled over them like a bower, and the soft verdant light diffused in the lush foliage cast a haze around them. The old man's eyes softened. They were part of the harmony and the peace of the place, at one with each other in a world of their own. Suddenly Cathy turned towards him and made him jump, as though a picture had unexpectedly come to life and spoken to him.

'You will come to me Mam's evening, won't you, Mr Stoddard?' Gilbert's father smiled sadly and shook his head.

'Ah, lass, I might want to, but you see I don't hold the whip hand!'

The 'whip hand' of the Stoddard marriage was, at that moment, staring vacantly out of the marital bedroom window. Her hopes fluttered helplessly in the air, like the last leaves of the sycamore at the bottom of the garden, falling to the ground at last, good for nothing but to be trodden into the earth. Her face was blank. She had no hope now. The girl had even won over her own husband. Against her wishes, James had shown he was on her side, leaving his wife without an ally in her fight. Catherine Straker would have her son. It was done. And whether or not she and James went to this ridiculous soirée at her mother's house was immaterial. Either way, the girl won. No. Nothing would stop this marriage now; she had far better bow to necessity and accept the situation as it was. She might not like it, but she was going to have to lump it all the same, and with as good a grace as she could muster Edith sighed and turned away from the window.

'My God,' she whispered bleakly to the walls of the room, 'what on earth am I going to say to May Cochrane's mother?'

CHAPTER THIRTEEN

It was 10 November. Cathy awoke feeling grey as the sky beyond her own dormer window. There was to be no work today. Miss Hutchinson had returned home, weak and pale after her discharge from the Ingham Infirmary. She needed rest and lots of it. Noise of any kind disturbed her, setting her nerves to screaming pitch, and they had to go about their business in the shop below the invalid's rooms in whispers, walking softly on the balls of their feet. Trade had slackened in the proprietor's absence too, so that Miss Hutchinson felt a day or two's closure would do little harm to her business but would do her shattered nerves a great deal of good. At least it meant that Cathy would be able to help her mother for the evening's entertainment, and even leave time to spare to 'titivate', as Hettie called it, doing and undoing her hair and generally beautifying herself for this very special evening.

'You look tired,' Lily said as they prepared the lodgers' breakfasts in the scullery. 'You want to have a lie down this afternoon. Take away them shadows under your eyes.'

Cathy said nothing, but took the tray into the dining room and served the boarders on the oilcloth that covered the trestle table for their mealtimes. Mr Miller smiled at her, as he always did. A young lad, on a short stay, snatched his plate and gobbled as though he hadn't eaten for days. 'Livin' on his breakfasts,' Cathy thought. Mr Miller touched the lad's arm and told him, with a look, to slow down. Captain Christiansen sat with his back towards her. Cathy leaned towards the table to set down his plate and her arm brushed the side of his face.

'I'm sorry,' she said, and her face betrayed her confusion. His grey eyes smiled up at her, and one side of his mouth tilted upwards as if to say it was all right, no need to apologise. Cathy looked away again and didn't hear as Mr Miller asked her to fetch the salt. Mr Miller looked askance at the Captain. He, in turn, shrugged his shoulders.

'I think Miss Straker has other things on her mind,' he said in his lilting Scandinavian accent.

But Cathy did not want to lie down, cooped up with her thoughts in her own room. What could it possibly do for her, lying on her bed, tossing and turning as she had done most of the night before?

'I'd like a bit of air,' she told her disapproving mother. 'Blow away a few cobwebs.'

Lily sighed and inspected her daughter's washed-out complexion.

'Eeh well,' she said reluctantly, 'it'll mebbes bring a bit of colour to your cheeks. What do you think, Hettie?'

Hettie shrugged. They could please themselves. She wasn't going to get dragged into a long walk. If there was any time to spare, she'd prefer to crouch over the stove with her books.

'Well, I can't go with you,' Lily snapped. 'I've got the pies to make. See if Mr Miller'll go with you, or the Captain. Aye, ask him.'

Cathy flushed angrily.

'Mam, for heaven's sake, I'm nearly eighteen. I want to be on me own.'

Lily frowned.

'If I didn't think better of you, hinny, I'd think you were up to no good.'

'Don't be daft, Mam. Why would I? I'm engaged . . . well nearly. You've not half got a suspicious mind these days.'

Lily pursed her lips and gave Hettie a sidelong glance.

'Aye well. That's as maybe. It's just not healthy young lasses walkin' on their own. Ask the Captain . . .'

'Mam! He'll think . . . well . . .'

Lily raised an eyebrow. She hadn't thought of that. In one way she looked on her daughter as a little girl, free to ask a respectable man to escort her, and in another she looked on her as a woman up to no good. Either she was a little girl or she was a woman. She couldn't be both.

'Well, don't be long then!' she snapped at last. And Cathy

rushed upstairs to change into her walking boots, snatching up a shawl to wrap around her before escaping up the hill for the tram, away from the quayside and the claustrophobic little streets, to head for the seashore and the windswept dunes.

The air was good. It forced itself into her lungs; it blew hard against her so that her body leaned against it as she walked, supporting her with the force of its blowing. The tide was out. Miles upon miles of open beach spread out before her, banked by the great dunes, which rose sharply to her left and hid the world from her. There was hardly a soul in sight; only a man and his dog, two tiny figures further up the beach, their shapes reflected in the wet sand as he threw sticks far out into the water so that the dog could swim after them. Cathy pulled her shawl over her head and stopped to watch them. The dog's bark came to her on the wind, distantly, and the man's voice, exhorting the creature on, rose echoing into the swirling air. Then the sticks were gone. The man held his empty hands in the air for the dog to see and the dog jumped round him, as if to see if any more were hidden behind his master's back. But there were none, and slowly the man walked on, away from Cathy, the dog jumping at his heels.

Gradually, Cathy's steps were drawn down towards the wet sand. It shone at her feet, mirror-like. She watched the bright drops jump from the toes of her boots as the dog had jumped at the feet of the man. And tired of that game, she looked up again to where gulls flew in from the choppy waves, battered on the currents of the wind, towards the land. One flew higher than the rest, a black-headed gull. It drifted on the upward draught of the squall, and plunged down, down, down towards the sea. Skilfully it sought a wave, billowing out, and it perched lightly as the wave swelled to its crest and seemed to stand there, at the height of its power, for an endless time before crashing downwards, its energy spent, expelled in a tide of bubbles foaming at her feet. The gull screamed, whipping away, to ride on the crest of another wave. Again Cathy watched the play of the gull, sensing the power in the swell, feeling the moment when it would break and burst from its peak, and then the bird would rise from its perch, fly along the sharp crest and then away as the wave was lost again.

The foam hissed at her feet and was gone in the undertow, dragged down back into the sea. The movement satisfied her. What did it matter that the wave was spent, that it turned to foam and was lost for ever, drawn back into the relentless waters? It had had its moment, there, before it broke, before its own energy, which had created it, turned against it to destroy it. Cathy turned her eyes up the beach towards the pools of dead water lying stagnant in the rocks. She felt her own energies returning. Her feelings rose in her like a surge, straining against her flesh, and she knew she could never deny this part of her. She had no power over this. It would swell up in her out of the tides of her being sooner or later. And if it, too, was to break and crash, throwing her onto the shore, dissolved into foam, then that was to be. At least she would have had that moment, she would, as dear Mr Stoddard had told her, 'get it out of her system'. If she married Gilbert now, if she forgot her nature for a while and Gilbert grew to trust her like misguided sailors trust a calm sea, she knew that this part of her would break through again, sooner or later. He would be hurt, and she could never forgive herself for that. Far better get it out of her system now, even though it meant risking everything she loved. Like the little mermaid, she would risk failing to gain the love of her man. After all, Cathy thought, the worst that could happen would be to die, dissolved into foam, and be dragged back into the sea. She stared at the bubbles surging round her feet. Their hissing drowned in the grate of pebbles grinding against one another as the tide heaved them, resisting, back into the waters.

Hettie went about her work for the evening's entertainment automatically. Lily had never dared to mention the business of Johnny Beale again after that terrible day when Joe had been and pricked the bubble of her illusions. She had wanted to, often enough, to offer comfort, counsel, anything. But Hettie did not encourage any such overtures. If she had cried, Lily would have understood it better. But she behaved so coldly, as though all feeling had died in her and left her stranded, alive but not alive, for the rest of her days. Lily found it hard to bear. She felt some guilt for what had happened, and resented her sister-in-law for refusing to allow her to expiate that guilt by being nice to her. Her presence was a constant reminder of Lily's thoughtless interference, and slowly but surely the resentment grew, gnawing at her, till it was like a live thing between the two women. But today, at least, Lily could put all that out of her mind. There was Cathy to think of; her future, her happiness. Deep down, Lily still had hopes of Gilbert's parents turning up. It would be such a feather in her cap if they did. Yet, even if they didn't, tonight would be a kind of celebration, a victory over Edith Stoddard and anyone else who dared to keep Lily Russell as was, removed from her rightful status in society. Cathy and Hettie were upstairs already, getting dressed for the evening. Lily removed her pinny and called in on the parlour to cast a proud eye over her work before going to her own room to prepare herself for the celebration.

A spray of camellias lay on Cathy's dressing table. Gilbert had called with them while she was out. A present from his father, from the conservatory. She touched them lightly. The delicate creamy petals felt cool and soft. Perfect blooms, without perfume, but with a calm virginal beauty that set off her own glorious vibrant colouring. She wore the cream silk of Gilbert's birthday party. Her neck and shoulders rose warm above the fragile lace. Her eyes were bright, the pupils large, dilated, and her cheeks were flushed. There was an air of expectation about her, and her emotions undulated gently as she gazed into her glass.

Hettie stared glassy-eyed, seeing and not seeing. Her face haunted her out of her mirror, like the face of someone she had once known, an old photograph, brown with age, of a woman long since dead. She reached for the artificial rose and pinned it to her blouse. Its colour glared against the blank whiteness of the linen cloth. She drew in a deep breath, then calmly rose and went downstairs to mend the parlour fire.

A glass of sherry warmed them as they waited for the guests to arrive. Mr Miller was the first, as ever, dressed in his best bib and tucker and on his best behaviour too. He sat, like a gentleman, in the least comfortable chair and tried hard not to wriggle as he engaged in polite conversation with Hettie. Cathy was in a restless mood, twisting this way and that, getting up and sitting down.

'You'll wear out the carpet, Cathy!' her mother objected.

'Ants in her pants!' the old sailor whispered in Hettie's ear and raised the ghost of smile on her lips.

Miss Liddell was the next to arrive, and, soon after her, young Mabel from the shop and a nice couple Lily had met at the Methodists, 'very respectable'. Then the Captain joined them and the party began to break up into little groups, easing the flow of the conversation, so that laughter rose into the air and the atmosphere warmed. Lily glowed. The evening had a good feel to it. She watched her daughter as she flitted from group to group, making their guests feel at their ease, smiling, laughing, rather excited, Lily thought, but none the worse for that. She was beautiful, her little girl. She was proud of her. Even Hettie seemed to be enjoying herself, though they'd have to watch she didn't drink too much of that sherry. She wasn't used to it and her voice was already getting a little shrill. Perhaps they should have stuck to tea, Lily thought, but still, you had to have a little 'something' at a supper party! She glanced at her watch. Gilbert was late. A frown chased across her brow then disappeared again. It might be a good sign. Mrs Stoddard might even now be getting into the cab and on her way there. Uninvited, Mr Miller had sat himself at the piano and began to play. The conversation subsided, and the entertainment was launched.

Mr Miller soon gave way to Hettie, who wanted her part in the affair to be over soon so that she could enjoy herself. Cathy attached herself to the old sailor and teased him into dancing with her as Hettie played her beloved Strauss waltzes. The room whirled as she danced. Cathy laughed with the pleasure of it, elated with the heady experience of flirting with danger. She felt the Captain's eyes on her, and knew he liked what he saw. He would have had to be blind not to have been drawn to the swirling skirts of the woman in the centre of the room, her hair blazing under the lights. From the corner of her eye, Cathy saw him rise from his seat and walk idly over to the piano where he whispered in Hettie's ear. And then the music stopped, and as Mr Miller retreated, panting, to his seat, the same uncomfortable one he had had before, Captain Christiansen took Cathy by the waist and led her in the movements of a much slower piece. Gently, carefully, they swayed and turned to the music, feeling in each other's bodies the same sensitivity that they had felt when practising the song, each knowing by instinct what the other was about to do, their movements harmonising easily as though dancing was the most natural thing in the world. And still his eyes laughed at her. She fixed her own steadily on his, challenging him, surprising him. And then the laughter went. He gazed back steadily, so steadily, that she now faltered and had to look away. His hand moved in the small of her back, he draw her closer in towards him as he swirled her round and round, again and again, his breath falling lightly on her cheek. Cathy's head swung round to face him. And she knew that he could see through the softness of her look, to know all that she was feeling for him. His eyes considered her. His head bowed imperceptibly in recognition and then turned as the door opened and Gilbert came into the room.

He was alone. He had driven up under cover of the music so that no one had heard him, and his entrance made the couple in the centre of the room start, as though discovered in some compromising situation. Cathy ran towards him, too enthusiastically, and as he kissed her on the cheek, Gilbert's eyes were on the tall blond sailor who even now was retreating to the opposite corner of the room. Lily bustled forward to ply Gilbert with sherry and draw him to the fire.

'Your mother's no better?' she asked acidly.

Gilbert shook his head and smiled apologetically.

'You're looking lovely, Cathy,' he said, staring up at her. 'The dancing's brought a bit of colour to your cheeks.'

'She was lookin' that peaky this mornin', Gilbert,' Lily put in. 'I thought she should have a lie down to tell you the truth, but no, she wouldn't have it. Went for a walk on the beach, if you please!'

Gilbert looked surprised.

'So that's where you were! Hettie never said, or I might have come out after you.'

'I felt like bein' on me own, anyway,' Cathy said softly.

A deep rolling note sounded on the piano. Gilbert seated Cathy on a chair and stood beside her, his hand resting on her shoulder. Captain Christiansen rose to announce his contribution to the evening. The highlight, as Lily whispered in Gilbert's ear, and then sat again, trusting no one but himself to accompany his excellent voice. Gilbert watched the Captain steadily. He had caught sight of him before on previous visits to Thrift Street, but had taken little notice of him. He was young, in his late twenties perhaps, blond, grey-eyed, and he had a strong frame. His ease in company had the feel of arrogance about it. He was a man who knew that he was attractive to women. And yet he seemed a gentleman, and he was obviously well educated. His playing was good, and when he sang, the strong tones of his voice soared with the extravagant music, bursting on their eardrums relentlessly, like the sea on the pier walls. He gave himself, heart and soul, to the music, and Cathy was transported by it. Uneasily, Gilbert looked down at her. She wasn't even aware of his presence. He took his hand from her shoulder and she didn't indicate by any movement that she'd so much as noticed. There was an energy between the singer and Cathy, an energy that bound them both, and which excluded him. When the singing had finished everyone clapped loudly, but Cathy most of all, and as the Captain rose to acknowledge their applause the shadow that had come between Gilbert and Cathy took flesh and blood and bowed before him.

Gilbert hardly listened as they talked. The Captain was explaining the essence of Nietzsche and of Wagner's thought to Lily, Hettie and Cathy.

'It's a kind of *liebestod*, Mrs Straker,' he explained.

'What's that?' Cathy asked.

'Sounds like a kind of fish to me,' Hettie shrilled, and Lily removed the glass of sherry from her hand.

'It's German, Miss Straker. It means, well . . . it translates so badly, but it means love linked with death. Like a deathwish, I suppose.'

'Ooh, it sounds better in German.' Hettie shivered.

'Wagner wrote all his operas about it. Love and death reaching a climax together . . .'

Lily coughed him into silence and spoke quietly but sternly.

'I won't have talk like that in the parlour, Captain Christiansen.'

The Captain bowed his blond head and apologised meekly, but Hettie sprang to his defence, animated by the sherry.

'It's very respectable, Lily,' she said. 'Christ himself was baptised in the love of the Holy Spirit by bein' totally immersed in water. He said you have to die to be born again.'

'What *are* you talkin' about, Hettie?'

Hettie opened her mouth to retort, but the Captain forestalled her by excusing himself. He wanted to go out into the yard and smoke his cigar. As he left them, Lily marvelled at his courtesy.

'You see that? He's a gentleman, isn't he Gilbert? Many a man would've just lit up here and now with never a thought.'

Cathy was like a cat on hot bricks during his absence. She kept turning edgily to the door in the hope of seeing him. Gilbert could not help but feel irritated.

'I need him to accompany me in my song,' Cathy explained when he questioned her, and Mr Miller whispered again to Hettie, 'Ants in her pants.' Each time he said it he got a bigger laugh, but Hettie was far gone by that time and had inveigled the old sailor into fetching her another glass.

Gilbert could hardly bear to watch them as Cathy sang her song. He wondered how no one else could see it. Cathy's body, her voice, everything about her poured out her love. And it hurt him to the quick. When the song finished and Gilbert rose to leave, Cathy's eyes, black with fear, pleaded with him to stay.

'I'll come tomorrow,' he told her, and making his excuses he left the party to finish in its own good time. The master of ships found himself all at sea. Cathy had taken on the colours of another man, and Gilbert felt the greyness of his own desolation.

The evening had been a huge success, and Lily went about her work the next day singing like a songbird. True, Gilbert's parents hadn't deigned to come, but so what? Let them sit on their horses, high as they were; her daughter was going to marry Gilbert all the same. And they'd just have to put that in their pipes and smoke it! Leftover food was stacked up in the larder. They'd be eating it for breakfast, dinner and tea for days ahead! Unless Hettie had any more midnight feasts, that is. Lily had heard noises in the night and had gone down to investigate. She'd caught Hettie at it, raiding the larder like a bairn. Eeh, but she was turning into a gannet. Lily shook her head at the memory. Still, if it cheered her up, who's complaining? And if she did end up the size of a house who'd be bothered anyway? 'Aye, let her,' Lily thought. She gave a box of food to Gilbert for his and Cathy's lunch. And she waved to them as they set off for a trip in the car. Aye, he was a canny lad.

Canny lad or not, Gilbert was not in the best of moods, and Cathy was quiet as they drove along.

'Got any preference where we go?' he asked her.

Cathy shook her head.

'Right then. I rather fancy the cliff tops.'

'But it'll be windy!'

'We could jump off together, eh? Lovers leap? Love and death? That suit you, would it?' His voice was hard and bitter. Cathy's heart jumped with fear. She hardly dared breathe, let alone speak. Finally Gilbert relented. His voice softened, sensing her distress. 'I'd die *for* you, Cathy. But I don't see any sense in dying with you.' He stopped the car. They were on the sea road, heading out to Marsden Bay.

Gilbert stared ahead blankly, and Cathy shivered. The silence between them was unbearable.

'I never heard such rubbish as that man talked!'

'What about *me*, Gilbert?' Cathy said. Gilbert turned to look at her. 'Don't you think I might want to feel that I could die for somebody?' Her voice was small, pleading. His hand reached out to touch her cheek and she leaned her face towards it lovingly. 'I do love you, Gilbert. You know that, don't you?'

Gilbert nodded. But there were tears in his eyes.

'I'll get over it, in time,' she sobbed, and he took her in his arms, comforting her. 'I can't help it. I know it's daft. I know that in the end it's you I want, Gilbert. But . . . but it's just something I've got to get out of me system. That's all.'

Gilbert thought for a moment.

'That's all right then,' he said.

Cathy's eyes lit up.

'You'll wait for me?' she asked. He nodded. 'You'll not let them keep you away from me!' Her hands gripped his now, desperately, hanging on to him.

'I told you before, Cathy. Nothing and nobody has the power to keep me from you but you yourself.'

And Cathy wept, salt bitter tears, as he held her, till gradually she calmed.

'Men aren't the only ones to have . . . feelings,' she said quietly. She couldn't look him in the face but fixed her eyes, instead, on his hands as she spoke. 'Do you understand?' Gilbert nodded. 'Mam wouldn't. That's one thing for sure. But it's true all the same. Some women are capable of feelings just as strong as men have. You should pity us, Gilbert, not despise us.'

'I don't despise you, Cathy.' His eyes searched for memories through her copper hair, over the fine lines of her face and the graceful arch of her neck. 'I love you,' he whispered.

At last Cathy looked up into his eyes.

'Thank God for that,' she said. 'I've just got to get it out of me system, before . . .'

Gilbert nodded. They lapsed into silence once again. Down below them, far below, at the base of the cliffs on which they stood the sea pounded relentlessly, cutting holes into the rock, making caves and shelves, overhanging places, where children played. They could hear it roaring now, the tide in, and their heads turned as a rock fell from the side of the cliff with a sonorous crash, smashing on the stones below.

'I'll wait for you, Cathy,' Gilbert said quietly, 'just so long as you want me to.' Their lips met in a long and gentle kiss, then Gilbert turned the car round and drove her home.

Cathy's birthday came and went. She was eighteen years old. There was a handsome spray of roses from Gilbert, and nothing else. Hettie and Lily exchanged glances, and up in Westoe Mr and Mrs Stoddard waited for the announcement. Nothing happened. Gilbert seemed down and Cathy hadn't been near the house in days. Edith Stoddard clutched at a straw of hope, and James sat in his conservatory, brooding. His orchids were coming to their best, soon they'd be past their prime. What could be keeping them from making the announcement? He itched to ask, but knew from Gilbert's face that he mustn't. It was Cathy. That much he knew. What had possessed the girl? What devil drove her to relinquish her hand when she had the aces sitting there ready to call? Gilbert knew why. He was hurt, deeply hurt. His face bore the marks of it, and his manner had changed. He worked long hours in the office on the quay and seemed to have no thought for anything but the future of the firm. Puffing his pipe at a vagrant greenfly that had forlorn hopes of surviving the winter in his glasshouse, James Stoddard sighed and held his peace.

Lily was not so forebearing, however.

'Well?' she demanded. 'Where is it?'

'What?' Cathy frowned.

'The ring. You *were* gettin' engaged, weren't you?'

Cathy sighed.

'We still are, Mam. It's not off or anythin'. It's just . . . well, it's just his Mam and Dad.' Lily gave her a sharp look. 'With them not comin' to the evenin' and that . . . well,

Gilbert and me just don't want to feel they're against us. That's all.' Lily snorted impatiently. 'We just want to give them, and us, a bit more time. Is that so terrible?'

'Time's just what you've not got, hinny!' her mother shouted. 'Don't you realise, ye great soft fool, you're playin' into her hands? Eh? You'll lose him. You will! And don't come cryin' to me when you do, that's all!'

Beside herself, Lily banged out of the parlour. She could strike the child, strangle her more like. But she couldn't leave it at that. Just when Cathy had breathed relief at her escape, her mother came back in.

'You want to just marry him, Cathy. Now! Never mind them. Elope if needs be. But for God's sake do it! Please! I beg you, pet. Please!'

Cathy turned miserably away, and her mother, feeling her hopes sliding from her grasp, went back into the scullery to take it out on Hettie.

It was almost Christmas. Gilbert had brought them a tree to put up in the Thrift Street parlour. His welcome there was more subdued than previously, but they were all glad to see him, Cathy included, and he felt more at home there than in his own house. The Captain had gone. He'd left the week before, to spend Christmas in his own country, and he wouldn't be back now till after the March gales. Cathy bore a sad, quiet look, and Gilbert couldn't help but feel sorry for her. Her eyes sought his comfort, and he gave it to her, taking her out as before, walking hand in hand, and talking quietly by 'The Sanctuary' fire. She still didn't visit them at Westoe. Not yet. Perhaps after Christmas, Gilbert thought. Meanwhile, they enjoyed just being together, sadder but wiser, each gentle and kind to the other, knowing what they both were feeling.

'I could maybe fetch you some logs,' Gilbert was saying. 'We've got plenty up at Westoe. A tree came down a few weeks back.'

Lily nodded her approval.

'Aha,' she agreed, 'that'd be nice and seasonal.'

Then all three lapsed once again into silence. Hettie was in the scullery, on her own as usual. She would be reading her romances by candlelight, snug against the stove.

And so she was, or she was till Joe knocked lightly on the window. Hettie jumped, saw him, then went to open the back door.

'Eeh, what a fright!'

'Sorry, Hettie. I didn't want to face Lady Muck, so I thought I'd come in the back way.'

'Come and warm yoursel'.' Hettie squeezed a cup out of the teapot for him and he put his hands round it thankfully.

'Anyway, I didn't think you'd want her to know.'

Hettie glanced at him sharply.

'Know what?'

Joe sipped his tea, then looked at her gently.

'I found him, Hettie.' She looked blank. 'Johnny.'

'Oh,' she said and sat suddenly in the nearest chair.

'Do you want to know, Hettie?'

Hettie nodded dumbly.

'He's livin' in Newcastle. Jesmond, with a young bit of stuff. That bloke in Cullercoats. Well, he just doesn't exist, that's all. I tackled him about the money.' Joe paused and looked at her, her knuckles were showing white against the sides of the table. 'How much *did* you give him, Hettie?'

Hettie seemed to have to gather herself to speak, dragging the words up out of a great depth.

'Nigh on fifty pound. I'd saved it from me palm readin' an' that.'

Joe bit his lips and sipped his tea before speaking again.

'Miserable little blighter!' he fumed. 'He said it were no more than fifteen quid.' He set down his cup and put his hand in his pocket, drawing out a small purse. 'I made him empty his pockets, her an' all. Whey, I mean she wasn't a lady, was she?' He emptied the contents of the purse onto the table. 'This was all they had on them. I should think they've spent the rest.'

Hettie stared at the coins and the few notes lying there.

'It comes to seven pound ten and a tanner, Hettie,' he said.

Hettie nodded and continued staring. Joe waited for a while, watching her, then quietly rose.

'Aye well. My job's done. And I can't say as I've liked it.'

Hettie looked up at him, her face was blank.

'I'll be back to see you, hinny,' he said, and patted her on the arm.

'Aye, Joe. Do that,' she whispered. 'There's not many as cares after me.'

Brusquely, Joe took his leave. He was glad when he was out again in the frost, looking up at the starlit sky. He'd added a pound or two of his own to the little hoard Hettie had on the table there. He had nowt left in his pockets. Not that he minded. He was glad of the walk home and a chance to settle his mind. He'd not relish another scene like that one in a hurry.

Hettie stared at the money for a long time. Then she collected it together and put it back in the purse which Joe had left behind him. She counted it carefully. It was as Joe had said. Seven pound ten and a tanner exactly. All that was left of a broken dream. In the parlour, Lily laughed. The voices were warm and welcoming, and the fire would be lit. Hettie heard them in the hall as she passed on her way upstairs, but she didn't look in on them. They heard the stairs creak as she went up to her room, and the door close behind her.

'What's the matter with Auntie Hettie?' Cathy asked. 'She's not gone up already?'

Lily snorted.

'Just bein' anti-social as usual,' she said. 'Well, let her. I'm not goin' to feel guilty about it!'

Cathy stared at her mother, surprised, and exchanged a puzzled look with Gilbert. And then they turned to watch the flames casting shadows on the walls of the room as they sat on in comfortable silence.

As Christmas came, Edith Stoddard breathed a sigh of relief. She was planning a small dinner party for Christmas Eve. She had the maid fetch her up a cup of tea to her room, and sat at her desk, pen in hand ready to write out the invitations. She smiled faintly as she took a sip of her tea before applying pen to paper.

'Mr and Mrs Stoddard, and their son Gilbert, request the

pleasure of Mrs Cochrane and her daughter May at a dinner party at their home in Westoe on Christmas Eve. Dress formal. R.S.V.P.'

May Cochrane shone with a reflected light. The still, cool surface of her waters drew men to her. For still waters were known to run very deep, and there was a fascination to unknown, even more to unplumbed, depths. She had no need to work at attraction. She simply was attractive. It was taken as a matter of course. So that Gilbert came as a surprise to her. With him she had to make conversation. With him she had to work merely to keep his attention. She held no natural magnetism for him. She was an intelligent girl, bored by normal social intercourse, but under-educated, and under-used. Gilbert, therefore, was a welcome relief and the challenge of him spurred her into unusual efforts to please.

But it was not Gilbert who greeted her and her mother at the front door of the house in Westoe Village. It was James Stoddard and his wife. Gilbert had not finished dressing. May glanced towards the stairs, then smiled graciously at the father who was only too glad to take the silver fox from her shoulders and present it to the maid.

'Gilbert will be down in a moment,' Edith Stoddard beamed. 'You know what these young men are . . . working late on his car engine, if you please!' The older women smiled conspiratorially at one another, 'boys will be boys' their expressions said.

May felt a frisson of anger and braced herself for a tough bout over the silver. She knew the competition. She saw the attraction. She would not attempt to equal the red-haired Miss Straker, however. For Miss Straker was the type of girl who could hold men for only a short time. They would lose their senses for her, but soon tire. May would net Gilbert in the end, she was sure of it. But, however long it took to haul him in, she would have to get her hook into his flesh tonight.

The maid was sent to tell Gilbert of their guests' arrival. There were presents to be opened by the tree, and they were waiting for him. He fastened his cufflinks, straightened his bow, and with a deep breath came down into the party atmosphere of the drawing room. May was standing close by the tree, tall and slender. She was wearing a dress of dove-grey chiffon, which seemed to have peeled away from her white shoulders, and floated round her ankles like a cloud. Her pale hair shone in the candlelight, and the silver ornaments gleamed from her hands and throat. If she had carried a wand, Gilbert would not have been surprised. She was, to him, exactly like an extremely tasteful fairy on the Christmas tree. Ethereal, and therefore unreal. As he went towards her to take her hand, she smiled an unreal smile, full of grace and charm, and well practised. It left him cold.

'Come along, Gilbert,' his mother encouraged him. 'Give May her present.'

'Ah yes . . .' Gilbert searched through the coloured tissues beneath the tree for the present his mother had bought on his behalf. 'Here it is.' He held it out to her, and May took it, as of right, looking him straight in the eye.

'I hope you chose it yourself, Gilbert,' she teased, pulling the paper away from the box inside. She opened the lid and saw a collar of fine Brussels lace. 'How beautiful,' she said, with genuine appreciation. 'Thank you . . .' she turned away from Gilbert, '. . . Mrs Stoddard.' Mr Stoddard laughed and the rest of the company followed suit. 'Its so right for me, it could only have been bought by *you*.' Gilbert smiled. May's wit was brittle but it sparkled and cheered him.

'I must confess,' he said to her, 'you're quite right, May. It's the first time I've seen what I bought for you.'

'And do you approve of your purchase?' she asked, seriously.

'I think . . .' he considered, 'I think, I have excellent taste. Don't you agree?'

'Oh I do! I do!' And her laughter rippled, like the shallows of the lake in Marine Park when a sudden breeze whips across its surface. 'And now I shall give you my present, Gilbert.' She glided to the table where the Cochrane contribution had been arranged, and picked out a small, flat parcel, which she held out to him.

'You shouldn't have bothered,' Gilbert was murmuring.

'Oh, Gilbert! I hadn't expected such urbanity from *you*!'

So reprimanded, Gilbert realised that he would not, as he had hoped, be able to wing his way through the evening. May had to be reckoned with. He would not be able to reply with polite commonplaces to cover his wandering attention. He would need all his concentration to deal with her.

'Thank you,' he said, and opened the parcel.

Inside was a small picture in a gilt frame. The subject was an arrangement of dried flowers, and at the centre of them was a sprig of May.

'She made it herself,' Mrs Stoddard said proudly. But May cut in sharply.

'Yes. I've given them to *all* my friends this year.'

'I'm honoured to be considered Miss Cochrane's friend,' Gilbert replied, 'but I rather thought it was supposed to be unlucky to bring May into your house.'

'Claptrap and superstition,' May objected. 'You're above such things, Gilbert.'

'I hope you're right,' he said and smiled his thanks.

Dinner was a grand affair, and, to his surprise, Gilbert enjoyed it. May didn't let up on him for more than a few seconds at a time. He admired her persistence. He enjoyed her humour, and entered into the spirit of what, to him, was a game. And May knew it was a game, but she believed that at the right moment games could turn serious. She was luring her fish, and the fish was responding to the bait.

Gilbert saw the sly glances passing from mother to mother. It irritated him beyond measure. But his response was to play harder. May's interest was as balm to his rejected soul. After the intensity of his relations with Cathy, light-hearted repartee, spiked with flirtation, refreshed his palate. 'Some women are capable of feelings just as strong as men have.' Cathy's deeper feelings were then engaged elsewhere, and she was playing with him as he, now, was playing with May. It was a dangerous game, but at least as far as May was concerned only her pride was at stake. Not her emotions. The affair of the presents proved that. So he did not reproach himself. 'All's fair in love and war.' And the world is full of walking wounded.

James Stoddard watched like an umpire at a tennis match. If Cathy could only see Gilbert now, the risk of losing him might drive her into saying 'yes' at last. James admired May. She was beautiful, a 'good catch', and could be charming when she wanted. He had never seen her as animated as she was tonight. She had a flush on her cheeks, and her eyes were bright and sharp as her brain. She and Cathy were chalk and cheese. The one was ruled by her heart, the other by her head. It was the judgment of Paris, forced to choose between Athena and Aphrodite. Who could say which goddess was superior to the other? Only the heart could tell which of the ladies was to be preferred.

Champagne and music followed dinner, and the two young people left their elders to their conversation while they danced in the billiard room. Gilbert had decided that May was 'a good sport'. He bubbled with exhilaration because he felt he could beat his mother at her own game. He grabbed his partner by the waist and whirled her round and round as the gramophone played. Gasping for breath they spiralled to a halt, both laughing uproariously. It was 'good fun'. Relieved of the tension of past weeks, Gilbert gave way to pent-up energy and put his hands about his comrade's waist and victoriously hoisted her up into the air, whooping.

'Put me down, Gilbert Stoddard,' May cried in alarm. Her dignity lay about her in tatters. Gilbert set her down in surprise.

'Sorry,' he said lightly. But when he looked into her eyes he saw that her pupils were dilated, the dark blue swamping the pale iris, and she was trembling visibly. Her shocked features silenced him, and her eyes held his as the gramophone whined slowly to a standstill. Her jaw dropped, and the mouth, which had curled itself into many a practised smile, suddenly gave way to surprising vulnerability. Her hook had sprung back on her and caught her in her own snare. Gilbert bent to kiss her on the forehead, as if to calm a frightened child. But, on an impulse, May jerked her head back, caught his mouth on her cheek and, swiftly travelling, Gilbert's lips found her open mouth.

In the drawing room, James Stoddard was playing the fool. May's mother and Edith, giggly as schoolgirls on champagne, clicked their tongues and raised their eyes to heaven as he shook another bottle.

'Stop it, James! We'll all be drenched!' But the cork popped, and the champagne gushed, spraying the room and its occupants who squealed with fright and glee.

'Christmas comes but once a year,' James announced by way of excuse. And the women enjoyed reprimanding him as though he were a schoolboy and they were not, themselves, tipsy.

The sounds of unaccustomed hilarity barely permeated the consciousness of the pair in the billiard room.

'I win,' May said quietly. 'But I lose as well.'

'How?'

'I think I love you.'

Her directness stunned him, and he could see by her face that she meant what she had said. A child somewhere in the world had said 'I *don't* believe in fairies', and suddenly May was a mere woman, with all a woman's feelings and confusions. Gilbert looked at her, and wondered what he'd done.

Christmas Day was something of an anti-climax. Edith Stoddard had a headache and griped endlessly about Persian rugs ruined by excessively high spirits and waste of good champagne. Both of Gilbert's parents knew that something had happened between the young people the night before. Gilbert was distinctly evasive and neither of them dared to probe. Gilbert itched to go down to Thrift Street but felt constrained to stay put, and wore himself out with the restless desire to be anywhere but where he was. By Boxing Day, he was seething with frustration. And in the afternoon, when his father slept and his mother pretended to read in the parlour though she in fact ate chocolates, he went out to tackle the fallen tree in the garden.

The deluge of emotion which Gilbert had experienced had taken him utterly by surprise. All the desire held back for Cathy's sake and then rejected by her exploded in him like a time bomb. He was attracted to May. And he knew, by the way she had looked at him, that he had damaged her. May love him? He was not such a fool as to believe that the woman who had happened to be there when the dam burst was the actual object of his desire. But if she believed so, then he was in real trouble. He was in danger now of using her, of turning to May on the rebound, and venting on her his feelings for Cathy, while May herself fell more and more deeply in love with him. He was ashamed to have played the dangerous game, and knew that he had done it, in part, to spite Cathy, to pay her back for her rejection of him.

He lifted the axe high into the air and let it fall with a crash against the trunk of the tree. The bark exploded, sending splinters everywhere, and the hollow thud of the impact bit into the bland atmosphere of the afternoon. He heaved the axe out of the tree, lifted it again, and crashed it down, to gouge a cleft into the wood. There was satisfaction in such labour after grappling for so long with the maze of confusions and desires within him. Again the axe fell and sunk deeper, gripped by the tree, which did not want to let it go. But Gilbert tore it out and let it fall again and again, and with every blow the conviction deepened. He could not wait for Cathy. She must give way to him. She must name a day, or else he would not be answerable for what he would do.

'I'll send the maid out to get him.' Edith, caught in the middle of the second layer of chocolates, was flustered by the sudden appearance of an unexpected guest. 'Nancy,' she told the maid, who came in tying her apron, 'Nancy, go and knock on Mr Stoddard's door. Tell him we've got guests. And when you've done that, go out to Mr Gilbert.'

Flushed with happiness, May had come, against her mother's advice, sure of her welcome. But now, standing at the window with a mince pie in her hand, her confidence ebbed. Gilbert's back was to her. But in it she read her own disillusion. The rise and fall of the axe bruised her spirit. For she knew that the lusty energy of the man in the garden would not be spent for her. He was hacking his way out of a situation in which he fervently wished he had never become involved.

PART FOUR

CHAPTER FOURTEEN

Events have a way of taking over the lives of people from time to time. Though 1914 began peaceably enough, and Cathy thought that she had all the time in the world, events were soon to prove otherwise. She and Gilbert had come to an understanding. They would announce their engagement some time in the spring, and would marry quietly, a small private ceremony, just their parents, Hettie, and Mr Miller, who would give Cathy away. But Mr Stoddard did not see the buds swell on the sycamore at the bottom of his garden that spring. He died towards the end of February from a thrombosis, leaving Gilbert in sole charge of the family business. Gilbert's mother was inconsolable. No one, including the widow herself, had been aware how much she had loved and relied on her husband. Gilbert was now her sole support, and he already had his hands full, for the business was in the process of expanding. He had opened up a new office in Liverpool in January and there were plans for an office in the port of London. This last had to be shelved, but his father's old friend, a retired captain who knew the freight trade well, came back to hold the reins in the Shields office on the quay, and Gilbert found himself divided between the new office in Liverpool and his mother's house in Westoe. He had little time to spare for visits to Thrift Street. So March came and went, and Gilbert was in a difficult situation. Mrs Stoddard suffered badly from her nerves. She grew hysterical at the slightest excuse and screamed like a fishwife. On his return from Liverpool at the weekends, Gilbert often found her ensconced with Mrs Cochrane and her daughter May, who had come to keep her company in his absence, and seemed content to stay when he was home again. He suffered their presence in the house, polite but unbending, making his way to Thrift Street when he could. Cathy understood. How could he spring their marriage on his mother now? They would just have to wait a little longer.

When April came and there was still no announcement, Lily began to fret. But Cathy was spared her constant prodding and jibing because Lily had other things on her mind. Hettie, who had been down all winter, went out one day in late March for a walk by the sea. She had lost track of time, staring out across the horizon, watching the ships come and go, and when she came back late that night, her feet wet from the surf and cold as Christmas, she already had the signs of a bad cold. The following day she had a high fever, and the doctor was called in. She'd caught pneumonia. The worst of it was that she had no wish to live. She lay there unconscious, burning up, in another world. There was no fight left in her. Lily nursed her day and night, refusing to allow her daughter near the invalid for fear of her catching the disease. Exhausted, Lily didn't spare herself, and when she thought Hettie was actually going to die after all her efforts, she cried, 'Damn her! Damn her! Damn her! Here's me worn to a frazzle and she doesn't lift a finger to help herself! Damn the woman!'

Joe came, soon as he heard, and Lily let him sit by her at the bedside through the night. Cathy brought them tea and sandwiches, went out to the fishmongers and brought back packs of ice for Hettie's head, bought new romances for the invalid to read in her convalescence; anything she could think of, Cathy did. Finally Hettie's crisis passed safely; reluctantly, she gathered strength and came back to the world.

Cathy felt she was surrounded by illness. What with Mr Stoddard dying, Edith Stoddard near to breakdown, so Gilbert said, Miss Hutchinson at work weak and frail after her operation from which she never seemed to recover properly, and then Hettie. Corruption hung in the air like a pestilence. She smelt it everywhere, and the spring, when it came, hadn't the power to shift it. She'd grown used to Joe coming and going, without fuss, using the back door always. She took little notice of him. He was Hettie's friend, and he had the power to cheer her up during her long convalescence. Even Lily had got used to him. He'd been useful in Hettie's illness, but though that gave him rights in the house, Lily didn't like it. She knew she owed him one, and she resented it as though Joe had come into their lives via the back door in more ways than one. He was a cuckoo in her nest, but he was there, and she just had to grin and bear it as best she could. He smelt of the ferry, and when he came back from a fishing trip in one of his mate's boats he stank of fish as well. Joe wasn't a gentleman. Neither was he a lodger. He was in no-man's-land, a queer fish, and he belonged nowhere. The back yard, the scullery and Hettie's room might harbour him from time to time, but the lodger's dining room and the parlour were barred to him. Still, Joe didn't mind. After all, it was Hettie he came to see, and he wasn't proud. Lily's sneers were like water off a duck's back to him. The only thing that bothered him was Cathy. She had seemed friendly enough, bringing the sandwiches and tea. She was a tender-hearted lass and in a state about her auntie being so ill. He could see that clear as daylight. Her gratitude reached out to him in great waves, nearly knocking him over, and his heart responded with like warmth. But once Hettie was back on the road to recovery, she went all stand-offish again. Aye, in some ways Cathy Straker was her mother's daughter and no mistake. Still, he couldn't help but sigh after that bright copper mane of hers and watch the lights that shone out of it in the sun. She stirred him, so proud, so beautiful, so cold, so warm. She had the power to turn him inside out, twist his heart round and then put it back again all adrift. She was promised to another. He knew that. Somebody far above him, an' all. But Joe watched and waited. If his chance came, then he'd not miss out. He'd grab it with both hands, and run off grinning. For Joe loved Cathy. In fact, he worshipped the ground she walked on.

As Joe carried Hettie up and down stairs, to sit with the family by the kitchen stove or catch the first sunshine in the yard, she saw the spaniel-eyed look that came across him whenever he saw her niece. She smiled sadly to herself. She loved Cathy. She wanted the best for her, and she hoped with all her heart that she'd marry Gilbert and live happily ever after. And yet she loved Joe too. Joe had taken up her cause, by choice, not through destiny. His quiet strength and love had brought her through her illness more than any of Lily's nursing, however devoted. And now Hettie clung to him, and would have liked to tie him to her by a stronger thread than friendship alone. He had given her back her life, and she would have liked to give him his heart's desire. Once, he caught her looking at him as they all sat deep in their own thoughts in the kitchen. She had looked away again quickly, not wanting Joe to see she'd read his thoughts. But Hettie was sensitive. She read the cards and people's palms; she read their characters too, so Joe shouldn't be surprised that she knew how he felt about Cathy. He felt the frail, beaten woman was an ally in the house, and he clung to her in turn.

For all her perception, Hettie had not noticed Captain Christiansen as he came and went like all the boarders did. His stay was marked by absences when he took to the sea again, coming back tired to reclaim his room for a few nights. He had returned in April. He played the paino amongst the dustsheets in the parlour, and sometimes Cathy was heard singing with him. Hettie liked to hear them. They brightened up the house, and lifted the spirits. And Lily was content to let them practise together. The Captain was a cultured man, a gentleman, far older than Cathy, at least ten years, and he had spoken of his family back in Norway. Yes, she could trust the Captain. And after all, Cathy was in love with Gilbert. So there was nothing at all to fear.

Cathy herself was low in energy that spring. She was having to work harder than ever at Miss Hutchinson's, and the girls all spoke in whispers now that their employer was so touchy. Ethel found herself tending to her more personal needs, doing for the invalid, and that left Mabel and Cathy with the workroom floor-sweeping and the tidying up to do. Cathy had the added chore of doing the books, having got the hang of it while Miss Hutchinson was in the infirmary, and she only took them once a week to the proprietor for inspection.

'We're runnin' this shop!' Mabel complained bitterly. 'But we're not gettin' paid for runnin' it!'

Then Gilbert was away so much. Cathy missed him, and she missed the going out, the fun they had together. When he was in Shields she saw little of him, and he was tired and preoccupied. She, too, needed some welcome relief from the miseries of the spring, and she found it with the Captain.

They didn't talk much, but when they did it was mostly about the sea and the various voyages he'd been on. Now his traffic was mostly local, Antwerp, Liverpool, London, Oslo, Le Havre, Marseilles, Stockholm, but in the past, before he'd been a captain, he'd travelled far further afield. He'd gone around the Cape, he'd seen the Far East; and best of all, he knew the South Seas. He joked with her about her insistence that mermaids lived in the warm southern waters. It was a fable from her childhood that she still clung to tenaciously. Of course there were no such things, he said, flying fish, yes, but not mermaids! And then Cathy laughed, for how could fish fly? And she'd gone on insisting that he must have seen a real live mermaid. So he answered her that yes, there were mermaids after all; there was one that a man he knew had caught off Tahiti. Perhaps one day he'd show it to her. And Cathy's eyes shone, pleading with him every time she saw him to show her the little mermaid. He teased her mercilessly, laughing at her, and watched her cheeks flush as she turned away in her embarrassment. For slowly the old feelings for the Captain returned; not with the same force as before, but stronger and stronger the more Gilbert stayed away. The Captain knew it and nurtured them with little attentions, which pleased both the girl and her mother. He brought them tiny bunches of violets when they first appeared in Shields market, and small gifts of food or chocolate which he pulled from his pockets like a rabbit out of a hat. But he looked in vain for the same ferocity of desire to shine out of Cathy's eyes. The edge had gone from her appetite. The hurt in Gilbert's face had done that. No, she hadn't got the Captain out of her system, but she no longer felt the old overwhelming need to do so. He tempted her but, tired and downhearted as she was, he had lost his power over her. The knowledge irked him. Before, when she had seemed so freely available, he had merely played with the idea of having her, but now that she resisted him he was determined to make her his.

And then, quite suddenly, a tidal wave came and swept through the gentler ebb and flow of their lives. They saw it coming far off on the horizon, and yet still couldn't quite believe that it was there. It was June. Hettie was just getting strong again at last. Joe's savings were nearly enough for his dream of a boat. Gilbert, the business now well under his thumb, had begun to turn his mind back to Cathy and their coming marriage. And Cathy, in her turn, and in spite of the Captain, was ready and willing to go along with him. Away in Holland the news struck the Captain with far more impact than at home in Shields. It had happened in Bosnia, in an obscure town nobody had heard of: Serbian patriots had killed the heir to the Austrian throne, the Archduke Franz Ferdinand. It was a sensation. Gilbert's heart jumped when he read it in the papers in Liverpool. Joe saw it on the hoardings in North Shields, and Hettie was told it by Mr Miller, who spent most of the day nose down in the papers in the library in Ocean Road.

It was sensational, but not really alarming. Such things happened, if not every day at least frequently enough in the Europe of that time. Then, on 24 July, there came the terrible announcement that Austria had delivered an ultimatum to Serbia of such brutality that, as the papers said, 'it can by interpreted only as a deliberate attempt to provoke war'. They all felt themselves shot out of their usual plane of existence and landed on a far bigger stage than the one they were used to. The days dragged, and people spoke hopefully of the Socialists in France who, under their leader Jaurès, might stop a coming war. But then he too was assassinated, and those who were left found themselves struggling against the tide as ultimatums were passed from government to government, and the outcome became inevitable. By 4 August the war was general in Europe, and young men flocked to join up and do battle for their country in the trenches.

Gilbert did not feel the general mood of fervour, the glorious patriotism that was sweeping everyone away. He knew what this war would mean to his business if it continued for long, and he knew that it would mean another postponement of his marriage to Cathy. Every day he felt her slipping further from him. His anguish brought back the memory of another day, when he had stood, handkerchief in hand, at the top of the hill and watched her descending further and further away from him. She could not have jumped off the cart and run back to him, not then, when they were children, but now? He arrived at Thrift Street in his uniform and waited in the parlour to see her.

The dustsheets were in place, and the half-drawn curtains let in the sunshine in streaming rays, in which he could see the dust dancing. The piano lid had been left up and music was still in place on the ledge. It was the overture to 'Lohengrün'. Gilbert snorted at the irony of it. He was going off to fight against the Germans, and here a lodger sat playing the music of a German master, Wagner. 'Death and Love', *Liebestod.* Well, there would be plenty of death, that was for sure, but love would have to take a back seat for a little while.

Cathy came in, pulling down her sleeves, her hair dishevelled. It was washing day and she'd been taking her turn in the washhouse possing in the tub. She was out of breath and flushed, embarrassed to have been caught out in her old dress and her pinny. But she stopped short in the middle of her apology when she saw Gilbert. He was standing, back to the light, a faceless soldier, with a glory of sunrays playing behind him on the white sheets which covered the sofa. She gasped, and her hands dropped to her sides in dismay.

'You've joined up!' she cried.

Gilbert shrugged.

'The sooner it's all over, the better,' he said gently. 'It won't last long if we all put our backs into it.' Cathy rushed to him and buried her head in the khaki cloth of his tunic.

'I don't want you to go,' she cried.

He eased her away from him and looked into her eyes.

'It won't be for long,' he said, 'and I'll be back on leave from time to time. It's not for ever.'

Cathy's face was streaming with her tears.

'How long will it last, Gilbert?' she asked.

'Weeks, a few months at most. You'll see. We'll be married by Christmas.'

'Oh I wish your Dad was still alive,' she sobbed. 'I wish, I wish, we'd got married when we'd thought!'

'Aye well. We didn't. And it's no good doing it now, when I might not . . .'

Cathy's head jerked up to stare at him. Her face was white against the livid colour of her hair.

'Promise me you'll be safe,' she demanded. 'Promise me.'

And Gilbert promised, easing her hands away from him and speaking softly of Christmas and when the war was over and how happy they would be.

As he left the house and his boots struck against the cobbles on the hill, he was surprised by a flock of gulls screeching overhead. They wheeled over the street, then turned back again out to sea. Gilbert hurried on to his car, glad that the leavetaking was over, and determined that by putting all he had into the war it would hurry past and be done, so that he would be free to resume his life where he had left off.

To Cathy, this war had seemed to rise naturally out of the spring's corruption. She wished that none of it had happened, that she could turn the clock back to that evening when Gilbert had come round and found her dancing with the Captain. For all the bad things had seemed to follow on from then. Her feelings had run riot in her. But now she was jaded, tired, and bore the guilt of hurting Gilbert, so that she simply hadn't the animal spirits left to feel the same way. Nor could she believe she ever would again. The stirrings in her belly, the dizziness in her head, and the feverish dreams were not the desperate calling of her soul. They were merely the calling of her flesh. They were a nuisance and nothing more. How could she have behaved so badly? she asked herself. And yet, at the time, it had all seemed so overpowering. Had she really 'got it out of her system' after all? Would she ever feel she could die for love of someone again? For all the shame, something in Cathy regretted this loss of feeling. For then she had been so alive. From the crown of her head down to her toes, she had seethed with emotion. Where had it all gone? Had the wave crashed down onto the shore, its time passed, and gone for ever? Or would it come again?

Joe had not signed up. Not yet. Lily kept dropping hints about 'some people not bein' man enough to fight', but Joe, as he usually did, ignored her, so that her aspersions were cast on barren ground. Alec MacGowan and Jim Webster, however, were not so easy to ignore.

'I said you were nae man!' Alec jeered at him, as they walked along the quay.

'Hadaway wi' ye, Alec! Joe'll come in with us, all in good time.'

'He's a bloody conchy!' Alec spat onto the sawdust floor of the pub to vent his feelings.

'Is that true, Joe?'

'There's no glory in killing.'

'Or being killed. Isn't that nearer the mark?' Alec asked him.

'No, it isn't Alec. And you know it. If a fight's worth fighting, then I'll fight it. If not . . . well I'm not goin' to rush into throwin' my life away. That's all.'

'Aye, you like a fight for the sake of it, Alec!' Jim laughed at him.

'Your woman'll think more of you if you go.' Alec knew exactly where to find Joe's soft underbelly. But Joe pretended to miss the Scotsman's drift.

'Madge? She's waved off half a dozen of us already! What makes *me* so special?'

'Aye, but Joe,' Jim intervened, 'that lass thinks a lot about you.'

'Madge and me've got an understanding,' Joe said.

'It wasn't Madge I meant. And well you know it,' Alec said. 'It was the other'n.'

Joe laughed and shook his head. 'It's not because of her I've not enlisted. It's because of me!'

'Everybody'll spit at you, man!' Jim warned him.

'Aye well,' Joe replied quietly, 'I'll just have to be man enough to stand it, won't I?'

Alec smiled. His hand reached out to touch Joe's back.

'You're an obstinate bugger. But I like you for it! It takes guts to go against the tide.'

Jim kept his own counsel but Joe was grateful for the understanding of the Scotsman. He let them go to their seats to talk about him as they would while he went up to the mission counter for their teas.

Madge had bought a brooch the shape of a Union Jack to wear in her lapel. She was gripped by war fever.

'Joe!' she cried. 'You not in uniform yet?'

Joe smiled and shook his head as he took the mugs from her.

'I've not seen you in ages.'

'I've been over the other side of the river,' Joe said.

Madge nodded.

'Hobnobbin' again, eh?' She cut him a piece of her cake. 'If she doesn't snap you up soon, somebody else will.' Her voice was teasing, but her eyes were serious. Joe put his hand over hers.

'I've never led you on, hinny,' he reminded her.

'I know. It's me own thoughts lead me, Joe. Me own thoughts.' Then she smiled. 'She must be quite somethin' to put *me* in the shade, mind!'

'Aye, she is,' Joe answered her with a wry smile.

'Then I hope she's got her head screwed on. Because I'd not like to see you gettin' hurt.'

'She's given me no sign of encouragement, Madge. So it won't be her fault if I do get hurt.'

'Aye well,' Madge said sadly, 'in that case you an' me's in the same boat, pet!'

Alec and Jim enlisted. Madge, realising at last that Joe Robson was not for her, gave in to the importuning of an Arab and agreed to marry him. He was a determined young man, with ideas of starting up a cafe on the quayside. He was going places. Madge thought about it a long time. She'd known a girl who'd married an Arab before. They made good family men, and good money too more often than not. Madge wasn't daft. She knew which side her bread was buttered and how to make the best of a bad job. All the young men were off to war. She'd better snap one up while she could! And Joe was glad for her. She seemed happy enough, and it relieved him to think she was being taken care of. Madge might sigh after him for a while, but she'd soon forget him, and then he'd be quite alone, apart from Hettie.

Hettie clung on to Joe. She, unlike Lily, didn't want him to go to the war. She hung on his arm as they walked along the harbour together.

'My girl!' he said as she smiled into his face.

'Not the one you want, though.'

'I've not got a look in, have I?'

'No, Joe. I can't deny it, pet.'

'I hear he's joined up?'

'Gilbert? Aye. He has.'

'I don't want to go behind his back.' Joe considered the situation. With Gilbert away, his path ought to be clearer. But it wouldn't be fair on Cathy to take advantage of his absence, let alone on Gilbert. And if she did turn to Joe at this time, then wouldn't it be just as a temporary stopgap? That wouldn't do for Joe. If Cathy was ever to have him, it would be because it was him she wanted, and then he would not run the risk of her regretting her choice afterwards. No hole-in-the-corner stuff for Joe. It had to be above board for one thing, and for another it had to be whatever was best for Cathy.

'Do you think he'll make her happy?' he asked.

'Aye. I do. All she needs is settling down. Once they were married, I think she'd be happy enough.'

'That's all I wanted to know,' Joe said resignedly. 'I might as well join up like the rest of them, I suppose.'

'Joe! No!' Hettie was horrified.

'The lads've gone, couple of weeks back. It's a pity, mind, we'd just about got enough together for that boat.' His eyes misted. All his dreams seemed to have dropped below the horizon, out of sight. His walk was despondent. Hettie hugged his arm to her.

'You'll get your boat, lad. After the war. It'll not last long!'

'Aye. Mebbe you're right. After the war.' He brightened up. 'I wonder if I could get into Alec's regiment. By, but I bet he'll be surprised!'

They walked along for a while without speaking. Hettie's throat ached with unshed tears.

'Are you comin' on Sunday?' she asked at last.

'Aye. I expect so.'

'It's nice weather just now, mind.'

'Aye.'

'Would you fancy a picnic on the beach? With the rest of them, like?'

Joe smiled. Good old Hettie. She'd make sure he had one last day to remember with her and, above all, with Cathy.

'Aye,' he said approvingly. 'That'd be grand.'

Cathy sided with her Auntie Hettie. She was dying for a bit of a day out and some sea air. She could go for a swim! Everyone knew the sea was warmest at the end of the summer, when the sun'd been on it the longest time. Oh how she longed for a swim in the sea. Lily was less than enthusiastic.

'I've got enough on me mind plannin' Friday!' she snapped. 'And now you want's to put up a picnic an' all!' For Lily had resumed the occasional musical evening, now that Hettie was up and about again. They'd taken on a patriotic flavour, too, since they were at war, and the same crowd of people, more or less, gathered to enjoy themselves one Friday in the month, sip a glass of sherry and indulge in polite conversation between the turns. Hettie went on about going to the music hall. Joe had finally taken her, much against Lily's wishes, as a treat last June and, said Hettie, 'It beats musical evenin's hollow!' But, just as Lily had turned a deaf ear to Hettie's objections to her 'evenings', Hettie and Cathy turned a deaf ear to Lily's objections to their picnic. They were having one and that was that.

When Joe turned up, Hettie didn't make a meal of it. It was just his usual Sunday visit, that was all, and of course he must be included in the party. So they all gathered up the bags and bottles and made for the tram that'd take them the longest distance along the shore. Joe had a wish to search among the rock pools, so they all made their way walking miles, past Gypsies' Green to Trow Rocks.

It was a lazy day. The war seemed a long way away as Hettie lay basking in the sunshine, feeling its warmth seeping down into her bones. Lily fussed over the food, and Joe wandered off looking in the rock pools, now and then pulling out some tiny crab or starfish. Cathy looked out over the sea. It looked calm as glass. Somewhere out there Captain Christiansen was sailing his ship, back from Oslo to Shields, somewhere in the great North Sea. She was warm; too warm. She pulled her boater further down over her face to shade her eyes from the water's glare and unbuttoned the top of her blouse. She glanced along the seashore. Joe was well off, straddling the slippery rocks, totally immersed in his search for crabs. She laughed to herself. 'Always the fisherman!' Lily caught her look and followed its direction to where Joe, overbalancing on a sharp rock, swung his arms around awkwardly in an effort to keep upright.

'Tut!' she commented. 'Eeh, I don't know why you had to invite him along, Hettie.'

'It'll mebbe be his last outing, Lily. Before he joins up.'

'That'll be the day,' she snorted. 'Tut,' she said again. Then she passed a sly look at her daughter who was staring out to sea. 'Have you noticed how he's always moonin' after wer Cathy?' Her lips curled into a sneering smile. 'Mind, a dog can look at a king, I suppose.' And then she raised her voice to ask her daughter, 'No chance of *him* gettin' you, is there hinny?'

Cathy frowned, nettled by such a stupid question.

'Don't be daft.'

'It's only a picnic,' Hettie said, put out by their snide attacks on her Joe. 'I don't know why you've got to be such a snob, Lily.'

'But he stinks of fish, Hettie! You must've smelt it on him!'

'Keep your voice down. He'll hear you,' Hettie hissed. But Lily only laughed.

'He's miles away. Look at him, nose stuck in a rock pool.'

'You'll laugh on the other sides of your faces when I tell

you,' Hettie volunteered. The other two women turned to look at her curiously. 'He *is* goin' to join up.'

'Well I never!'

'Stop it, Lily. And you know why? Because of our Cathy.'

There was a shocked silence. All three of them turned to stare at the ungainly figure slithering about the distant rocks.

'You're havin' me on, Hettie!' Cathy said at last.

'No. True as I'm sittin' here. He told me last Friday. He's goin' to the recruitment place the morra.'

'But he must know, Hettie, he's not got a chance of havin' my daughter!'

'Of course he knows, Lily. That's why he's goin'!'

Lily snorted again but said nothing, and Cathy looked away.

'Just think, Cathy. Gone to be shot at in Flanders and all because of you! Mind, don't let on I told you. He'd kill's.'

Both women shook their heads and assured Hettie they'd not give the game away. After a while, having got used to the idea, Lily struck up an attitude towards the situation.

'Best thing, an' all!' she affirmed. 'I'm glad he's goin'! He's like a dog on the scent. It's disgustin'.'

'Aye well,' Hettie said airily. 'In that case who's on heat?'

'I beg your pardon!' Lily had never heard Hettie speak so coarsely. She could hardly believe her ears and Cathy had gone quite red.

'There you see? Look at her. She's gone the colour of beetroot!' Hettie exulted.

'Get away with you, Hettie. Our Cathy doesn't even know he's there half the time. Do you, pet? Her mind's on better things!'

Finally Hettie subsided, and the three of them shuffled uncomfortably on the hard rocks. Suddenly Cathy asked if her mother had packed her swimming costume, and Lily dragged it out of one of her bags and threw it across to her.

'Come on Hettie. Get off your backside,' Lily insisted. 'We'll have to screen her from view!' And like an Arabian princess Cathy disrobed behind a makeshift screen of rugs, held up by an anxious mother and auntie to keep the eyes of a man, barely within sight, from her unspotted flesh. At last she was ready and picked her way carefully over the stones, in her bright knitted swimsuit, towards the sea.

'Enjoy your swim, pet!' her mother called after her, then turning to Hettie with a sudden fury, she spat, 'You shouldn't talk like that in front of the bairn! Such smut, Hettie! We're not all like you, you know!'

With that the two women left on the shore sank back into a mutual sulk.

The sea, warm on the edge, chilled the further Cathy waded in. She gritted her teeth against it and forced her legs against the weight of the water, deeper and deeper, till, with a gasp, she plunged down under the water, diving to the bottom, before emerging further out from the shore. Cathy could swim like a fish. Her father had taught her when she was little never to be afraid of the sea but to enjoy lying on the rollers, letting herself go with the upward and downward movement of the waves. The salt tasted good on her lips, and her skin stung with the bitter cold of the deep waters. She could imagine herself lying across the wet rocks, mermaid-like, if only her legs weren't so hairy, or her swimming costume so baggy. For when it was wet it sagged in the water and, if she wasn't very careful, she could walk out of the sea, revealing all she had, the knitted top sagging to her waist! Hardly the stuff that a mermaid's dreams were made of! She wished she could take the knitted monstrosity off altogether and feel the flow of the water against her bare skin, free of the drag of sagging wool which impeded her movements. Still, it would hardly be decent. She must simply try to forget she had it on and lose herself in the buoyant, flowing sea.

Back on the shore, Joe looked up and saw her floating on the water. The sun glinted around her, and he could see that, lying still as she was, she was drifting further out. He frowned and dropped a starfish from his hand to walk back, as quickly as he could, across the jutting rocks. Hettie and Lily, intent on sulking, saw nothing at all. Cathy was a good swimmer. There was nothing to be concerned about.

The swell beneath her lifted Cathy's body to a crest and let it down gently with a dipping motion that turned her stomach deliciously. Her hands played in the water at her sides, and she stretched along the lips of the waves, lending her movement to the tide. Her mind drifted far away. She saw herself dancing with the Captain, and entered once again the dizzy elation of her feelings then. Her energies rekindled, and a sensation of great bliss came down on her, flooding over her head and down her body like a deeply felt shiver. She smiled and turned on her belly to dive down into the depths again.

Coming up, the water beating in her ears and swishing by her limbs, Cathy burst through the sea's surface to see Joe standing on a high rock. He seemed to be calling to her. But she couldn't hear him for the water throbbing in her ears. Hettie and her mother had turned to look at him surprised. And then, laughing, Cathy turned tail to dive again, searching with her hands through the murky water for the seabed; filled with joy and light, Cathy felt happy. The feelings weren't dead after all. They were very much alive! And she was glad! Glad! And she knew that it was worth all the pain and hurt, the periods of numbed sensations, to feel this surging life inside her, dying for love, *Liebestod*, the seeking for divine union, when, like the little mermaid wished, 'his soul would flow into thine, and thou wouldst become partaker of eternal bliss'. The words came out of her memory as though she had heard them yesterday. Again she broke surface, and this time saw with some annoyance that Joe was running towards the sea, his legs bandy like a frog's, and he was going to join her. Cathy turned to swim away, but as she turned her legs sank beneath her for a moment, and she felt a strong pull dragging at them. Quickly, she turned back, throwing her legs up towards the surface of the water, and she began to swim against the pull. She had been lost in her dreams and had let herself drift into a current, but the dreams meant nothing to her now. All that mattered was her life; she didn't want to die. She fought, pushing against the undertow, struggling to keep a steady rhythm to her breathing and her eyes on the rocks ahead. But then she seemed to swirl round, suddenly, and they'd gone from her.

She righted her body to swim again on a new course, making for a rock further out. She was losing ground. Suddenly she screamed, and frantically searched the surface of the water for Joe's head, bobbing up and down, as he swam out to her. 'Joe! Help me!' But she was under, bubbles over her head and swirling water blearing her vision. Her hands joined and prayed her way back to the surface. 'Joe! Over here!' And then she was down again. Her legs felt heavy under the water, though she tried to kick them, to fight back upwards. She gasped, and a sudden belch of water entered her so that she spluttered and her nose was full and she couldn't breathe, and then suddenly there was light and air that she couldn't breathe for the salt water in her nostrils and she knew she was sinking. But a hand grabbed her, hurting her. She struggled against it automatically, and then there was darkness.

The first thing Cathy felt was the pain in her chest, then it was the burning roughness of her throat. And then other sensations crowded in: Joe pressing hard down on her back; a limpet digging into her right breast; water spurting out of her mouth; and cold drops dripping from the man who had saved her. Her lips moved. There was sand on them. She felt sick. Her head was spinning. Her costume sagged like a sponge full of water, and she heard her mother speaking.

'That's enough now, Mr Robson. She'll be all right, now.'

And Hettie was saying over and over again, 'Eeh! Eeh! She could've died! Eeh our Joe! Eeh. She could've died!'

Cathy coughed, barking out drops of water, raw with salt.

'It's all right,' Joe was saying soothingly. 'Come on, Miss Straker, let's get you comfortable.' And he turned her over. Cathy tried to focus on the man. Who was it? Was it Captain Christiansen? Or someone else . . . yes, Gilbert? 'It's me, Miss Straker. It's Joe. Joe Robson.'

Somehow they got her dried and dressed, refusing Joe's help even to hold up the screen. They could trust him to save her life but not to refrain from peeping. So he went off searching way down the beach towards the prom for a bogie to cart the lass back at least as far as the tram. She couldn't be expected to walk after that!

Still coughing and spluttering, Cathy had no option but to suffer the indignity of being pulled by Joe back to civilisation in a bogie, her hair a mess, shivering with cold and shaking with fright. Joe's trousers were beginning to dry out. He had been wearing his best suit . . . well, it *was* a Sunday! Luckily his jacket had been removed much earlier in the day and had lain safely by the bags with Hettie and Lily, along with his shoes and socks. He'd carefully rolled up his trouser legs so's they wouldn't get wet while he prowled among the rock pools, but, partly out of a sense of decency and partly out of haste, he had failed to remove them when he'd dived into the brine after Cathy. And now they were drying, creased and shrunken, so that his ankles, in their socks, stuck out beneath and his big feet were displayed to view like a clown's. Lily and Hettie walked at the back of the procession, Hettie excited by the drama of the day and Lily desperately trying to dissociate herself from the exhibition in front of her.

Cathy lay in bed for several days and so missed the arrival of the Captain, back in Shields after his last trip. He had brought Lily a salmon, a whole salmon, fresh from the sea! Lily had been overwhelmed. It was like a dream come true, and Hettie hurried down to Comical Corner to meet Joe on the ferry and give it to him for the smoking sheds. Lily wanted smoked salmon for the 'evening', and would he please hurry with it so that it was done in time. Obliging as ever, Joe took the salmon to a smoking shed on North Shields fish quay. He had friends there who'd do it for him free, and he'd get it back in time to bring to the Friday do.

Cathy had her feet up, being mollycoddled by her mother and her aunt, when Joe came his usual way, via the back door, into the kitchen. He took off his cap as he entered the room and bowed slightly at the ladies present. Lily's eyes fell at once onto the brown paper parcel in his hands. Her hands went out to grab it even before it was offered.

'Is that my smoked salmon?' she asked greedily.

'Aye.' And Joe let her have it. She tore at the paper, throwing it aside in her haste.

'Eeh, Joe, it's good of you to have gone to so much . . .' But her voice failed her as she stared at the fish. Her forehead puckered and she bent to smell the flesh. 'By, d'ye not think it's a funny colour, Mr Robson?' she asked.

Joe shrugged his shoulders.

'What d'ye mean, Mrs Straker?'

'D'ye not think it's a bit, kind of . . . well . . . yellow?'

Joe looked relieved.

'Oh that's nowt, man. It's just the iodine.'

'Iodine?'

'Aye. That's reet. Ye kna they paint the herrin' with it, when they turn them into kippers like?'

'Kippers?' Lily asked, unbelieving. There was a pregnant pause. Cathy couldn't help smiling, and Hettie raised her hand to her mouth in fear. Then the torrent broke upon them. 'Do you mean to tell me, do you really mean to tell me, Joe Robson, that they've gone an' painted my good salmon with iodine!'

Cathy burst out laughing then, choking, she held it back, going red in the face, till Hettie had to bang her hard on the back.

'It's still the sea water,' Hettie explained to Lily's white, angry face.

'I don't see anything to laugh about!' And then Lily turned back to the astonished Joe. 'Do you mean to tell me that they've treated my good salmon like it was a kipper?'

Joe stared back bemused, simply not knowing what all the fuss was about. And Hettie stopped bashing Cathy's back long enough to say, 'What do you think they smoke at North Shields sheds, Lily?'

Lily's mouth dropped open. As usual she was thwarted. Whatever she wanted she got thwarted. She wasn't even allowed to let off steam. How could she? The damned man had saved her daughter's life! Throwing the ruined salmon onto the table, she rushed upstairs to her room.

Nobody wanted Joe that night, but he stayed on anyway. It seemed he couldn't tear himself away from Cathy's side. Having saved her, he felt he had to continue to protect her, and she was embarrassed by his presence, knowing very well the Captain wouldn't come near while he was there, hogging her company. His ears were burning from the talk, too. In the opposite corner Hettie and Lily rowed under their breaths and his name could be heard clearly spat out from amongst the whispers from time to time. He knew he looked daft. His trouser bottoms were half way up to his knees, but it was his only suit, and he wasn't ashamed of how it got that way. Hettie, as usual, sprang to his defence.

'Would you rather he'd stood there watchin' her drown while he took his trousers off, Lily, eh?'

Unable to answer that one, Lily contented herself with a general protest.

'He's ruinin' the whole ambience of me evenin'!'

'Lily, they shrunk in the course of true love!'

'Ye great soft jelly! Look at him! It doesn't give him the right to stand over my lass as if he owned her!'

The two women gave Joe sidelong looks and he shifted uncomfortably.

'And that salmon,' Lily went on, 'I'll never forgive him for that. I could cry.'

'It's only a fish, Lily.'

'Only a fish!' And she watched with shame as Captain Christiansen frowned and peaked inside the bread to inspect the salmon. 'Eeh, his lovely salmon. He'll think I know no better!' But the Captain merely smiled and laid the offending sandwich aside before approaching the ladies. Cathy watched him, Joe still glued to her side. He was asking after her. She knew by the way he kept glancing back at her. And he looked at Joe too, his eyes dropping to the level of his knees and trying not to smile. And then he came towards her after all. He bowed slightly to Joe, who nodded his head in return.

'So this is the hero of the hour,' he commented, smiling at Joe.

'Yes. We owe Joe many thanks,' Cathy said graciously.

'Oh, any time!' he volunteered.

The Captain's eyebrows rose and fell again.

'I only wish it could have been I who saved you, Catherine,' he said quietly. Cathy smiled at him. 'And the hero is also to be a soldier.'

The Captain's look challenged Joe, though Joe was at a loss to know what he had to challenge him about!

'Aye,' he replied. 'I'm off tomorrow.'

'So, poor Miss Straker will be losing her gallant rescuer. Such a pity! Well, we must cheer her up!' Cathy looked at him expectantly, no idea what he might have in mind. And then he whispered, 'Do you remember that mermaid I told you about?' Cathy nodded, round-eyed. 'Well, I shall take you to see it. Yes I shall! My first mate this trip is Gustav Meyer who owns the little creature.' Cathy gasped. 'I have already asked your Mama, and she has said it will be fine for you to come and see round the whole ship. Perhaps on Sunday?'

'Oh yes, please!' Cathy smiled eagerly. 'I've been dyin' to have a good look round a ship and Gilbert wouldn't let me. He says it's no place for . . .'

Her face fell and she looked aghast at the Captain.

'It's all right. It'll be a Sunday,' he said and Cathy nodded.

Poor Joe could only stand and stare, a good deal of his attention caught up, anyway, in the region of his crotch, where the shrunken trousers strangled his manhood most unmercifully. And then Hettie added to his embarrassment by striking up 'Goodbyee' on the piano in honour of his leaving them the following day. He'd begged her not to let on to anybody, but they all seemed to know, and he had to suffer countless handshakes before he left that evening.

Next day Hettie went alone to join the crowds in Ocean Road as the troops marched along it for embarkation. When she saw Joe she jumped up and down, waving and shouting, and it heartened him to hear her, though he never actually caught a glimpse of her, and any one of a number of waving hankies might have been hers. He wondered if Cathy had come along with her, or whether she thought of him at all, as he marched along in his khaki, feeling anything but glorious, in step with the blaring music of the band.

CHAPTER FIFTEEN

Sunday dawned bright and cheerful. Cathy put on her Sunday best, a white flounced dress with a big hat, to be escorted by the Captain over his ship. She was as excited as a schoolgirl over the outing and felt proud as she leaned on the Captain's arm from the cab to the quayside, where the ship was in dock. The *Odin* it was called. It was named after a god, a god from the old days when the Norsemen roamed the world in their boats, pillaging and worse, so he told her. They'd come to Tyneside too, and left their mark on some of the community, families alive even today bearing the old Norse names, anglicised a little through the years.

It was a big ship, much bigger than Cathy had expected. She was quite overawed by it, and the seamen on board all saluted the Captain as he boarded it with a lady on his arm. What matter if one of them winked when he thought she wasn't looking? She would pretend she hadn't seen, and walk on regardless. The boat rocked gently in its harbour, and she had to feel her way along the wooden boards. New smells assailed her nostrils. There was tar, but fresher than the smell she was used to, and oil, though not as fetid as the ferry. There was a lingering trace, too, of foreign tobacco, and creakings, dull thuds from down below, and the talk all in Norwegian, which was strange to her. Her father must have sailed on just such a ship. She loved the little doors with the portholes in them, and the aroma of strong coffee when they visited the galley. He took her everywhere, to the bridge, to the engine room, to the sailors' cabin with its hammocks, to the foot of the mast, to every nook and cranny of the ship. And Cathy loved it. She wished she could stow away, go to sleep hidden in the freight hole, to wake with the rolling waves beneath her and the crying gulls above. But still she hadn't seen what she most wanted to: the little mermaiden. The Captain looked quizzically at her, then laughed. Again he offered her his arm.

'Come along, Madam,' he said. 'There is one thing more, and then we shall have tea.'

He led the way to the private quarters, small cabins, and knocked on one of the doors before going inside.

'Come on in, Catherine. No one will bite you.' And Cathy crept over the step and into the dingy cabin, where the smoke of tobacco lay heavy in the air. Captain Christiansen spoke first in Norwegian and then in English.

'Miss Straker, may I introduce Mr Meyer, our first mate.'

Cathy held out her hand, but the older seaman merely nodded gruffly at her.

'You wish to see my merman, do you?'

Cathy nodded, politely refraining from commenting on the sex of the creature. It would surely be a mermaid! The first mate eased himself off his bunk and pulled a box out from underneath. The Captain smiled encouragingly at her as the seaman slowly opened it up. Cathy frowned. It was small, no bigger than a tool kit or the size of a doctor's bag! How could he possibly get a mermaid in there? And then she thought perhaps it was a child still, and so she waited patiently. Carefully, he took hold of a handle and pulled out a glass case. Cathy felt a shiver of revulsion pass through her as he set it down on his table.

It was no more than eighteen inches long. It had a fish's tail, and its body, the human part, if such it could be called, was hard and leathery. The wizened face was bearded; where there should have been arms were gills, and there on its chest, quite unmistakably, were two distinct breasts.

'Would I open it for her?' he asked Cathy in his bad English. Already he was taking off the lid. The overpowering whiff of formaldehyde almost knocked her out. Cathy shook her head violently, and put her hand to her mouth before scurrying out of the cabin to be sick.

Her legs were shaking. She felt faint. The two men came out after her and watched her as she retched over the side of the ship. When she had finished, Captain Christiansen took her arm.

'Perhaps some tea would restore you. After all, you have not been well . . . the shock of the accident. We will go to my cabin and there you can lie down for a while.'

The first mate shouted something at him. The Captain seemed annoyed and shouted back, but the older man glared after them as the Captain slowly walked his charge along the ship towards his own private cabin. His boy was close at hand, a Scottish lad he'd taken on at Aberdeen when the last one walked off.

'Bring us some tea, lad,' the Captain shouted as he pushed the door open for Cathy to enter. 'In half an hour or so. Use your discretion, eh?'

And the lad laughed, running off to the galley as Cathy sank back onto the narrow bunk.

She felt so terrible. Her head swam. Was it the formaldehyde? Or just the sight of that hideous little thing they called a mermaid. She shivered involuntarily at the memory of it. And the Captain sat in a chair close by, taking her hands to warm them in his.

'I'm sorry,' she whispered. 'You . . . he . . . must think I'm very rude. It was just . . .'

'Sh. Sh. Close your eyes now.' And she felt the cool touch of his fingers on her eyelids as she closed them, soothing, calming. 'Come now. Let me make you more comfortable,' he said.

Her eyes opened again as he fiddled with the buttons at the top of her blouse, and her hand rushed up to stop him.

'No. You need more air . . . let me loosen it just a little.'

So she let him and sank back again, her breathing easier as her throat was freed. She was so dizzy. How her head swam! He stroked her brow, her head, loosening her hair, and his face seemed very close. Again her eyes opened, and he closed them with his cool fingertips.

'It's all right. Trust yourself to me. Trust me,' he said. And his hand soothed her neck, slipped behind and caught the nape. Alarmed, she tried to sit up, and found his arms round her holding her there on the bunk. Weakly, she leaned against him. She liked the strong feel of his arms about her. She shouldn't allow him to hold her so, she knew she shouldn't, but she felt so ill, and then, oh, as his hand searched again for that place at the nape of her neck she groaned.

Immediately, he pressed his lips on her, kissing her again and again, on the throat, the face, his hands wrestling with the buttons of her blouse. And Cathy began to struggle.

'No. No. Please. Stop it. Please!' And he seemed to let her go, but only to push his hand against her belly and throw her back against the bunk. He was speaking to her, all the time, small soothing phrases in Norwegian, '*Lille elskling . . . Jegelsker deg sa . . . kam til med na . . .*'

His hands were everywhere. She couldn't believe there were only two of them, he seemed to have grown some more since they first boarded the ship. She could have fought harder. She wanted him to kiss her. He stirred her feelings, and she knew her resistance was but a token affair. She felt her body answering his desire, answering the movements of his hands and lips, though when suddenly he lunged his hand beneath her skirts she gasped, and made to shout out loud for help. And then he moved her body as though it were a sack, to make himself more comfortable, before the shock, the terrible hurting brutish thing that he was doing to her. She cried out, and tried to push him off, but he held her hands fast. And the waves under the anchored ship rolled him further into her, and he pressed down hard on her, making such noises, like a pig. '*La osselske hverande. Kom!*' But it had nothing to do with her; any of it. It was happening to her and yet not to her. She lay lifeless beneath him. '*Kom! Ga med meg . . . Cathy! Ga! Slik . . . Kom jente . . . Ligg ikke bare der . . . Ga med det . . . Kom . . . Kom . . .*' Cold as marble, Cathy remembered, 'Then his soul would flow into thine, and thou wouldst become partaker of human bliss.' But this was not his soul that was flowing into her, it was something wet and sticky, and as he slumped against her she smelt again the smell of the formaldehyde and was sick all over him.

Cathy could hardly walk as she left the cabin. Her legs splayed out without control and trembled badly. All the strength seemed to have gone out of her, and if she felt dizzy before, she felt much worse now. The gallant Captain took her arm and supported her past the glowering eyes of the first mate and the amused glances of the other sailors. He had changed his own clothes in the cabin, but hers were creased, and matted with sick which she'd been unable to remove.

There was little sympathy for her at home. She had gone out too soon after the nasty incident at Trow Rocks and had come over badly. Cathy did not enlighten them. She felt too weak, too hopeless, and she knew that she had only herself to blame. Or so she thought. The weight of guilt was enough to keep her silent on its own, but the nausea, the feeling of defilement and filth made her simply want to hide away. The Captain was kind. He carried her up to her room and laid her on her bed, but Cathy refused to allow her mother to undress her. And so Lily left her to it, apologising all the way downstairs to the Captain for his spoiled jacket and shirt, and the great inconvenience her daughter had been to him.

She longed for a wash. After a long sleep, when the daylight vanished, leaving her cold on top of her bed, Cathy rose and looked in her basin. The bowl was filled with cold water. Slowly, feeling bruised and stiff, she removed the dress at last and dropped it to the floor. She wished she could burn it, and the petticoats, and the underpants, and her stockings too. There were weals on her body where the whalebone from her stays had dug into her under the onslaught. Strange how she hadn't noticed it at the time. Everything she wore lay on the floor at her feet and, shivering, Cathy began to wash.

She felt better, cleaner afterwards, at least outside. But inside . . . how she wished she could flush her insides out. Suddenly another wave of nausea overcame her and she was sick again, into the dirty water in the bowl. Downstairs she could hear someone playing the piano. She giggled, a painful convulsive giggle, which contained sobs. Was it always like that? Was that why her mother had seemed happier when her father was away than when he was home? Was that . . . ? Cathy remembered a darkened room, a wing chair, a present on a table and her father pressing her mother for something that he wanted so badly. And then she'd given in to him, 'just this once', and they'd gone up to bed where not even Hettie would disturb them, and she, their child, was forgotten. Cathy had known about sex, and yet not known. It was a fact wrapped up in fairy tales, and now that it had happened to her she could not equate the two. Perhaps with Gilbert . . . Cathy picked up her hairbrush and yanked it through her curls. Gilbert? How could she think of him? Would he know? Could she ever tell him? She stared at herself in her mirror, pale in the darkness, and she knew that she could not. She could never tell Gilbert about this. Perhaps he would blame her, too, if he knew. He had seen how she desired the Captain. He would blame her for what had happened. He would lose all respect for her. It would hurt him terribly. And, after all his own forebearance, to be landed with soiled goods? Standing naked before her mirror, Cathy's hands moved to cover her private parts. Like Eve before her, she had eaten of the apple and she was ashamed.

There was a knock on her door. Alarmed, Cathy reached for her wrapper.

'It's only me!' Hettie's voice reached out to her through the door, wanting her to hear but not disturb her if she still slept. A sob burst through Cathy's gullet.

'Oh Hettie! Hettie, come in, come in.'

Hettie opened the door and came in quickly, an anxious look on her face.

'What are you doing up? You'll catch your death!' But Cathy was crying, sobbing, incoherent. 'I'll fetch your Mam!'

'No! No! Not her!' the girl pleaded. So Hettie put down the cup of foaming chocolate on the chest of drawers and hurried her niece into a nightdress before bundling her into bed and holding her still in her arms. 'What's the matter, my little mermaid, eh? What's the matter?'

'I'm not a mermaid, Auntie Hettie. I'm not.' She cried like a child.

'There now. What is it, pet? You can tell me!'

Cathy hiccuped.

'I can't. I can't tell anybody. It's all me own fault anyway.'

Hettie frowned and sighed, then got up to fetch the steaming chocolate.

'Here. Get this down you. It'll warm you and mebbe bein' sweet you'll keep it down.'

Cathy took the cup and drank obediently while Hettie hurried downstairs to fetch up a hot bottle for her feet. She slurped up the foaming bubbles on her tongue as she had done when a child, feeling small and longing to hear the old fairy stories again. Only there weren't any fairy tales any more. Torn between an old need and a new knowledge, Cathy felt marooned in a kind of no-man's-land between childhood and the sudden reality of the adult world.

Hettie was as quick as she could with the bottle, and she hurried into Cathy's attic room, without knocking, to slip the stone warmer down into the bed for Cathy's feet. It was scalding to the touch, so Hettie drew it out again to wrap it in a towel before Cathy could tolerate it and warm herself. Her teeth chattered, and she felt an overwhelming sense of loneliness. Shyly, she looked at her worried aunt.

'Hettie, will you come in beside's for a minute?' she asked.

Hettie said nothing, but removed her boots and her skirt to slide in under the bedclothes and put her arms round the girl. Together they lay there for some time, till Cathy fell asleep again, and Hettie eased herself away to go to her own room and lie awake wondering about Cathy.

As she lay, thinking, it all slipped gradually into place, and a horrible suspicion came into her mind. Hettie sat bolt upright on her bed and stared at her reflection in the mirror. Surely, it couldn't be? Lily said he was a gentleman. And Lily knew about these things far better than her, a woman who'd slipped up so badly. She relied on Lily's judgment. Maybe too much, she thought. Lily was inclined to see only what she wanted. She had no real experience of men, whereas she . . . Oh yes, Hettie had had only too much! Her mind raced through the history of Cathy's relationship with the Captain. She had been on the verge of an engagement with Gilbert when he came to them, and the engagement had been postponed. Gilbert looked unhappy, stayed away from them, until the Captain went home for Christmas. He had always liked Cathy. They all knew that. And Lily had entrusted her daughter to him. But surely Cathy loved Gilbert? A confusion of ideas swept through Hettie's mind. It all hung on the character of Captain Christiansen. They knew so little about him, when it came down to it. He behaved like a gentleman, a cut above the usual seamen. He spoke of his family at home. He played and sang like a professional. But what did they actually know about him? Hettie's mind raced back. It had been Lily who'd taken him in. Yes, when Hettie had been rushing out to meet Johnny Beale! She had imagined Lily would ask all the usual precautionary questions before admitting him into the house, to check on his respectability, a job Hettie usually did, being as it was her house. But had Lily? Hettie was daft, she knew that. A man'd pulled the wool over *her* eyes, but surely Lily would never fall for a bit of flannel? Would she? Who was this Captain Christiansen? She'd offered once to read his palm for him, when he was worried about the weather a few months back, and he'd had a long trip ahead. He'd refused her point-blank. Why? Why? Unless . . . a man's hand flashed before her memory. It had long fine fingers, unusual in a seaman. She had commented on those fingers at the time, for they were the hands of a philosopher or a musician. Yes, and they were curved, misshapen, and the palm was hot, she remembered that, and there were many lines issuing from his Line of Heart and it was weak, whereas the line above it was strongly marked. She could see it clearly now. How had she not connected it before? Too wrapped up in her own affairs! It must have been him. It must have been Captain Christiansen! How could she have been so blind? But surely he would not . . . ? Surely not? Hettie's reflection stared back at her from the mirror, ghastly in the light from the moonlit window. She had to find out. She had to know. There was no time to spare. She got up from the bed and dashed upstairs to Cathy's room.

Cathy was sleeping. She didn't stir as the doorknob softly turned and Hettie came into her room. The girl's clothes were littered about the floor. Quietly, Hettie bent down and picked them up one by one. They smelt of sick, and something else, a strange smell, not unlike bleach or . . . yes, a man's semen. It had to be. She took the pants to the window and through a slit in the curtain looked at them by the light of the moon. They were stained. Quickly, Hettie took the clothes out of the room, closing the door behind her, and padded softly along the corridor and down the stairs to the Captain's room. She listened at the door. There was no sound. She tried the knob and the door opened. The curtains were not drawn and the room was light enough to see that there was no one in the bed. Where was he? She checked the drawers in the chest, and looked for his bag. He had gone. But surely he wasn't due to leave till the following night? Hettie's heart beat fast as she went down to the scullery and washed out the girl's clothes and waited till the hour was half way decent to venture out onto the streets.

It was still dark when Hettie threw a shawl over her head and softly closed the front door of 15 Thrift Street behind her. It was too early for the trams, so she walked quickly, past the shadows at the corners of the streets, lurking in shop doorways, and giving a wide berth to seamen, still drunk from the night before, lurching their way back to the quay. But no one bothered much about her, too intent on her purpose and under the camouflage of the workwoman's shawl. There were a few ships in dock. Hettie searched for the names written on the sides. And, at last, she found it, the *Odin*, gently rocking in harbour after all. At once Hettie felt relief and an increase of her anxiety. For now she had to face him, on her own, and her heart quailed at the thought. She wished she had Joe with her to back her up. It needed a man, did this. If only Henry had still been alive! But then, if he had been, none of this would likely have happened! The gangplank was up and no one was stirring, still soporific from last night's booze. Hettie called up, and her voice sounded shrill in the early silence of the morning. She called again, and a man, half undressed and hardly decent, looked down at her from the deck.

'You're too late, Missus!' he shouted down at her. 'We're

none of us capable!' And then he belched and turned away laughing.

'I must see Captain Christiansen,' she shouted back. 'Tell him it's Hettie Straker.'

The man hesitated, muttered something incomprehensible and then went away. Hettie doubted very much that he was going to do anything about her at all. So, after a while, she shouted up again. The first mate looked over the rail at her this time, and again Hettie shouted that she had to see the Captain. The seaman gave her a long hard look, then traipsed off and Hettie heard some banging going on somewhere on the ship. There were raised voices. The Captain was angry and Hettie felt very alone and weak. This was hardly a good start to their meeting. Then, finally, Captain Christiansen looked over at her.

'Who is it?' he called.

'Hettie Straker. I've got to speak with you, Captain Christiansen!'

'What about?'

'Do you want me to shout it from the rooftops?' Hettie shouted back.

Cursing her, the Captain let down the gangplank, and Hettie walked nervously aboard.

He denied everything, of course. Would he do such a thing? A married man? He had children back home, and he had too much respect for Miss Straker to harm her in any way. His answers were so easy that he had Hettie close to believing that the whole thing was all her own imagination, that the stained underpants were nothing more than the girl's monthlies coming on, that she was being, in short, a fool. But he was too easy, and Hettie knew it. She'd heard Johnny Beale charming the birds off the trees, and the whole thing sounded all too familiar. But even if she was right, what could Hettie do? And what would be the point? The man had a wife, or so he said. She challenged him on that point and he produced a family portrait from one of the drawers in his locker. He seemed amused at her discomposure, and when finally accused of doing a moonlight flit, the Captain laughed outright and said, 'But I settled up with

Mrs Straker herself, yesterday afternoon, when you were upstairs tending to poor Miss Straker. Ask her, if you don't believe me?'

Feeling defeated and foolish, Hettie left the jetty and caught the tram home to Thrift Street. She had not wanted to leave it at that, to let the man get off scot-free, and yet she'd had no choice. What else could she do? Lily was getting the breakfasts on her own when Hettie wearily walked into the kitchen.

'And where d'ye think you've been, Hettie Straker?' she demanded angrily.

Hettie said nothing, but set about putting on her pinny to help.

'Wer Cathy ill in bed and you walkin' out an leavin' me to it! You're crackers! Where've you been, at this time of the day!'

'A walk.'

'Eeh! You're simple. You are, honest. Simple!'

'Captain Christiansen's gone, Lily. Did you know?'

'Aha. He came in and settled up yesterday when you were up with wer Cathy. Why?'

'Nothin'.'

Lily spat a few more words at her, and then the subject was dropped.

Later, when the seamen had all been fed and watered, Hettie went up to Cathy's room with a mug of tea. The lass was sleeping soundly, her head buried deep under the blankets, only the bright hair showing on the pillow. It seemed a pity to wake her. Hettie watched her for a minute, then sadly touched the bright head gently, and whispered, 'Rise and shine.' Cathy stirred, stretched, and then, even before opening her eyes, she remembered, and frowned.

'I've brought you a cup of tea, pet,' Hettie said gently. 'And then I want you to talk to's.'

It was a relief to tell someone. Over the shock, Cathy felt low and despairing. She seemed to hope the Captain loved her on the one hand, and on the other, she feared Gilbert would know, would find her out on their wedding night, and no, she couldn't bear to tell him. He was so good, so kind, and she had hurt him too much already. Hettie cheered her up as best she could and, sworn to secrecy, she promised Cathy she wouldn't tell her mother. There was little point in telling her. The deed was done, and Lily would go mad; everybody'd hear her shouting at the lass and put two and two together, and she'd go on and on world without end, for the rest of Cathy's life. Hettie had stood enough of that from her sister-in-law herself not to wish it on her niece now. No, they must just hope for the best and, in time, Cathy would get over it.

But Cathy did not want to get over it. She loved the Captain. Didn't Hettie understand. Hettie soothed her gently.

'Yes, pet,' she said. 'I loved somebody once.'

Cathy looked up at her plain, miserable-looking auntie.

'I did,' Hettie insisted. 'I thought he was marvellous. Your Mam didn't understand, of course. Neither did your Dad, come to that. They thought . . . well . . . that women don't feel the same way as men do.'

Cathy looked away in embarrassment.

'What happened to him?' she asked quietly.

'Nothin'. He went away. That's all. Just like him.'

Cathy looked at her again, sharply.

'What do you mean, "like him"?'

'He's packed up and left, pet.'

Cathy suddenly tried to get out of her bed but Hettie held her there fast.

'No. It's no good followin' him. You've got to forget him, Cathy. Believe me, it's no good lookin' back, because he'll only have you for a sucker a second time!'

Cathy was beside herself, thumping Hettie, crying and shouting, 'But he loves me. He loves me. I know he does!'

Hettie bore the attack patiently, then calmed her down.

'Maybe he did, pet. In his way. It just depends what you call love, that's all.'

'But he'll come back, Hettie. He'll come back.'

Hettie sighed. 'Eeh pet. I wouldn't bank on it. That's all.'

Stroking the girl's head, Hettie rocked her gently in her bed.

'They showed me a mermaid. Horrible it was, dead, preserved in formaldehyde in a glass case, Hettie!' And then Cathy wept and wept, and Hettie said not a word but bore with her till the crying finally stopped.

Lily never knew a thing about it, and when the month had passed and the Captain didn't return to claim his room, she let it to another seaman, muttering about the lack of consideration, not even letting her know, when they could have had a boarder all this time. And Hettie quietly watched and waited for a sign of Cathy's monthlies. Finally, it was Lily herself who mentioned that.

'She's not come on this time,' she said in a confidential whisper. 'It must be the shock of that drownin's upset her.'

And Hettie had nodded in a knowing way and kept her thoughts to herself. After all, it might be true, and Hettie had other things on her mind. There was a war going on. Cathy had heard from Gilbert three times since he'd gone away, jolly letters, telling her not to worry, which had had the effect of making Cathy burst into tears. Lily interpreted this display of emotion as 'missing the lad'. And it was true, Cathy missed Gilbert now more than she ever had before, desperately wanting him there to lean on and cheer her up. He complained that she'd written only once, and she was forced to sit down and write about the events at Thrift Street, or at least those events which she felt she could write about. But Hettie had not heard from Joe. Gilbert was an officer, but Joe was only a private, and he'd been sent straight to the front line after his training period. She supposed he didn't have time to write, and anyway, unlike Gilbert, Joe was hardly in the habit of writing letters.

The Western Front followed the defence of the Channel ports and, early in October, Joe Robson found himself part of the British advance at Armentières. He met up with Alec in Dieppe; part of the 19th Infantry, waiting to be brought up to the front line.

'What're ye doin' here, Geordie?' Alec demanded when he first saw Joe.

'We're a crew, aren't we?' Joe asked.

'Aye, but we don't all go to sea,' Alec returned.
'Thought you were spoiling for a fight?'
'Ach, this is no fightin'!' Alec snapped. 'Have ye heard them talk?' He nodded over in the direction of a group of men going home on leave. 'Ye can't get to grips with the enemy. They're over on the other side of no-man's-land. It's inhuman, lad. That's what it is. You can see the whites of their eyes when the moon shines on them and that's about all.'
'Have ye heard anythin' o' Jim?' Joe asked.
'He's gone. "Wipers". He'll be seeing action now.'
Joe looked across the fields in the direction of Ypres. He could see smoke, a mist, like the early fog over the North Sea.
'Funny,' he said, 'Jim was the one that wanted to stay on land.'
'Eh?' Alec looked at him as though he'd gone daft.
'Nothin'. Here . . . Hettie sent me some cake. Do you want a bit?'
Alec took a piece and savoured it thoughtfully.
'What happened to your pacifist principles, Joe?'
'I never said I was a pacifist. I only said there wasn't any glory in killin' folk.'
'There's one thing, Joe, lad . . .'
'What's that?'
'You're in no danger of any glory here.'
'What d'ye mean?'
'You'll not be killin' anybody.'
'Don't be daft, man.'
'You got ammo for that gun there?'
'Not yet. No. Why?'
'Ye canna kill anybody without ammo.'
'But I'll be gettin' some . . .'
'We hope.'
Joe looked over towards that haze on the horizon.
'What about Jim?'
'Their ammo's rationed. One round an hour. That's all he'll get.'
The wind blew chill. Joe shivered, and stared at the bleak faces of the men going home to Blighty.
'What the hell are we doin' here, man?'

'Playin' lotto as a matter of fact. Fancy a game?'

Joe spent most of his off duty time reading by the light of a candle. Bede's *History of the English Church and People* was his current favourite. The monk from the Jarrow monastery reminded him of Tyneside and taught him about his roots in the north. If ever he got back there he'd look at the place with new eyes. The other lads wrote letters home, read and re-read the pages sent to them by loved ones. That was the favourite pastime. Every day at five thirty reveille sounded, and every day they asked themselves if this was the day they'd be sent to the front. Alec, in an earlier draft, went first. Joe thought he'd have at least a couple of weeks longer to wait, but only two days later he was sent for, with the rest, for a medical. Some failed and were kept back at base. They were the envied ones. Joe did not fail. His whole draft was in a state of tension. None of them had had experience of warfare. No one had seen action in Flanders. Each tried, at first, to cover his fear with bravado, jokes, high spirits. But as the day wore on and they were kept busy going backwards and forwards to the Quartermaster's stores, spirits flagged and silence descended. Each man was wrapped in his own thoughts, the dread in his mind growing heavier in relation to the growing weight of the pack on his back.

Fear and exhaustion heightened sensation. After days in cattle trucks, on crowded trains, on the march, Joe's draft finally approached its regiment. It was dusk, the no-man's-land of time, when neither night nor day predominates, when objects seem to disappear into the greyness and men are inclined to believe in apparitions. The sky ahead flickered with bright lights. A firework display to welcome them to the front line. They stumbled across rough ground and at last they arrived at the unit. Tethered horses shifted restlessly, and here and there amongst the tents was the welcome sight of a camp fire. There was no one to welcome them. Nowhere for them to sleep. They walked about all night or huddled under greatcoats, trying to keep warm. Joe wondered where Alec was. Asleep in the warm, no doubt! And then came the dawn. Joe's stomach hurt with hunger.

With the others, he made his way to the field kitchen. But no rations had come for the new draft. They were forced, instead, to scrounge for hard biscuits.

'Not a patch on the mission, eh, Joe?'

Joe whirled round and found himself face to face with Alec MacGowan. The two men embraced and were embarrassed to find tears in each other's eyes.

'Have ye seen owt of Jim Webster?' Joe asked him.

'Only went an' blew off the top of his finger!'

'Eeh, poor old Jim!'

'Poor? What's poor about it? He was at Passchendaele, son. The rest of his mates had their bloody *heads* blown off! He always was a jammy bugger!'

It was a joke. Amongst all the carnage, it was a relief to know a man could be saved by something so ridiculous.

All around them was devastation. Craters, greenish yellow from the explosion that caused them, groups of wooden crosses, broken lines of wire, blasted trees, all bore witness to the previous bombardment. Bombs, unexploded mines, lay in wait for the unwary in one line of broken trenches. The stench of the rotting German bodies rose sickeningly from a mine shaft which had once been behind enemy lines. The noise of the artillery juddered the ground, cracked in their ears. But at night, bivouacked together, Alec sang the sea shanties while the guns were quiet:

'Who'll buy caller herrin'?
They're bonnie fish an' halesome farin';
Buy my caller herrin',
New drawn frae the Forth.

Alec's voice, soaring out of the darkness from the circle of a candle's light, had the tang of the salt air in it and Joe's heart ached for the freedom of the seas as he stared out across the barbed wire.

Cathy continued working at Miss Hutchinson's, though she missed Mabel. Miss Hutchinson had been ill again. The pain in her side returned, and her temper flared frequently. Mabel had grown increasingly fed up with complaints about her work and felt overworked and underpaid in any case. The war had given rise to all kinds of other jobs, and if it was less ladylike to work on munitions, still, it was far better paid. And so she left her old employer, and left Cathy feeling more and more friendless and alone.

Cathy's birthday seemed a turning point in an avalanche of bad fortunes. She had wakened in the night with a violent pain and had been sick. It was the best birthday present she could have wished for. She knocked lightly on Hettie's door, and the pair of them cried on each other's shoulders. They'd been kept in suspense for the best part of two months, and finally Cathy had been reprieved. It was three in the morning, but the two women went down to the scullery and celebrated with hot cocoa and a drop of brandy from Hettie's medicine chest. It was cosy and warm, like an oasis of security in a desert of trouble. The stove was still warm from the night before, and Hettie poked it back into life for the kettle. Apart from the cocoa, Cathy needed a hot bottle. Her pain was dreadful. She leaned against the oven for relief, and the waves of pain and nausea made her faint. But she didn't mind. It was a familiar pain, and welcome. She began to make plans again, and those plans would surely include Gilbert after all. She must and would put the Captain out of her mind. Everything seemed more hopeful, more possible that morning, and feeling grey and sick Cathy went off to work believing in God's great goodness as never before.

Miss Hutchinson had baked a cake for her, and she and Ethel sang 'Happy Birthday to you'. There was a present too, a new hat, made by her employer's 'own fair hands' as she put it. It was navy, her favourite shape, like a man's trilby but softer and flatter on the crown. She pulled it sideways on her head so that the matching ostrich feather swept dashingly across the side. Ethel's head tilted as she smiled her admiration, and Miss Hutchinson looked pleased as punch. Cathy took it off and went to kiss her on the cheek.

'Thanks, Miss Hutchinson. It's the nicest birthday present

I ever had.' Sent home early because of her continuing pain, Cathy was greeted by a large basket of flowers. Somehow, Gilbert had got someone to order them for her and include his message. 'I love you. See you Christmas. Gilbert.' Cathy went to bed early, a smile on her lips, worn out with her pain but full of plans for Christmas and Gilbert's homecoming. And then, the next day, Hettie received a card from Joe. It was a printed card, with a choice of sentences. 'I am quite well. I have been admitted into hospital/am sick/wounded, and am going on well/and hope to be discharged soon. I have received your letter/telegram/parcel, dated . . . Letter follows at first opportunity/I have received no letter from you/lately/for a long time.' There were instructions that the soldier sending such a card was to write only his name and the date of sending, and a warning that anything else added to the printed choice would be erased. It made Hettie's spine shiver. He'd tackled the card with a pencil, and Hettie gathered that he was quite well, had received her letter and that a letter from him was following at the first opportunity. Well, it didn't exactly give a lot away but it was a blessed relief all the same. Hettie was forced to remove her glasses and wipe the tears from her eyes after she'd deciphered it.

The advance from Ypres had been accomplished. In the dark days of October, Joe and Alec marched on to La Bassée. The battle for Armentières had begun. Tiredness blunted fear. Long periods of waiting were interspersed with short bursts of frenzied activity. Menial tasks, digging trenches, filling in potholes, were welcomed because they were jobs that could be understood. They had some relation to real life. Joe and Alec worked side by side, digging in. Their comradeship was an anchor in a shifting landscape. They talked as they worked, about the boat they'd be getting just as soon as the war came to an end. They wondered if a way could be found of getting a message back to Jimmy. Had he gone home to Blighty? Could he put his ear to the ground and pick up a bargain for them so there'd be no time wasted on their return? The excitement brought colour to their cheeks, animation to their voices. They didn't hear the whine as the shell approached.

'Run for cover!'

Joe ran, dropping his spade. Alec slithered in the mud and fell back into the hole. Joe slid to a halt, tore back, and fell as the shell came home. It was all over in a flash.

'Alec!' Joe reached up out of the mud looking for his friend. But he was dragged down by the searing agony in his shoulder and never saw the bloody remains of what had been Alec MacGowan spattered all round him. There was no glory. Only darkness.

'Breath is life. You control your breath, you can control your life and you can control your pain.' Alec's voice haunted the hours of waiting as Joe surfaced into consciousness. All around him were cries and moans. Nothing he could do about it. Better ignore it and concentrate his mind on his own agony. 'Breath is life.' Joe drew in a deep breath and held it for long seconds. Then, slowly, he let it out. Again he breathed and held the air in the pit of his lungs. His head began to feel light, the pain distanced itself from him. Yes. He would think about his breathing. In. Hold. Out. Pause. In. Hold. Out. Pause. He found he was not part of himself, but outside. He was looking down on Joe Robson as though he was a separate being, reviewing the body of another man.

'We'll have to have that arm off,' the surgeon told him.

Joe moved his fingers.

'No!' The force in his voice surprised them.

'It'll go gangrenous.' The doctor was tired, didn't want any trouble. It was easier to cut it off and have done with it.

'Stitch it up,' Joe insisted. And Alec's voice said, 'You can control your life.' The surgeon sighed. He was wasting his time. He knew it. The arm would never be any use, the wound would go septic, and the patient would die. He'd seen it all before.

'Go on!' Joe told him.

'On your head be it!' And Joe breathed deeply as the surgeon began to stitch. 'You can control your pain . . .' Alec whispered.

* * *

A few days after the postcard arrived at Thrift Street news of Joe's wounding came from the other side of the river. Even as Hettie had been sighing with relief at her card, Joe was already lying in that hospital bed, his shoulder blown out. Even Lily gasped in horror at the news. He had only just gone out there! How could it have happened? The papers said things weren't so bad, that British casualties were light! And if it could happen to Joe, it could also happen to Gilbert! That was the thought that really terrified Lily. Having sent him off with phrases about doing his bit, and 'we're proud of you, son', now she couldn't wait to get him safely home and the war over. For, if anything happened to Gilbert, then Cathy would never marry him and Lily would never get back to Westoe after all! She had nightmares for days following the news about Joe, and drove Cathy mad asking if she'd heard from Gilbert lately. Having at first mourned Joe's terrible wound, now she said he was lucky, and had probably got it on purpose in order to get a discharge. A suggestion which greatly distressed poor Hettie. Lily kept on, too, about Captain Christiansen. She wondered why he never came back to see them, and supposed he must be docking in Hull these days instead. 'He might've sent us a postcard,' she said.

Cathy was thinner. She was pale and drawn looking, and often sick. It was put down to shock, and pining for Gilbert. Even Hettie said it must be that. What else could it be? Besides, she was working too hard, for not only had Mabel left them, Ethel had given in her notice too, with the intention of going with the Red Cross to train to be a nurse. Miss Hutchinson took the news in brooding silence. She knew it would be hard to replace her. Mabel she might manage to replace, some girl who'd need training, but not Ethel. For Ethel had been a skivvy, and skivvies were very thin on the ground now that there was war work. Everyone complained about the lack of servants, even Mrs Stoddard in the village, who found she had to do the housework herself for the first time in her life.

It was the beginning of December. Cathy had not seen Mrs Stoddard since before Gilbert had gone away. She knew she wasn't welcome at the Westoe house, and yet Cathy felt she ought to have gone up to see his mother, for his sake. She was a widow now, and often ill, and what Miss Hutchinson had said about servants made her wonder how the 'old faggot' was getting on. There was a frost on the ground as Cathy closed the shop door behind her. She heard Miss Hutchinson shoot the bolts behind her, and Cathy turned to walk briskly towards the tram stop. She felt tired and queasy, but she had decided she'd go and see Gilbert's mother and go she would. Her mother wasn't expecting her home till late, and she'd ignored her duties to the old lady too long. As she waited in the queue, Cathy pulled the collar of her coat up high about her ears. It was fur, an old piece off a coat of her mother's from the 'good' days, rescued from the treasure chests in her bedroom. Perfume clung to the fur, and it still smelt of the oil she had used on her hair months before. The summer now seemed like a bad dream, like a part of someone else's life into which Cathy had strayed by accident for a while. But it was over now. She must try to re-establish relations with Mrs Stoddard. If she was going to marry Gilbert, and she was certain now that that was what she wanted most in the world, then she must show some willing. And this was the best way she could think of showing it.

So Cathy climbed into the steamy tram as it dragged its way along Ocean Road and then turned up the hill, past the new town hall, towards Westoe. It was a steep climb, but the tram ground on and on, while the passengers silently listened to the sound of its struggling. Then, at last, they were at the top and Cathy climbed out onto the sparkling pavement. The air was crisp and fresh. She'd felt so weary in the cab, but now she was outside again Cathy revived and enjoyed the walk round the corner and into the village street.

In her heart, Cathy loved the tree-lined avenue. Here there was room to move, air to breathe, and a rural beauty and peace which always made her feel content. She couldn't blame her mother for wanting to get back here. She had begun to see how hard it must have been for Lily to leave her old home, feeling cheated and humiliated, and descend the hill to the lowly quayside. And yet she had adapted, finally. Cathy half laughed to herself. They say you can get used to anything in time. God help Gilbert, she thought. She doubted if he'd ever get used to his trench. She shivered and made her way to the front of the house.

It seemed very dark in the house, and no one answered the bell. Cathy frowned, and made her way round to the back to see if there was any sign of life there. The conservatory door was swinging open. Cathy hurried up to it to shut it, knowing how the tropical plants inside needed the constant heat. Mr Stoddard would have raised the roof if he'd seen the door left open like that. Her hand was on the handle, ready to push it to, when she missed the warm draught of air that should have been coming from the glasshouse. Puzzled, she looked inside, and her heart sank. It was quite obvious that no one had been looking after it. There was still some green left in the hardy aspidistras, and a few green leaves among the ivies, but the African violets had disappeared, the bottom leaves of the Monstera, that had climbed so high up to the roof, were wizened and brown. She picked one off in her hand. It was like parchment, all the moisture gone out of it. The frost had attacked the Umbrella plants and the palms; and the orchids, Mr Stoddard's fine orchids, were withered on the bark. Cathy leaned over to touch them. One small bloom, pale cream, tinged with green, bravely struggled against all the odds to blossom on the dead bark. It was one of those which Mr Stoddard had wanted her to wear at her wedding. She could hear his voice now, 'In any relationship, there's always one who loves, and one who allows themselves to be loved.' How right he was. Well, now she had done the 'loving'. Though as Hettie had said, 'It depends what you call love.' She'd risen on the crest of her wave and crashed down again. But, thank God, she had not turned into foam, and her orchid still lived, just. She loved Gilbert. She was sure of that now. She had been so afraid when she'd heard about Joe. A terrible fear had gripped her stomach at the thought that she might lose Gilbert. And she knew then that she'd do anything for him, anything at all to make him happy. Yes, she smiled, perhaps even die for him. The tiny waxlike flower seemed to wither at her touch. The petals came apart in her hand and fell to the floor at her feet. Killed by the frost. Yes, she would do anything to make Gilbert happy, even visit his mother!

Cathy found Mrs Stoddard in the parlour, playing patience. She jumped when Cathy came into the room, searching for her.

'I pulled the bell,' she said, 'but no one answered.'

Mrs Stoddard shrugged.

'It's my housekeeper's night off and the scullerymaid's deaf. *I* never answer the bell.'

Cathy nodded understandingly.

'No. Of course not. May I sit down?'

'If you're staying.'

And so Cathy sat, and coughed to fill the ghastly silence.

'I suppose you've heard from Gilbert,' she said at last.

'Writes me every other day!' The mother's reply challenged the girlfriend to better it.

'I'm glad. He seems very well.'

'As well as can be expected,' Mrs Stoddard said, and pushed a printed card, one much like the kind Joe had sent Hettie, under the playing cards on her table.

'Mrs Stoddard,' Cathy said at last, 'I hope we can be friends.'

The woman stared at Cathy. There was something different about her. Her gaze was steady and direct, she sat upright in her chair, her back straight, and her face was still.

'I *am* going to marry your son, you know.'

Mrs Stoddard shuddered. All of a sudden, her body seemed to give, and she sobbed. Cathy jumped to her feet and touched her gently on her arm. But the woman shook her off, and reaching for her handkerchief wiped her eyes.

'I'm all right, dear,' she said. 'I'm quite all right. Don't worry about me.' But Cathy stayed close by, where she was. Mrs Stoddard had called her 'dear'. Was it possible? Was it really possible? 'All I want is for my Gilbert to come home safe . . .' And then she sobbed again, unable to continue speaking.

Cathy waited till she was composed, and then Mrs Stoddard spoke again.

'I saw a lad from the cricket club, last week, home on leave. Eeh he was a mess, pale as you like, and jabbering on. Scared to death of going back, he was. And he used to frighten the daylights out of everybody when he had a ball in his hand. They live in mud trenches, and people dyin' all round them, and it could be their turn any minute.'

Cathy looked at her in horror. Gilbert had said nothing about all this.

'It can't be so bad, surely?' she whispered.

'Oh, he doesn't write the truth . . . not what it's really like. He thinks to spare us, lass. But I keep dreamin' . . . I keep dreamin' they've got him and he's dead, and I'm left all on me own in this great house!' And then she sobbed again, trying desperately to keep control of herself. Cathy knelt at her feet and leaned her head against her hand. 'Eeh lass, I don't care if you marry him or not so long as he comes home safe!'

Cathy stroked the hand, twitching nervously on the knee, and then rose.

'I'll peep into the kitchen, shall I?' she said. 'Ask the scullery maid to fetch us some tea?'

'That'd be nice.'

As Cathy left the room, she heard the blast of Mrs Stoddard's nose against a lace handkerchief.

It was like a truce. Mrs Stoddard didn't like her or approve of her any more than she had done before. Cathy knew that well enough. But if God would give her back her son, safe and sound, then she'd make this sacrifice and tolerate his marriage to Catherine Straker. It took a war to bring about such a change of heart. But it had happened, and for that Cathy was grateful. Older and wiser now, Catherine Straker was not going to look any gift-horse in the mouth.

CHAPTER SIXTEEN

It was almost Christmas when Joe Robson crept back from the front. There was no fanfare of trumpets, no civic reception, nothing at all. Hettie was up in arms about it.

'The Corporation should've done *something*!' she said indignantly. But the truth was that no one at home really wanted to know about the first casualties of the war, limping back in dribs and drabs. They were still in the jingoistic euphoria of sending them off by the battalion and closed their ears to any rumours about the harsh realities the lads would have to face. The truth sank in only very slowly. Returning soldiers couldn't bear to speak of the horrors of the trenches, and their relatives would not have believed them if they had. So a great chasm grew up between the men away at the war and those they had left behind, a gap of bitter experiences, of nightmare visions and shattered illusions which was the real no-man's-land between the two sides, the soldiers and the relatives at home.

Joe would get his pension of course, a small stipend that would have to be supplemented somehow, and he would get his campaign medal, but that was all. Hettie was sure Joe would be given the V.C. But, and it seemed strange to her, he didn't seem to care whether he did or not. All he wanted was to settle down in peace and forget. He'd come back alive and that was something. There was a celebration tea at Thrift Street. 'The Sanctuary' was opened for the occasion, on Hettie's insistence, and Joe sat in the chair of honour while Hettie cut the cake, resplendent with a Union Jack in the centre of the white icing, like an Everest conquered. Hettie tried desperately hard to create a party atmosphere. She had bought Joe a present, a pair of fisherman's socks, wrapped up in gaudy paper, with South Shields' motto crayoned on the front. It was the commemorative gift that she felt ought to have come from the Corporation, and she had gone to great trouble to get the official crest and motto right. In the centre was a drawing of a lifeboat, the first one which was built in Shields by Wouldhave and Greathead, and under it was the Shields byword, 'Always Ready'. Joe looked at it for a long time before removing the wrapper, and then smoothed it out with his hand, intending to keep it. The socks were inspected amidst a collective silence, and he nodded appreciatively before kissing Hettie on the cheek. And the socks and wrapper were laid aside carefully till the party was over and he went home.

Hettie pulled her glasses away from her face and wiped her eyes with her hankie.

'I thought the socks might come in for when you get your boat,' she said quietly.

Joe nodded.

'Aye. They will, Hettie. Thank you. It's a nice thought.'

Lily sniffed and stared at the loose fabric over the shoulder.

'You'll not be goin' in for a fishin' boat now, though, surely?'

Joe's jaw stiffened.

'I will. I've saved for it, and when the war's over, I'll gan in for it.'

His left arm hung limply inside his jacket and Cathy could not help but look at it. Joe smiled at her reassuringly as he followed her gaze.

'Aye. It's all right. They wanted to cut it off, like. But I wouldn't let them. Aye, said it'd go gangrenous. It hasn't. I'm provin' them wrong, and I'm gettin' more use out of it every day.'

A soft smile played about Cathy's lips. It drew her to Joe, made him look at her as though for the first time. She was the same old Cathy, and yet not the same after all. She was pale, thin in the face, and there was a sadness about her eyes. Joe wondered what had happened to her to have caused this change. Cathy felt a deep compassion that took in Joe's suffering, his courage and his determination to make the best of what was left of his life. Whatever her own worries might be, nothing so terrible as Joe had suffered could ever happen to her. And he had come through it, a better man. It gave her hope, for perhaps she would do the same, through her own troubles, and learn not to care what the world thought, in the same way as Joe. She felt a fellowship with this man, and just as he was seeing her as though for the first time, Cathy was seeing Joe in the same fresh light.

For Cathy's troubles were not over after all. The pain and bleeding of the month before had been a false dawn of hope. And now she was sure that she was, after all, pregnant.

'Are you all right, Miss Straker?' Joe's voice was gentle, considerate. Cathy blushed to think that this man, who had been through so much, should concern himself over her. 'Only you're lookin' a bit peaky, like.'

'Oh I'm fine, Mr Robson, thanks,' she said gratefully.

'Aye. You'll be worried about Mr Stoddard, I daresay.'

'Yes I am.'

Lily glanced at her daughter.

'To tell the truth, Joe, Catherine's not been the same since that drownin' business.'

Joe nodded understandingly. Cathy wished they'd all stop looking at her. She folded her arms across her stomach and turned away from Hettie's searching gaze. Aye the lass *was* looking drawn. In the moment of their eyes meeting, Hettie also knew. Cathy was pregnant. The joy in Hettie's mouth turned suddenly to dust and ashes. At the moment of her relief at Joe's return came the realisation that Cathy's life was ruined. Fate had dealt them a cruel bit of irony. It had mocked them with false hopes, and now it was too late. Cathy was three months gone.

Lily couldn't understand it. Both Hettie and Cathy seemed to find so much to do that night. It was late, and she was tired.

'I'm droppin' on me feet,' she complained as Cathy pulled out some stockings to darn. 'They'll wait, won't they?'

'No, Mam. I need them for tomorrow. Me otherns've got a hole in the heel.'

'You go up to bed, Lily,' Hettie said kindly. 'I'll do the other one while she does that.' And Lily had been glad to be let go. She said goodnight and left them to it, a warm bed beckoning after a long day.

They waited till they heard her door close. Then Hettie spoke quietly.

'Have you come on?' Cathy shook her head silently. Hettie sighed. 'How do you feel?'

'A bit sick, nothing much now, not like it was at first.'

'You look tired.' Again Cathy nodded silently.

'When were you due?'

'Five days ago.'

'You're pregnant, pet.'

'I know.'

There was a long pause. Each of them applied themselves to darning a stocking. Then Cathy spoke again.

'Hettie, do you know a way . . .'

Hettie's lips tightened.

'No,' she said sharply.

'Please!' Cathy's voice was desperate, near to tears.

'Definitely not!' Cathy had not expected such a tone from her kind and sympathetic aunt. She looked at her, nonplussed. 'You're three months. It's too late!'

'It's me only hope, Auntie Hettie. Please, please help me!'

'No!'

Cathy returned to her darning, almost blinded by the panic that was rising in her.

'Why Hettie? Why won't you help me?' she sobbed.

Hettie sighed, and stared ahead of her into the past.

'I wouldn't wish that on you, Cathy.' Her hands were trembling. Memories flooded back and cast a shadow over her features. Cathy saw them on her face, bitter and dark, full of pain. 'I nearly died,' Hettie whispered.

'You?'

'Aye. Did you not guess?' Cathy shook her head. 'Your mother wouldn't have told you, of course. Not fit for a young girl's ears. And she was right. She wouldn't let me near you for a long time. And I wanted to . . .' Hettie began to cry, tears long suppressed. 'I wanted to be close to you, to a child, so badly. Oh God, Cathy. You don't know. You see, I wanted to have that baby; I was driven by the fear of bein' cut off from Henry and you. I thought Lily'd never let me in the house again if I had . . . a bastard.' Hettie laughed. 'By, but she nearly did that anyway, only Henry brought me back into the fold, slowly like.' Hettie's face softened at Henry's kindness. 'He was a good brother to me. Anyway, what sort of life would the bairn have had? Bearin' the stigma? So I . . . murdered it. And by God I paid. After that, even when I got over it, if I ever really did, I could never have children again. I don't want any of that to happen to you, Cathy.'

'I'd rather die!'

'Aye, that's what I thought an' all when I was lyin' there, in pain, burnin' with fever, but God has a way of makin' you pay, Cathy. Or that's what I think. I lived to regret what I'd done. And so would you.'

'But . . . but what sort of a life will *this* child have?' Cathy cried.

'Your Mam'd get over it. And you've got me and this place. I'll leave it to you, when I go. Well, it's better nor nowt.'

'But . . . Gilbert . . . ?'

Hettie looked at her.

'Aye. That's possible. He's a good lad. He loves you. Mebbe he'll swallow it and . . . Is there any chance it could be his?'

Cathy shook her head.

'I couldn't tell him about this, Hettie.'

'It's worth a try. I would.'

'I couldn't. That's all.'

Hettie said nothing.

'Do you think if he were found Captain Christiansen would marry me?'

Hettie looked at her in horror. Cathy didn't know. Hettie had never had the heart to tell her he was married all the time.

'He'll not be back.'

'No. But if he was found. If someone found him, and told him?' Hettie shook her head. 'Maybe Joe . . . ?'

'He's got enough on his plate.'

Cathy looked downcast. It was true. How could she ask him? And yet who else was there to ask?

'Do you think he would?' Cathy insisted.

Hettie sighed.

'It's not worth tryin', pet. It'll do no good!'

'How do you know?'

'I just know that's all.'

'I've got to try, Hettie. I must. What else is there?'

It was Cathy's last hope. Hettie shook her head miserably and said nothing. There'd been so much pain, so much trouble, how could she be the one to dash Cathy's hopes. She couldn't bear it, hadn't the courage. And so she let it go, putting off the evil day when, at last, the lass must find out the truth.

And now Cathy could think of nothing else. They must see Joe and ask him. The sooner the better. There was no time to lose. She wanted it sorted before Gilbert came home on leave, so that she would know what to say, what to do. Hettie allowed herself to be dragged along miserably in Cathy's plans, knowing the extra pain that the discovery would give her niece when she learned that her Captain already had a wife. Hettie felt cowardly, but having refused the fence once, she knew she couldn't jump it now. And so she found herself at Comical Corner, the old meeting place, waiting with Cathy for poor Joe, about to be sent on a wild-goose chase, and all because Hettie hadn't been woman enough to come out with the truth.

Joe came willingly enough, glad to be of service to beautiful Miss Straker, and led the ladies into the snug of a public house where they might sip porter and speak privately. The porter brought a little colour back into Cathy's cheeks, and she drank it down quickly, needing its extra courage before she could broach the subject. Hettie was very talkative, and bright; nervous, Joe thought. Cathy just stared at him bleakly. Joe began to feel uneasy, wondering what was on their minds.

'I want you to do something for me, Joe,' Cathy blurted out at last.

'You've only to ask, Miss Straker.'

'You remember that Norwegian Captain we had staying with us? Captain Christiansen?' Joe nodded, his face closing up against a name he did not like. 'Well, I want you to find him for me.' Joe was postively astonished.

'What for?' he said at last. Cathy flushed scarlet, and Hettie drank down her glass quickly. Joe looked from one to the other. 'Why? What's the beggar done?'

'He's got her pregnant. That's what!' Hettie suddenly said, in a voice much louder than she'd intended.

'Sh, auntie!'

Joe went white, and could not look at either of them. After a long pause he got up to refill their glasses, drinking down a glass at the bar before coming back to the table. Hettie grabbed her drink and swallowed it down, giving him back her glass, wanting more. Cathy's face was hidden as she stared down at her boots, unable to look Joe in the eye. When he came back, Hèttie took her third glass and drank it down also while Joe sat in his place between the two women on the bench.

'I don't believe it,' he said at last. And then, finally, he looked at Cathy. Cathy raised her eyes to his, and he knew that after all it was the truth. 'Did he . . . ?'

Cathy nodded then shook her head. Joe sighed. It was obvious the lass didn't want him to press the point. His mind raced with questions he would like to ask but which he knew were too indelicate. Did Gilbert know? Did Lily? How long ago did it happen and how? Suddenly Hettie giggled. Both Joe and Cathy looked at her in amazement. The giggling continued. Tears ran down Hettie's cheek, and she held her side with the pain of it. After a bit, Joe turned away from her and spoke quietly to Cathy.

'Don't you worry,' he said, 'I'll search him out.'

'There's no point!' Again, the other two stared at Hettie. She was rocking on her stool, in an agony of laughter. 'He's married.'

Cathy felt sick. The colour drained from her face and she swayed on her stool. Quickly Joe rose to catch her weight. Unable to carry her because of his shoulder he was forced to kneel by her as she rested against him, till her senses returned. Hettie was wiping her glasses with a hanky and crying now.

'I'm sorry,' she moaned, 'I'm sorry. I just couldn't tell ye before. I know I should've but I couldn't. And then there's Joe. I couldn't let him just go, all that trouble for nothin' and him with his shoulder blown off. I know I should've said before, but I couldn't.' Then Hettie hiccuped and was silent.

Gently, Joe raised Cathy from her seat and made her lie flat across the bench. He was holding her hand. His eyes never left her face. Hettie was silent now and sober as a judge. She sat still on her stool, like a naughty schoolchild put in the corner with a dunce's hat on its head. She'd stay like that till she was told she was forgiven. Slowly, Cathy recovered, and Joe raised her to a sitting position, holding her there till her head stopped swimming and she was able to drop her feet to the floor. Her hands were cold and clammy, but her clothes were sticking to her and she was shaking visibly. Joe swallowed hard.

'Miss Straker, there's one thing I've got to ask,' he said. Cathy focused on him with difficulty. 'Mr Stoddard . . . I mean Mr Gilbert . . . ?'

Cathy shook her head vehemently.

'That's over.'

Hettie hiccuped again. They both glanced at her before Joe resumed.

'Miss Straker, I'm at your disposal,' he said awkwardly. 'I've always admired ye from afar, like, and now . . . well, what I mean to say is, I'd like to marry you.'

And now it was Cathy's turn to laugh, and Joe looked hurt, feeling his presumption strongly.

'No, no,' Cathy giggled, 'It's not you, Joe, it's all this . . .' She looked around her. 'I've never been in a public before in me life. I mean, you're on your knees and all that, but it's not how I imagined it at all.'

Her laughter subsided at last. Joe shuffled at her feet, his knees hurting on the stone floor.

'Did you mean it?' Cathy said suddenly.

Joe shrugged in an embarrassed fashion.

'Aha,' he said.

'I don't love you, Joe.'

'I know.'

'Just so long as you know.'

The pair of them looked at one another as though sizing each other up. Hettie, jaw wide open, looked from one to the other.

'Eeh!' she said. And then she laughed. Then Cathy joined in, followed by Joe. And then Joe suddenly stopped.

'You mean you will?' he said amazed.

'Aha.'

And then all three of them rocked with laughter, so that in the public they all thought there was a party going on, one man and two women; by but he was a lucky dog and no mistake!

In the cold light of day, none of them looked quite so cheerful. There was Lily to face, for one, and Gilbert for another. Joe kept having to pinch himself to see if he was still awake, and Hettie kept on asking Cathy if she was sure she was doing the right thing. It had been a decision taken on the spur of the moment, with a full glass of porter inside her. Joe wouldn't keep her to it if she wanted to change her mind. But Cathy shook her head. Better a bad decision than indecision, the terrible agony of not knowing what to do. She'd had enough and clutched at the first lifebelt that offered itself. It just happened to be Joe, in the right place at the right time.

'He's a good man,' Hettie told her. 'He's had a bad time.'

'Don't worry, Hettie. I'll make it up to him. I'll be a good wife.'

And Hettie saw from her face that Cathy meant it. She was determined, and nothing would sway her.

It was decided to say nothing to Lily till Cathy had had it out with Gilbert. Joe waited with bated breath, half hoping, for Cathy's sake, that he would take her in spite of her predicament, and half fearing it too. It was a quirk of fate that at the very moment when Joe had entirely given up all hopes of winning Cathy, when, because he was no longer an able man, he felt he had nothing to offer her, she should have come to him in need. He had thought to raise himself to her level. The war had put paid to that. It had killed Alec: and Jim, the one they'd thought had got away, had died of lockjaw from the wound on his finger. A joke gone sour. Alone, Joe could never have raised enough to buy a boat, even if he had been able bodied and fit to crew it. So he came home, devoid of all such ambition, ready to accept his fate. Then, like a bolt from the blue, Cathy was toppled from the crest of her wave and fell right into his arms. It had the feel of a dream, a sweet dream following straight on from a nightmare, the one as unreal as the other. And yet it was not a dream come true. He grieved to see his love brought low, nor would he believe she was his until the interview with Gilbert was passed.

Gilbert had thought of nothing but seeing Cathy again all the time he'd been away. Unlike Joe, he hadn't been on the front line, and he returned home very much the same Gilbert who had gone away in the summer. He had only a few days' leave, but his first thought, on his arrival at Westoe, was to get himself down to the hat shop and take Cathy in his arms. His car was in cold storage. Petrol wasn't easy to find and, in any case, it seemed hardly worth it to reassemble the greased parts just for a few days' use. So he took the tram, a novel experience for Gilbert, and armed with a bunch of roses he had picked up at Fowler Street on the way he barged in through the shop door, clanging the bell joyously as he did so.

Miss Hutchinson and Cathy were on their own when he arrived. Ethel had gone the week before, and as custom was slack the two women were sitting quietly in the back room, tidying the drawers of trimmings. The drawers were stacked on the work table before them, and slowly they worked through each one, sifting and arranging the contents and stacking them on the bench behind them. They both looked up at once when the bell clanged. Miss Hutchinson was pleased. It might, after all, be a customer, and she rose before Cathy and made her way into the main shop. She recognised Gilbert at once, and shouted through, 'It's your young man, dear!'

Cathy's heart was in her mouth. She couldn't move for a

second. Here at the shop? She hadn't expected this. She had thought Gilbert would come to Thrift Street.

'Catherine!' Miss Hutchinson called again.

Quickly Cathy checked her hair in the mirror and pinched some colour into her cheeks. Her legs were giving way under her, and her pulse was racing. Would he notice a difference in her?

'Catherine!' her employer called again.

'Coming!' And Cathy took a deep breath and walked through the dividing curtain into the shop.

He looked so happy, so handsome, too, in his uniform, that Cathy couldn't help herself. Even Gilbert was surprised as she rushed straight into his arms and clung to him, weeping.

'I love you, Gilbert. I do love you,' she said over and over again. Miss Hutchinson, still hovering in the background, coughed.

'Miss Straker . . .'

'Oh I'm sorry, Miss Hutchinson . . .'

'No. No need to apologise. I just wanted to say that I'll be closing the shop now, so . . .'

'But . . .'

'No! I won't hear another word. You run along now, the pair of you.' Miss Hutchinson looked round the shop. 'It's not as if there was anything spoiling,' she said sadly. 'She's been pining for you, Mr Stoddard. See how thin and wan she is.'

Gilbert lifted Cathy's chin and looked at her face. He frowned.

'Have you not been eating properly?' he asked. Cathy opened her mouth to reply but he wouldn't let her. 'I know what we'll do, we'll take you out for a good feed, right now!'

Cathy stared up at him silently. All she could say was, 'I love you.'

The restaurant was half empty. It was the middle of the afternoon. Gilbert guided Cathy to a quiet seat in a bay window, overlooking King Street. They had hardly spoken in the tram. They had just sat quietly holding hands.

Gilbert's firm grip had calmed her, and Cathy knew, as she sat by his side, that here was a man who could indeed master her, and be her lord. It seemed to her then such an amazing, precious thing. Now, after everything she had experienced, too late, she could see the difference between Gilbert and the Captain, and all the other men she had ever met! Gilbert shone out in contrast to them. For he was a man she could respect. It was an irony that she could never have learnt of Gilbert's value without losing him. How could she know what the day was, unless she had also experienced the night? But the experience of the night had made the day forfeit. Gilbert was a rare bird indeed and she would never meet his like again. As for Joe? Why, Cathy hardly knew him, after all. Now, alone in the restaurant with her master of ships, Cathy began to cry.

'What is it, Cathy?' Gilbert asked anxiously.

'I love you.'

Gilbert looked at her, puzzled. They were words he liked to hear, but she had said them once too often.

'It's all right, love. I've not even been near the front line yet.' Cathy shook her head. 'Ma couldn't believe it either. She took a lot of persuading. Oh, by the way, it *was* good of you.'

'What?' Cathy sounded surprised.

'To visit her like that. Do you know, I think in her heart of hearts she was quite touched.' Gilbert laughed. 'You are a good girl.' Again Cathy shook her head and blew her nose loudly. 'Yes you are. I think she's quite lonely really. May Cochrane's given me up in disgust. She never goes near Westoe these days!'

'She shouldn't . . .'

'No. You're right. She shouldn't.'

Cathy bit her lip. He had misunderstood her. She had meant to say that May Cochrane shouldn't give up hope.

'She's a cold fish,' Gilbert added.

'Who?'

'May Cochrane.'

'Oh.'

And then the waitress came to take their order. There was

nothing for it; Gilbert *would* have champagne. He was in high old spirits. And the longer the charade went on, the harder it was for Cathy to burst his bubble. Instead it just grew and grew, and Cathy began to see how hard it had been for Hettie to break her bad news to her, and why she had left it till the last minute, as she had; it was so much easier just to let things ride.

It seemed to Cathy that she was watching herself spin out the last act of a play, reluctant to allow the curtain to close and bring the dream world to an end, knowing that when she left the theatre she would have to face the cold dank night air of the real world outside. Both of them, for their different reasons, found themselves talking too much, loving too much, laughing on the edge of tears, as though desperate to cram the rest of their life's emotions into a few hours. Gilbert was aware that a Jerry bomb could demolish everything for both of them in a moment. Cathy, on the other hand, knew that her bombshell, just as destructive in its way, would blow their relationship to smithereens, for ever and ever. The evil moment was postponed, and they drank their champagne and ate their lemon sole with the maxim that 'sufficient unto the day was the evil thereof'.

When Gilbert dropped Cathy at Thrift Street Hettie knew at once that nothing had been said. Cathy was avoiding her eye, and Gilbert was far too full of himself. Lily, too, was all over him, and another soldier's coming-home cake was eaten in 'The Sanctuary', as though part of some well-rehearsed ritual. Reluctant to go, Gilbert nevertheless rose at half past eight and said his goodbyes. His mother would be deeply wounded if he didn't spend at least some of his first evening at home with her. Everyone understood and sent their best to Mrs Stoddard, along with a piece of Gilbert's cake, wrapped in a napkin.

'I'll call in in the morning,' Gilbert said quietly to Cathy. 'If it's fine we could go for a walk?'

Cathy nodded silently. He tweaked her under her chin and winked. Her spirits had flagged noticeably since her return to Thrift Street. She knew that the last act was finally over, and tomorrow would bring the curtain down at last.

'Goodbye Gilbert,' she said as they stood at the front door. He smiled and bent down to kiss her. Cathy folded him in her arms and her lips clung to his more passionately than ever before. When she let him go at last he simply said, 'Phew!' raised his eyebrows, smiled, and left.

That night Cathy got undressed and ready for bed as usual. But the morning found her sitting up in bed, dark circles under her eyes, and her candle gutted. She hadn't slept a wink. She rose, feeling a dull, steady determination inside herself, and sat at her mirror, brushing her hair, ready for the day. She knew that what she was about to do was a kind of suicide. But she had to do it. She had questioned herself closely through the long sleepless night, and she was sure that she was right. She wasn't going to tell Gilbert the truth. She wasn't going to tell him about Captain Christiansen or the baby or anything. She was going to set about killing Gilbert's love for her in the only way possible. He had seen with his own eyes how flighty she could be. That day he had walked in on the Captain and herself dancing, he had seen that she loved another man. He had been hurt, very hurt, but he had borne it and loved on, his respect for her undiminished. But if he thought that there had been others . . . ? He would surely dismiss her as flighty, unworthy of his love, and be glad to let her go. Then it would be easy for him. And that was what Cathy wanted; not because she didn't love Gilbert but because she loved him so much.

Cathy did feel some guilt for what she had done, or rather what she had felt. Her mother would never have understood such feelings, and no lady ever admitted to them. It was well known that only women of the streets desired men in 'that' way. And Cathy had transgressed the bounds of decency, not so much by what she had done, especially since she had not been entirely a willing partner in the act, but by having allowed herself to entertain such feelings at all. And so she felt a strong compulsion towards self-punishment. But she knew that though Gilbert would marry her in spite of everything, would stand by her and bring up her child as his own, continuing to love her, their relationship could never be the same again. He would surely lose all respect for her.

His love would rather bear the mark of pity than the love a man bears for his equal. The marriage would therefore be soured. Her own spirit would rise up against his pity, and there would be friction between them. Cathy had no intention of subjecting either Gilbert or herself to such a marriage, and so she would turn him against her and marry Joe. At least Joe knew what he was getting when he'd asked. And she'd make sure that he never regretted having asked her.

Cathy was calm as she sat in the scullery waiting for Gilbert to call. She was wearing her new hat, the one Miss Hutchinson had given her on her birthday, and she had taken pains with her appearance, even borrowing some rouge from Hettie who kept the disreputable article secreted amongst her underclothes, away from Lily's gaze. Cathy needed the right costume and the right make-up to play the part she had in mind today.

Gilbert was late. His mother had caused difficulties about his coming down to Thrift Street. She had cried when he'd insisted, but after all Cathy was going to be his wife and she'd better just get used to taking second place in his life. Cathy smiled up at him, and together they walked out and took the tram to the beach, where they could walk along the prom and be alone together.

'You've got a better colour today, Cathy,' he commented. Cathy gave a teasing tilt to her head.

'Can't you tell why?'

Gilbert shrugged and answered that he couldn't.

'I've got rouge on.'

Gilbert frowned and leaned closer to stare at her cheek.

'So you have!' he said surprised. 'Why, that's not like you.'

'How do you know what I get up to when you're not there?' She laughed at him. Gilbert felt uneasy, thrown off balance by such a remark. It wasn't like Cathy at all. She was playing with him, surely? 'Well, you wouldn't want me to be miserable and sit at home all the time, would you?' she pouted.

'No. Of course not.'

'Well, then.' And she was all smiles again, and took his arm, stepping out gaily beside him.

He was silent for a while, and then he asked, 'Have you been out and about much, then?'

Cathy nodded feverishly. 'Oh yes. We often go out. Music hall mostly.'

Gilbert gave her a sharp look. He knew very well that Lily usually put the kaibosh on that particular form of entertainment.

'It's all right, Mam lets me go with Hettie . . . and . . . Joe.'

'Joe?'

'Aha. You know . . . that good-lookin' lad. Cousin of Hettie's. He's very nice.'

'Is he now?' Gilbert was bristling already in spite of himself. 'And what about that Captain?' he asked.

Cathy felt as though Gilbert, her own Gilbert, had dealt her a body blow. He'd never so much as mentioned the Captain before, too gentlemanly to bring up the painful subject. How right she had been in her thinking. How sour their marriage would be if he knew the truth. Even Gilbert could not have lived with the knowledge that he was bringing up another man's child. His reaction spurred her on still further in her efforts to alienate.

'Him?' She laughed. 'Oh, I'd forgotten about him. Aren't you funny? No! It's Joe I love really.'

Gilbert dropped her arm and stopped in his tracks. He was speechless.

'What's the matter with you, Gilbert?' Cathy asked innocently. 'I only said I was in love with Joe. I mean . . . you know what I'm like. I can't help it.'

Gilbert just couldn't believe it. Had he been blind all this time?

'Cathy?' He spoke quietly, a puzzled look on his face. 'Cathy? This isn't really you, is it?'

His look cut her in two. She loved him. She always would. If he only knew how much she loved him. But she couldn't tell him, not ever again. The words might rise to her lips, but she would brush them aside with a bright smile. The moment was passed.

'Of course it is!' she laughed. 'Who else would it be?'

Gilbert shook his head. He looked away towards the sea, as if searching for the answer there.

'I don't understand,' he said at last.

'There's nothing to understand, Gilbert. When are we gettin' married?'

He swung round on her and spoke with such suddenness that Cathy was quite alarmed.

'Do you love me at all, Cathy?'

It was the last question she wanted to answer. Of course she loved him, her insides screamed out; but her tongue replied, 'Of course! When I'm not *in* love . . . you know I do!'

'I see.' He looked down and kicked at the sand under his feet. 'You mean you love me when you're not loving Captain Christiansen, or this Joe bloke, or somebody else, eh? That it?'

His look was angry when he raised his eyes to hers. Cathy flinched, but her tone remained playful as ever.

'Come on, Gilbert. You're not the only pebble on the beach.' And she laughed then, her hands taking in the breadth of the shore that lay before them. Gilbert stared at her, searching in vain for the Cathy he thought he knew, but he couldn't find her there.

'Cathy,' he said at last, 'do you really think you could be happy with one man?' Cathy shrugged. 'Because if not . . . if not, then I really think we should give up any idea of our getting married.' His eyes pleaded with hers to reassure him, but she avoided his eyes and watched instead a dog playing with another on the sands.

'They're having a mock fight. Look,' she laughed. Gilbert glanced at the dogs then looked despairingly back at Cathy. She assumed an angry air.

'I am what I am, Gilbert. I can't help it. I thought you loved me for me, not for some wild dream you've got tucked away somewhere. I mean, I'm not your blasted mother!' She spat the words at him. Gilbert's jaw dropped open. Suddenly he closed it again.

'Then that's that!' he said. Stiffly, he offered her his arm and escorted her back to her tram. Cathy continued teasing him all the way, complaining of his ungentlemanly behaviour in not going with her to Thrift Street to drop her at her door. And then the tram pulled away, and his face slid out of sight behind the glass of the cab window, and in full view of the entire tram Cathy burst into a fit of agonised weeping.

And now there was only Lily to take care of, and Joe had promised to help with that. Hettie made a point of inviting him to tea the following day. Lily couldn't understand it. He'd been given his hero's welcome once, surely he didn't want another one? And was she expected to provide another cake, with a flag on top as well? Well, he'd just have to make do with the leftover pieces from Gilbert's and think himself lucky at that! And Joe did think himself lucky. He turned up in his best bib and tucker, and an odd pair of trousers, bought second-hand to replace the shrunken pair that went with his suit. Lily looked askance at his legs but was grateful for small mercies that at least he wasn't showing his knees! Cathy was stiff as a board in anticipation of the expected storm. Hettie was talking too much. But Joe was calm and steady as ever. Cathy couldn't help remembering the crest and the motto Hettie had drawn for him on his present, 'Always Ready' and a lifeboat. That was Joe all right. And it wasn't the first time he'd come to her rescue either. Good old Joe. She smiled encouragingly at him, and he smiled warmly back. It wouldn't be long now and the worst would be over.

The sandwiches were finished and the cake reduced to crumbs when Joe decided that the moment had finally come.

'Mrs Straker,' he began in a strong formal tone that made Lily look up quickly. 'I'll come straight to the point.' Lily frowned and set the tray down on the table. 'I think you'd better sit down.' Lily looked at her daughter for enlightenment, but Cathy looked away, and her mother began to smell a rat.

'Here, what is this?' she began.

'I've come to ask for Catherine's hand in marriage,' Joe said and looked straight at the mother. Lily gasped, stared at him and then burst out laughing.

'Eeh, that wound's turned your brain, Joe!' she said. 'Don't be so daft.' And then she rose to pick up the tray again but was stopped by her daughter.

'Mam. Please. Sit down and hear him out.'

Lily sat with a thump.

'I know I'm not much,' Joe went on, 'and I know you don't like's us. But I've got a future . . .'

'My daughter's engaged to Gilbert Stoddard, Mr Robson, or have you forgotten?'

There was a long and awkward silence.

'Tell him, Cathy.'

Cathy shook her head.

'What's happened?'

'Just hear Joe, Ma. Please.'

Lily went cold as ice. All of them sitting in the room at the time felt the temperature drop at that moment. Joe cleared his throat and bravely continued.

'I've got me savin's still, and eventually I'll be goin' shares in a boat of me own . . . a fishin' boat.'

'And what use would *you* be on a boat Joe Robson, with your shoulder blown off!'

Hettie sprang to the defence.

'Joe lost his shoulder in the service of his country, Lily!'

'It may be that the other lads'll have to do the crewin' for's, like, though I'm hopin' I might be able to go out sometimes. Anyway, there'll be my share of the catch, I've got me pension, and . . . and I've been after a job.'

'Who'd have you?' Lily spat. 'Disabled man!'

There was an embarrassed pause. Then Joe spoke up quietly.

'The Corporation have offered me a job. As a . . . as a lavatory attendant.'

Lily's horror was so great that both Hettie and Cathy couldn't help themselves. They just had to laugh, smothering down their mirth as best they could under coughs and nose blows, knowing that it wouldn't help Joe and could only make Lily more angry than ever.

'Lavatory attendant!' she screamed. 'Lavatory attendant!' She turned to Cathy. 'You can't be serious?'

'Yes, Mam.'

'But . . . but . . . but . . .' Lily was reduced to babble, and they began to worry for her in case the shock might bring on a stroke. Cathy went to her side and gently smoothed her mother's forehead with her hand.

'I'm not goin' to marry Gilbert, Mam. Ye see . . .'

'I'm not lettin' you marry . . .' and Lily pointed directly at Joe '. . . him! Look what he did to my salmon!'

And then Hettie spoke up.

'You'll have to tell her, Cathy.'

Cathy bit her lip, but Lily ploughed on regardless.

'Mr Robson,' she said, 'I was born and brought up in Westoe Village. A far cry from where you see me now! And you expect my daughter to marry a lavatory attendant!'

'Mam. I'm pregnant.'

Lily might have turned to stone. All four of them were suddenly still, like children in a schoolyard playing statues, waiting for the whistle so they could move again. It was Lily who blew the whistle.

'I don't believe it! What do you know about all this Hettie? I bet it's all your fault!' she said almost all in one breath. And then she turned to Joe. 'You rat! You lousy filthy stinkin' rat! Do you realise what you've done?' She was standing now, and screaming right into his face. 'You've spoiled my little girl, you animal! You've spoiled her! You've spoiled everythin'! Everythin'!'

The words disintegrated in her mouth, ending in an incoherent, screaming babble. Joe rose from his chair and gripped her by the arms; finally raising his one good hand he struck her across the face and she fell to the floor senseless. For a second they stood looking at her, paralysed. Then quickly Joe picked her up with one arm and slung her across his good shoulder. Hettie raised her hand to her mouth, fearing Lily's wrath if she ever learnt that she'd been treated in that way, and then the two women followed Joe up the stairs, where he laid the unconscious woman on her bed. Like conspirators round Caesar's body, all three stood round Lily's bed, wondering whether to flee or stay for the inevitable wrath to come.

CHAPTER SEVENTEEN

Lily lay on her bed unconscious all through that evening and the night. The next morning, when it was obvious that she hadn't moved, Cathy went out to summon Dr Hollom and sent a message to Miss Hutchinson to tell her she couldn't come in. She felt numb with panic. It was all so unreal, as though everything, the baby, Joe, and her mother's illness were all part of someone else's life, which she had stumbled into by mistake. She kept wanting to laugh over the silliest things, and couldn't understand why. Joe came at dinner time and sat with her for a while by Lily's bed He told her how they'd sat in the trenches cracking jokes 'In a world gone mad, you've got to laugh, Cathy, or else you'll cry.' That made her feel better, removing at least some of the guilt from her shoulders as she watched on, half hoping, half fearing that her mother would wake.

Dr Hollom came at last, at nearly four o'clock, and went straight up to examine Lily. He thought at first she must have had a stroke. But after a while he wasn't so sure. He asked Cathy for a pin and began inserting it in different parts of Lily's body. Cathy had to look away, feeling squeamish, but there was no reaction from Lily. Nothing at all. He shook his head and lifted her eyelids to look at her eyes.

'There's nothing we can do,' he said, 'but wait and see.' And with that he snapped his bag shut and left them to it.

It was the darkest time of the year, the days leading up to Christmas. Hettie and Cathy sat on in the growing twilight, only rising to make pots of tea, see to a lodger, or answer the door. Joe returned, late in the evening, and joined the vigil. Cathy began to feel she'd always lived in this room, that her mother had never moved, and that this state of affairs was in fact normal. Hettie too got used to it, and brought up some mending; Joe read aloud from the papers, and Cathy began to wonder, of all things, what she would wear for her wedding. It had become a cosy scene, and Lily's stillness was simply part of it. In fact, had any one of them dared to admit it, it was pleasantly peaceful.

Now and then Hettie or Cathy rose to stare into Lily's face or feel the pulse which was weak and very, very slow. Then they'd bend their ears to her mouth and listen as Lily's breathing continued in shallow breaths, coming only at very infrequent intervals. They had piled blankets over her and kept a hot bottle at her feet, but she was still cold as ice. She seemed only half alive, and they were helpless to do anything for her.

Had they but known it, Lily knew exactly what was going on. She had come out of the deep unconsciousness early that morning, but something in her had refused to come round altogether. She did not want to come back into this world. She refused point-blank to face what must be faced eventually. Perhaps it wasn't true, and she had dreamt it all. But then, what was Joe doing, sitting with them all beside her bed? She listened to him reading from the papers, solved a clue in a crossword puzzle that none of them daft beggars could get, and heard herself and her condition discussed at some length, as though she wasn't there at all. Her thoughts were slow, but Lily had no sense of time; she was living half out of the world in a different dimension, left only with an awareness of what was being said and done around her apparently comatose body. She knew that her breathing was slow and shallow. It amazed her, in fact, that she could continue to exist on such meagre rations of air. And there was a slight pain around her heart, as though each tiny beat cost such a superhuman effort that it cried out in protest.

Slowly, too, Lily became aware of extreme coldness. And she realised that she couldn't continue like this for very much longer. Either she must live, or she must die. But which was it to be? They had taken away her dreams, her hopes; what reason could there be for living now? She was no better than a skivvy in this miserable house, she who had been brought up to be a lady. She would grow old here, and die here, and they'd all gloat over her grave. Revenge seeded itself in Lily's cold body. It was nurtured by bitterness and regret, and watered by anger. She had thought only of others, done her best for them, given what she had, even her last few jewels had been sold for Cathy's good, and she'd thrown it all back in her face. Her daughter was a slut, like her aunt; bad blood the Strakers had, and it was in Cathy. It would be in her baby too, his baby, Joe's. But there would be something of herself in it too. It would have some Russell blood in its body. Would it be enough? Children learn by example. Cathy had learnt from Henry, and from his sister, Hettie. Cathy did not deserve to rise. She had fallen back into the gutter where she belonged. But her baby? If Lily was to die now, it stood no chance, none at all. But if she lived? She would take it on herself to make sure of its education, its upbringing. And they would be forced to let her. Cathy would have to work. The child would need its grandmother, and this time Hettie would be kept well out of the way. Yes! That'd teach them. They thought she was as good as dead and buried. Well, they had another think coming! So the seed grew into a seedling as Hettie darned on and Cathy's mind picked its way through the debris of her life. Joe finished reading the paper at last and folded it, wondering whether he should stay the night with them, or go back to his own lodgings. And finally the seedling became a fine, healthy plant. Lily's chest rose to take in a deep breath. Her lips parted and formed a word, 'Brandy'. Joe, roused from his reverie, stared at the body on the bed.

'I thought her lips moved,' he said.

The two women stared at the still figure, then Hettie rose and held the candle to Lily's face. The chest heaved again, and another breath, deeper than the last, was drawn into her lungs. Again the lips parted, and on the exhalation of the air Lily breathed, 'Brandy'.

'Brandy!' Joe cried.

'There's some in me medicine chest in me room,' Hettie said and scuttled out to get it.

'Why didn't we think of that before?' Joe said, wringing his hands in concern. 'Get something, a hanky, Cathy, that'll do; we'll need to drop the spirit into her mouth bit by bit.'

Cathy searched her mother's drawers and found an old hanky, the embroidery laundered white round the edges. She gave it to Joe, and he soaked it in the liquor Hettie had brought back with her.

Cathy stood at the foot of her mother's bed, watching through the iron rails, her face white and her eyes black as Hettie and Joe performed the operation. Hettie lifted Lily's head gently and supported it against her own body while Joe held the soaked corner of the handkerchief to Lily's lips, so that the drops slipped between them and down into her mouth. Some liquid oozed from the sides of Lily's mouth, but when there was enough she swallowed. Joe nodded to Hettie, who laid the head back on the pillow, and they waited for some result. It was only a matter of seconds. Lily's eyes sprang open. She breathed long sighs of relief, and the colour flooded back into her cheeks. There at the foot of her bed she saw the white, intent face of her daughter, staring at her through the rails. Their eyes met, and Cathy shuddered at the enmity that had poured into her from her mother's look. It was only a moment, as Hettie settled her against her pillows, and then Lily was giving out orders, in her usual strong voice, about beef tea, and chicken, and poached eggs on toast, which she wished to consume in order to build up her strength.

Instinctively, Joe and Cathy left Hettie to tend to the patient and crept from the sick room, silently, to find refuge in the scullery. Cathy felt tired and weak after the ordeal. And Joe sat her in Hettie's chair by the stove, while he set about getting her something to eat. Lily wasn't the only one in need of building up, he said. Hettie came down and fussed, excitedly, as she prepared Lily's tray. She couldn't stop talking.

'Eeh, it was just like Lazarus!' she kept on saying. 'I'll never forget it as long as I live! Eeh! Lazarus come to life!'

The image did nothing for Cathy's stomach. She shuddered again, and in her mind recalled her mother's eyes as they'd met her own across the bottom of the bed. But surely she was reading her own childish fears into it? She was a grown woman now, not a baby. She would be married soon, and have a child of her own. What could her mother possibly do to harm her, and why? Joe passed her her cup of cocoa. It had no froth on it. He didn't know how she liked it, but she took it gratefully and drank, picking at the bread and cold meat he also laid before her. He watched her as she ate, encouraging her with a few words now and then, till she had finished the last crumb, and he took the plate away.

'I'll stay,' he said. 'You go up now. Get some rest. You're tired.'

A sudden unreasoned panic gripped Cathy.

'But where will you . . . ?'

'I shall be all right on the sofa,' Joe said gently. 'Go on now.'

Ashamed of her suspicions, Cathy made her weary way back up the stairs, past her mother's open door. She hesitated a second in the ray of light that escaped from the room onto the dark stair. She had a memory . . . a distant memory of another time, there had been darkness and loneliness. Yes, and there had been fear, terror, on the stairs, and her mother had not been her mother at all; she had wanted to kill her! Cathy's feet quickly passed on and further up to the top of the house and her own room. Quickly she undressed in the darkness and crept in between the cold sheets. She had been a child then. She had fallen down the stairs and banged her head. She hadn't been thinking straight. There was no such excuse for her fears now. No. It was all in her mind. She had imagined the hatred in her mother's eyes. It would be all right tomorrow. Huddled under the bedclothes, Cathy closed her eyes and slept.

Hettie had given Lily a bell, and the next morning, early, Lily used it. She had orders for the day. Cathy must help with breakfasts and then go off to work. They needed her pay packet and Cathy should make sure she got it while she could. Hettie would have to see to all the heavy work, and she herself would have her breakfast and her lunch in bed where she was, getting up that afternoon to take a little air in the park, before retiring early.

'What about Joe?' Hettie asked.

Lily frowned.

'What do you mean, what about Joe? He's not still here is he?'

'It's all right, Lily. He slept in the scullery. He was still a bit concerned about you, like.'

'Rather late in the day, don't you think!' Lily snorted. Hettie looked puzzled. 'Never mind. I don't want to see him. Tell him he can set about cleanin' his lavatories or whatever it is he wants to do!'

'Yes, Lily.' Hettie was at the door, ready to get to work on Lily's orders, when she was recalled by a hiss from the bed.

'When, Hettie? That's what I want to know. When did they . . . *do* it?'

Hettie's mind raced. What should she say? Joe'd already told her they weren't to enlighten her about the real culprit, Captain Christiansen. It'd only make it worse for Cathy if they did, for there was no hope of her marrying *him*. And now Lily'd decided that Joe was the father, better all round she should continue to think so. But when *could* they have 'done' it? Hettie gabbled a reply.

'Mebbe when he was . . . you know . . . life savin' her. He was almost on top of her, Lily!'

Lily's mouth dropped open. Her voice was harsh.

'You needn't pretend your innocence with me, Hettie Straker, because I know better!'

'Eeh, well, I don't know, Lily. It must've been round about then.'

Lily's eyes narrowed. 'Sly little minx!'

Even Hettie was taken aback by the venom. Silently, she left the room and looked up the stairs to Cathy's room. After a moment's hesitation she went up and opened the door.

Cathy was sleeping soundly, one arm flung out above her head, but a frown creasing her brow. Hettie bent over her and smoothed it out with her hand. It seemed a pity to wake her, and in her condition too. Cathy stirred and sighed before opening her eyes. Hettie smiled down at her.

'Rise and shine,' she said lightly.

Cathy raised herself and tried to move her arm. It was dead, so Hettie helped her and rubbed the life back into it, muttering sympathetic little noises as Cathy writhed with the pain of returning feeling.

'How is she?' Cathy asked at last.

Hettie raised her eyebrows.

'She seems in fine fettle to me. You wouldn't think there'd ever been owt the marra with her.' Cathy nodded, sensing something behind the words. 'She says you're to go to work this mornin', pet.' Cathy sighed. It was actually a relief to think she wouldn't have to be near her mother for the rest of the day. 'In fact, if I was you, I'd not look in on her at all. Leave well alone for a bit.'

Cathy stared at Hettie, then looked away.

'She'll never forgive's, will she, Hettie?'

Hettie said nothing, but rose from the bed and left her, saying she had a lot to do.

The mother of the bride did not attend the service. Only Hettie and Mr Miller escorted the couple as witnesses, and Mr Miller gave Cathy away. There was no organist because there was no congregation to sing, and there was no reception because there were no guests to invite. But there was excitement in the air. It was New Year's Eve, and shotgun weddings were a common occurrence during the war. So neither Joe nor Cathy felt their ceremony to be so very unusual after all. The bride wore her best suit and navy hat, with a small veil added, through Miss Hutchinson's kind services. In her hand she carried her prayer book and a small bunch of chrysanthemums, thrust into her hands at the last minute by Joe. They stopped off at a public for a drink on the way home. None of them admitted it, but it was part Dutch courage to face Lily, and they stayed there longer than intended. It was half past ten when, having satisfied hunger with pies and peas, the wedding party finally arrived back at Thrift Street, with a bottle for Lily to see the New Year in.

But Lily wasn't there. She'd gone out visiting early in the

afternoon, and stayed out purposely to avoid seeing them on their return. She had taken herself to the theatre, best seats of course, and with the money from one of her last real pieces of jewellery, sold that very morning, she treated herself to an excellent supper at the best restaurant in town. She finished her meal with a small brandy to fortify her and then went on to midnight mass at Saint Hilda's Church in Market Square. As Cathy and Joe shyly undressed by the candlelight in Cathy's room, Lily kneeled with clenched fists and bowed head, praying for strength, as the incense swirled about her head. It was one in the morning when Lily finally arrived home by cab. Hettie greeted her with relief.

'Eeh Lily. You might have said! I was worried sick!'

Lily snorted and went into the scullery.

'I take it the newlyweds have gone up?' she snapped.

Hettie nodded.

'Tut! Goin' to bed with a lavatory attendant, if you please, and under *my roof*!'

Hettie drew herself up to her full height.

'The roof is mine, Lily. And they're welcome!'

Lily gave her a sharp look but held her peace. Hettie watched her with a feeling of dread in her heart as Lily systematically prepared her own cocoa, gathered her things together, and went up to bed. There she undressed, drank her cocoa, and put two wodges of cotton wool in her ears before getting into her bed.

Gilbert was winging his way south in the train. Tomorrow he would be embarking for Europe, his leave ended. He felt uneasy. Again and again he played back the scene by the beach in his mind. He could not believe that that was Cathy. She had been wilful and contradictory in the past but never hard, never hurtful. She was warm, compassionate, loving. Whatever her faults, they were never calculated to bring suffering to others. So what had she been playing at? It was she who had forced him to break their engagement, goaded him till he eventually rose to her and was angry at last. Who was this Joe she'd talked about? Why, she'd never looked at him before! It just didn't make sense.

The more Gilbert thought about it, the more uneasy he

felt. His whole being fought against the moving train, wishing he could stop it, get out and go back to discover what lay at the bottom of Cathy's incomprehensible behaviour. If only he wasn't going back to the front. Not today. Not yet. All through his short leave he had fought against his own softness, as he called it, his weakening, when he thought of Cathy, and he had told himself that he must harden himself against her. He had almost given way. Two days after their break-up he had gone down to the shop to find her, only to be told that Mrs Straker had been taken badly and Miss Straker would therefore not be coming in. His mind had told him that he'd had a lucky escape, that it would be a good thing when he was back at the front and out of harm's way. But now that he was indeed out of harm's way, his heart spoke up and told him that he'd been wrong to give in so easily, that something was at the bottom of it all, and that Cathy did truly love him. So that now, instead of fighting against the urge to see her, he was fighting against everything that was taking him away from her. The communication cord above his head drew his eyes again and again. And yet he knew it was no good. He had to go on. He would be done for desertion if he didn't. But he would write to Cathy at the first possible opportunity in the hopes that her reply might bring them back together again or at least enlighten him. The decision made, Gilbert's eyes closed. The train rocked him southwards in an uneasy sleep, in which nightmares alternated with periods of wakefulness in half-lit stations along the way.

And so the year 1915 had begun. It had a desolate feel to it. Hopes of an early end to the war were fast fading. And though the people at home held on to the belief that, after all, it wasn't so bad out there in the trenches, there were growing numbers who could tell them otherwise. The full extent of the horror of that war would penetrate little by little against great resistance from the civilian population and from the government itself. There was inconvenience, of course, shortages both of goods and of labour. Miss Hutchinson found her business slackening. She had in any case lost two of her workers, and the third was pregnant. There seemed little point in continuing the unequal struggle. She said nothing to Cathy as yet. She would battle on till the spring, till after the Easter processions, and then see. But Cathy sensed the impending closure of the business. She knew that once she showed, Miss Hutchinson wouldn't want her serving in the shop, and her employer showed no signs of finding replacements for either Mabel or Ethel. Miss Hutchinson often sat in silence as they worked in the back room, withdrawn and weary. Her thoughts were drawn to Whitby and her sister's house by the bay, to peace and quiet and an end to labouring with her needle for hours on end in Ocean Road. They were a sorry pair. Cathy with her aching back, Miss Hutchinson with her nagging pain in her side. Sometimes they caught each other's eye as a hand strayed to the affected part, and they laughed.

At home it was hardly more cheerful. It seemed to Cathy that she was surrounded by a wall of silence. Miss Hutchinson brooding at work, and her mother ignoring her at home. Lily hardly ever spoke to her, except to say 'Pass the sugar' or 'Get this lot ironed'. Her silence was almost tangible, affecting even Hettie and Joe, who spoke little in Lily's presence. The web of taciturnity grew threads, cocooning Cathy, making her withdraw from everyone. And when she spoke, her voice sounded strange and cracked. She read a lot, cooped up with Hettie in the scullery, Cathy with her books, Hettie with her magazines, neither speaking. And Cathy wondered if, after all, she, like the little mermaid, had been stricken mute for loving a man she could not have. And so the days passed with a dead, numb monotony. She became uncaring. Nothing touched her feelings, and she slept for long hours, dropping off over her books by the kitchen stove. Even in bed there was little human contact.

That first night, when Cathy and Joe had undressed so shyly, Joe had averted his eyes until his wife's nakedness was covered by her nightdress. She had turned her back while he removed his trousers. And when he got in beside her they lay together, side by side, for some time without moving or saying a word. Cathy was stiff as a board. He sensed it, and, turning his head on the pillow, told her that she had no need to worry. He wouldn't touch her unless she wanted him to. Then Cathy had cried, and he had taken her in his arms till she felt better. Then the newlyweds turned, back to back, and slept till morning. It became the habit of their bedtime. So that Cathy remained wife in name only to Joe Robson throughout her pregnancy. Neither had she seen him, his slumped shoulder, and the arm hanging by a ribbon of flesh and muscle. He was as much a mystery to her as he ever was. Sometimes she lay awake, hearing his breath ebbing and flowing gently as he slept. And she wondered why he had allowed her to use him in this way. She marvelled at his great forebearance, knowing that he loved her. She felt that for Joe she existed only in his imagination; he did not, could not, truly know her as herself, could not love her for herself. She began to lose all sense of her identity, swamped by the ever-growing presence in her womb.

It was early in February when the letter came. Cathy found her hands shaking as she took it from Hettie. Joe watched her troubled face as she took it upstairs to their room to read it. She expected anger, recriminations, a demand for explanations. But it was too short a note for any such thing. He simply said:

Dearest love,

I have waited so long for your reply to my letter, and received none. I persuade myself rather that you did not receive it than that you chose to ignore it. But I cannot leave our future lives to silence. I once said to you, Cathy, that nothing would part us, and I would never leave you, unless you yourself sent me away. And this is what I ask of you now, dearest. Either you must tell me that you love me after all, and that you will be my own Cathy once again, or you must tell me, leaving no doubt in my mind as to what you want, you must tell me to go away. Till I receive some reply from you, I shall be in such suspense, Cathy. Please put me out of my misery one way or another.

I love you.
Gilbert.

A sob wrenched itself from some hidden place in Cathy's numb body. Anguish overwhelmed her, splitting the cocoon in which she was imprisoned with a sudden burst of emotion that shocked her entire system. The other being, the one inside her, kicked out to protest, fighting its mother's feelings, instinct pitted against instinct in one flesh. Sitting on the edge of her bed, Cathy calmed herself, holding the baby still in her belly with her hands. And then she rose, went down to the scullery for paper and a pen, and climbed back up the stairs to draft the reply Gilbert demanded. He spoke of a letter, some letter she had never received. Thank God! she thought. At least fate had been kind enough to spare her that. But what could she write? What could she say to him? She sat on the bed, her writing desk on her knee, and stared at the blank sheet of paper. Better be quick, and to the point. She lowered her pen onto the paper and scrawled:

15, Thrift Street.

Dear Gilbert,

I do not want to see you or hear from you ever again. Please do not write.

Yours,
Catherine Straker.

She laid down the pen with a shudder, folded the paper, and pushed it into an envelope which she addressed with care, copying the numbers and words on the top of Gilbert's letter. Avoiding the temptation to read what she had written, she sealed the envelope, and put on her shawl and flew out of the house to post it before she could change her mind.

Cathy's letter, written with such urgency, languished unopened in Belgium. Gilbert, who had joined the Royal Engineers as a second lieutenant, was now with the 177th Mining Company on active service at Hooge. One kilometre up the Menin Road was a spot the men had nicknamed 'Hellfire Corner'. An old railway embankment stood to the left; further on was a wood and a lake. In peacetime it was perhaps quite a pleasant place, but as the men trudged up the hill from base camp they knew the meaning of the words, 'Abandon Hope All Ye Who Enter Here'. Everything that mattered had been left behind them, in the rear trenches, sealed in an envelope, to be sent home in case of accident, and any letters were held over until their return, if they returned at all.

Morale was low as the column marched on to the front. The thirty men of Gilbert's platoon looked up to him for encouragement, advice, instruction. Gilbert, after all, was one of the ruling class. They were used to believing that such a man would therefore know how to rule. But Gilbert recognised his own inadequacy, and turned for guidance to a sergeant, Bill Wright. Bill was an old soldier. He had been in the trenches for three months, and that was old in terms of the war in 1914. He had survived longer than most, and knew all there was to know on the subject. He was twenty-nine and looked much older. He had a wife and five kids at home in Durham, and he spoke with a heavy Geordie accent. His presence was a source of comfort to the young officer, who had been thrown so suddenly into the deep end of a murderous war. For Gilbert's manual might tell him all about the mechanics of his gun, but it said little about the mechanics of pain and fear.

German aircraft flew overhead, too high for the reach of British guns. The men looked up. Some jeered. Most, too deep in thought to care, ploughed on, scratching every now and then as the lice crawled on their skins and in their hair.

'Ye know,' Bill said, 'I think them creepy crawlies are a blessing. They take your mind off things.'

Gilbert smiled. 'Things' covered a multitude of sins.

'Aye,' said Gilbert, in an attempt at the dialect, 'but the rum ration takes your mind off them better!'

They were going into an unreal land. Stunted trees, potholes, mud were the signposts to it. And fear lived in Gilbert alongside a strange joy, which grew stronger as they approached the trenches and settled down to wait the next attack.

When it came, the joy reached a fever pitch and sent each man over the top as though desiring his end. There in the smoke, under incessant fire, Gilbert knew that he could face his own death, and he was charged with an energy that drove him and in turn drove his men. Normal feelings were numbed in him. And when, after the first attack, some of his men looted the bodies of two German soldiers, bayonetted in the fighting, he felt no revulsion. And yet, inside himself, Gilbert knew it was all wrong. But knowing and feeling were two different things.

Then came the waiting time, before the next assault, and the memory of what he'd seen hurt him. It was as though he had become two men, one he recognised, the other he could not. Struggling inwardly, he sought out Bill Wright.

'Aye,' Bill said, 'I know what you mean. We've all got it. It's called the instinct for survival. You've got to go. It's the only way to do it, otherwise how else could you force yourself over the top?'

There were fifteen minutes to go till the time of the next attack. Gilbert felt the skin on his face tighten. The pulse in his throat throbbed along with his heart, too fast, too loud. The silence made the minutes drag. But as each one passed, he approached closer to that inner world of unreality, and his eyes burned with the knowledge that it all had to be gone through again. And again. And again.

Afterwards, the wounded lay close to their own trenches. Their cries could be heard, pleading to be helped back amongst their own. The screams lasted sometimes for hours. But no one could go to help them. They might lie for days and some of them might even be rescued and recover. But the stench of death was all around. There were to be eight days of Hellfire Corner, knee-deep in mud, soaked to the skin, cold, and only the rum ration to warm them. After the dawn stand-to, when the men stood on the fire-step in case of attack, there was a brief lull; a tacit agreement between the two sides not to attack during breakfast. Gilbert organised fatigue parties to repair trenches, and after the dusk stand-to he had to inspect his men. Rations and stores had to be brought up the communicating trenches, latrines had to be sunk where they had caved in, and always mud clung to them, inches deep, making every job hard labour. Battle fever brought on nervous exhaustion. Labouring brought on physical exhaustion. Gilbert would not shirk his share. But the work he hated most was paperwork; everything in triplicate, and such a waste of time. Cathy and Shields seemed far away from Hellfire Corner. Perhaps Gilbert thought, they had never existed at all.

The world wasn't made in a day,
And Eve didn't ride in a bus,
But most of the world's in a sandbag,
And the rest of it's plastered on us.

Bill Wright's grin, on his rum-rosy face, cheered Gilbert. He was an anchor in a sea of mud and fear. He alone had the power to brace and comfort. He was always there, solid and warm and the one real thing in the whole rotten mess. He knew about women, too. Gilbert had talked to him before they were moved up. 'Your trouble, son,' he had told him, 'is that you put them on a pedestal. They're only human, ye know. Like you an' me. Flesh and blood. They need a bit of slap an' tickle. Ye want to thank your lucky stars she likes the idea. And if you don't do somethin' about it, she's bound to go funny, go off you, or find some bugger else!' It certainly brought Gilbert down to earth. 'Ye want to take a leaf out of our book, working classes like . . . bed 'em first, marry 'em after. She'll come round. You'll see.' Thinking about it, Gilbert wondered if he could be right. He had been hampered by his feelings of respect for Cathy. But did it mean he had to respect her less because they made love to one another? The strain of waiting had played on him. Maybe it had also taken its toll of her. He should have taken the bull by the horns and insisted she marry him, or, if she prevaricated, at least shown her his love, fulfilling her and himself, so that afterwards their marriage would seem simply the natural course of events. Brought up by Edith Stoddard, Gilbert was attracted to the passionate nature of a Cathy Straker and yet expected her to behave as rigidly and coolly as his mother! Even May Cochrane had surprised him with the depth of her feelings. He knew that she, who was a lady in even his mother's eyes, would have followed him to the ends of the earth. Then Gilbert was glad of Cathy's wildness, and knew that pushing him from her was the result of a repression of her own too deep feelings for him. She loved him. That was all that mattered and he had been a fool to allow her to push him away. Her strength must be equalled by his own. When his next leave came, he would go home and drag her, resisting if she must, to their wedding, and he would make her sing with the pleasure of it. He would never meet her like again, though he waited the rest of his life, and his passion for her soared through his flesh as though released from a long term in prison.

And it troubled him in the rear trenches, like all the men. But in the front line of fire it was forgotten. Two men drowned in the mud, and the platoon was already down to nineteen. Three days to go. Gilbert did the round of his men's feet. Trench foot, due to constantly soaked socks and boots, was rampant. He managed to get a supply of grease for them to coat their feet.

'Kitchener's thinkin' of enlistin' ducks, ye kna,' Bill laughed. It wasn't funny, but Gilbert laughed all the same.

'Keep on changing your socks. Three times a day if need be!' Gilbert told the platoon. And the sickening odour of the feet mingled with the smell of the lime and rotting vegetation, the latrines and the stench of the dead.

'The ducks wouldn't come,' Gilbert said to his sergeant. 'They'd have more sense.' And Bill's eyes smiled.

Then came their last assault. Gilbert had felt feverish for two days. A result of infection from the lice. But he had shaken it off and kept going. And then they went into the fifteen minutes' silence before zero hour. The fever burned higher as the now familiar battle joy rose in him. The niceties of his mother's parlour were a joke to him. A tear stung his cheek as he smiled grimly in remembrance of it. So 'nice' she was. Cathy was not 'nice'. There in that fifteen minutes, Cathy became real to him again. She would understand all this. She was not afraid of the depths of human experience. She lived. And he too would live, for her. In the frenzy of death, Gilbert thought of life. Then the time came. Over the top into no-man's-land, Bill Wright at his side. Overhead the roar and clamour of battle, almost tangible. It was the backcloth to hell. Gilbert screamed and went into it.

Bayonets, grenades, shells, gunfire rained and drummed at them. The litter of no-man's-land tripped their feet, tin cans, barbed wire; and Bill Wright caught his foot and fell, and a German, with bayonet raised, speared him into the mud. Gilbert heard his agony but could not help him. He thrashed about him, slipped, fell, rose, shouted at his men, fired into nowhere and heard the answering cry when, by chance, some target was hit. And then it was over. And the worst of the litter was left; bodies, and one of them was Bill Wright's. No advance had been made on either side.

But Bill was not dead. Not yet. Gilbert, exhausted and shocked, stumbled over the corpses towards him. Bill's rosy face was now white. His hand lay across a mess of blood and entrails. His eyes, black and round with pain, opened onto Gilbert's blackened face.

'Do's a favour,' said the sergeant. 'Finish's off.'

There, in the middle of no-man's-land, Gilbert wanted to cry. He stared back into the pain-dark eyes of his friend, raised his gun and fired into Bill's head.

Dusk was falling. He was a target where he stood. Gilbert tore himself away and staggered off, blindly, in the wrong direction. He had to get back to the trenches, to what was left of his platoon. He stumbled on and his foot slid on the edge of a shell hole. In his exhaustion, his balance gone, he fell into it. And he felt the mud pulling him down, dragging his flesh, and he could neither cry out nor breathe for fear he would be sucked down for ever. Slowly, he sank. Hours passed. And the unreality struggled in him with his instinct to survive. On the one side oblivion called him, on the other life, and the passion for it that he knew was in Cathy Straker fought against the encroaching darkness.

Six men returned to the rear trenches from Hellfire Corner. Gilbert was not among them. Two days passed. A brother officer took it upon himself to open and read the letter that had been waiting for him. He shrugged. It wouldn't matter now. Gilbert Stoddard was missing, presumed dead. He handed the letter to the chaplain, who kept it, and wondered whether to send it home to Gilbert's mother. But as the next platoon in the firing line advanced, they stumbled on the head of a man sticking out of the mud, and a hand two feet away which appeared to belong to it. They cleared the mud from its nose, and Gilbert opened his eyes.

Unhurt, but suffering from exhaustion, Gilbert rested for a week in hospital before returning to the rear trenches. There the letter from Cathy finally caught up with him. He had thought himself safe at last, when life itself dealt him a blow. He would not mind going over the top. Not any more. His reason for staying alive had been taken from him.

The first Coalition government came to power in May. Gilbert had spent his last leave in London, in spite of his mother's demands that he return home and her plans for himself and May Cochrane. Instead, she was forced to visit him in London and attend some of the suppers and parties that Gilbert was invited to. She stayed for two days and then went home; she seemed to have lost all hold over her son and felt more lonely than ever.

Cathy's baby was due in early June. But it seemed sluggish in coming, content to stay where it was for a while longer. Hettie was quite excited at the prospect of a baby in the house. Lily seemed unaware that any such event was about to take place, and so Hettie expected to have the care of the child often when its mother was out at work. Cathy was afraid. As her time grew nearer, she was drawn to Joe's shadow, as though for shelter, and he was glad of it. His hand reached out to hers in bed, and they lay silently, not needing words, growing closer as the time approached. But the baby wouldn't come. Every day Joe came back from his work at the public convenience near Marine Park and gave his wife an enquiring look. And she just sighed and shrugged. Then, finally, on 15 June something happened. Exasperated with the stalemate in France, the Germans launched a zeppelin attack. Five bombs fell in Shields. It was the trigger that shocked Cathy out of her lethargy and silence. Hettie helped her up to her room and sent Mr Miller out for the doctor first, and then Joe. Cathy was in labour.

The house was like a battleground. At the top of it, Cathy howled in pain; in the kitchen, Lily laid into Joe; and in between, the lodgers cowered in their rooms, hoping that a bomb wouldn't fall on them from the Jerry raid. At one time Joe pushed his way past his mother-in-law and up the stairs to Cathy's room. He stood by horrified as he heard her scream, the sweat pouring down her face. Lily came on after him and stood by him watching her daughter. Only Hettie held her hand and wiped her forehead with a wet flannel from time to time.

'It's God's punishment,' Lily said as Cathy's eyes, black and unseeing, seemed to fix on her. And Cathy wondered whether it would have been any easier if it had been a rich man's bastard that she was bearing.

Lily turned to Joe and said in a loud voice, 'You'll have to leave her alone after this, aye, and for quite a while. She's havin' a bad time. And mind you do, Joe Robson! Or I'll hear you! The walls are thin in Thrift Street!'

All the lodgers must have heard her. Joe hung his head and left the room, to sit, knuckles clenched and white over the kitchen table, waiting.

'You're holdin' back,' Hettie whispered in Cathy's ear. 'You'd think you didn't want to give birth, lass. Let it go.'

Cathy moaned and sobbed and then, at last, one more pain, more terrible than all the rest, and the baby's head came into the world.

'Where's the doctor? Where's the bloody doctor?' Cathy screamed.

The doctor was too busy seeing to casualties from the bomb, and Hettie had no time to answer her. She held the baby's head in her hands. It blinked once. Then one more final effort and its body slipped out of its mother into Hettie's arms.

'Give it to me,' Cathy reached her arms out towards it.

But Lily held up a cloth. She took it from the aunt and wiped it clean, billing and cooing at the infant.

'Go on Hettie. She's got the afterbirth to come. Pummel her belly. Go on!'

Hettie laid the mother back against the pillow, and her hands gently massaged the sore, swollen flesh.

'Harder woman! Harder!'

Cathy moaned, but driven on by Lily's eye, Hettie went at it like a wrestler; it felt like a punishment for doing wrong. Satisfied as Cathy's body finally ridded itself of the afterbirth, Lily turned back to the baby. It had fine blonde hair on the crown of its head, and its eyes were dark.

'It's a girl,' Lily said, nodding and pleased. 'Who's a pretty little lady, eh? You are! And who's goin' to grow up to break all the men's hearts, eh? You will! Yes! Yes! Your Nana says so!'

She held the child to her, laying her cheek against its head, smiling for the first time in months. Exhausted, Cathy lay back watching her.

'She needs a name, doesn't she?' Lily said.

'Yes, Cathy. What are you going to call her?' Hettie smiled. Cathy shook her head. She hadn't thought about it, hadn't even taken in the reality of the child until the moment it had separated itself from her. Lily's hand brushed lightly over the baby's head.

'It's hair's so pale, almost silver.' She smiled indulgently at the child. 'I know what we'll call her, we'll call her Sylvia!'

PART FIVE

CHAPTER EIGHTEEN

Gilbert's eyes opened. He had survived. The chatter of the guns, the whining of the shells had stopped. The screaming and the shouts had given way to moans. He was aware of a cold wetness beneath him, and above him the weeping skies of the Somme. He tried to move his leg, and could not. A pain shot up from knee to thigh. He smiled. It meant that at least his leg was still part of him. His mind began to drift. He became aware of a heavy smell. It was wood burning. The very trees were on fire. Suddenly he began to shake. He couldn't still himself. It was uncontrollable. The shaking caused unutterable pain in his leg. He vomited and then fainted, lying back in a pool of mud.

At first he saw only the red cross. It frightened him. The redness of it jumped out to attack his nerves, and he cried out. But gentle hands came down and held him still, till he could focus better. It was a woman, a tired woman, with rings under her eyes. She was speaking to him, but he couldn't hear her for the guns rattling in his head. He watched her lips moving. Her hand raised to touch his head, but he flinched from her. Her expression showed her hurt. And he was sorry.

'Are you English?' he shouted.

The nurse nodded, and smiled. Then Gilbert laughed, tears rolling down his face, and she was telling him to sleep. He tried to sit up but swooned at the attempt, and when he next came round she wasn't there.

And so Gilbert rocked between periods of equal nightmare, whether awake or asleep. But gradually the guns in his head quietened, and he began to hear the relative peace of the hospital barracks. Once, he heard them again, he heard the familiar whine of a shell, the last sound before he had been thrown from the trench and flung into no-man's-land.

But this time the guns were real. The nurses packed up and the patients were moved on to another, safer place. He thought he wouldn't see her again, the one whose lips had moved without any sound. But suddenly she was there. She smiled at him and lifted the cover at the bottom of his bed.

'Still got it then?' Gilbert said.

'Your leg? Yes of course you have Captain Stoddard.' She smiled and removed the dressings from his knee and his shin.

'What's the matter with it?'

'Shrapnel.'

'Please can you speak up. I can hardly hear you for the noise.'

She looked at him in some surprise.

'What noise?'

'The guns.'

She frowned and took his wrist, watching the quivering hand that hung from it.

'It'll go away,' she said, 'in time. It's shell shock. That's all.' But she didn't look at him. She couldn't bear to see the fear in their eyes when they had been shocked. It was a panic that easily transferred itself, and she must remain calm and collected.

'Haven't I seen you before?' Gilbert asked her.

'That's an obvious line!'

'No. Really!'

'You probably won't remember. I was with you in the other place.'

Gilbert nodded.

'Where do you come from?'

'Norwich.'

'Oh! And what's your name?'

'Duncan. Nurse Duncan.' Gilbert looked at her. 'First name Anne. Married. Thirty-one years old.' With that she slapped a new dressing on his leg and left him.

Gilbert liked her homely, down-to-earth attitude. It made him feel easy with her. It even made him smile. She got teased a lot, and under pressure the only thing that cracked were her jokes. She was in good spirits, though very tired, because she had leave coming up and her husband had wangled his at the same time so that they could meet in Paris. She desperately wanted a child, and, she laughed, they'd never manage it on the scraps of leave she and Peter managed to get together. Gilbert wished her luck and waved her goodbye with some regret. Without her the dreams got worse, and he woke up sweating, calling up for help in the middle of the night, the guns and shells howling and clattering in his ears. His leg hurt too, and he was afraid of gangrene. But they were all so busy. He would wait. He would put up with it and try to sleep. Maybe when he woke the nightmare would finally have ended. He tried not to think of Cathy. She was, in any case, so far away, in a different world which was hard for him to remember. Sometimes he wondered if it was still there, and whether he'd ever be able to fit himself back into it on his return, even if it was. He felt dishevelled and dirty. With heavy casualties coming in constantly, they'd had no time in the past few days to bother with shaving him, and his hand shook so much that he couldn't do it himself. He spilt tea down his bedclothes, and pricked his nose with his fork. He had become afraid of trying. And then Nurse Duncan came back.

'You look more tired than ever,' Gilbert laughed.

'Second honeymoon,' she smiled. 'What do you expect? I'm sleeping on my feet!'

Then she thrust a bowl of water towards him, followed by a shaving brush, soap and a razor.

'Try,' she said. 'Come on. I'll steady your hand.'

She set the mirror before him, and a white face stared back at him.

'That's not me,' he said.

'Yes it is,' Nurse Duncan replied sadly.

Cathy stared in the mirror, her brush halted in mid-air. It was as though she was seeing herself for the first time in years. She looked somehow different. Her face was thin and pale. Dark rings circled her eyes, and her hair was drab. She leaned forwards, closer to the mirror, and stared at the strands of hair falling before her face. It was red, but not the same red. It had grown dull, and lost its vibrant colour. Her eyes fell away from the glass and a tear fell on her hand. Joe stirred. Cathy looked at him lying in their bed. His face was puckered, not at peace. He, like her, had grown used to sleeping against the ceaseless crying of the child. The wads of cotton wool protruded from his ears. Cathy snorted with laughter at the sight. Poor Joe. She knew she ought to love him. If any man ever earned a woman's love, then Joe had earned hers, again and again. And yet she couldn't, she just couldn't love him. She'd gone cold, numb. She stared down at the tear still resting on her hand. She hadn't cried in months. And what a thing to cry about . . . her hair had lost its colour! As if there was nothing worse! The hand itself was red and chapped. A red weal crossed the back of her left hand where the knife had slipped, for she had been taken on over the river, on the fish quay. She was a filletter.

Hettie tapped gently at the door, then opened it.

'It's time,' she whispered, and handed in two mugs of tea, heavily sugared.

'Thanks, Hettie.'

'The bairn's sleepin' then.' Both women looked across at the sleeping baby. A frown creased its brow permanently. It was moody and bad tempered, and had spurned its mother's milk, so that her breasts were sore and swollen. Cathy sighed.

'Thank God for small mercies,' she said.

Hettie bent forwards and picked the child up.

'I'll take her down to Lily, then,' she said and gingerly carried the bundle down the stairs to Lily's room.

Cathy was grateful to be rid of the child, though she felt it was also a kind of defeat. For Lily was the only one of them who had the power to quieten Sylvia. She screamed and screamed till the house shook, disturbing their sleep, lodgers and family alike. They were exhausted from nights of wakefulness, their nerves shattered by the din. In the end she had let Lily take her off her hands, and went out seeking work instead. It was Hettie's relations who'd come up with the job over the river. Miss Hutchinson had shut up shop long ago and gone down to Whitby to live with her sister, and after all, as Hettie put it, 'beggars can't be choosers'. So Cathy had rolled up her sleeves and begun to learn how to use the sharp filletting knife.

'Joe.' Cathy touched the sleeping man, lightly, and he woke with a start. 'Your tea's there.'

'Ta.' Joe stretched and yawned, then flopped back on the bed. 'I don't like you gettin' up so early, pet,' he said.

'I'm not too keen on it meself, hinny!' Cathy laughed a tight little laugh, which was becoming something of a habit with her. Downstairs in Lily's room they could hear Sylvia crying.

'She's started,' Joe said.

Cathy took no notice, but continued dressing.

'D'ye not think ye should go down?'

She sighed.

'Let her get on with it. It's what she wants.'

'She's your baby.'

'She's not yours.' Joe looked hurt. 'I'm sorry.'

Joe shrugged, and raised himself to drink his tea.

'Ye never used to be so . . . cold, Cathy,' he said.

Cathy looked at him a long, long time, and then left the room.

Down the cobbles past Comical Corner to the ferry, coming and going across the river, morning after morning. What did he expect? What did any of them expect? Downstairs in the kitchen Hettie waited with a slab of bread and dripping for her to eat as she dashed down the hill to the quayside. She went with Cathy to the door, and they stood outside in the dark for a moment.

'Do you know, Hettie,' Cathy said, 'I think it'd have been better if we'd told Mam the truth. About the baby I mean, and . . . and the Captain.'

Hettie frowned.

'Better in what way?'

'Better for Joe.' Cathy paused staring down at the cobbles. 'I'll never be a wife to him, Hettie.'

Hettie said nothing for a while.

'Give it time, pet,' she said at last. 'You're still low after the baby. It's just . . . well, you need takin' out of yourself, that's all.'

Cathy didn't answer her. She looked up at the stars overhead between the house tops.

'Maybe if we told her now. Then Joe'd be free to go, if he wanted.'

Hettie shook her head.

'He wouldn't go. No, pet. If we told her, you'd never hear the end of it. She'd ruin even what memories you've got. You hang on to your dreams, pet. Because dreams is all you've got. I should know.' Hettie's voice wavered. Cathy pulled her shawl over her head and tossing a 'Tarrah, Hettie' over her shoulder she clattered on down the hill.

The early morning on the river, the first ferry across, morning after morning, without end. Leaning over the rail she watched the cold waters churning away behind her, and smelt the salt tang from the sea. Lizzie MacNaughton came across with her, both half asleep, dead to the world, silent as the grave, as the boat chugged over the dark river. She was a canny lass, was Lizzie. She sang too, like a bird.

Cathy listened to her sudden outbursts of song among the tar and the fish smells, but she didn't join in. She thought of Joe over in his public convenience on the south side, and her on the quay on the north side, and never the twain shall meet. At least, not till each was exhausted and ready for sleep again. Their real lives were separate. No wonder they found it hard to get to know one another. And then, off the boat, Lizzie and Cathy walked together to the fish quay, clattering a bogie between them, fetching boxes of fish, bought at a good price, and setting down to gut and fillet them ready for sale. Dead fish eyes stared up out of the offal bin, and the stench of the glue factory made the air rank. No, the little mermaid didn't turn to foam, she lived on, a living death, cold as marble inside and out, her tail cut off and flung with the rest of the offal in the bins, ready to be made into glue. And, so Cathy thought, 'the best place for it an all!'

Then it was home again, back over the river, and up the cobbles, home to Thrift Street. Aye, Hettie was right. Dreams were all she had to live on.

Joe was late home that night. Hettie's eyes questioned him as he came in, and his answered with a twinkle and a nod. Lily, nursing the baby, sharp as a new pin, caught the look.

'And what's goin' on here?' she enquired. 'Or is it a secret?'

'Pity if it was, Lily,' Hettie snapped back.

Cathy sat, away from the fire, sipping her tea, her hands packed with lard to relieve the soreness.

'It's a treat. For Cathy,' Joe said. 'Hettie and me are takin' her to the Queen's.'

Lily was furious, though she could think of nothing to say in reply.

'She needs takin' out of herself, Lily,' Hettie explained. 'She's miserable an' low since the baby. She needs liftin' up.'

Lily snorted.

'And what's on at the Queen's?'

'Oh, just a bit of music hall!'

They all thought Lily would explode. Her cheeks bulged and her tongue flickered out menacingly, but then, like a faulty balloon, her anger deflated and she shrugged.

'Huh! She cannot fall much further, I suppose!'

Hettie was enraged.

'The nobility go to the music hall, Lily. There's no need to be so snotty about it!' But Joe touched her arm and glanced uneasily at Cathy. She hadn't looked up once during the interchange, and, after all, it was all for her.

It was to be a gala occasion. Hettie wanted Cathy to wear her brown velvet suit. She shook her head.

'Past glories, Hettie,' she said.

'Hadaway wi ye!' Hettie snapped. 'You're gettin' me down, lass. We've gone to a lot of trouble for you.'

'I don't know what for, Hettie. Honestly, I think we should let Joe go.'

'Don't talk so daft.' She held the skirt in front of her. 'Try it on, now.'

Cathy looked at the waist. It looked ominously small.

'Coward!' Hettie jeered at her.

So Cathy took the skirt and slipped it over her head. It fell gently round her hips, but the waist wouldn't meet.

'It only needs lettin' out a bit.'

'A bit!' Cathy protested. 'It's all of two inches! It'll spoil the lie of it!'

'No it won't.' And Hettie set to, altering the costume.

Cathy remembered getting ready for another occasion altogether when she had reached for Hettie's rouge. This time, it was an essential part of her toilet. It warmed her face, and even made her feel better as she looked at herself in the glass. The skirt didn't hang so badly after all, and she could leave the jacket hanging loose. No one would notice. Joe smiled at her approvingly.

'You look a cracker, Cathy,' he said. 'By, but I could fancy you!'

Cathy looked quickly away, and he could have bitten out his tongue for such a slip. But it was soon forgotten as they left, arm in arm, for the tram and then on to the theatre.

There were khaki suits everywhere. Faces were brilliant with smiles and laughter, all too much, too brittle, and filled with shadows of barbed wire and sandbags, bodies torn and bleeding in the mud. The determination to enjoy themselves was close to hysteria, and it frightened Cathy, who still could not be persuaded to emerge from her chrysalis. She sat between her aunt and her husband and listened to the dirty jokes and the roaring laughter. She could feel Joe's leg, warm against hers, and when she glanced towards him to see his laughing face he looked back at her, aware of her every movement, and put his one good arm round her protectively. As she looked at him she saw, over his shoulder, a woman threading her way towards them. Cathy did not know her, had never seen her in her life before. But there was no doubt she was coming towards them. Joe was looking at Cathy and did not see. Cathy frowned and opened her mouth to speak, but then the woman was on them. She poked Joe in the back, and he turned in surprise to see a white feather held in her hand. His mouth dropped open, and he looked from the feather up to her face. She pressed it towards him with a smug expression.

'Excuse me, young man. This is for you,' she said in a posh voice. Then she held it up for all to see and handed it to him. Joe took it quietly. 'I suppose you *have* noticed you're the only man here not in uniform.' Then she spat at him 'Conchy!' All around them people began to hiss, 'Conchy, conchy conchy!' Joe stared at the woman, unbelieving, the cloth of his jacket sagging over his empty shoulder. Suddenly Cathy found her voice. She shouted loudly, so the whole audience could hear.

'He's lost his shoulder! He was invalided out ye filthy, foul-mouthed bitch!'

Then Hettie joined in. 'You tell her Cathy! An' come to that, Missus, why aren't *you* at the front?' The woman backed away, falling over the feet of the seated audience. 'If you feel as strong as that about it, why don't you go dig a trench an' sit in it!'

Joe's head hung low on his chest. Tears streamed down Cathy's face. She took his arm, lovingly.

'Come on, Joe,' she said. 'Let's go home.' Then he rose, and Cathy, followed by Hettie, left the theatre, close behind him.

Cathy couldn't stop crying. All the way home on the tram the tears kept falling, and her body shook. She sat between the pair of them, and they held her comfortingly, but it was Joe she wanted. And, when they got home, they went straight up to the attic without so much as calling on Lily. Joe helped her undress and Hettie brought up some whipped cocoa, which made Cathy begin crying again. So Joe held her in his arms, and she leaned against him, burying her face in his chest, till the sobbing was over. And then he picked her up and put her into bed, crawling in after her to hold her tight. Gently, he rocked her.

'Oh Joe! Joe, I could've killed her! I could honest.'

'She doesn't matter. None o' them do. Even your Mam!'

Cathy laughed and sobbed at once.

'Silly old faggot!'

'Aye.'

And then Cathy looked at his face in the light of the candle. Her hand touched his cheek, and she shook her head and kissed him lightly on the nose. He smiled, and brought her in close to him again, stroking her back, her shoulders

CHAPTER NINETEEN

Gilbert's recovery was slow. But he didn't mind it. He had no great desire to get back home, his world was quite complete where he was. He enjoyed Nurse Duncan's presence on the ward. They all did. And he found himself feeling her joy for her when her letters arrived, and her fears when they didn't. He was living life by proxy, which was about as much as he could bear. She had told him that he would be sent to a nursing home for officers for a little while, to help him recover from the shell shock. His nightmares kept on recurring, and his hands still shook. The slightest sudden noise sent him into a wild panic, gasping and crying out like a child. He felt ashamed of these displays of emotion afterwards, but no one else seemed to mind that much. They were merely . . . an aberration. 'Stoddard's off again,' they said. But she knew, Nurse Duncan, how to cope with him. She was strong, firm, and warm. He admired her hugely.

And then, one day, Nurse Duncan missed her duty. The ward was shortstaffed. He asked if she was ill, and they told him that she had a headache but would be back with him in a day or two. Gilbert was due for discharge and he found himself panicking in case he didn't see her again. No one would tell him the truth. He was sure there was something more. His day of release came. He asked for Nurse Duncan's private address, but they refused to give it to him. Feeling low in spirits, Gilbert left the hospital, believing she had gone out of his life for ever.

They sent him to a nursing home near Cromer. He stayed inside for the first week, but he hankered after the sea air. He had been born and brought up by the sea, it was his home, not so much Tyneside itself as the North Sea, always there, always the same and yet not the same. They let him go for walks along the beach. At first the rattling of the pebbles, drawn down the shingle by the receding tide, sent his nerves to screaming pitch and Gilbert ran back to the home, shaking. But he forced himself to suffer the sound, telling himself time and again that it was only pebbles, and there was no need to run. And gradually he was able to stay out there for some time, walking along the Norfolk shore. He walked a long way some days, over as far as Sheringham and the golf course just beyond. The air brought colour back into his face and he breathed it in in deep gulps, and felt the strength returning to him. His shin ached, though, when the wind was cold, and he had to wrap it in layers of wool or else it pained him badly, a nagging pain, that set his teeth on edge. And his knee was stiff. But like Joe, with his arm, Gilbert managed to do more than anyone would have thought possible with his gammy leg.

A woman emerging from the hotel near the beach saw Gilbert striding out along the shingle. His leg seemed stiff, giving him a slightly rocking gait. She was sad and withdrawn, and her eyes followed him for some time before she made up her mind. Suddenly, she made off across the back of the hotel and came out beyond the bathing huts to cut him off. She stood in the middle of the path, her arms extended, grinning at him. He stopped in his tracks, and the concentrated frown on his forehead gave way to a broad smile.

'Nurse Duncan! I presume!' he laughed. And then they hugged one another like long lost acquaintances. 'Another second honeymoon?'

Anne Duncan's face fell. She shook her head.

'Didn't they tell you?' But she could see by Gilbert's face that they hadn't. 'Peter was killed.' Her face creased, and a long howl issued from her. It cut Gilbert to the bone. He took her hands and held them hard, looking intently at her, till the pain had gone again. 'I'm sorry,' she sobbed. He held on to her hand and they walked on across the golf course in silence.

They met every day after that, stopping for tea in Sheringham to eat dressed crab and stare out of the steamed windows at the sea outside. It was their favourite stopping place, and they became well known to the lady proprietor who served them. Anne told him all about Peter Duncan. He was from Northampton, they had met at a race meeting where her father, a gambling man, frequented the course. She and Peter had hit it off right away. He was a gambler too, though not as bad as her father, or, at least, he was better at it. He had won the money for her engagement ring on the Derby. And they had married in Liverpool after he'd lost his all on the National. They had a tiny flat in Islington, and she took up nursing and tried to keep them on her wages. And then the war came. He made a fine soldier. But he had gambled once too often. And now she was alone again. Her father had been forced into steady employment and was quite happy pushing a pen, well behind the lines, in the army food stores.

She, in turn, heard all about Cathy, and the story troubled her. Gilbert showed her Cathy's last letter, and she stared at it a long time.

'Whatever the reason she wrote it,' Anne said, 'I think you have to abide by what she says. Perhaps, one day, you'll find out what really happened.' And then she had smiled softly at him, and he had taken hold of her hand and kissed it. It was the first moment that they knew that although neither of them had been the other's first choice, still, they might do. Neither of them said anything, but each left the restaurant that day feeling a lightness of heart that they hadn't experienced for some time. The grey drab days of the dregs of war had given way to light and colour at last.

There was an announcement in *The Times*. Mr Miller, who had never given up his old practice of reading all the papers in the public library, saw it, and came back to Thrift Street with the news. Cathy was larding her hands in the scullery, and Lily and Sylvia had gone out for some air. She took it calmly.

'I'm glad,' she said, and set about preparing tea for her Joe. She and Joe seemed happy enough. Their love grew, as if to spite the harshness of their lives, not to mention Lily.

Year in, year out, long after the war ended, Cathy chugged across the river in the *Ha'penny Dodger,* as adept with her filletting knife as Joe was with his lavatory brush. But they both had their separate dreams still. Cathy, watching the dolphins playing in the Tyne waters, saw the dawn light, struggling through the early morning mists, her shawl tight over her ears, water freezing from the end of her nose, and relived the old dreams. But even those faded in time, died in Sylvia's cold, grey eyes, froze inside her on the fish quay, her hands blocks of ice, up to her armpits in fish scales. The last flip of the mermaid's tail, and Cathy was lulled by the Tyne waters into accepting her lot.

Joe saw that contentment, for her, was a kind of defeat, and it irked him. He wished he could make it better for her, for himself. Sitting in his warm little room, down in the lavatories on Ocean Road, reading the paper, Joe might also have appeared to be content. He struck up friendships with some of his more regular customers, and on a fine day he would emerge from his cosy underground world to stand in silent companionship with one or other of them, staring out to sea as the seagulls reeled overhead and the ships disappeared over the horizon. His eyes strained to follow them and Fred Reed, standing at his side, read the longing in them.

'You want to think yourself lucky you've *got* a job!' he said.

Joe looked at him in surprise, wondering what was behind the remark. He had known Fred for years now. They had shared many cups of tea together in Joe's little room under the road, reading their papers, exchanging the odd remark about the weather, the state of the nation, or the health of their wives, leaving more dangerous topics, their dreams, unspoken, by mutual consent. What now had occasioned Fred to break their pact?

'I've been laid off,' he said. So that was it! It took a personal calamity to break the pattern of years, to disrupt the cosy habit of their friendship.

'I'm sorry, Fred,' Joe answered him simply.

'The shape of things to come, Joe lad.'

'Aye, it looks like it.' The two men riveted their eyes on a fishing boat as it emerged from the river, and plodded out to sea. 'I read in the papers this morning there was a slump coming.'

'Aye,' Fred sighed, and began to roll a cigarette. 'I'll have to give this lot up,' he said, indicating his tobacco. 'Not thirty yet, and on the scrap heap. By God it makes you wonder.'

Joe's heart ached for him. The tragedy of wasted lives! He hadn't the words for it.

'There must be something we could do!' he said at last. Fred Reed snorted, his bitter disillusion drawing Joe up sharp. 'Well, there must, man! We can't just give up!'

'There *are* no jobs!' Fred almost shouted, but Joe topped him.

'Then we've got to *make* them!' he said. At last the two men were looking at each other, eyeball to eyeball. It was their first real contact in all their years of friendship.

'All right.' Fred's tone changed. 'You tell me how. You tell me, Joe.'

Joe looked away, afraid, almost, to give his own dream a voice at last.

'I wasn't always like this . . .' he began, then cleared the frog from his throat before continuing. Fred watched him expectantly. 'I used to be an active sort of a man. I was a stoker on the ferries for years, Fred, shovellin' coal, and by, it's a hard job that.'

Fred grunted his agreement. He was a welder in the dockyards till a few days back and he knew what hard work was like, same as the next man.

'But I wasn't doin' it for the fun of it, you know,' Joe went on. 'I had ideas, Fred. I was savin' up.' Joe paused dramatically. 'There were a few of us then, with the same idea.'

Fred bit his tongue to stop himself blurting out, 'Get on with it, man.'

'We were savin' up to go shares in a fishin' boat.' Joe's eyes were fixed straight ahead of him and Fred followed his gaze, out to sea, where the little fishing boat cut a lonely figure as it progressed outwards, getting ever smaller. 'I've still got them savin's, Fred.' A frown crossed Fred's forehead. What was Joe getting at? 'The trouble is, it's not a venture you can go into on your own,' Joe explained. 'And the other lads . . . well, the war . . .'

Fred understood the unfinished sentence. Then suddenly he was surprised as Joe's eyes turned on him.

'Have you got anything? Savings, like?'

Fred backed off momentarily.

'I've got a bit, but . . .'

'There must be others, Fred, other men, who'd like to join us.'

'You're talkin' about me life's savin's man.' Fred's voice was shaky. 'My family's only security!'

'I know,' said Joe calmly, 'but how long do you think the money'll last out? A lifetime?'

'No.' Fred shook his head.

'Fred, this'd be an investment in the future!'

Fred stared at Joe in amazement. This man, this lavatory attendant, had a fire in his eyes, and eeh by, that fire was catching!

Cathy thought so too, but like Fred she was afraid.

'My Dad died at sea,' she said. 'And there's you with only one shoulder. You're at a disadvantage to start with. It's too dangerous!'

'Better a bit of danger than a dead-end job!' he answered her. And she was answered. This idea of Joe's had shocked her into the realisation that their lives were indeed 'dead-end'. Without knowing it, they had been dying slowly in Thrift Street. They needed shaking out of their complacency.

'I don't know what me Mam'd say!' she said.

'Sod your Mam!' Joe said with great conviction.

Joe couldn't wait to get his plans off the ground. He and Fred began to put out feelers to their acquaintances, testing their possible response to a full approach. Rollo Cook, a pitman and a customer at the 'gents', was sick of the everlasting darkness; he was ready to swap one danger for another and put in his savings to boot. Fred's old comrade in arms, Charlie Ockenshaw from Lancaster, was game, and Cathy whispered the idea to her partner on the quayside, Lizzie MacNaughton, whose man had been a fisherman before the war. Excitement grew and Joe's heart was full as his dream looked to come to life at last. The conspirators met in pubs, scanning the papers for boats for sale, going off to inspect them, arguing on the price, the size, the condition of each one; till, finally, they came upon their boat, lying in dock up at North Shields and looking sorry for itself.

'She needs a lick of paint!' Charlie said.

'She needs a bit more than that,' said Bob MacNaughton.

'How d'ye weld wood?' Fred asked. And they all laughed, sizing up the work they needed to put in before the boat could be declared seaworthy.

The time for a family conference was fast approaching. 'The evil hour', as Cathy jokingly called it. But Joe bided his time until Lily was in as good a mood as they could get her before broaching the subject. It was Hettie's birthday. 'The Sanctuary' had been opened up as of old, and tipsy on sherry, Hettie was tinkering at the piano as Sylvia, showing off her lessons in deportment, gave them a rendering of 'Madam, Will You Walk?' Mr Miller had been let in on the secret, and slyly he kept on topping up Lily's glass till she too was smirking with pleasure. Mr Miller winked, and Joe took the hint. The 'evil hour' was upon them.

'I've got some good news!' Joe's voice rose above the applause as Sylvia took her place at her Nana's side. All eyes turned on him. Joe faltered for a second, and Cathy put her hand in his to encourage him. 'I *hope* you'll all be pleased anyway!'

'Well, get on with it, man!' Lily was not as forebearing as Fred Reed!

'Oh, sorry, Mrs . . . er . . .' Joe, as usual, was at a loss what to call his mother-in-law. He couldn't call her Lily, and couldn't bring himself to call her 'Mother', and Mrs Straker now seemed too formal, so where possible he avoided calling her anything at all. 'I've been doin' a lot of thinking lately,' he went on. 'And, it seems to me that things are goin' to get worse in this country before they get any better. And, well, it's time we made an investment in our future.'

Lily's back stiffened, and the smirk left her face. She had heard that word 'investment' before and it hadn't done her any good then.

'What do you mean by that?' she asked sharply.

'Look, my job . . .' Lily snorted and Cathy darted her mother a warning look. 'My job's what you might call "dead-end". It's not even really necessary and there's blokes bein' made redundant all the time. It could be my turn next. And even if it isn't, I can't see the Council puttin' up me wages in the present economic climate, can you?' There was general assent. 'So, as prices rise, what I bring in's goin' to buy less and less.'

'What *are* you drivin' at, Joe?' Hettie was sobering fast as the threat of the slump was brought home to her.

'It seems daft to me to keep my savings, which you all know about, gettin' mouldy in the Post Office when they could be put to some good use.' Lily's alarm grew. 'Originally, like, they were intended to cover my share in a fishing boat, and I don't see why they couldn't be used to the same purpose now.'

'You've not got enough for a fishing boat!' Lily put in triumphantly.

'Aye. But we've formed a syndicate, like, a few of the lads . . .' A squeak issued from Lily's strangled throat. 'We're goin' to do it, Mrs er . . . we're goin' to buy a fishin' boat.'

'But that money's wer only security!' The words were carried on an anguished wail. Lily grasped her granddaughter by the waist and rocked her to and fro in an agony of fear. They said life kept on repeating itself, didn't they? She couldn't believe it. That the good Lord should smite her twice, and that some man should again gamble her all on the sea. Oh no, she couldn't bear it. She couldn't!

'Don't you think you should hang on to the job you've got,' Hettie asked anxiously. Joe looked annoyed at this remark. 'I'm sorry, Joe, it's just that, supposing the boat sank, and you were lost at sea . . .' Her voice wavered and

Cathy turned her eyes away. Her aunt had voiced her own fears. 'What'd happen to the rest of us?' Hettie went on.

'She's got a point, lad,' Mr Miller put in.

Joe glowered and Cathy felt her hand clammy in his.

'There's a bunch of you,' Mr Miller went on, 'more than enough to crew a boat like that one. Surely you can't all go out in it can you?'

Joe said nothing, and Cathy at his side kept her silence too.

'You've got nae shoulder, Joe,' Hettie said gently, 'why don't you leave the crewing to the other lads?'

There was a long pause. Cathy held her breath. It was what she wanted, but she knew what a sacrifice it would mean to Joe, left behind in his underground room, while the other men tasted the salty dangers of the North Sea. Man as he was, he could not contain the sob that rose to his throat and swallowed hard. They were right, of course. He had his responsibilities. So had the other men, but they *were* whole men, not a useless cripple like himself! Cathy followed his thought, reading it through the flesh that touched her own.

'You go out with them, if you want, Joe. Nobody's goin' to stop you,' she said.

Joe smiled sadly.

'No,' he said, 'I'll not go.'

'I gather from Mr Miller that you've already got your eye on some boat or other,' Lily broke into the following silence.

'More than that, Lily.' The use of her Christian name shocked her. 'We've already bought it.'

Sylvia was astonished to find herself thrust aside as her grandmother flew out of the parlour and up to her room where she threw herself on the bed to wail helplessly against her fate.

'Well,' said Mr Miller. 'That's that!'

Joe's mouth betrayed the ghost of a smile.

'Aye,' he said.

It was full steam ahead now, if that boat was to make the most of the summer's fishing. Mr Miller went down to lend a hand from time to time, and a comradeship grew amongst the men and their wives, filling a gap in Joe and Cathy's life. They had a common goal, a future to work for, and hope, above all, hope.

'We'll have to think of a name for her,' Lizzie said as she and Cathy came down to watch the progress after their morning's work on the quay. Many names were suggested; Lizzie fancied 'Lucky' or 'The Good Hope', but Fred said Lucky sounded more like a dog's name and they didn't want to tempt fate with a name like 'The Good Hope'. Then Joe surprised them all by telling them the tale of Saint Cuthbert and the dolphin, and how the saint had been saved from drowning one day by the kindly fish, laid to rest on the shores up the coast, by Holy Island.

'By, but you tell a good tale, Joe lad,' Rollo said, 'and if you want to call it the "Saint Cuthbert", well, I'm right behind you.' Gradually they all gave their assent, and Mr Miller's shaky hand painted in the letters on the side of the boat.

Hettie joined them on the quay for the launching. It was an emotional moment, not least for Joe, as he saw the other men gathered on the deck. He had a bottle of brown ale in his hand, they couldn't afford champagne, and all waited for Joe to name the ship and crash the bottle against its side.

'No,' he said, 'it's a job for a lady, this.' And he handed the bottle to Cathy. She in turn hesitated then passed it on again to Hettie, who stood effacing herself behind the wives of the other men.

'Eeh, no!' she protested. But they all pushed her towards the boat, and giggling and blushing she came forward at last, her voice high with excitement, and shouted, 'I name this ship the *Saint Cuthbert*!' Then they all cheered and clapped as she swung the bottle against the ship's side where it smashed to smithereens, leaving a scratch under the brown stain. Mr Miller hid his chagrin at the spoiled paintwork and smiled his congratulations.

'Pity the bairn wasn't here to see it,' he said. Cathy sighed, but in her heart she was not sorry, for Lily and 'the bairn' would only have spoiled their joy, wet blankets that they were. A tear came to Joe's eye as the boat slid into the water, and the women behind him fell silent as the men on board set about their business and set course out of the safety of the harbour and onto the open sea.

'Happy landin's,' Lizzie said sniffing back her tears.

'Aye. Happy landin's,' the other women echoed.

It was an anti-climax. Cathy had to go back to her filletting and Joe to his 'gents'. Had anything really changed? Of course, when they came back with the first catch there would be the excitement of filletting their very own fish and selling it, with the possibility of a profit. But now? Joe looked at Cathy's crestfallen face and smiled.

'I've got a surprise for you,' he said.

Cathy looked up in anticipation.

'Oh? What's that, Joe?'

'There was some money left, Cath. And I tell you what, hinny, I've squandered it!'

'Eeh no, Joe!'

'Call it another kind of investment . . . in our future, Cath. You see, I've spent it on a holiday!'

Hettie, walking on ahead, heard the shriek and looked back. Cathy's hands were on her mouth and Joe was grinning. She waited till they caught her up.

'Eeh, Hettie, our Joe's taking me on a holiday.'

Hettie's eyes opened in astonishment.

'You mean on a day out?'

'No,' Joe said triumphantly. 'I'm takin' her away, properly, for a whole week!'

'Eeh never!' Hettie had heard of people going on holidays, but didn't actually know anybody who had done it. 'Where're you taking her?'

'Up to Bamburgh. It's a village up the coast, opposite Holy Island.'

'Oh!' was all Hettie could say in her rapture. 'It'll be like a second honeymoon.'

'A first one, Hettie!' Joe put in and Cathy laughed.

Mr and Mrs Robson were booked in at the Percy's Arms, a little pub which had been recommended to them by the MacNaughtons, for they had spent their honeymoon there. And, according to what Lizzie had said to her, it hadn't changed a bit, Cathy thought, as she and Joe sat in the snug. They didn't speak much. Silence was golden as far as they were concerned, drinking in the luxury of Lily's absence with the beer. And there was more to come, for upstairs a room awaited them, a room all to themselves. For at this time they still shared Cathy's garret room in Thrift Street with their Sylvia, the child's single bed jammed up at right angles to their own, so that there was no privacy for them. Joe had spoken to Hettie about it, on the quiet, and she had said she'd be willing to let them have a room on their own, further down the house, just as soon as one was free, but Lily had vetoed the idea. They needed money for this or that and they'd be losing the rent. Even Sylvia tried to persuade her Nana, complaining of the 'fishy smell' her mother had.

'Eeh, me Mam stinks of fish and me Dad stinks of sh . . .' she had said, but Lily had cut her short with a reprimand about 'language' and would hear no more about it. So Cathy and Joe had had to put up with things as they were, while Sylvia grew daily, older and 'wiser'.

Still, tonight at the Percy's Arms there was no Sylvia. She had pouted about her Mam and Dad going away on their own, and Lily had called it selfish. Surely they could take the child with them? But Hettie had hissed at her sister-in-law, 'Don't be silly, Lily! Two's company!'

And Lily had muttered darkly, 'Aye. That's what I'm afraid of!'

The lights in the snug glowed warmly as Cathy and Joe turned to look at one another. Joe's face questioned her. Cathy nodded, and they put down their empty glasses and went upstairs to their double room. It was cold still, early in the year, and the stone walls of the pub held the chill in them, so that it seemed to emanate from the very plaster. But Joe thought the little shiver Cathy gave as she undressed was one of excitement. She was shy, as though they had never seen one another naked before, and they stood, in the dim light from the tiny window, each looking at the other, their flesh luminous in the shadows. Cathy's eyes searched the map of Joe's body, seeing how his big toes sloped in, his calf muscles bulged, his hips, so lean, seemed to continue the legs till they met the torso, where the ribs bulged out and dark hairs stood proud from his skin in the cold. She traced the muscles of his chest as they fanned out strongly along one shoulder and down the workman's arm, and then she allowed herself at last to see the slope where the flesh covered the absent bone on the other side. Her hand reached out and touched it.

'It's not so bad, Joe . . .' Joe smiled. 'I mean . . . you'd hardly notice if it didn't droop lower than the other one.' Her hand caressed the place, smoothing over the empty flesh, and Joe found his other arm rising to hold her. Cathy's lips curled into a smile as she met his eyes.

'Stroke the back of my neck, Joe,' she said.

Joe shook his head in mock disapproval.

'Eeh, but you're a fast cat,' he said.

Cathy laughed.

'Not too fast, mind,' she said. 'I want to remember this moment for ever.' Then, slowly, her mouth dropped to touch the empty shoulder, savouring the taste of the flesh, and the smoothness of the skin, while her hand traced the folds of scar tissue across Joe's back. 'Oh I love you, I do love you,' Cathy murmured. And when Joe's arm drew her in to him she felt she could die of the joy that flowed through her flesh. He was searching her out as they stood on the cold lino of the floor, and her lips parted to meet his as they swayed towards the welcoming bed and allowed the flood of their sensations to carry them far away.

The fish from the Seahouses fish shop tasted all the better because Cathy hadn't had to fillet it herself. She sprinkled vinegar on it and ate it with her fingers with evident enjoyment. Her cheeks bulged with greed, and Joe laughed at her.

'You'll put on weight!' he jeered, but thought secretly that that would be no bad thing after all. They ate from newspapers, the wind behind them as they walked back along the shore towards Bamburgh.

'By, but we're gettin' good air in our lungs!' Joe said.

'We can hardly avoid it!' Cathy grinned as her hair flew

loose and slapped her face, flying out in front of her. 'Are you happy Joe?' she shouted above the wind.

'Yes!' he yelled back.

'So am I!' Then Joe's arm came round her and they fought the wind together, forcing their way onwards along the beach. Out at sea they could see the outline of the islands, the inner Farnes.

'There's a lot of wildlife on those islands,' Joe told her. 'Rare birds and seals!'

'Seals! Oh Joe, I'd love to see them! Oh Joe, can we?'

'I don't know. We could mebbes ask a fisherman to take us out.'

They laughed at the irony of it. The little harbour at Seahouses was filled with fishing boats, safely anchored out of the wind, for the sea was choppy. They turned back and sought the sailors on the jetty for a likely-looking man, mending his nets.

An old sailor had watched their approach from some way off, raising his head from time to time as his hands busied themselves mending the holes. 'Honeymoon couple,' he thought to himself as they drew nearer. And he smiled at the proud stance of the man and the admiring sparkling eyes of the woman. No, he wouldn't mind taking them out. He wouldn't mind at all!

By the third day the weather had improved and the old man at last consented to their trip. Cathy packed a picnic and Joe borrowed some binoculars from their landlord so he could do some bird spotting, and they hurried back along the beach on the bright cold morning. The seaman was waiting for them.

'I thought you were never coming!' he said, pretending annoyance. Cathy smiled disarmingly, and he helped her into the boat, already tamed by her.

The gulls followed them out, wheeling overhead, gulls of all sorts, and Joe's binoculars followed them as the old fisherman pointed out the different species. He took them close in to one of the islands, refusing to attempt a landing but near enough for Cathy to see the colony of puffins crowding all the rocks around. But the high point came when they reached the seal island, and Cathy slithered dangerously over the slimy rocks, screaming with delight as she saw first one seal, then another, sliding past her, bobbing up out of the water, looking for all the world like old men, whole families congregating in little groups and all of them fascinated by the human visitors. She would have to get a postcard of this for Hettie, Cathy thought. The seaman watched them, quietly amused as he puffed on his pipe. Like a pair of school kids, he thought indulgently. Then tired and hungry they came back, and Cathy opened up the packets of sandwiches she had brought with them.

'Will you have some?' she asked, holding them out to the old man.

'I wouldn't say no,' he answered, and all three dug in, sitting in the stationary boat and fending off the marauding gulls.

'Eeh,' Cathy said, as she and Joe made their tired way back to Bamburgh that evening, 'I have enjoyed meself.'

'So've I.'

'Mind, we'll sleep tonight . . . all that fresh air.'

Joe agreed again and cast a sly look at her.

'Just how tired are you?' he asked.

'Not *that* tired,' she said and started off at a jog trot. 'Last one there's a Jessie!' And he had to run to keep up with her.

The last night was a sad one. The week had flown for them, and the idea of Thrift Street loomed larger by the minute. After their supper they left the pub for a last wander down to the beach. The dunes loomed high in the dusk, and Bamburgh Castle stood proud above them, looking out to sea. They stopped and looked up at it.

'It's a grand building,' Joe volunteered.

'When I was little I used to think it would be smashin' to live in a castle.'

Joe looked at her, trying to read what was in her mind.

'And don't you now?' he said at last.

Cathy shook her head.

'Too draughty,' she said.

CHAPTER TWENTY

When Cathy found she was pregnant she was overjoyed. She had begun to think she would never have another child, one that she and Joe could really call their own. For Sylvia was her Nana's little girl. Lily dressed her like a doll, with outfits for this and outfits for that, all of them beautifully made out of the best materials. Like the bottomless jar, Lily's trunks never seemed to run dry, and her finery was cut down to provide for the child. It all went to Sylvia's head, and it nauseated Cathy to see her preening herself in front of mirrors, and fussing if Joe creased her dress when he tried to show her some affection. There were times when Cathy wondered how she could have spawned her. The little hands were always grasping out for what she could get, and yet Sylvia could not be all bad. It was Lily's influence that had spoiled her. Lily had never hidden the fact that she despised Joe and Hettie, and even her own daughter, and Sylvia had caught it from her like an infection. Without her grandmother's interference, the child's cold nature might have been trained, made more gentle, more considerate of others. But she was taught to be selfish, materialistic, and she was spoiled, knowing that if she screamed hard enough she'd get whatever she'd set her greedy little eyes on. Everything, that is, except a room of her own. This was the only point on which Lily was adamant. But surely now that Cathy was pregnant, Lily would see the necessity of changing the sleeping arrangements?

'Mam, I'm expecting.' Cathy had braced herself to tell her news.

'Oh?' Lily's voice lacked interest. 'Expecting what?'

'What do women usually expect, Lily!' Hettie said, exasperated.

Lily turned on her daughter with such force that Cathy actually backed away.

'What?' she shouted. 'A baby? You mean to tell me you're expecting a baby?' Cathy nodded. 'I see. I knew you shouldn't have gone on that holiday. That's when it happened, isn't it?'

'Probably.'

'Eeh, congratulations, pet,' Hettie beamed.

'Joe's hoping for a boy . . . for the first one, anyway, so's he can take over in the boat when he's old enough.'

'And how many do you intend to have, might I ask?' her mother demanded.

'*I* don't know!'

'You just don't think, do you? Just as long as you get what you want. No thought for anybody else.'

'What do you mean, Mam?'

'It's another mouth to feed, isn't it?'

The light dawned on Cathy. Lily looked through the window to where young Sylvia was playing in the yard. 'Taking the bread out of the bairn's mouth,' she said in a whimpering voice.

'Oh don't be so silly, Mam!' Cathy raised her voice to her mother for the first time and Lily's mouth fell open in surprise. 'And I should think, while we're on the subject of our Sylvia, that Joe and I might have a room to ourselves now, don't you?'

Lily pursed her lips and muttered something that Cathy could hardly catch.

'What did you say?' she asked.

'She said, why not, it'd be like shuttin' the gate after the horse's gone,' Hettie interpreted, smugly.

Cathy looked at her mother for a long time. Lily had turned away her face and was ironing for all she was worth.

'Do you mean to say that that's why you've kept Sylvia in our room all this time?' Cathy demanded, her voice wavering with emotion.

After a long pause, Lily looked up and said, 'Well you couldn't be trusted *not* to behave like animals!'

Mother and daughter glared at one another across the laundered sheets.

'No wonder Dad always looked so unhappy. Crumbs from the table was all he got, wasn't it?'

'Cathy!' Hettie reprimanded. 'That's not like you!'

'No, it isn't, is it?' Cathy said darkly and left the room.

Lily's face had crumpled, it had fallen in a heap like the rumpled sheet at her hands, and Hettie rose to put her arm round her.

'It *is* like the animals!' Lily sobbed through her tears. 'It is, isn't it, Hettie?' Hettie said nothing, and her hand stroked the shaking back of her sister-in-law in an attempt to comfort where she could not explain.

'I was brought up to think . . .' Lily gulped, 'to think it wasn't nice . . . not ladylike, and it isn't, is it?'

'I'm not sure what a lady is, Lily.'

'No well, you wouldn't!'

Hettie's hand dropped to her side as Lily recovered herself.

'I did love your brother, Hettie,' she said, 'in my way.'

'I know you did, Lily. The trouble was, it wasn't his way.'

Lily's temper did not improve as Cathy's pregnancy progressed. Her daughter positively bloomed with approaching motherhood, and Lily acidly remarked that Joe would pop his shirt buttons if he swelled with pride any more.

'If it's a boy, we'll call him Alec.'

Cathy had looked at Joe and seen tears in his eyes. Something had told her not to ask why. And she agreed to the name without a murmur.

Hettie, a new aim in life, worked away at mittens and bootees and matinee jackets, patterns garnered from back numbers of her magazines, while Mr Miller tried his hand at carving a rocking horse, if you please! Sylvia had never had a rocking horse, and Lily didn't see why it was necessary to make one now! Sylvia herself, who had made friends at school with one Mabel Weston, thought it faintly disgusting that an old woman like her mother should be having a baby. And Mabel sympathised.

Cathy seemed to grow stronger as her pregnancy became

more apparent. It was as though the life inside her lent her its strength, and Joe and she demonstrated their mutual love more openly in the family circle. Seeing it, Lily grieved somewhere deep inside her. She would light her candle early and leave the parlour or the scullery to go upstairs to her own room, leaving them to it. As she lay in solitary splendour, Lily remembered a night when Cathy had barged into her bedroom. She had flung her arms round her neck and told her she loved her. She cherished that memory, even now. Cathy had loved her once, and Henry . . . surely Henry had loved her long ago? Misery crept through her soul, like a grey creeping paralysis.

'Doesn't anybody love me any more?' she whispered.

'I love you, Nana,' Sylvia's shadow whispered back.

'Cupboard love,' Lily answered her. Still, it was better than nothing.

Cathy was getting very near her time. The long hours standing on the quay became too much for her, and she had a little stool to sit on beside the bogie while Lizzie called their wares. The boat was doing well. Lily need not have worried about a shortage of cash, and Cathy enjoyed dealing with the fish when it came in and would not for the world have given up her work unless it was thought necessary. But the doctor seemed to think she was fine. She enjoyed Lizzie's company. They had a lot of laughs together. After all, she had been her only friend, apart from Hettie, for years past. So Cathy stayed on, teased by one and all and enjoying every moment of it. One young lad, Willie they called him, used to go for the ice for them. He was a born practical joker and this time as he handed over the package of ice Lizzie noticed a twinkle in his eye.

'What are you up to, Willie?' she asked suspiciously, then, before she could stop him, he slipped a great lump of ice out of his pocket and dropped it down the back of Cathy's neck.

It was at that moment that Cathy felt the first, searing pain. She toppled forwards into Lizzie's arms, groaning.

'Your waters have broken!' Lizzie gasped as she felt the wet on Cathy's skirt.

'Don't be daft, Lizzie,' Cathy giggled, 'and get that lump of ice out of me knickers before I'm swimming in it!'

Relieved, Lizzie shook the ice out of Cathy's clothes and sitting her on the bogie, alongside the fish, she wheeled her friend down to the ferry to get her home before it was too late.

Dr Hollom, older now than when he had attended Lily, came to help at the birth. Hettie fussed about with towels and sheets and water, and Sylvia was sent to her friend's house for the night. The baby was early by almost a month, but Dr Hollom did not expect any serious complications. It was, after all, Cathy's second child, and it should have been a much easier business than the time before. It should have been, but it wasn't.

'You're holding it back,' the doctor told her.

'I'm not!' Cathy moaned as she strove to expel the child from her body. Joe, unable to bear the suspense, came into the room and sat at Cathy's side, holding her hand and urging her on with comforting words.

'This is no place for a man!' Lily told him.

'Hadaway an' shite,' the gentle Joe answered her.

Dr Hollom now told Cathy to hold back. He wanted to make another examination. Yes, the head was down all right, but there was something wrong. He hesitated for a second, then placed his stethoscope on Cathy's belly. Quietly he said, 'Go on, Mrs Robson. One more gallant effort.' And Cathy heaved and strained and the body of her baby slumped out onto the sheet.

The chord had wound itself round the baby's neck. It would have been a girl. It had red hair sticking out from its head, and Joe wept openly to see it.

'Oh Cathy,' he cried. 'Oh my Cathy, my Cathy.' And they clung to each other as to a lifebelt.

Quietly, Hettie hid the baby clothes away in the back of her wardrobe. They might 'come in', as she said to herself, and the lass wouldn't want to see them lying about. The rocking horse was burned on the scullery fire and Sylvia was brought home again, to her old bed in her parents' room, because there was still no room spare in the house. But after

Sylvia was asleep Joe's hand reached out to Cathy's, and they found the warmth and trust each was seeking in the other's arms. The joy Cathy had so longed for became as familiar to her as her morning tea. She and Joe might never ride to the crest of the wave, their love ebbed and flowed in a calmer sea, less exciting, but it was infinitely safer. Joe's arms formed Cathy's harbour, and she was glad to stay in them.

In some ways this little death had touched Hettie more than any of them. She had an air of aimlessness in whatever she did, and she seemed pale and distant. Spring was just around the corner, and Cathy remembered their trip of the year before.

'Do you think we could go away again, Joe? Just for the day? And take Hettie with us?'

Joe nodded, and one day he came home from Ocean Road with a lady's bike in tow.

'Who's that for?' Sylvia asked eagerly.

'For your Mam, greedy guts.' Then he winked at Cathy. 'There's another one where that came from an' all.' Sylvia's eyes brightened again. 'And that one's for Hettie.'

'Eeh!' Hettie squealed. 'I'd never ride a bike!'

'Come on, Hettie, I'll teach you,' Cathy said, and persuaded her to get on it, then laughed as Hettie wobbled down the back lane.

But Hettie did learn, even though she insisted on giving bystanders a running commentary of the road ahead as she went along.

'Now there's a left turn comin' up. I've got to slow down, pull the brake, steady, put me hand out, don't wobble! . . . then ease the bike round . . . and I've done it!' It was the same at every bend in every road. But it was worth it. It was an escape for the three of them. They took off into the countryside, up the coast, and explored the further reaches of the River Tyne on days snatched from the jaws of Thrift Street and the quayside. They were days when light dappled through green branches and the rain sparkled on eyelashes, and beer went down a treat by the roadside along with the pork pies. As they settled, basking in the sunshine or huddling together against the wind after their picnic, Hettie would wander off on her own, 'to look at nature' as she put it. Though as Joe and Cathy well knew, she was being 'diplomatic'.

Sylvia felt her exclusion from these trips keenly, even though she would much prefer a shopping trip in King Street with her Nana and Mabel Weston to any of the sights of nature you could care to mention! And Lily felt herself obliged to buy the child a small bicycle of her own, so that she could tag along. Fortunately, Sylvia soon grew weary of trying to keep up, complained about the insects, and fell in the river, ruining her best frock. So she did not seriously interfere in their plans and the three continued to enjoy themselves on their own. In any case, Mabel had been sent to piano lessons, and Sylvia, desperate to keep up with her, nagged at Lily to send her along too, to which, seeing it was a ladylike accomplishment, Lily was obliged to agree. Sylvia now spent much of her free time at the piano in 'The Sanctuary'.

Another miscarriage followed on from the stillbirth. This time the baby was gone almost before Cathy knew it was there, and she began to think that Joe was fated not to have his son after all. Then Mr Miller died suddenly of a stroke in the public library, and with his departure Cathy and Joe sensed that their world was about to change.

To Hettie it was not so much a change as the end of her world. It was called The Riverside Development Scheme, and it meant they were going to knock down Thrift Street. Hettie couldn't understand it. It was explained to her that they wanted to extend the docks, that it was 'progress', but she worried about her boarders. Where would they go? And she clung to her little corner by the scullery stove, where she sat, night after night, all on her own, reading her romances by the light of a solitary candle. It was her entire world. She had retreated into it soon after the war. They had put up memorials to the dead of the Great War, 'the war to end all wars' as they called it. They had all gone and looked at it, reading off the names of people they had once known. There, in the second column under the Bs, Hettie saw the name of Johnny Beale. She turned away from the dark stone monument and withdrew into herself. It was as though she was still living in her past, and even on the bicycle she kept to her long skirt, refusing to show more than an ankle, and she was horrified when Cathy had her hair cut off, the red waves smoothed round her head in the new look. But Hettie did have her teeth seen to. They'd given her trouble all her life, and when, in the late twenties, she couldn't bear the nagging pain any longer, she took herself to the dentist and had them all taken out. Joe sent her for a holiday, a whole week, the first of her life, and she came back feeling very much better. But the false teeth stayed in their jar, and Hettie cut the crusts off her bread, chewing the soft bread with her gums, eating on her own in the kitchen while 'the family', as Lily called them, now took their meals in the 'sitting room'.

And then came this news that the Corporation were going to demolish her. Hettie's brain refused to take it in. She went on as before, leaving everything to Joe and Lily. They were offered a pittance for the house. They said it was a slum and not worth buying anyway; the Council was doing them a favour. But Joe had done well with the *Saint Cuthbert*, and he and Cathy had put a fair bit aside. They would have enough to buy a terraced house further up the town in Tyne Dock. Hettie wouldn't come to look at it, but Lily and Sylvia took the tram to Rosamund Street with Cathy and Joe, to see what it was like.

It was a grey day, inclined to dampen their spirits, but all present were determined to make the best of things. Rosamund Street was made up of terraces, tall, narrow buildings which gave straight onto the street, and with back yards behind. The house was already empty, the previous occupants having died, and it was in some need of decoration; but they exercised their imaginations as they walked round it, seeing it as it could be.

'There's enough bedrooms to have one each,' Joe said, innocently. Lily pretended she hadn't heard, but Sylvia squealed with delight.

'Ooh, can I decide on the wallpaper and that, for mine then?'

'I don't see why not,' her mother agreed.

'I want roses everywhere, on the wallpaper and the curtains, and I want laces up at the window, in festoons . . . oh, and pillowslips with embroidery on them . . .'

'You'll make do with the ones from Thrift Street, my lady. We'll have hundreds of them, unless you want to embroider them yourself.'

'Which room do you think Hettie'd like?' Joe asked, his voice echoing round the empty house.

'This one'll get the sun in it.' Cathy stood at the back window staring out. 'And it's a good size.'

'It wants to be for all *her* stuff!' Lily said with a snort. 'And she's not storin' it in the guest room!'

'What guest room?' Joe asked.

'What do you mean, "What guest room?" I mean that little box room on the landing. We've got to have a room for guests!'

'Oh.' Joe pondered and winked at Cathy. 'I'd been thinkin' of something else.'

'Oh?' Lily challenged him.

'Well, it's just . . . I thought it'd be ideal for a bathroom, like!'

Lily whooped with joy! Such luxury. She rushed out searching for Sylvia.

'Eeh, d'ye hear that, pet? Eh? We're goin' to have a bathroom!'

They were full of the joys of spring when they got back to Thrift Street, but Hettie would have none of it. She refused to listen to their descriptions of the house. What did she care whether Sylvia had roses or forget-me-nots on her walls. It was all the same to her. She stuck her head in the sand and refused to pull it out. As Joe sat on in the scullery doing his sums, Hettie sat in her usual corner, reading by the light of the fire. Lily kept hovering in the scullery, dying to know if there was enough left over to cover the cost of a bathroom, her long-cherished dream.

'We might have to wait a bit,' Joe warned her. And Lily, crestfallen, had gone from the room, only to return ten minutes later with a triumphant look in her eye and a small box in her hand. Even Hettie glanced up as the box was laid on the kitchen table in front of Joe, with the explanation, 'That's my contribution, Joe.'

Joe cautiously picked up the box and slowly, as though there might be a bomb inside, opened it up. His face showed no expression, and Lily's confidence wavered.

'It's me diamond pin, Joe, and a bracelet. They're all I've got left.'

Joe looked up seriously, and said, with as much awe as he could muster, 'Are you sure, now?' Lily nodded. 'Well, thank you.' Then he closed the box once again and carefully placed it in his pocket.

Lily looked across at Hettie, who was once more nose down in her magazine.

'I don't know, Hettie Straker. You might show some enthusiasm. After all Joe's doin' for us.' Her voice had respect in it, and Joe smiled with amused tolerance at this sudden change. 'I mean, compared with this place,' Lily looked about her with disgust, 'the house in Rosamund Street's a palace! It's got runnin' water, Hettie, comin' out of the taps, and electricity!'

Poor Hettie's only answer was to bundle up her book and rush sobbing from the scullery to her own room.

There was packing to be done, lodgers had to be given notice, arrangements had to be made for the removals. And most of it fell on Joe and Cathy. Cathy fought down her own nostalgia for the old house, trying to look to the bright future Joe had promised them, and got on with it. Orange boxes, tea chests and cardboard boxes littered the hall. And as the pictures came down, a bare desolate look came to the house. Voices echoed eerily, and the place felt suddenly cold. The great day was almost upon them. But Hettie's room remained intact. Lily knocked imperiously on her door.

'Come out of there, Hettie Straker! Or we'll leave you behind, mind!' She spoke to Hettie as though she were a child, half threatening, half coaxing her out from behind the closed door. 'If you don't open up I'm comin' in anyway!' There was no answer, and Lily tried the handle. The door was locked. 'I've got a key fits this lock, Hettie, so don't think you can skulk in there for much longer!' And Lily went away muttering darkly about how 'some people' ought to be left behind, because they were more nuisance than they were worth. Hettie tried to shut out their voices, smothering her head under a pillow, but it was no use. For Lily was back within minutes and she heard Lily's spare key in the lock. But still the door wouldn't give. Hettie stared at the piles of furniture stacked against it. She had barricaded herself in.

Lily was furious, and Sylvia thought it a huge joke, running off to tell her friend Mabel, in highly dramatic tones, that her daft auntie was causing trouble. But Cathy and Joe exchanged sad glances.

'She wants to go down with the ship,' Joe whispered.

Cathy nodded, and tried to restrain her mother's harsh remarks, shouted through the door.

'Come on out, you daft faggot you! You want to think yourself lucky Joe's willin' to give you house room after this exhibition!' Joe couldn't help smiling. My, but she'd changed her tune. Before it had been how lucky Joe was that Hettie gave *him* house room! 'You're only comin' on sufferance in the first place!'

'Mam!' Cathy drew her mother away, gently. She knew very well that Lily was only getting her own back. After all the years of living 'on sufferance', as she put it, in Hettie's house, the tables had been turned, and her son-in-law now owned the house they were all to live in. Hettie would be the 'guest', not Lily this time. And how she gloried in it. It did her shattered pride good.

Under her pillow, Hettie heard the muffled sounds of Lily's departure and breathed deep sighs of relief. The onslaught was over for the time being. She lay back on her bed and looked round the familiar room. It had been her father and mother's. She had known it as a child, and it had the same furniture still. She looked up at the ceiling above her head. The plaster was grey and cracked, and the hole she had made in it as a child, playing with a ball, had been filled in. But it was still visible. She remembered her mother's fury and her father's amusement when she had done it. It had been her mother's birthday, and she had been full of the joys of spring, rushing in to her parents' bedroom in the morning, her offering, a box stuck all over with shells, in her hands. Her mother had been pleased. It was a beautiful box she had said, she had admired it again and again, and how clever little Hettie had been to make it herself. And Hettie, in a sudden burst of delight, had thrown her ball up high into the air, and it went clean through the ceiling, showering her mother in the bed beneath with bits of broken plaster.

As she lay in that same bed in her mother's place, Hettie's sad mouth curved into a smile. What she would give now for a taste of her mother's anger, let alone her love, her praise. She had been her mother's little girl, and when she died, the bottom had gone out of Hettie's world, for no one had ever loved her like her mother, nor ever would again. No one would ever call her 'little Hettie' now. Her stern father withdrew into himself and Hettie found her only consolation in her big brother Henry, who promised he would look after her always. But always is a long time. A very long time. Hettie's vision of the ceiling above her head misted over, and a tear trickled down her cheeks. They had taken everything away from her. Henry, Johnny Beale, her child. The sad tale of her life was written in her palm, as crazed with lines as the ceiling in this room. And now they wanted to demolish her. To them it might be just a house that they were razing to the ground. But it was more than that. They were demolishing Hettie's childhood, her only security, everything. They were demolishing *her*. And nobody cared.

But Joe cared. On the other side of the door, he waited silently and listened anxiously for a sound from within the room. A strangled sob told of the heartbreak Hettie suffered, and Joe felt inside himself the pain that was this final betrayal of Hettie Straker.

'Hettie,' he called softly, 'Hettie, it's Joe.'

Hettie's head turned towards the barricaded door. Ah yes, there was Joe. There was always Joe.

'Can I come in, Hettie? I want to talk to you.'

Hettie made no response. He could almost feel her eyes on the door between them.

'I love you, Hettie,' he said at last.

That was too much. Hettie burst into a fit of convulsive sobbing, a violence sped through her and she sprang from the bed, tearing the furniture from the doorway, so that Joe fell into the room.

'Oh, Hettie, Hettie. Let Joe look after you, eh?' he said, rocking her in his arms.

'You're all I've got left, Joe,' Hettie cried. 'You won't ever go away from me, will you?'

'No, no, Hettie. I'll never let you down. I promise you. Never.'

Then Hettie moaned and sobbed, gripping the slack cloth of his shoulder like the grieving widow clinging to the insubstantial ghost of her past love.

'You're all I've got,' she said again and again. 'All I've got.'

At last the tears were spent, and Joe laid her on the bed to rest.

'I'll be back,' he reassured her as her childlike gaze followed him to the door. And she knew he would. Joe could be relied on. 'Always Ready.' Hettie remembered the crest and motto she had drawn on the wrapping paper the day he had come back from the war. She could trust Joe, if she could trust anything in this life.

Downstairs in the kitchen Joe was laying down the law. Cathy was instructed to make a cup of tea, well sugared, and take it up. She and Joe would see to Hettie's packing. Lily and Sylvia were to keep out of the way and never mention the incident of the barricade, ever. As the pair left the kitchen, Joe turned again, and said, 'Now, mind what I told you. No remarks!' And he followed Cathy back up the stairs to Hettie's room.

As the three sat bleakly, unable to think of anything to say, Hettie drank down her tea. Little noises, moans and sobs, punctuated the silence, and she looked about her with a mournful air. At last, she sighed.

'Eeh,' she said, 'I'm glad life *isn't* eternal. Because, you know what? It'd kill me.'

Cathy and Joe couldn't help but smile. For somehow, tragedy, or at least Hettie's tragedies, always seemed to verge on the ridiculous. And that was a tragedy in itself.

Cathy would have done all her aunt's packing for her. But Hettie wouldn't allow her. They positively fought to unpack the big wardrobe. And when they reached the bundle at the back of it Cathy understood why. Wrenching open the newspapers tied around with string, she saw the bootees, the mittens, the little dresses, so carefully crocheted for her by Hettie.

'I wondered what happened to them,' Cathy said quietly. The two women exchanged a look, an understanding, and Hettie stuffed the things back inside, securing the bundle tightly, before stowing it in one of her many boxes.

'You never know!' she said. Cathy smiled and shook her head.

On moving day, those many boxes of Hettie's were heaved out of her room in never ending succession and lifted onto the bogie to take to Rosamund Street. Lily, constrained to silence about the barricade business, let go her tongue on the subject of the boxes.

'You've got everything but the kitchen sink in them, Hettie!' she reprimanded her, but Hettie ignored her and went on producing more and more. She had packed up her life in those boxes, and not only hers, her parents' life as well, mementoes of her and Henry's childhood, the silver horseshoe from the piece of wedding cake she'd brought home from Lily's wedding, the little shell box she'd given her mother, photographs, post cards, broken vases, and candlesticks that might 'come in'. It was all there, somewhere. But the last boxes were the heaviest of the lot. Joe came out of the house staggering under the weight of them.

'What have you got in there?' Lily exclaimed as she sat waiting on the bogie.

Then poor Joe, exhausted, the thin muscles of his shoulder giving way, fell forwards, dropping the box heavily onto the pavement. The string broke and magazines spilled out onto the road.

'Romances! Would you believe it?' Lily cried. 'You can't take that lot, Hettie!' But Hettie stuck her chin in the air and looked at Joe as though challenging him to live up to his promise.

'I'm not budgin' without me papers!' she said defiantly.

Joe gallantly picked them up and put them back in their box, and Cathy helped him lift it onto the cart. Hettie sniffed the tears back up her nose and put on a dignified look as she joined Lily on the cart, ignoring Sylvia's sly comments. Joe went for a final look round the house before locking up 15 Thrift Street for the last time.

The cart jolted off, Joe and Cathy walking behind, and Cathy was reminded of her mother when they'd set off from Westoe, and how it nearly broke her heart to leave the old home. Hettie's face was bleak and wet as the cart heaved up the cobbled hill and turned the corner at the top, Hettie's last sight of her home. Tarrah to the quayside, tarrah to the lodgers, and the fortune-telling. Tarrah to independence. She burst into tears and moaned, 'What'll I do all day, with only you for company, Lily?'

'Thanks very much!' Lily pursed her lips. 'Some people,' as Sylvia would say, 'weren't half selfish!'

Sylvia took up most of Lily's time now. She was growing up and was everything her Nana'd hoped she'd be. She was taught how to set the table properly, and was kitted out in natty little suits and hats, with lace gloves, walking beside her elegant Nana down Rosamund Street for a stroll in the park while her mother scrubbed collars at home for a few pennies a dozen. She changed her music teacher to a woman who lived near the 'Chi', and the halting strains of 'I'll Take You Home Again Kathleen' disturbed Cathy's afternoon sleep after her return from the fish quay, interspersed by more perfectly performed scales as Sylvia prepared herself for exams. It reminded Cathy of her own endeavours when she'd gone for singing lessons to Miss Liddell. But Sylvia had no urge to go on the stage. No surge of emotions disturbed her sleep. No, Sylvia dreamt of being a model and marrying a millionaire who had fallen in love with her photograph in some glossy magazine. The lessons were merely a necessary preparation for her future social status. The ripples of Sylvia's life ebbed and flowed as her Nana would have wished, free from any dangerous undercurrents of emotion. But, once again, events were to form themselves into a tidal wave and take matters out of Lily's hands.

It was 1933. Sylvia was up to grade five in the London College Examinations, and she had been summoned to Toc H House in Westoe Village for her practical hearing. Lily took fright at the idea of going up into the village again. She hadn't been near the place for years, not since the Stoddards had last invited her. Cathy didn't want to go there either, but somebody had to accompany the girl; Joe was working all day, while she had time off during the afternoon. The trams had finally given way to yellow trolley buses, 'canaries' they liked to call them, as they sang their way along the wires. Holding her music under her arm, Sylvia, accompanied by her mother, boarded the bus that would take them to Westoe.

Cathy hesitated at the entrance to the village. It was so different from the rest of the town. There was now no countryside separating it from Shields. It had been built up, all round. But there was still a different atmosphere about the village and she felt it as she passed through what had been, at one time, a gate, and into the wide, tree-lined street. The trees were tall now, high over her head. They met in an arch, shading out the sun. It gave the village a sombre look. It felt like walking into a churchyard filled with ghosts, and her voice lowered as a matter of course. The houses seemed smaller to her than they had done before, older and shabby. The green, where the horses had grazed, now had a bus shelter in the middle of it, and institutions had taken over many of the private dwellings. The Toc H was close to the village entrance on the left. Cathy hurried her daughter inside and sat with her in the waiting room as another sufferer went through his or her paces in the examination room. Cathy's hands shook with nerves for her daughter, but Sylvia was cool as a cucumber sitting there beside her.

Cathy marvelled at her composure. She herself would have been in a state of high excitement and anxiety. But Sylvia took everything in her stride, living on one flat plane, unaware of the highs and lows of her mother's experience. The girl seemed alien to her. Not of her body at all. And, in her turn, Sylvia despised her mother's rough chapped hands and humble manner.

At last a lad came out of the examination room, white-faced and shaking. He and his mother exchanged a look, and went out of the place without a word. And then it was Sylvia's turn. The bell rang and she walked to the door, knocked and entered. She'd be in there half an hour or so, longer if she did well. Cathy sighed and prepared herself to wait.

The lad and his mother had forgotten to close the door. A cool draught swept in, chilling Cathy's feet. She got up and went out into the hallway to close the door, but stood instead, listening to the wind rustling in the trees outside. The sound drew her, like the whispering sound of the sea in a shell she had once had. She walked slowly out of the porch and into the street, savouring the fresh air of the village, where little traffic passed. Her head turned to look further down the street, and her steps followed her gaze, taking her on into the centre of the village. She stopped for a moment outside the Stoddards' old house and wondered idly if they still lived there, then she went on and looked up above the walls to the house where she had spent her childhood, far less grand than the Stoddards', far smaller than she remembered, and derelict now. A 'For Sale' sign protruded from the top of the wall and through the gate she could see the garden was overgrown. No one had lived there for a long time, and it looked almost past repair.

She drew her coat round her. There was a chill breeze, but it wasn't time to go back yet. So she wandered along the green on the other side, feeling the springy turf under her feet.

A curtain was pulled back in an upstairs window of the Stoddard house where Gilbert had his desk. He stared out at the woman on the green. She looked to be in her early forties, tall and slim, with a fine ankle, but she carried herself badly, her head bowed low, looking at her feet. She was walking in the shade of the trees. But, as she stepped out from under a spreading beech tree a ray of the sun found its way through the overhanging leaves and lit up her hair. It was red, and shone in the sudden light. It drew Gilbert up short. He stared harder at her. He wished he could see her close to. But she was walking further away from him towards the end of the village. He dropped the curtain and ran down the stairs, his leg dragging behind him. A thin voice called to him from the sitting room.

'Gilbert? Gilbert? Where are you going?' But he didn't answer. He flung open the front door and stared down the street. The woman had disappeared. Gilbert frowned, and made his way to the garden gate and caught sight of her again, going into Toc H House. He was smiling now and out of breath as he chased along after her. She turned and seemed to see him before she went through the doors, or perhaps she just saw a man hurrying along behind her.

Through the window he could hear someone playing the piano and a man's voice, tired and patient, calling out instructions. He waited. The man spoke for a while and a girl answered him in a monotone. Then a door opened and closed. After a while he heard a bell ring, and then the woman came out of the house beside a young girl. She was mousey-haired and smaller than the woman, and she walked precisely down the steps ahead of her, turning back impatiently for her to hurry after. The woman looked up. She caught Gilbert's eyes, looked away automatically, then looked again, startled. She stopped suddenly.

'Come on, Mam!' the girl cried.

'Wait a minute, Sylvia!' Cathy frowned at her daughter and smiled at Gilbert.

'Yours?' he asked. Cathy nodded. Gilbert looked at the girl. She seemed be almost grown up, pretty, but quite unlike her mother.

'She's been in for an exam,' Cathy explained, embarrassed.

Gilbert nodded.

'Musical!' he said. The words sounded so ordinary. They carried no meaning at all, and there was so much each wanted to ask and to know.

'How are you?' Cathy asked at last.

'Fine. How are you?'

'Fine.'

Sylvia shuffled impatiently beside her mother.

'Come on, Mam. It's nearly tea time.'

Cathy ignored her.

'I saw you'd got married,' she said.

'Yes.' Gilbert looked shyly at her. 'And you?'

'Yes. I'm married.'

'Of course.' Gilbert looked embarrassed at his *faux pas*, both of them only too aware of Sylvia standing close by. He would have liked to ask them for tea, but Sylvia gave him an impatient look and his mouth closed against the words.

'Ah well. Got to be off.' Cathy hesitated, then turned to go.

'Nice to see you anyway.'

'Yes.'

Gilbert watched them as they walked away down the avenue of trees. It was as well the girl had been there. He would have surely asked Cathy to stay otherwise. And she was married now. No good raking over old embers. And Gilbert? He had told Cathy he had married, but he hadn't told her that his wife had died, five years back, after a long spell working in Dean's Isolation Hospital in the town. She had contracted rheumatic fever which had left her heart weak, and, older than Gilbert by some years, she had died, leaving him alone to run his business. Cathy and her daughter turned the corner and left the village. Gilbert stared at the emptiness at the end of the road, and then went back to the house.

The incident disturbed Cathy. Joe, too, noticed she was out of sorts for a few days after the trip to Westoe. He put it down to visiting the old haunts and said nothing about it. As time passed there was, in any case, plenty to occupy their minds. The row in Europe was hotting up, but it was hotting up in Rosamund Street as well. Hettie had kept up her old habits of reading in the kitchen. She didn't like to sit in the sitting room with 'the family' because not only was there Lily's sneering to contend with, but Sylvia acted like an echo chamber to her Nana, so that Hettie felt she wasn't wanted in there and preferred to keep her own company. But Lily had begun to get on her high horse about the electric light bill. And one day she really had a go at her sister-in-law.

'The waste,' she said, 'sittin' in there all on your own. The sheer waste of the electric. You must think money grows on trees!'

'It wouldn't matter,' Sylvia chimed in, 'if she was readin' somethin' improvin'.'

'It'd be different if you paid the bills!'

Joe was out at work, and Cathy, unwilling to get involved, had sat silently through the row till now. But she couldn't stand it any more.

'And who do you think *does* pay the bills, Mam? Not you!'

Lily sniffed.

'I gave him me last bits of gold, that little gold bracelet of mine and a diamond pin, for the deposit on this very house!'

'Mam! That pinprick of a diamond, as you called it, hardly covered the cost of the light bulbs, let alone the light bill!' But Cathy was sorry as soon as she said it. Lily winced, and her dignity crumbled before her eyes. Her only way out was to attack Hettie further.

'All I ask, Hettie, is a little common sense!'

When Joe came in that night, worried to death about the news in Europe, he found Hettie snivelling in the scullery, trying to read with her fading eyesight by the light of one candle.

'I'm sorry, Joe. I'll not be beholden to *her*,' was all she'd say when Joe questioned her. And he turned on Lily for the first time, calling her names, all the names under the sun, till she too was crying, and said she knew where she wasn't wanted, then went up to her room to pack, knowing full well Joe would give in and say he was sorry in the end. And he did. As Cathy dried his damp socks by the fire, he sighed loudly.

'I suppose I'll have to go up to the old faggot.'

Lily forgave him, but Sylvia didn't, and the rift in the family grew larger as a result, with Lily and Sylvia top dogs in the cold war. But then things changed. There was a real war. Lily and Sylvia panicked at the news that not only were young men to be conscripted into the services, but young women also would be sent away to work. Sylvia was going to have to choose between a hasty marriage and an early pregnancy, or buckle down to labour as a land girl or a hand in a munitions factory. At first, marriage seemed the only answer, but no one 'suitable' presented themselves, and so, preferring industrial muck to pigs' muck, Sylvia opted for the munitions factory in Birmingham. Lily lost her main ally in the camp.

CHAPTER TWENTY-ONE

The war gave Hettie a new lease of life. Suddenly she found herself needed by the community. The able-bodied had all gone to war, or into service in the factories, or on the land. Joe, given a choice between the Home Guard and going out with his own ship, sweeping mines, volunteered for the latter. For him, too, the war was an opportunity to blossom. Hettie had found work close to home. She took on the job of air warden. It meant a different attitude to life. The uniform, which she loved, had a short skirt. Her hair, too long to go comfortably under her hat, was cut to a shingle, and she wore her teeth every time she went out. Johnny Beale wouldn't have recognised this new, positive Hettie, with status and an aim in life. She became almost bossy, pestering the life out of Lily, and out of Sylvia when she was at home, chivvying them out of the house and down the shelters, drilling them in the use of gas masks, nagging them to follow her example and do more for the war effort.

'Get your skates on, Lily,' she'd chide as the sirens sounded, 'and get yourself down that shelter. I can't wait all day ye know. Some of wer've got responsibilities!'

'Aye,' Lily muttered under her breath, 'and don't some of wer make a meal of it an' all!'

The trouble was, Lily was feeling redundant. Everybody else was busy but not Lily. Cathy, when she wasn't filletting fish on the quayside, had her washing to do and the housework. Joe's sea socks and Cathy's shirts and collars permanently festooned the fireguard in the sitting room, and Hettie was always hogging the iron to press her uniform. There was nothing left for Lily, except to live for the day when her grand-daughter came home on leave from Birmingham.

Lily had been saving rations for the occasion, and a high tea awaited them in Rosamund Street; the best cloth spread over the drop-leaf table supported a feast of real ham, tinned peaches, bread with actual butter, and a proper chocolate cake.

'You'd think it was Christmas!' Hettie said.

'Just mind nobody touches any of it till I get back!' Lily warned. 'That poor bairn probably won't have had a proper meal since her last leave.'

Cathy snorted as she smeared the paste on Joe's sandwiches, knowing how he would turn his nose up at them when he got them. He was out sweeping mines, and all he could get for his tea was paste! It wasn't right! Not that he said anything; he didn't need to. Cathy knew what paste sandwiches in your bait meant, didn't she? She'd had enough of them in the days of Miss Hutchinson's hat shop. She cast sidelong glances at the plate of ham, and as soon as she heard the front door bang Cathy slipped a knife between the slices and prised a piece out. Victory! By, but he'd be pleased! She slapped it between two slices of bread and marge, spiked it with mustard, and laid it carefully inside his box for a surprise. Hettie watched her greedily.

'Do you think she'd miss a peach slice?' she asked.

'Yes. She counted them,' Cathy answered her.

The 'poor bairn', a slim, elegant creature, with unnaturally blonde hair, teetered along the platform under the weight of her suitcase. Lily saw her from the barrier and waved, but Sylvia's pale eyes could not pick her out. She strained to distinguish the faces in the crowd, the intensity of her effort making her head jut forward and giving her face a pinched look. There was a permanent and deep furrow in her brow, a remarkable feature in a face so young. But it was still young enough to look pretty. She was almost on top of her Nana before she saw her.

'Eeh, lass, you want to get yourself a pair of glasses!' Lily fussed, rubbing away at the frown with her finger as if she could rub it out. 'You'll marr your looks.'

'Gerroff, Nana.' Sylvia shrugged her off.

'I've only got your interests at heart.'

'I know.' Sylvia's irritation quickly gave way to enthusiasm. 'Come on. Let's go to Carricks for wer tea!'

'But . . .' Lily was dismayed, 'but we've got it all laid on at home.'

'Ah come on, Nana, I'll buy us a cake between us.'

'But I've made chocolate cake for you, specially.'

'We can eat it later, man! I've got somethin' to tell you.'

Sylvia's confidential tone implied the juiciest of news and Lily's eyes brightened.

'I don't want *them* around when I tell you.'

Lily nodded, and like a pair of conspirators, grandmother and grand-daughter deposited the case in left luggage before scurrying off to their favourite tea shop.

The furrow deepened on Sylvia's brow. Her concentration was intense. Lily held her breath, and the knife split the one eclair with precision. Both women smiled up at one another, satisfied at a job well done. Like a queen dispensing maundy money, Sylvia slipped Lily's half onto her plate before raising her fork to attack her own. Her lip curled in distaste.

'It's artificial cream,' she said.

'Tut. It took enough coupons an' all,' Lily remarked. 'Never mind, pet. It's very nice. Now, tell me your news.'

'Well, Nana, I've met this man . . .' Sylvia's eyes rolled, and her voice dropped to a confidential whisper.

'I know, pet.' Lily was perplexed. 'You've been engaged to him for months.'

'Oh no. Not *him*.' Sylvia dismissed her fiancé with disdain. 'This one's mature.'

'Oh,' Lily said knowingly. A sudden suspicion entered her mind. 'He's not married, is he?'

'Of course he's not. I'm not daft, Nana.' And she wasn't, either. Lily should have known better than to ask. Now if it'd been their Cathy . . . 'He's called Michael. Michael Burns. He works in the Air Ministry.' Lily looked suitably impressed. 'He's gettin' on, I mean he's thirty, but he's, well . . . he's established, if you know what I mean.' Lily knew. Michael Burns was 'comfortable'. 'He's quite high up, something hush hush, based at the airport. He's got a car, and his hobby's local politics. Oh, and he's not in the army because of his hammer toe.' Sylvia paused to allow this information to sink in.

'And he's asked you to marry him, has he?'

'Well . . . not yet. But he will,' Sylvia smiled, 'if I want him to.'

Lily considered the candidate. 'He sounds all right.'

'Mind, it'd mean me going to live in Birmingham, Nana.'

Lily was saddened at this news; still, any sacrifice was worth it if it meant Sylvia's happiness.

'The thing is, Nana, should I tell Peter Wood?'

'Eeh well, you can hardly be engaged to two of them at once, pet.'

'I know!' Sylvia snapped, 'but what I thought was, maybe I needn't tell him just yet.' She paused, hoping Lily would get the point. 'Keep him danglin', like.'

'Well, I suppose you don't want to count your chickens . . .'

'Exactly. I could keep him as a standby, eh?'

'Aha.' Lily bit into the artificial cream thoughtfully. 'Thirty, did you say?'

'Aha.'

'Mind, pet, watch him. He might be after what he can get.'

'Oh he is, Nana! But he's not gettin' it! Not till I get what *I* want anyway!'

The waitress turned in surprise as the two ladies by the window broke into guffaws of vulgar laughter.

Peter Wood, 'a canny lad' as Cathy thought him, called on Sylvia several times during her leave. His eyesight was poor, which is why he had been excused service, and Cathy and Joe thought he and Sylvia made an ideal couple, if only because neither of them could see the other properly.

'As long as they don't get glasses and see what the other's really like, they'll be all right,' Joe laughed. 'No, but seriously, she could do worse!' And Sylvia knew she could. Peter's father owned a grocery business, and he was shy and therefore malleable putty in Sylvia's hands. Hettie liked Peter too, and he obviously adored Sylvia. So, as planned,

Sylvia played him along, leaving him none the wiser when she left them for another spell at the Birmingham factory.

But if Peter was kept in the dark about Michael Burns, Michael knew all about Peter. It didn't hurt for him to know that he was in competition for Sylvia's favours, and she used her fiancé both as a defence against improper advances and a stick to spur on the Burns passions. She was walking a tightrope, but practice makes perfect and Sylvia's skills increased as time went on. She enjoyed exercising her powers on Michael, sensing just how hard to get she should be, while yet promising delights to come. She played him like a fish on a hook, and the more he wriggled, the deeper the hook bit. On her next leave, Michael drove Sylvia all the way to Shields, and Hettie had to sleep in Cathy and Joe's room to make space for the house guest.

Joe was away when this visit took place, and Cathy was glad, for all she worried about him. She lay in bed listening to the foghorns and thinking. She did not like Mr Burns, and she didn't like the way Sylvia played with him, either. His eyes followed her everywhere, and Sylvia knew it. His hands reached out to graze against her bottom as she passed, and she pretended not to notice. But then, of course, Sylvia was a lady. Hettie moaned in her sleep and turned over. Dear Hettie. She didn't notice anything. Too many stars in her eyes. Even now she was dreaming of the things she'd never had, orange blossom, white frothy veils, everlasting love; in short, she was dreaming of romance. It was better than the pictures or her magazines because it was happening in her own house, and she had a ringside seat. Even Hettie hadn't given a thought to Peter Wood. Not that there was any danger of him coming round and upsetting the plans. Sylvia had taken the precaution of not informing him of her impending leave. He would be kept dangling till the last minute. Cathy's heart grieved for the lad. Still, he was better off. Far too good for her, deep down. Yes, their Sylvia and Michael Burns deserved one another. The whole thing was a business transaction from start to finish, and all this teasing merely part of the negotiations. Mr Burns wanted something Sylvia had, and she wanted a posh house and his high income. She would trade her assets off against his.

Cathy blamed herself. It was all her fault that Sylvia had turned out the way she had. The truth was, she had never wanted her. During her pregnancy she had felt as though she was carrying a parasite, an interloper, and after the birth she had been too tired and depressed to cope with all that crying. She had allowed Lily to take her away from her, and by the time Cathy felt better it was already too late. She was Lily's child. But even then she could have, should have, objected to the ideas Lily put in her head. It was not really Sylvia's fault at all. She was a victim, used by her grandmother as a tool of vengeance against her mother for having let her down. The child never had a chance. And deep down Cathy had felt she deserved to be punished for what she had done, deserved her own child's disdain, Sylvia's rejection. Looking back now, Cathy could see that her guilt was in fact a selfish thing, an indulgence. For Sylvia's sake, Cathy ought to have raised her voice against the way Lily was bringing her up. And Joe at least was blameless. Why should Sylvia despise him? 'Eeh, me Mam stinks of fish and me Dad stinks of sh . . . ' Cathy could hear the childish sneering voice of her daughter and felt the injustice against Joe keenly. If only Sylvia knew the part he had played. He was a hero. A real one. And Sylvia would never know it.

Thoughts of Joe drew Cathy's mind back to the foghorns, blasting out over the sea. There it was, close in, the warning note from the land, and then the answering note from the ship. She hoped Joe was all right. She hated it when he was out at night. But she couldn't blame him for going. The *Saint Cuthbert* was their ship. It had been requisitioned, and with some of the hands gone off to fight he was needed, watching over the vessel, sweeping mines instead of netting fish. And he enjoyed it, after all.

'It's better than sweepin' the lavs, Cathy,' he had said when he told her. And she had understood. Poor Joe, trapped underground, while outside the gulls screeched overhead and the years passed, and the tides came and went, in and out, without him. But now she had to suffer the agonies of the other wives, waiting for their men to come home from the sea. It was the least she could do for him, and though he read the anxiety in her eyes, she never gave it voice.

Hettie stirred and surfaced from her sleep.

'I'm sorry, Hettie. Did I wake you?'

'No no. It's all right, pet.' She drew in a deep breath and stifled a yawn. 'What's the matter? Can you not sleep?'

'No.'

'It's Joe, isn't it?' Cathy murmured a yes. 'Try thinking of something nice instead, eh? Tell you what . . . you can work out what you want to wear for the wedding!'

In the darkness, Cathy smiled. Thank God *somebody* was getting some joy out of it!

They all waited with bated breath for Mr Burns to 'pop the question'. Sylvia was only on short leave. Both she and Mr Burns had to be back to their various duties in Birmingham. Lily began to wonder if the golden moment had come and slipped by after all. The weather was against them, what with the sea fret and the fog. It was no weather for walking out, and the petrol shortage meant there was nothing spare to take Sylvia out in the car. And there was no peace in the house. One of them was always in and out. Cathy saw how her mother fretted, and couldn't help but feel sorry for her.

'Maybe he's waiting till they're back in Birmingham,' she said to her.

But Lily shook her head.

'No, Cathy. I know. It's me feminine intuition. It'll happen here, if at all.'

Then finally the weather broke and Sylvia suggested Mr Burns might like to take a look at the pier before going back to Birmingham.

'There's an interesting story connected with the lighthouse,' Sylvia told him as they rattled along in the trolley. 'You'll never believe this, Michael, but there's a doll stuck in the cement in its side!'

He looked at her in admiration.

'You're a mine of information, Sylvia,' he said.

'Well, Michael, I do believe in keeping up with the local community.'

Michael, who had his eyes on the mayor's office in Birmingham, thoroughly agreed.

'I'm glad you feel that, Sylvia. Personally, I think service to one's community is every man's duty.'

'Oh yes. I'm right behind you there, Michael.'

'That how you see yourself, is it? The power behind the throne?' he teased her.

'What do you mean, Michael? I don't even know the king,' she said archly. And he liked it.

It was a fresh day, and Michael used the chill in the air as an excuse to hold Sylvia close to him with his arm. She felt his hand slip under her right breast which jogged against it as they went. Anglers lined their route, young men and old sitting on the edge of the pier, silently intent on their fishing.

'Did I ever tell you about my friend Mabel?' Sylvia asked her escort.

'I think you've mentioned her once or twice,' he replied absently.

'I thought so.' Sylvia paused, and let the hand slip further, till it was almost supporting her breast. 'Well, she's getting married soon,' she said, as she gently eased the hand away and put it round her waist.

'Ah,' Michael said.

'I suppose I'll have to make up my mind too . . . about Peter . . . that man I told you about.' She waited till this had sunk in, then went on. 'Really, he's so pressing. He wants an answer, you see. His last letter made that plain enough. His father owns a grocery business, you know.'

'Ah.'

'I didn't know what to say to him. That's why I didn't tell him I'd be home this time, what with you coming, and . . .' She trailed off. They had run the gauntlet of the anglers and were standing by the lighthouse. His hand strayed upwards till a finger touched the tip of her breast. Sylvia smiled and pulled away from him to show him the place where the doll was embedded in the cement.

'A miner found it on the pier when the lighthouse was just

being built and he stuck it in the wet concrete. That was in 1895, and it's still there to this day.'

Michael had come up behind her to look at the doll. She could feel his breath hot on the back of her neck. His hand touched her hip.

'Will you marry me, Sylvia?' he said.

'Me?' She looked up in amazement. 'Why, this is a surprise!'

He smiled. 'So, what's the answer?'

Sylvia paused, enjoying the moment.

'It's all so sudden, Michael. I mean, I do . . . love you.' He bent down to kiss her lightly. 'Oh dear,' she giggled. 'I suppose I'd better, after that!'

Mr Burns looked suitably pleased and took her arm as they walked back along the pier home. As they walked his hand strayed up under her breast; it hesitated, fearing the usual banishment, then eased higher up. Sylvia ignored the whole proceedings and looked the other way as the hand turned, palm upwards, holding the weight of the breast as if to say, 'Mine. All mine.'

'A wedding in the family!' Hettie was cock-a-hoop. 'So romantic! A war bride.'

'He's not a soldier, Hettie,' Cathy said with some irritation, but was sorry straight away, sorry to dampen Hettie's high spirits. But Cathy had a lot on her mind. There was Joe to be told for a start, and then there was Peter. Cathy begged Lily and Hettie not to blab the news as soon as Joe came home.

'Leave it to me,' she said, 'till I've got him on my own.'

But Hettie wasn't capable of hiding the bubbling excitement she felt at the prospect and gave the game away over tea.

'I was going to tell you, Joe,' Cathy told him as he sat on the edge of their bed, dangling his feet thoughtfully over the side. 'I wanted you to settle down first, have a bite to eat, take a breather.'

Joe sighed and shook his head.

'What's he like?'

'Tut.' Cathy's face told him all he needed to know. 'I don't like him.'

'So I gathered.'

'I don't think he'll be good to her, Joe. That's my worry. It's me mother's fault.' Joe couldn't help smiling. Everything was always Lily's fault. 'Given her ideas, she has. You know, our Sylvia may think she's worldly wise, but she's not!'

'Worldly wise, at *her* age!' Joe snorted.

'Oh yes. She thinks she's got this Burns character all sewn up. But if you ask me, she might be in for a bit of a shock.'

Joe, in his underpants, considered his bare feet and sighed.

'I blame myself,' he said.

Cathy looked at him, startled.

'Aye.' He sighed again. 'I should have made a stand in the beginning, but no, I was too soft with Lily. I suppose I was keen to keep the peace, for your sake.'

'We're none of us the same people as we were then, Joe.' Joe smiled and nodded, acknowledging the truth of that. 'It's funny, Mam seems to have shrunk somehow.' Joe laughed. 'She has! And I don't mean just, well, her height and that. I mean, if anything she's got stouter, but, oh . . .'

'I know what you're saying. She's got meaner, Cathy. Sometimes she's like a cartoon of herself, like she's shrunk to fit behind a mask.'

Cathy stared at her husband. Joe was a man of few words, but by God when he did speak it was worth more than a lifetime's gossip.

'Aye,' she said. 'She's got smaller, Joe, and you've got bigger. You've grown and developed.'

'So have you, Cath,' Joe said gently.

Cathy sat on the bed beside him and nestled into his arms, familiar as the foghorns that comforted her nights when he was away. She felt his chest rise with a deep breath and settle again.

'Maybe Sylvia'll grow as well.'

'Maybe,' Cathy answered him doubtfully. 'But if she does, by the looks of it it'll be a case of learning the hard way.'

'Like you did.'

In the pause that followed Cathy saw herself as someone

else might, from the outside in, watching the scenes of her girlhood as she might watch a picture at the Queens. The new Cathy looking back on the old, after a lifetime's battering.

'Yes,' she said at last. 'Like I did.'

Slowly he turned her towards him and kissed her gently on the mouth. A surge of joy, warm and generous, flooded through her, and he marvelled at the answering passion that never seemed to fail him.

'Come to bed,' he said. But he didn't need to ask.

In the cold light of day irritation took the place of acceptance. Peter called. He had had a letter from Sylvia in Birmingham and wanted to speak to Joe 'man to man'. The lad was upset, but what could Joe do? Tell him he'd be better off without her? It might be true, but it wouldn't help him.

'There's other fish in the sea,' Joe said at last.

Peter said nothing at first, he seemed to be struggling within himself. Suddenly his resentment and disappointment screwed up to such a pitch that he blurted out, 'I thought it was only soldiers got "Dear John" letters! I know it's happening all over the place. But usually the women go for the men at home and give up waiting for the blokes in uniform. Not the other way about.'

'This Burns bloke isn't a soldier,' Joe told him softly. 'You're every bit as much of a man as he is. Probably more.'

'Then why?' Peter wailed.

'Who knows,' Joe said vaguely, 'with women?' And with that poor Peter Wood had to be contented. Joe could not have told him his loved one was after another man's money; the pain of learning of her worthlessness would be worse than his dismissal. He slapped the lad on the back with a gesture of male solidarity against the inexplicable hankerings of the female sex. And Peter was comforted by it.

'Me Dad gave me this for you, from the shop.' He handed Joe a parcel and turned to go.

'Thanks, lad. Be seeing you.'

'So long,' Peter said, and went out of their lives.

Even Lily felt some shame when she opened the parcel. Inside was a bag of sugar, half a pound of sausages, and two eggs. She looked at this bounty, and was forced to admit, 'Eeh, but he was a canny lad.'

Nothing would get Hettie down, and her excitement at the approaching wedding was contagious, making them all happy. She had been saving her clothing coupons for ages, and nothing would do but that she had to buy herself a new hat for the occasion. Lizzie and Cathy both took a day off from the fish quay to accompany Hettie on the hat-buying expedition. All three laughed and giggled like a bunch of schoolgirls on an outing. Hettie had had her eye on a wide-brimmed hat, 'so romantic' as she said, but when she tried one on, her small face was swamped.

'Eeh, pet,' Lizzie gasped through her laughter, 'it looks like you've put on a dustbin lid!' And Hettie had to agree. She sighed, her eye hovering over the other creations on display. Cathy's hand reached out to something that had caught her eye. It was a toque, in pale blue silk, and it had a white osprey feather trailing down one side. It was absolutely beautiful.

'Ooh!' Hettie breathed, holding out her hand.

'Try it on, Hettie,' Lizzie encouraged her. Carefully, Hettie raised it like a crown and lowered it onto her head. Cathy approvingly set to arranging it for her.

'There, it frames your face nicely,' she said.

'You know,' Hettie sighed, 'the Queen's got one like this.' She stared at her reflection in the glass, assuming an air of regal authority as she did so. The other two women looked at one another and smiled. 'How much is it?' Hettie took off the hat and gasped at the price ticket. 'Oh no, it's too much. I couldn't.' And she set the hat aside, marching away with a set expression on her face.

But during tea at Carricks, the set expression wavered.

'Eeh, it was just you!' Lizzie told her.

'And after all, you don't spend much on yourself,' Cathy eased the prickling conscience.

'Do you think I should?' And with that Hettie was escorted back to the shop, heart quaking with fear in case someone else had bought it in the meantime. But they hadn't, and taking a deep breath, Hettie fished out all her coupons and handed them over with the money. As they waited for the assistant to pack it up and for the change to come winging its way back to them on the pulley, Hettie shook with nerves.

'Eeh, what have I done?' she said. 'What'll Lily say?'

'Never mind her!'

'But it's so expensive!' And then, at last, the parcel was ready and, glowing with pride, Hettie took it out into the street.

She giggled all the way to the trolley stop. Cathy laughed.

'Do you know, auntie, I don't think I've ever seen you look so happy in all my born days!'

It was a fine day, but there was a slight breeze. All three of them felt exhilarated as they looked up at the gulls screeching in from the sea.

'Must be a storm out there,' Lizzie observed. She was thinking of her man, and of Joe, who had gone out again in the *Saint Cuthbert*. Hettie frowned. She knew how Cathy worried when he was away. It reminded her of the times when Henry used to go to sea, and how she had worried then. Cathy saw that Lizzie's remark had put a damper on Hettie's day. She tightened her lips, then smiled.

'Try your hat on again, Hettie,' she urged. 'I want to see you in it!' Hettie giggled, but with Lizzie to back her up Cathy persuaded her to get the creation out of its box, so they could admire it all over again.

'Eeh, it's just like that one of Queen Mary's. It's real osprey, you know!' Hettie held it over her head, ready to place it on her cropped hair, when a sudden gust lifted it out of her hand. She squealed, and her arm reached up after it, but it danced away, Hettie chasing after as Cathy and Lizzie tried to stop her. But Hettie's eye was on the white feather, her osprey, hovering over the road. Her arm reached out.

'Hettie!' Cathy screamed. But her cry was drowned in the screech of brakes, and Hettie fell, her body broken in the street. Her hat, hovering like a will-of-the-wisp, came to rest a foot from her hand and was trodden on by a rescuer.

The memories flooded back as Cathy keened inwardly for Hettie. She remembered the stories she used to read her and the hot chocolate, whipped up to a froth, and she knew that with Hettie her own childhood had died too. But as she and Joe stood side by side, watching them lower the coffin into the earth, Cathy slowly smiled. Borne on the light breeze, like the osprey in the air, Hettie's soul was freed at last, and a feeling of great joy came over Cathy. She had no words to describe it, and later, accused of unseemly behaviour by her mother, Cathy could only pass Joe the old book and show him the passage at the end. He put on his glasses, and read it aloud in the privacy of their room.

'. . . our little mermaid was scarcely sensible of dying. She still saw the glorious sun, and over her head hovered a thousand beautiful, transparent forms; she could still distinguish the white sails of the ship, and the bright red clouds in the sky. The voices of those airy creatures above her had a melody so sweet and soothing . . . they hovered around her without wings, borne by their own lightness through the air. The little mermaid, at last, saw that she had a body as transparent as theirs; and felt herself raised gradually from the foam of the sea . . .' Joe's voice thickened as he reached the end and handed the book back to Cathy.

'That's what it was like, Joe,' she whispered. 'That's what I felt happening at Hettie's graveside.' But Joe was too full to answer her with more than a nod of understanding.

Hettie had missed the wedding. But she didn't miss much because, in any case, Sylvia didn't get married in Shields. She and Mr Burns tied the knot in a Birmingham registry office. Cathy and Joe weren't invited, though they were not actually asked to keep away. But Lily went down and stayed in their new, spacious house in Edgbaston. She sent home letters, extolling the virtues of the quiet, secluded streets, the large rooms, the luxurious bathroom and the kitchen with all its modern gadgets. Cathy wrote back, encouraging her mother to stay on a little longer. And when Lily, in her next missive, mentioned that Mr Burns was converting his attic into a 'granny flat', Cathy and Joe both wrote, telling her how they'd miss her, but how they would sacrifice the pleasure of her presence in Rosamund Street knowing how much Sylvia needed her in Edgbaston. For Sylvia, having become pregnant soon after her marriage, was excused war work and was at leisure to keep her Nana company.

And now Joe and Cathy were alone. It had come so suddenly that they felt quite lost for a while, with so many empty rooms in the house. Cathy felt lonely when Joe stayed out in the trawler. She missed Hettie badly and felt her alienation from her daughter more keenly than she had expected. She especially felt Sylvia's undisguised contempt for Joe, and she longed to tell her the truth about her origins at last. But Joe wouldn't let her.

'It'll do no good,' he told her. And he was right. It might even drive Sylvia further away from them, and it would break Lily, who had only just finally got what she had always wanted. She'd got back to where she came from, for Edgbaston was even posher than Westoe, and she was content at last.

And so Joe and Cathy let it ride, and sat out the war on their own in the house in Rosamund Street. They were happy in each other's company. Only when Joe was away through the long nights did Cathy lie awake in the big bed, listening to the foghorns, and wondering. She hoped that after the war Joe would give up the sea, and then her mind would be more at rest. But he only said, 'If I can sweep mines, I can net fish!' Nothing would stop him now. He, like Lily, had got what he wanted and he wasn't going to give it up. Nor would Cathy ask him. She enjoyed what time she had with him, and didn't tell him of the nights she lay awake fearing for him. 'It's better than sweepin' lavatories, Cathy!' he'd say with a wink, and they'd laugh. They had days out on their bicycles. They went to Penshore Monument, and Blyth, Durham and Roker, picnics packed in their saddlebags. That was the summer following the war. When winter came and the weather worsened they didn't go out any more, but sat at home reading to each other or listening to the wireless.

And then March came. March 1947. It showed signs of spring early that year, and Joe and the lads went out in the *Saint Cuthbert*, spreading their nets as far as Iceland in search of the herring.

Who'll buy caller herrin'?
They're bonnie fish an' halesome farin';
Buy my caller herrin ,
New drawn frae the Forth

The cold bite of the wind stung Joe's memory. Jim and Alec! Aye, but they were grand lads! He wondered what they'd think if they could see him now, married to Cathy, going out in his own boat, everything he wanted Joe had, even if it wasn't in just the way he'd wanted it. Still, he had no complaints. He had taken the bad along with the good and that was the way of things.

When ye were sleepin' on your pillows,
Dreamt ye aught of our puir fellows,
Darkling as they face the billows,
A' to fill your woven willows?

Aye, Cathy would be asleep by now. Joe felt a great contentment, a great peace, as he always felt on the sea. At one with everything that ever lived or died. He looked up at the dark sky and felt the change as the wind veered round from the west.

They had been gone a week. And Cathy did not sleep. She lay cold and stiff in her bed on the dark nights, listening for the sound of the foghorns. Each one sounded like a friend to her, warm and comforting. It made her feel less alone. Memories flooded in in the silent hours. Memories of her father, and of Hettie, Thrift Street and Mr Miller, Sylvia and her mother, all of them crowding in on her. She heard Hettie asking at the door, 'Lodgin's or consultation?' '"Dead March". They always come in March, Lily. "Dead March". Always a boat lost in March.' Cathy sat up suddenly, panting for breath. 'Dead March' and her Joe was out in it. He was late back. They should have been home by now!

Lizzie joined her in her watch at the Lawe. Together they gazed out over the horizon, neither speaking as their eyes scanned the water for a sign of the *Saint Cuthbert*. Lizzie started singing softly. But Cathy was mute with fear. She drew her shawl over her head. 'Eternal Father strong to save, whose arm doth bind the restless wave.' The words were carried away on the wind. And then the clouds parted and a misty ray of sun shone through onto the water's surface. Cathy remembered Hettie's voice, and how she'd felt at her graveside.

'The sun rose from his watery bed. His beams fell so softly and warmly upon her that our little mermaid was scarcely sensible of dying. She still saw the glorious sun, and over her hovered a thousand beautiful, transparent forms.' Aye, the mermaid, bottled in formaldehyde, trapped in a glass case for display. But not her Joe. Not Hettie either, really. Hettie hadn't faded away into foam. It had taken a double-decker trolley bus to mow *her* down. Joe had survived the minefields. And she too would survive, whatever happened. 'Love and death', '*Liebestod*'? She'd long ago stopped believing in that romantic twaddle. Passion died, no doubt about that, but love? Cathy stared out over the sea, knowing that somewhere out there Joe, her Joe floated on the ebb and flow of the tide. He would come home to her sooner or later. And she knew, too, that their kind of love would never die.

Jack MacNaughton was washed up at Cullercoats. And Joe, lighter by a shoulder, came in a mile further on. They were buried in North Shields with the rest of the crew. 'The men of the *Saint Cuthbert*. Together in life, together in death.' After the service, Lizzie and Cathy went back over the river one more time on the *Ha'penny Dodger*. Lizzie was keening softly the tune of 'The Waters of Tyne'. 'Aye, Joe,' Cathy thought. 'Always end up on the wrong side of the river, don't we?'

CHAPTER TWENTY-TWO

The leaves were falling in Westoe Village. They rose on the air and drifted gently into mounds of yellow and brown and russet. It was a warm day, with the kind of mellow sunshine that comes at the back end of the year, gentle and healing. Cathy had been drawn there by an auction. It was the Stoddard house up for sale with all its contents. She had said goodbye to so many things, she couldn't let this one last memory go without some mark of her respect. And so she made her way towards the village in the late afternoon, when the sale would be almost over, for one last look.

There were a lot of cars in the street, and people came and went through the open doors of the house as though it was some kind of a party. They looked happy and smiling, their arms laden with newly-bought objects, chattering about the price, and the weather, leaving behind them a trail of excitement. It was impossible to feel sad in such an atmosphere, and Cathy hoped that whatever the reason for the sale it would mean a new and happy start for Gilbert and his wife. She did not want to go into the house for fear of bumping into any member of the family, and so skirted round the garden walls into the haven she knew as a child. There was the old sycamore at the bottom of the garden, still clinging onto its leaves, always the last to go. There were the bushes where she and Gilbert had played together, and the old swing. A woman came out of the back of the house bellowing to the child who sat on it, and he jumped off guiltily and went indoors after her. The swing continued swaying long after he had gone, its chain rusty and creaking against the bar at the top. For a moment Cathy wondered if the boy could have been Gilbert's son. But surely he was too young. She herself was a grandmother, God forbid! A young grandmother maybe, but still a grandmother. Her red hair had darkened over the years and had wisps of white over her forehead. But she had kept her slim figure, and when she remembered to keep her head erect she retained the old grace too. She longed to go and sit on that swing, but didn't dare, because she feared she would be seen from the house.

Cathy smiled up at the sun and looked around her, savouring the memory of the garden for future years; then she turned to leave it to its new owners. As she was passing the conservatory she glanced inside. She was surprised to see someone in there. She could see his head above a row of geranium slips, the only plants in the delapidated old building now. It was Gilbert. She knew it was, though she could only see the back of his head. He had a mug in his hand and he was drinking from it. Cathy hesitated. She could go on and leave, and Gilbert would never even know she had ever been there. Or she could go in and speak to him. The moment would never come again. Still she hesitated, half hoping he would turn and see her, taking the decision out of her hands. But he didn't. He just sat, very still, taking sips from his mug from time to time. She could see some grey in his hair through the dirty glass. They were getting older. They had missed their chances so many times. Suddenly she turned and stepped briskly towards the door of the conservatory. Gilbert looked up alarmed at the approach of footsteps, and rose to his feet as she came in to face him.

'I thought it was you,' she said.

'Cathy! Well I never!' He half laughed and stared at her.

She looked round uneasily.

'I probably shouldn't've!'

'No! I'm glad you did. I'm all on my own.' Cathy's look questioned him. 'Mother's dead . . . long while ago now.'

'Oh. But your wife, won't she . . . ?'

'Annie? Not unless we hold a séance.' He laughed.

Cathy was flustered.

'I'm sorry. I didn't know. When?'

'Years. Before the war. It's all right. Here, have a chair.'

He unfolded a deckchair and set it out for her.

'This was the only place I could get any peace. Have a mug of tea with me, eh?'

She nodded, smiling. And Gilbert disappeared out to the kitchen to fill a couple of mugs.

The glasshouse seemed so small. Cathy was surprised. When it had been filled to bursting with all those plants it had looked huge, but now it was bare it seemed to have shrunk to half its original size. She lay back and watched the sun as it broke up into rainbows, refracted in the broken panes of glass. The effect was dazzling, beautiful, and she was smiling as Gilbert came back and stood at the door. He stopped for a moment, looking at her. He seemed to be deep in thought. And then he walked in and gave her her cup, which she held in her two hands like a chalice.

'You have the air,' he began quietly, 'of a woman at a loose end.' Cathy smiled and drank her tea. 'Someone at a loose end is usually on their own. Are you?'

Cathy was surprised. The question was so direct that she was taken aback by it. But she nodded all the same.

'Good,' he said. 'Now we know where we stand.'

There was a long and awkward pause.

'I'm sorry . . .' she began.

'Don't.'

Cathy drank her tea and rose from her chair to go. But Gilbert also rose, alarmed.

'You're not going, are you?' Cathy didn't know what to say or what to do. She looked back uncertainly at him. 'Please. They'll be going in a minute . . .'

'Is the house sold?' Cathy asked, sitting again.

'Yes. Now they're on to clothes lines and chamber pots, I think.' Cathy smiled. 'Fetch a good price now, you know . . . the old ones.'

'But what are you going to do?'

Gilbert shrugged.

Cathy looked anxiously at him. 'Surely you've got somewhere to go?'

'Not in Shields,' Gilbert replied. 'There's a small flat in

Liverpool, but, well . . . I'm on the look-out for some digs!' He laughed.

'I don't believe you!'

'I'll be staying in a hotel tonight, unless I camp out in the house. I don't suppose they'd mind.'

Cathy had plenty of room down in Rosamund Street. It was on the tip of her tongue to ask Gilbert if he'd like a room there, temporarily of course. But the memory of Joe filled all those rooms. It didn't seem right, somehow.

'Are you leaving the area, then?' she asked.

'The main operation's in Liverpool now. But I don't know. Once a Geordie always a Geordie. I'd like to keep a foothold in the old place.'

'Then why . . . ?'

Gilbert sighed and looked round.

'On the practical side, it's too big, and it's falling to pieces anyway. Needs rewiring, a new roof, decent heating system. It's cold as Christmas. And . . . well, it's dead. That's all. It's been like living in a mausoleum. I should have made a break a long time ago.'

Cathy nodded.

'My place's much the same, Gilbert. Eeh, I don't know. We all thought it was the bees knees when we moved into it, but now . . . Times change, eh?'

'Where would you like to live?'

Cathy shrugged. 'Pair of drifters now, aren't we?'

He smiled sympathetically.

'My manager tell me there's some lovely houses being built along the cliff top. "The Broadway" they're calling it. Looking out to sea.'

'I wouldn't care if I never saw the sea again.'

Gilbert looked at Cathy, surprised by the tone of bitterness in her voice. She stood and stared out at the garden through the broken panes.

'I think that's why I came up here today, really. I mean, I wanted to say tarrah to the old place, but . . . eeh, I don't know. When you're in Westoe, the sea feels a long way away. You could be bang in the middle of the country somewhere, not in Shields at all.'

Gilbert rose and stood behind her; after a moment's hesitation she felt his hand, warm and comforting, on her shoulder. Her voice broke.

'I think if I hear one more foghorn, I'll go mad!' She was almost crying. Gilbert longed to put his arms round her, but he was afraid that perhaps she didn't want him.

'You've had a hard life, Cathy,' he said quietly. Cathy nodded. 'Why did you?'

'I don't know. It just seemed to happen. Or maybe it was all my fault. Me mother always said I had a tendency to cut off me nose to spite me face.' She turned towards him laughing at herself.

'And do you still have that tendency?'

'God, no! I got over that a long time since. No!' She shook her head sadly.

Gilbert said nothing. She felt him, standing so close to her yet not touching, and she could not bring herself to look up at him, knowing that his eyes were on her, searching for the Cathy he used to know.

'I'm not the same, Gilbert,' she whispered.

'The same, but different.' He laughed, and then she looked up and caught his smile.

She nodded.

'Aye. I suppose you're right. A bit older and wiser maybe. And about time an' all.'

Gilbert's hand rose and touched her hair. Cathy flushed. 'It's not what it was. It's gone dull and lifeless. I'm gettin' old.'

'You're still a beautiful woman, Cathy.' She shuffled uneasily. 'I'm sorry. I didn't mean to embarrass you.' His hand dropped as though he'd been burned.

'Oh no, Gilbert! I'm embarrassed, but only because of what I am now, and what I did to you, though God knows I did it for the best, and I've paid since. But look at me. I'm not the bright-haired lass I used to be. That's all gone.'

Gilbert looked down and then grinned teasingly back up at her.

'You've got nice ankles, mind!' and winked.

'Gilbert Stoddard! I never knew you had it in you!' And they both laughed.

'Annie, my wife . . . she unbent me a bit. Ma never liked her you know.'

Cathy roared with laughter.

'Tell me another one!'

'No! Her father was a gambler. He was! And she . . . well, don't get me wrong, she was a nice woman, you know, but not so stiff. She said I needed loosenin' up a bit.' Cathy raised her eyebrows in some surprise. 'So you see, it wasn't just you. I was a bit backward in coming forward myself!' His eyes twinkled at her, and suddenly they were both back in Miss Hutchinson's shop with the gaslight flickering, one of those lost moments between them. Cathy shook her head, and smiled.

'I can't tell you what a relief it is to hear you say that, Gilbert. Eeh, and to think, all these years I've been blamin' meself. I thought it was all my fault.'

'We didn't know, Cathy. Not then.'

'I didn't deserve . . .'

'Rubbish!'

Suddenly they became aware of steps on the gravel outside. They turned to look through the grimy glass like two lovers disturbed in a guilty act. It was the auctioneer, come in search of the vendor.

'Eeh, he'll think we've been up to no good,' Cathy giggled.

'I should be so lucky!' Gilbert teased. And they both were laughing as Mr Nagler saw them and bent his head to come through the door of the glasshouse.

'Em . . . it's all over, Mr Stoddard. If you'd just like to . . .'

'Yes. All right. I'll come in.' Gilbert nodded and the man turned back to the house. 'Come on,' Gilbert whispered, 'you can't leave me on me own now.' Cathy smiled.

'I'll follow you inside.'

Gilbert bent to kiss her cheek, and then hurried in after the auctioneer.

Cathy wandered out of the conservatory and looked down the garden. Her eye lighted on the swing again, and feeling like a grown-up in a child's playground she walked over towards it, stealing a look over her shoulder, before settling herself on its seat and swaying gently to the rhythmic squeaking of the chain. She could have been seventeen all over again. Joy bubbled up inside her, making its way through the dark patches, coursing up in spite of the years between. The air felt light and warm on her cheeks as the afternoon sun faded behind the sycamore, casting long shadows at her feet.

A sound caught her attention. Gilbert was calling her from the house. She heard a car start up outside; the auctioneer leaving, no doubt. She jumped off the swing and felt the wooden seat sway back against her legs before walking across the lawn to the open French windows at the back of the house. Gilbert was holding a bottle in his hand and looked very pleased with himself.

'I found this in the cellar,' he said, 'behind some old boxes. Bubbly! Come on.'

Cathy went inside. She felt like an uninvited guest in the place, Mrs Stoddard's shadow lurking behind the huge arch which linked the two halves of the room.

'Do you remember me coming to your party without any knickers on?' she asked. Gilbert laughed. 'By, I learned to keep them on since!'

Gilbert gave her a look which made her blush. Eeh, but he *had* come on! He was digging in his pocket for a penknife. He found it and pulled it out victoriously.

'South Shields motto, "Always Ready"!' He laughed. Cathy looked round for glasses, and saw a thermos on the table. 'Yes, they'll do,' he said. So she took the two plastic cups from the top and held them ready as Gilbert pulled out the cork. It exploded from the neck of the bottle and spattered them. Champagne dripping from their eyelashes, they were helpless with laughter.

'I must've shaken it when I brought it upstairs.' Gilbert tried to get as much as he could into the flask tops, and then licked the stuff from his soaking hand. Their laughter rang through the empty house, and Mrs Stoddard's shadow fled aghast.

'To a new life!' Gilbert said.

Cathy nodded. 'I'll drink to that.'

The light was fading at the windows. Cathy sat on the window seat, looking out across the tree-lined avenue.

'Won't they miss you at home?' Gilbert asked.

She shook her head. 'There's no one there.'

'Then why don't you stay?'

Cathy hesitated, then turned from the window to look at him.

'Would you like me to?'

'Yes.'

Their faces were in shadow. They felt, rather than saw, the other sitting in the empty room.

'I feel like I'm playing truant.'

Gilbert got up off the floor. 'Well, I don't know about you, but I think I've been good for far too long.'

He helped her up and looked quizzically at the cushions on the window seat.

Cathy followed his gaze and then his thought. 'Gilbert Stoddard!'

'I know! You didn't realise I had it in me!' His arm brought her in towards him, his face came towards hers, and she lifted her mouth to meet his lips.

Hand in hand they sought out the stub end of a candle, and then, while Cathy arranged the cushions on the floor, Gilbert retrieved the rug from his car. The wind was getting up. It blew a hollow sound down the chimney, and in the street, leaves scuttled across the paving stones. Gilbert banged the door as he hurried back with the rug. The sound reverberated through the building, making her aware of the rooms upstairs, of the presence of previous inhabitants. Gilbert saw her face in the light of the candle, and paused in the doorway to the drawing room.

'It's all right. It'll do the old faggot good,' he said loudly. And then he came towards her and took her once more in his arms. 'Where's your old faggot, eh?' he whispered in her ear. 'Pushin' up the daisies?'

'No. My old faggot lives in Birmingham now, with me daughter.'

'Oh yes. Your daughter.' He pulled back from her and looked at her. 'She doesn't look much like you.'

There was a second's pause before Cathy spoke again.

'No,' she said. 'She takes after her father.' Gilbert's eyes questioned her. Cathy smiled. 'You remember you told me once that a ship wasn't the place for a lady?' Gilbert nodded. 'Well . . . you were right!' They stared at each other and then burst out laughing. 'I was expecting her when . . .'

Gilbert sighed.

'When you broke it off with me?'

Cathy nodded.

'That Norwegian sea captain. Do you remember.'

'How could I forget!'

'I'm sorry.'

'Sh . . .' His hand reached up to her head and stroked the cropped hair gently.

'It was me own fault really. He took me for a look round his ship, and . . .' she snorted. 'I got more than I bargained for. That's all.' The hand stopped stroking Cathy's hair. 'Me Mam never knew. She thought it was Joe . . . Joe Robson. Well, he offered to marry me, and . . .' She was crying now, and his hand resumed the gentle, soothing movements on her head. 'I've been a good wife to him. And I loved him, Gilbert. I did really. It broke me up when he . . .'

'Sh . . .' Gilbert sighed. 'I love you, Cathy. I'm sorry I was so backward . . .'

'In coming forward. Yes I know. But we didn't realise what it was all about, Gilbert. Not then. We did our best and, well, here we are now. That's all.'

Suddenly he pulled her close to him. She clung to him, pressing her face hard against his. 'I can't believe this is happening, Gilbert.'

His hand reached behind her hair to find the place he remembered on the nape of her neck. Cathy's body gave against him and she sighed as the old surge of feeling swept through her.

'Do you think we should?' she asked quietly.

'Do you want to?'

'Yes.'

'Then we definitely should. You've got to grasp the moment, or it's gone for ever.' He tilted his head towards the shadows upstairs. 'This'll shake her!'

'My knees have gone,' she said.

'Good.' He bent to lift her from the floor.

'You can't! Your shoul – Sorry.'

He lifted her in his arms and dropped her gently onto the cushions. Slowly, he began to undress her as the flame of the gutted candle flickered and went out. There was all the time in the world. The tide of their sensations rose and fell, taking them along with it, unresisting, till, rising to its peak, they stood on the crest, daring gravity, before its overswell, its own energy which had created it, broke through the tension of the wave and the waters fell crashing back towards the surface of the sea.

Cathy stirred and woke, but Gilbert's arm tightened round her, refusing to let her go. Her head turned towards him, and she kissed him lightly on the forehead. He groaned and stretched, releasing her only to catch her back again with the other arm. Their lips met as though they'd never really been apart. And then Gilbert rose and flung the rug from him.

'I shouldn't think this room has seen the like,' he said, 'since you turned up without your knickers on!'

Cathy fell back against the cushions laughing, then remembered there were no curtains at the window.

'Gilbert! You'll be seen.'

Gilbert ducked down and reached for his trousers, then looked up again at the window.

'I doubt it,' he said. 'There's thick fog outside!'

Cathy twisted round and stared out at the mist. She frowned.

'It's a wonder they haven't been blowing the foghorns!'

Just as she said it, a horn blew far out to sea.

'Oh no!' she cried.

'They've been blowing half the night,' Gilbert told her. 'Didn't you hear them?'

'No. They sound further away up here.'

'Not far enough, though, eh?'

Cathy smiled and shook her head.
'I wonder if they can hear them out at Rowland's Gill.'
Cathy propped herself up on her elbows, 'But that's out near Hexham, isn't it?'
'Well no, not quite, nearer Gateshead.'
'They can't hear them over there, surely?'
'Exactly.'
'Oh. I see.' Cathy looked at him shyly. 'I think.'
'There's some nice houses there. We could take a look at them today, if you like. I've got the car outside.'
Cathy looked out of the window.
'But it's pea soup, man!'
'It'll be gone by the time we're out of Shields. Bet you.'
He was buttoning up his shirt and looking intently at her. Cathy sprawled back against the cushions.
'Gilbert Stoddard,' she said, 'what are you asking me?'
Gilbert shrugged. 'Well. I just thought it might be a nice place for us to live, like.'
Cathy laughed and picked up a cushion. He backed away, but it caught him against his chest, toppling him down towards the makeshift bed.
'What are you asking me, Gilbert?' Cathy whispered in his ear.
'Will you marry me, hinny?' he asked smiling.
'Yes, please, pet.'
'It's high time,' he said.